LONE STAR
LEGACY

LONE STAR LEGACY

WILLIAM W. JOHNSTONE

AND J. A. JOHNSTONE

KENSINGTON
PUBLISHING CORP.

www.kensingtonbooks.com

KENSINGTON BOOKS are published by

Kensington Publishing Corp.
119 West 40th Street
New York, NY 10018

Special book excerpts or customized printings can also be created to fit specific needs. For details, write or phone the office of the Kensington Sales Manager: Kensington Publishing Corp., 119 West 40th Street, New York, NY 10018. Attn. Sales Department. Phone: 1-800-221-2647.

PUBLISHER'S NOTE: Following the death of William W. Johnstone, the Johnstone family is working with a carefully selected writer to organize and complete Mr. Johnstone's outlines and many unfinished manuscripts to create additional novels in all of his series like the Last Gunfighter, Mountain Man, and Eagles, among others. This novel was inspired by Mr. Johnstone's superb storytelling.

ISBN: 978-0-7860-4877-9 (ebook)

ISBN: 978-1-4967-3590-4

First Kensington Trade Paperback Printing: May 2023

10 9 8 7 6 5 4 3 2 1

Printed in the United States of America

LONE STAR LEGACY

Chapter 1

The big, old cottonwood's great arm wagged up and down in a slow, easy rhythm. It was not a balmy south Texas breeze riffling through its leaves that made it do so. It was the thick hemp rope flung over it long minutes before, a rope, now taut and creaking, that led down, down, down twenty feet to a man's head canted hard to the left, unnaturally so. The head's sweaty hair, sandy in color and matted to the man's reddening scalp, jostled with his huffing, squealing efforts.

His wrists were bound tight behind him with another rope that wrapped several times about his lean waist before trailing down his legs, nearly rigid and bound at the ankle. He was bootless and his brown socks, spotted through with holes, wagged and roped off his jerking toes. The man jerked, his body whipsawing rigid, save for a hint of a bend at the knees. With each jerking movement, his plight grew worse.

Joss Keeler was a lean man, always had been. A husband to one woman, a father to four children, a son of a pap and a mama back in Kentucky. He and Edna had pulled up stakes and hauled westward three years before to farm a bone-dry patch of land he'd regretted buying sight unseen from his smarmy cousin Merle. Should have known better, as Merle had always been a lying jackass.

The move, the relentless, blistering, hammering of the sun, the snakes, the lack of water, the rank-tempered, scrubby cattle, all of it had conspired to make Edna a bitter little thing, old looking far before her time, and Joss a curl-backed, beaten man also long before he had earned the look and feel of it.

But he was, by God, a family man and he'd done what he had to do to feed his family. They had already packed the squawk-wheeled work wagon with what of their broken, battered possessions he thought the remaining drudgery critter, a toothless mule name of Melvin, might pull.

They were headed northeastward, and though Edna never said a thing about it, Joss knew she'd not eaten that day, nor maybe the night before. They'd gnawed through the last of their wormy flour and cornmeal, and he'd seen her boil up the remaining dry black beans earlier in the week.

He'd lost the last of his cattle—the rangy, wild cattle dotting the land in these parts—to some sort of haired dog beast, coyote or wolf or Comanche wearing a dog skin he knew not. He'd only seen it from too far to do a thing about it.

Trouble was, Chaw Perkins, Ambrose Dalton, and the biggest cattle hog of them all, Regis Royle, wanted all the land and all the beasts on it, no matter who else might be there, no matter if they were there legally. And those cattlemen rode their hired hands hard to scour clean the land of any small holders thereabouts.

Joss was a hard learner, though, and when several nighttime visits failed to run him and his off, well, here they were. One more day, he thought, and I would have been shed of this place.

But now here he was, kicking and pumping at the end of a rope, as if this least, last effort might somehow save him. Joss's final thoughts, quickly burning in his brain like paper in fire, were of Edna and the boys and wee Ess, the youngest, at two years of age already so like her mother. They were now to go on in their lives without him.

The thought had never come to him before. He'd instead always pictured being the papa in their lives, the man his wife turned to for help, to bring in firewood, to bring home meat for the table. And that's what he was doing, taking one last head of rangy cattle, one he was sure was unbranded, therefore unclaimed, therefore attainable by anyone for any purpose at all.

Especially, thought Joss, himself and his family. After all, he owned the land on which he'd seen the beast, eh? Why not drop one last mangy longhorn, skin it out, and take along as much as they could carry and eat, which was likely most of the beast?

After he'd shot the heifer, certain it belonged to none and thus all, he'd set to skinning it out so they'd have meat for the trail. At least something to fill their bellies while they began their long journey of failure and shame back to Kentucky.

But that's not how it worked out.

Now here I am, thought Joss, dying, and my wife will get the word from a fat-and-happy rancher who made our lives hellish for three years running.

"Least I can do," said Ambrose.

That was big of him. Joss did near everything he could think of to get away, even tried to run for it, but they shot him in the heel. He bet it was Royle, but he couldn't be certain.

"I never did take nothing in life that wasn't mine to take, damn you all!" Then he'd told himself to calm down, that taunting and cursing these fools wasn't about to get him anywhere. Then he pleaded all the while they jerked him around and roped him like a bellerin' calf and trussed him whilst he bled from the foot and yowled and thrashed.

Finally, he did the thing he'd always told himself he'd never do to another man in life, the thing he vowed to his Pap he'd never do. Joss begged. Begged like a ganted-up old street creature in a city somewhere with his cupped hands out, too poor even to buy a hat. He begged for his life.

Wasn't for him, and he believed that. It was for Edna and the young'uns. They did not deserve to trudge through their days thinking their own Pap was a cattle thief. Because he wasn't.

"That cow didn't have no brand, damn you!" he'd shouted, but two of the three men kept a cold eye on him, and Royle looked over his head, as if not looking at him kept him from being tainted by their intended crime. He told them as much, too.

Now, jags of hot lightning pain lanced up and down his body, his throat having given over to some feeling far beyond agony. The last of his efforts were reduced to jerking and working his body back and forth, stiff as a plank, as the rope spun him slowly in a circle.

Joss's mind blackened and puckered about the edges, curling in on itself like a delicate fist of paper. What about Edna and the children? Oh, what about them? Think of them, he told himself, this is all you have left, this last scrap of a moment . . .

Chaw Perkins and Ambrose Dalton stared off beyond the thick trunk of the cottonwood, the first packing a pipe, Ambrose working a quid of chaw, both employing the full intent of a man bent on doing anything at all but what he should.

The third, Regis Royle, worked no chew in his mouth, but did flex his jaw muscles, as if he were chewing something that might never be swallowed, and he did eye the dying man, long after the fellow, all chiseled bone and ratty clothes and callused hands, ceased to live.

Not for the first or the last time did the thought occur to Regis Royle that maybe, just maybe this time he'd been wrong. Maybe this man was telling the truth. A truth deeper than the idea that he hadn't killed, gutted, and halfway butchered a range cow, one nobody'd laid claim to yet, anyhow. Maybe it had all been a mis-understanding. Maybe, maybe, maybe. . . . A long, slow sigh leaked out of his mouth.

He noticed Ambrose was riding away from the scene, slow and in no hurry. "Where are you headed, Ambrose?" he said. There was no way he was going to shoulder the fat man's share of the burden of stringing up a man and dropping him on down again.

"Like I told that fellow. Promised him I'd tell his wife and young."

"Not without toting home his body, too."

That got Ambrose to stop. He didn't turn. But he did move his head to one side and let fly a brown stream of tobacco juice. "Seems to me we're partners here. Ain't no call for you to tell me what to do, now is there, Regis?"

"There is if it looks like you forgot the deal, Ambrose."

"Fine." The fat rancher turned his horse back to face the dead man and his two comrades. "I'll help you cut the sumbitch down, then you, by God, can drag his body back to the wife." He spit again, then resumed his upright post atop the horse.

Ambrose looked from Chaw to Regis Royle, and back again. "What's got into you two? We agreed this here part of the job was going to be no different for those who have wronged us and sought to bilk us out of our herds. You know as well as I do that's the way it has to be. Hell, we agreed on that! Elsewise, what are we doing out here, stringing up folks like they was runaway slaves?"

Regis couldn't help this feeling of disgust rising in his gorge, threatening to choke him from within. He got this way each time after he helped hang a man. Granted, it had only happened three times since he and the other ranchers formed the Cattlemen's Justice Consortium in a reaction to the increasing numbers of bold-as-brass thievery they'd all experienced of many head from each of their herds.

Even if he was a rustler, it was a raw way to go out, swinging and gagging. The worst was always seeing their heads, swelled up to twice their normal size. The tongues did the same, so much so they burst right out of their mouths, all purple-black like nighttime storm clouds, like something not of the body had been stuffed in there, but didn't quite fit. They looked like they'd been caught choking down a cow's tongue.

Sometimes their lips split. And the eyes, lord, but the eyes bulged, popped forward like a frog's will do if you squeeze it to death from the legs up. Sometimes a man's eyes would pop right out and trail down a swollen cheek.

And then the filth—most of the men would mess themselves, all of it, front and back, staining their trousers and leaking down legs, running off the end of grimy bare feet, where their boots had been kicked off in their throes, bucking their last ride, on the grim steed of death.

Regis wondered if it was kinder at the end to just shoot a man. Cover his eyes and shoot him. But he had to keep in mind, had to keep reminding himself, that these men earned their deaths. They'd been caught like willfully rotten boys filching from the cookie jar, no excuses could work, no reasoning would provide excuse enough to steal another man's property. At least that's what all the ranchers had agreed on. If they let just one thief go free, the rustling would never end.

When he'd helped form the Cattleman's Justice Consortium, a fancy name, to be sure, Regis hoped it would one day soon outgrow the need for hanging thieves, and instead the men would sit around a table and hash out the details of how to get their cattle to far-off markets safely and without losing half their weight on the trail.

He'd heard rumor of two, some said even three, rail lines considering expanding their ranges, looking for wider markets and reasons to justify the expense of laying track through days' worth of open, raw land just to get to some back-of-nowhere settlement. But that was the point, wasn't it?

The railroad tycoons, just like the ranchers, were looking, likely itching, for the excuse to flex further the elongating fingers of their empires' grasp. And if that were the case, then Regis, by God, wanted the Cattlemen's Justice Consortium to be at the forefront of the lobbying efforts to attract them to their far-off corner of Texas.

Regis wanted to ride point on an organization with so many powerful ranchers representing so much beef on the hoof, so much potential money for all involved, that the railroad men had no choice but to take notice.

He was convinced that a great deal of money could be made for all involved, from the cattlemen on up through the railroads to the meat buyers and packing companies in far-off cities such as Chicago, where the end was met by much of the beeves shipped from all over the West.

Yes, the appetite for beef was becoming a most impressive thing, at least back East, so said four different men he'd chin-wagged with. Regis trusted them as reliable sources of information. After all, he'd worked with them for years in his role as half-owner and working partner in a coastal and river shipping firm with his longtime partner, Cormac Delany.

It had long been Regis's business to sniff out solid founts of information about potential markets, and to discard any that were useless or dried up. Those four were among his most trusted and longest-known.

A fifth, and the most trusted, was Cormac, a man who in many ways had been a father to him for a long time. Their acquaintance had begun on a fall day many years before when Cormac had found Regis stowed away belowdecks, among the rats in ankle-deep bilge water, on his sidewheel paddler.

The fiery Irishman could just as easily have tossed him overboard, but he'd seen something, Regis liked to think it was a look of boldness nested in his dark, untrusting, unbroke-mustang visage.

According to Cormac, who was raised devout Catholic, his sainted mother ("God rest her!") would never forgive him from beyond the grave if he'd chucked a starvling off his boat. So Cormac had fed him.

Regis remembered with a grin, and red-cheeks, at the rich memory, that he'd wolfed down more food than three men could put away. Then Cormac had set him to work.

And here he was, all these years later, a rancher and a co-owner of a bustling shipping fleet. But it was as a rancher Regis was most keen, most proud, and most busy.

Since riding through the Santa Calina range a couple of years before, and deciding that if it were at all possible to possess that stunning range, he would do so, no, he must do so, the young man's life had barely been his own, so much had happened. And yet, the memory of that first slow trip on horseback, alone, through the Santa Calina range, flanking the river and seeing tall grasses sway in a light breeze, haunted him and comforted him.

He often smiled at the memory. It had been an awkward ride, since he hadn't, to that time, had occasion to sit a horse for more than an hour at most in his life, being more accustomed to life on the water. But all that had soon changed when he and Cormac bought the Santa Calina range and, with the help of his good friend, the Texas Ranger Jarvis "Bone" McGraw, and his reluctant, sometimes difficult, sometimes refreshing, nearly always annoying little brother, Shepley, Regis had set about hiring men and building a ranch.

Now, roughly fifty hired men, some with their families, the Royle Ranch had grown to include two hand-dug reservoirs for watering cattle, a solid, if small, ranch house for him and Shep, a big bunk house that was already filled, a sizable dining hall and camp kitchen, corrals, two barns, a relocated village of Mexican workers who Regis convinced to move to the Royle range once he'd bought their entire town's worth of livestock and he realized they'd have nothing to live on the next year.

And there were roughly more than one thousand head of cattle, surly, wiry, bawling, bucking, downright rowdy Texas Longhorns more comfortable grubbing in the brush and stomping rattlesnakes than being herded and branded.

But that's what they'd been doing, rounding up all the feral beeves they could on their range. They were there for the taking, after all. They'd done the same with the vast herds of mustangs, whose magnificent yet brute savagery made the Longhorns look like tame rabbits.

Though to Regis, the most important of all of his ranch undertakings had been and continued to be the acquisition no matter the costs, of more land. He had sworn early on that the only way he was going to devote his entire life to ranching was to be the best at it.

And the only way he knew for certain how to do that was to be the biggest rancher the world had ever seen. And the sure-fire way to be that man was to buy land. Lots of it. As cheap as possible, but he'd pay more if he had to. Anything for land. That abiding thought had guided Regis since the very beginning. Land was all.

Chapter 2

By the time the man had ceased to be a living man and swung slowly on an unfelt breeze, Regis Royle had sifted and sorted through the same various concerns about the people he was helping to round up and teach lessons to. When he'd first approached Ambrose Dalton, Chaw Perkins, and Dubber Jones, and a few of the other ranchers in the region about ways to deal with the rustler problem, he'd been far more fired up about the task. After all, he'd lost many hundreds of head in the last year to rustlers.

A significant number were lost in the cover of night to filching border wolves, gangs of vaqueros, and gringos with no more pride than a saloon drunkard begging for coins.

The Santa Calina range was too large for Regis and his men to patrol in full in a way to prevent this theft. The other ranchers had the same problem with their respective spreads, but together, by loaning each other men, and by paying lone riders to lurk the ranges, keeping an eye out for depredations, then tracking the thieves, they were able to slowly nibble away at the poaching problem.

They damn sure couldn't count on the law to help them, and the newly reformed Texas Rangers, back together and in action in part to help ranchers deal with rustlers, were useful but not yet numerous enough to do the job alone. Until then, the ranchers

agreed, they would do the job themselves. And that meant doling out justice as they saw fit.

That was the part about which Regis had been uncertain. He
didn't like the idea of giving away his hard-won cattle to thieves,
no sir, but neither did he relish killing men for the crime. But the
problem had gotten bad enough in recent months that he had
said to hell with it and ridden along.

Ambrose, his closest ranching neighbor, had told him it would
get easier, that he had to do it otherwise he might as well hand
over his ranch, give up on his beloved Santa Calina range. That
unthinkable notion was the final straw for Regis Royle.

Regis rode alone to deliver the body of the Consortium's latest
poacher to the man's family. This was a task he had never shirked
when it came time to do so over the past few months, but it was
not a job he enjoyed.

That was but one of many ways he and some of the other men
differed, particularly Ambrose, who seemed to relish delivering
vicious news. The fat rancher would ride in well-heeled and
never without at least two of his own men, each armed more than
any man needed to be.

But Regis Royle rode alone, and it was never easy, and from
what he was seeing up ahead, it would never be as difficult as
today. He saw in a clearing ahead, a woman seated on the ground
before a listing work wagon hitched behind a droop-ear mule.

There were the children huddled about her, all but the oldest,
a boy about twelve years of age. He stood apart, poking about the
harness on the mule as if rechecking the buckles and straps that
had already been checked. They were waiting for someone, waiting for the man he now escorted back to them.

As soon as he saw the little family clustered about the scantily
loaded wagon—two worn, oft-mended chairs, a broken cradle
filled with mothy bedding, casks lashed to the sides with rope—
Regis suspected they may have made a terrible mistake.

The bitter bile of regret tickled his throat. Had the man been as innocent as his beseeching, rage-fueled protests swore? Had his high-pitched, unbelieving cries that rose in desperation with the look of terror in his eyes, been true? Had his screaming, howling, and thrashing been the actions of an innocent man? Had his final begging, sobbing moments, at the very end of his life, at the very end of his rope, been those of a wronged man?

The woman saw him before any of the children did. She stiffened, feral and alert, her innate sense of protectiveness pulled her arms tight about the three small ones close to her, drawing them closer. Her eyes narrowed as she eyed him.

Regis rode King, his buckskin gelding, and carried the man draped across a pony Ambrose had brought along on this outing, for such a purpose.

They always knew where they were headed, and trusted the word of their lone scouts to pick out the rustlers, with preference given to encampments of thieves, usual among the more brazen gangs, of which there had been many of late.

It seemed that most thieves, once they found a place of bounty, weren't clever enough to vary their attacks. They went to the same spot, the same river crossings, the same narrow tracks, night after night until they'd exhausted the supply of beeves. Then they'd move on.

They didn't realize that once the cattlemen got wind of such operations in a certain section, they seeded the area with cattle knowing they were likely to catch the thieves in the act. This strategy had worked with some success for months. On this day they had followed up on a tip by a fellow named Tomas, a new ranch hand of Ambrose, one he swore confidence in.

Now, looking at this woman and her children, and the oldest, looking up from fiddling with the harness, Regis felt the air leave him. Even the mule swung its grayed old head around and looked his way.

Regis slowed King's pace as they rode forward. He kept his gaze on the woman, kept a hand on the saddlehorn, holding the reins in his fingertips, the other hand, his left, held the reins of the pony carrying the man's body. He stopped twenty feet from the wagon.

He began to speak, but his voice cracked. He cleared his throat and began again. "Ma'am," he should have taken off his hat, but he did not have enough hands. "I am Re—"

He saw she'd looked wide around him, and must have seen something she recognized. She stood quickly, knocking down to its backside a small child, four or so years old. The shocked child began to weep as the woman rushed to the pony.

The bairn was still clutched in her left arm, but it was as if she had forgotten the little, squirming thing. He saw it had been nursing at her breast.

She ran right by his right leg and began saying, "No, no, no!" before she reached the dead man. He saw her free hand snatch the dead man's sweaty, hanging topknot, and lift. She knew, finally, without doubt what she'd suspected, perhaps when Regis had first ridden slowly into view.

The other children, walking singly, approached their mama.

When he'd awakened that morning, Regis did not foresee his day untying itself like this. This is not how it should have gone. Not how any day should be.

"Ma'am . . . might I have a word, without the children?"

"No!" she shouted, then looked up at him, hurt and anger and confusion warring in her watery, red eyes. Strands of long, auburn hair wisped from beneath the loosely tied bonnet. "No, you say it now, you say it here, right now. What's happened? What's happened to my Joss?"

He swallowed down more of that bitter, clotting mess in his throat, the cruel tang of wrongfulness and regret. Children, thought Regis, unable to avoid their still-wondering eyes. This had been an impoverished man who needed a job and a free side of beef, not a rope around his neck. God in heaven, what have I done?

As this thought haunted him, he realized this incident was night-and-day different from every one of the hangings of the past few months. To this point, not a one had they been uncertain about. They'd all been caught in the act, and had died for it, as rustlers, some of them mewling and whining, one or two silent and stoic, but most left life cursing and spitting hatred.

They'd been thieving from—what Regis believe himself and his fellow cattlemen to be—honest businessmen whose workers depended on them for everything. The thieves threatened the food in the mouths of the children of those workers.

But this man Joss, he was not like the rest. He had been telling the truth. They were indeed loaded up to leave the territory, having lost their meager holdings on a failed farming venture. Why here? This was no place to make a go as a farmer.

As the woman's rage and grief battled before him, the business mind of Regis Royle searched for a way to make this right. Somehow he had to do something to set this situation right.

He cursed Ambrose Dalton and Chaw Perkins for not riding along with him. Then as quickly as he thought it, he was relieved they weren't there. For they were callous, especially Ambrose, who would have tried to shame the woman before her children. The thought made Regis bite down hard, pulsing his cheek muscles.

No, he had to be here alone. There would be nobody here to interfere with him trying to make things right. He had to try.

It wasn't easy.

The woman was inconsolable, and he could not blame her.

"What did you do? How . . . how?" She looked up at him, more confusion than anger in her eyes. "What did you do to him? What have you done to my Joss? He's hurt, is all, just hurt . . ."

She hugged the dead man's face to her bosom, laid her cheeks across the back of his head. "Joss, oh Joss, we'll get you down from there, get you fixed up. A poultice. I can do that. Jeremy, get my medicinals out of the wagon. Jeremy!"

Regis glanced at the youngsters, at the silently sobbing boy stroking his papa's head. He'd have to be the man of the clan now. He looked far too young to shoulder such.

In that moment, looking down into her face, Regis made a decision that might dog him for the rest of his days. But in that fragile moment, he felt he had no other choice. He would be weak, weak as water.

He'd do what he could to not admit he was an active participant in the man's death. He told himself the truth would only make a horrible situation worse by having to subdue the angry woman or her equally rage-filled children. Perhaps he could make her think he had merely been charged with bringing him to her. Even as he let his mind weigh this thought, he hated himself for it. Knew it was a mewling, cowardly way out.

"He was found, caught, ma'am." Regis looked at the young boy who was now staring at him unblinking, tears rolling down his dirty cheeks, nothing but raw anger in his eyes.

God, but he had to convince them of . . . of what, Regis? Stick with the truth, as you've tried to live your life all these long years, as you're trying to teach your brother, Shep, by example. And he, not a youth inclined to telling the truth himself. Do it, Regis, he told himself, for the truth will find its way. It always does.

And so Regis Royle swallowed, sat as straight in the saddle as he could, handed her the reins of the pony, which he would leave with her, damn Ambrose. He'd pay the market rate for it.

"Ma'am," said Regis. "This man was found a mile or so from here, butchering a cow."

She nodded, some sort of misplaced hope flickering in her eyes. "Yes," she nodded. "He was going to kill one last of our beef animals, for food for our journey. We're going home." She almost smiled, but it was a reflex spurred by memories, happier times. "But we have got no food."

Regis regarded her. "He was found butchering the cow, ma'am, but it was not his to butcher. It was . . . not his. He was found and judged to be a . . . a rustler, ma'am."

"I don't understand." She looked to her dead husband as if he might look up at her and provide a simple explanation. But he wasn't moving.

He had expected the sort of rage that instant grief spawns, and in this Regis was not disappointed. The oldest boy, red-faced and teeth-gritted, tearful and spitting, rushed him, punching him on the leg with fists that flailed and inflicted no harm.

Regis, still in the saddle, held the horse from dancing and tried to offer words, any words he could think of that might somehow help, though knowing they would do nothing.

The boy interrupted him with a shout of "Shut your mouth!" every time he tried to speak.

Holding her dead husband's head cradled against her bosom, stroking his lank hair, the woman wept in near silence, only her shoulders shaking revealed her plight. The younger children howled because something in their already difficult lives had somehow grown worse, and now their mother, their source of consolation and love, was upset.

"Ma'am, please let me help . . ."

"Go." She shook her head, not looking up, not looking at anything. "Just go away. Leave us be."

He sat in silence on the horse a moment longer, then tried once more. "Ma'am . . ."

She turned her face toward him then, with red-rimmed eyes and wispy hair strands stuck to her tear-soaked cheeks, her mouth a rictus of rage revealing stained teeth. "There's nothing left to do! You've done it all! Go! Go!"

He reached inside his vest to an inner pocket and tugged out his leather cash pouch. It wasn't laden, but it contained more money than he usually carried. He'd neglected to store it in the safe box at his cabin at the ranch when he'd returned there from town the day before.

He tried to hand it down to her, then to the boy, but neither paid attention to him. He tossed it as gently as he could, tough when it thudded to the dusty earth, it seemed an indecency, an offense on top of an awful offense.

He dropped the lead lines of the horse bearing the dead man and tugged his horse's reins, urging the beast around, away from the lamenting family.

He half expected the boy to rush at him, or shoot him in the back as he rode away, but nothing happened except what he could hear—louder crying now from the woman, and her brood.

I helped create a fresh widow and her fatherless children. This has to change, he thought. It cannot go on this way.

Some shadowy beast that he'd never before felt now tracked Regis, and he knew it would never again leave his trail. The only thing he could do would be to never make this mistake again. Or the beast would draw closer, and closer again until one day it would overtake him.

Oh, but the woman had been inconsolable, as he reckoned he would be were someone to bring home his closest loved one, dead.

His thoughts turned to his younger brother, Shepley, draped over a horse, dead. Shep, who was forever pulling some mad stunt that clenched Regis's guts and set his teeth together in anger and frustration. But that didn't mean he could stand to lose the young rascal from his life.

They were, after all, alone now in the world, save for distant relations back East. He and Shep had been separated enough that he didn't think they could ever regain the time apart, but Regis had vowed to try.

When they'd started the ranch, he'd agreed to make his little brother a junior partner in the new, fresh promise of the ranch if he stuck with it and worked hard. It had been all guns firing at the time, but intention, Regis knew from his own experience, was a short-lived thing.

It required dedication to grinding through and sticking with a task, no matter how long range, each day, day on day, night on night. And that was something Shep had proven he was not very good at.

Chapter 3

"Frederico, how goes it, my good amigo?"

The squat, broach-chested man plunked his straw hat atop his black-haired head and smiled, with his mouth. "Good to see you, Señor Shep. What brings you to our home today?"

"Well . . ." The younger man slid down out of the saddle and stood holding the reins of his horse. He fiddled with the ends, looking past Frederico toward the still-open door to the kitchen.

He'd not been in the small adobe home, but he knew what it looked like, because they all looked the same. The small cottage, as Regis insisted a dwelling be called, shared the same construction and layout as all the rest they'd built for the villagers they'd relocated from many miles south, in Mexico.

The plan had been for the Royle Ranch to begin to establish the number of workers that Regis and Bone had been certain, especially Regis, the ranch would need in the coming months and years. At the time, Shep hadn't much cared one way or the other.

Though he was Regis's younger brother, and though Regis had made him some sort of junior partner in the ranching enterprise, Shep had decided he was going to light out after whatever it was his future offered to him.

The ranch, he'd told himself plenty of times, was his brother's dream, not his. And a year and change in, he was nibbling at eighteen years of age, and he wasn't certain what he wanted to do with himself. But he did know one thing for certain: Ol' Frederico—actually, now that Shep saw him close up, he wasn't so certain the Mexican farmer was any older than Regis—had one fine looker of a daughter.

As with her daddy, Shep wasn't entirely certain how old she was. But he'd rummaged around, asking questions of Bone, ranch foreman, legendary Texas Ranger, and all-around solid fellow—especially when it came to dealing with bull-headed Regis—but Bone hadn't known much about the girl.

Course, Shep had cloaked the question in general terms about the entire family. Then he'd asked other questions he didn't care about regarding other of the Mexican families they'd relocated to the Royle Ranch.

Somehow Bone had suspected what he was really asking about. "Shep," he'd said, eyeing Shep with those rocky gray eyes, "where their families are concerned, those fellows from south of the border can be a downright caution, like a head-caught snake." He'd leaned forward, narrowed his eyes, and nodded once, as if Shep might be able to read what was on his mind. Nope.

"I reckon that's good," said Shep. "Last thing we want is a bunch of ranch hands who don't give a fig for their kin." He had hoped that sounded acceptable to Bone.

He wasn't certain if it had been, because he rode off without looking back, in part because he didn't want Bone to beckon him back with one of those long fingers and a sly grin.

That nearly always meant he was about to be handed a pick-axe and a shovel. There was more post-setting to be done. Always more. And digging! That never ended, and it always seemed as if Bone knew where Shep was. Shep couldn't say the same about the Texas Ranger. He'd pop up just when a fellow found a good spot of shade to stretch out in.

"So, boy, what you want here this early?" Frederico smiled again with his mouth.

But not, Shep noticed, with his eyes. He knew. Shep felt his face redden.

"I uh, well, sir, I was just wondering if . . ."

But he couldn't do a damn thing, couldn't get up and ride away for fear of looking like the jackass he felt himself to be. He couldn't make up a lie, not because he was opposed to lying, though. Hell no, he did it all the time to Regis, but because his mind was, all of a sudden, a dried-up thing.

No, actually it was all mush. Just plain mush. All he could do was not look Frederico in the eyes and keep on worrying the curled ends of the leather reins in his hands.

Frederico saved the moment for him by stepping forward, closing the distance between them. He kept stepping. Shep was backed up to the horse, felt the right stirrup nibble his spine. He was about half a head taller than Frederico, but he wasn't half as wide at the shoulder. And those arms, ending in those hands, he could not recall ever seeing hands as thick, as wide as those two brown, work-hardened paws.

Frederico stepped even closer, glanced once over his left shoulder, toward the house, where the doorway was still dark. No morning sounds came from within. Maybe the family's already up and out, thought Shep.

Or maybe they're in there watching and listening. Oh boy.

"Hear me good, Señor Shep."

Señor Shep, thought the young man. He calls me that, even though I'm a junior partner in the ranch. But he calls my brother "Señor Royle," and we have the same surname.

Frederico's breath, inches from his face, dragged him back to the moment as though he'd snatched Shep's shirtfront in one of those ham-size hands and pulled him close.

Frederico still smiled with his mouth. His voice was low, even, like gravel being ground between two flat stones. "My wife and I, we have four children, sí?"

Shep figured the pause meant he should reply. He nodded.

He also tried to swallow, but something lumped in his throat. He nodded again, just in case.

"And the eldest is Mariella, sí?"

Again, he nodded, a lot. As if it were a competition.

"Even though she is the oldest, she has only seen fourteen years." Frederico stopped talking and his dark brown eyes stared unblinking straight into Shep's.

Fourteen. The number echoed in Shep's head. Fourteen? He just said Mariella's age was fourteen? He was nearly eighteen himself. That girl looked, in all the ways a man might tell from a distance, to be at least his own age. But fourteen? Oh, boy.

Frederico was not smiling with his eyes or mouth. He was just staring at Shep from that close. Finally, his gravelly voice curled out and up at him once again. "You know, sometimes I think to myself, 'Frederico? You have done a good thing here, taking Señor Royle up on his offer to build a life with your family and the others from your village, all now here on Texas land.'

"For this used to be Mexican land, too, but anyway. I tell myself that this could be a very good thing for me and my family. After all, we work hard, why should we not also find reward for this? The one thing I have seen though, and it bothers me a little, is the number of coyotes about the place." Frederico paused.

Now Shep was really confused. He nodded again. It had worked a few minutes ago. Maybe it would again.

"Sí, sí," Frederico nodded, his head bobbing, but his eyes never left Shep's. "So I tell my wife to keep the children safe in the house. Because once you get coyotes sniffing around the place, the only thing you can do is shoot them. Shoot them in the ass or the face. Or both. I don't care." He shrugged.

"Anything to keep them from sniffing around my children." He pulled a frown and dipped his head to the side as if deciding on a course of action. "Yes, once you let a coyote come sniffing around your place, you might as well say goodbye to your daughter and sons. Because once a coyote is around, sniffing, he will come back.

And back again, until the very reason he had to come around in the first place is gone. He will have destroyed it. You see?"

Shep nodded, though he wasn't certain he was breathing.

Frederico finally stepped back, and Shep let out a long, stuttering breath. Then, with a quick smile, the man walked to the little house. He turned in the doorway. "Have a good day, Señor Shep."

Shep nodded and leaned against the horse for a moment, thinking. Then he came back to himself and mounted up and galloped on out of there.

Two days later, Shep was seated at the table at the small cabin he shared with Regis, at least when Regis was out at the ranch from Brownsville. His ranch visits were becoming a more frequent thing these days, not a development Shep was all that fond of, truth be told. He liked living alone. Nobody around to tell him what to do and when to do it.

Regis doled out two eggs apiece, and a sizzling steak that smelled pretty darned good. He wasn't about to give Regis a compliment about much of anything, but he'd been close a time or two when it came to the man's cooking. It had to be said that Regis had a touch for preparing vittles.

As Shep sliced off a bite off that hot steak and commenced to chewing, he closed his eyes and might even have grunted. He opened them and saw Regis was doing the same. The older man finished his piece and pointed his wagging knife at Shep across the table. "As long as the only grunting and sniffing you do is here at the table."

Shep jammed in another wad of meat, dripping in egg yolk. "What's that supposed to mean?"

Regis finished slicing another bite of steak, chewed it, swallowed, then finally looked at Shep. "I heard a rumor that you were sniffing around Frederico's daughter, and that's not something that can or will be tolerated by me or anyone. Least of all

Frederico. Man is a hard worker and built like a bull. He'd take you apart with one hand, boy."

Shep let his fork drop with a clatter on the pewter plate. "I can't believe you. Any of you! All I did was—"

"If you're tempted to lie to me, Shep, then skip it. Don't you ever get tired of such shenanigans? Forever running off at the mouth, doing things you know will only lead to headache?"

"For you, maybe."

"What's that mean?"

"You make your own headaches, Regis, that's what I mean."

They ate in silence for a few moments, then Regis said, "And no, Frederico didn't say a word to me. I won't have you thinking ill of that man."

"Never thought he did. Besides, we talked."

Regis hid a grin behind his coffee cup. "Uh-huh," he said, and sipped.

He was smiling, Shep saw over the rim of the cup, with his eyes.

Chapter 4

"We get any more kids sprouting up around here we're going to need a school." Bone rasped a big hand across his jaw and chuckled, looking toward the ragged edge of the most recent gather of beeves in the distance. That particular crew of a dozen men had been at it for days and had brought in fewer head than he'd expected. Rustlers again, he bet.

"And a teacher," said Tut, eyeing Bone with an intensity he usually reserved for the noonday meal.

"What are you getting at, Tut?"

The young man smiled. "Well, here's what I'm thinking. You see . . ." the chunky young ranch hand made that funny sound he always did with his nose when he was about to launch into some long, involved explanation.

The only thing that kept Bone from rolling his eyes was that whenever Tut got that devilish look, he was about to make a decent point. His oddnesses had often resulted in good ideas. Man was a candidate for more responsibility on down the road—he was already the one the men deferred to when Bone wasn't about—provided he didn't eat them out of vittles first. He could pack away the food, could Tut.

"The last time I was in Brownsville, I passed a lovely time with young Miss Belinda Orton. In fact, we had a grand time, walking along the waterfront. She packed a picnic basket and we made a day of it."

Bone nodded. "That's great, Tut. Any chance you could get to the point of the story? I have to talk with Tupper about those beeves they brought in yesterday."

"Oh, yeah, Miss Orton," Tut's face mooned bright and red once more, and his eyes took on that glossy look so common with young men in love.

Bone wondered if he appeared the same way to folks he talked with when he brought up Margaret. It still grated his teeth to think back on how they met—he and the boys, Tut vital among them, having saved Margaret and a handful of other women from being shackled in boxes in a cramped wagon, treated like less than starved, kicked dogs.

And yet she'd flourished once he'd brought her and the others to his own little ranch, left to him unexpectedly by old dear friends, Mack and Martha Deemworth, some miles from Royle Ranch proper. She'd made the place into something he could never have imagined.

It was prettier, if possible, than it had been when old Mrs. Deemworth was alive, with all her gardens and pretty curtains and touches of womanly kindness about the place. Even old Ramon, his hired man, seemed to like having her around, not to mention the critters, for the horse and cattle and sheep all looked happy and well fed, a feat in this dry, dusty land.

"Bone? You listening?"

"Huh, oh, yeah, go ahead, Tut."

"Well, Miss Orton, as I said, she's a schoolteacher, see. Only thing is, if I was to . . ."

"To what, Tut?" Bone still had no idea what the kid was on about.

"To . . ."

Bone raised his eyebrows and canted his head forward, waiting to hear what the red-faced fellow wanted to say.

"To . . . ask her to marry me . . ." Tut said it in a wheezing whisper. "My word, Bone. I never thought I'd say that in my life."

"I know the feeling," mumbled Bone.

"What's that?"

"Nothing. So you're asking me if you was to drag poor Miss Orton out here to live, would we be able to set up a school for the children of Royle Ranch?" Bone smiled, looking once more at the herd of milling beeves, rangy and gnarly though the Longhorns were.

"Well yeah, that's about what I'm asking, yeah. Dang it, Bone, it's a good idea."

"Never said it wasn't, Tut. Just sets me to thinking about how much things have changed here in the last couple of years. You and your pard, Percy, were here nearly from the start, so you know what I mean. Doesn't it ever amaze you to look around and see what we've done here? The lives that have changed because of it?"

Tut shrugged. "Never thought of it that way, but yeah, now you mention it, we've brought a pile of folks and critters here."

Bone nodded. "Yeah, but it's more than that. Look at the buildings we've put up, too. I don't know how many cottages and cabins, loafing sheds and three barns. Those corrals yonder and more back that way toward the river."

"And the stock tanks."

"Yep. The water's likely the most important thing about this place. We'll be able to irrigate more of the land, too. And it'd be nice if we could harvest hay enough to keep the cows from starving in the winter months."

Tut was silent, and Bone saw the younger man was red-faced again and thinking. "You really think it's bad, for a lady, I mean? Miss Orton, you think she'd hate it out here? Because I . . . well what I mean to say is cattle is all I know. All I want to do. If you thought she might not like it, well . . ." He shrugged again, letting the gesture finish his sentence for his mouth. It was one of those traits he'd always had and the men had gotten used to.

All but Regis. He hated it when Tut shrugged. Called it waffling. And he said waffling was a sign of weakness. But hell, Bone had seen Regis shrug as much as any man.

"Doesn't matter what I think, Tut. What matters is what your Miss Orton thinks."

"How will I know?" said Tut.

"Only one way to find out."

"What's that?" The eagerness shone on his face. Kid was desperate for answers.

Bone sighed. "Ask her, Tut. But not until you help me get those new beeves counted." They fell into a fast stride, side by side. "Oh, and Tut?"

"Yeah, Bone?"

"You feel you need to sweeten the deal with Miss Orton, you tell her we're planning on building a right fine little schoolhouse here. With a bell and everything."

"Yeah?" said Tut, smiling wider than any lunch spread could have made him.

"Why not?" Bone smiled himself, for he, too, had just decided something. It didn't involve a schoolhouse, but it did involve plans for the future.

Something that until he'd talked with Tut he hadn't been certain about. Now he was. And it excited him and set his guts to fluttering, all at once.

Chapter 5

"How long you plan on doing what you're doing?"

"Huh?" said Regis, looking at Bone. "What, pouring bad coffee down my throat?"

"I heard that," said Percy the cook.

"Good," said Regis. "I hoped you would. We pay decent money for these beans and you go and ruin them. I've never tasted coffee like this. A curious blend of sock stink, beef tallow, and"—he sipped again, his nostrils flaring and moustaches twitching—"unwashed hair? And thick as pitch. My god, man."

The cook, who rarely cracked so much as a smile, unless he was seen reading one of his many books while he stirred his ever-present stewpot, on this occasion smiled broadly. But he still did not look up. "You've discovered my secret recipe, boss."

Though his mouth held its down-pulled pose, Regis knocked back another slug of the vile brew.

Bone, despite the seriousness of the topic he'd brought up, could not help but smile. "I'll give you this, Regis. You're as headstrong in your pursuit of downing a cup of coffee as you are in just about everything else."

Regis dragged his wrist across his moustaches and tamped down a belch. "I'll take that as a compliment," he said. "Now, what was that you asked me? How long I plan on doing what?"

Bone looked about them. What he intended to talk with his boss and senior partner about required they be away from the peeled ears of the crew.

"Well, what I mean is . . ." Bone rasped a big hand across his jaw.

"Out with it, Bone. We know each other well enough to not hold back when something's on our mind. And you have the look of a fellow with a mind full of something." Regis grinned and lost it as soon as he sipped from his cup again.

"Okay, then, here it is—that Cattlemen's Consortium of yours."

"What about it?" Regis tried to keep his tone light, but Bone detected a hint of guardedness.

"You know the Rangers are getting back together, right?"

"I do, yep."

"Well, they've asked me do I want to give it another go."

Regis smiled. "I hope you told them you're too busy, Bone. We need you here, at the Royle Ranch. On the Santa Calina range." He waved an arm wide to indicate the broad sweeping views of waving grasses. "Besides, that's a young man's game."

"Just how old do you take me for, Regis?"

"Easy now, Bone. I don't mean to offend you. I just meant . . ."

"I know what you meant, thanks. And whether I do or don't Ranger up again is not something you have to worry about. And it isn't really what I wanted to talk with you about."

"Well, what is it, then? Been a long time since I was a mind reader, Bone."

"As I said, it's your Consortium, Regis."

"Not my Consortium. It's a group of ranchers who've banded together to—"

"I know what you do. It's how you do it that I have a problem with."

"Well now just how do you expect us to deal with rustlers? You know as well as I do that they're no different than those border trash and bands of desperates who kept trying to run us off when we first set up shop here. And from what you've told me, we still get them."

"Not as much, but yeah, they're still around. But it's not the same thing, Regis."

"Why? Because we take the fight to them instead of waiting for them to show up on our door step?"

"No. It's because you are playing judge and jury. Big difference."

"It's not like the law is doing anything about it."

Bone sighed. "You know as well as I do the law's stretched thin in these parts. That's why they're regrouping the Rangers."

"And I'm glad they are, but what am I—and the other ranchers—supposed to do in the meantime? Shout at these fools? Shoot over their heads?"

"Nope, but you could lock them up."

"Lock them up," Regis snorted. "Where? And how?"

"We're building everything else here at the ranch, why not a jail? You said yourself you want this place to be its own town."

"Eventually, yeah, but why should I pay to feed and house a cattle thief?"

Bone closed his eyes and rubbed them hard with a thumb and fingers. "You know what? Doesn't matter, Regis. No matter what I say, you'll have an answer, one that makes sense to yourself, at least."

"You taking the side of the rustlers, Bone?"

"Pull them horns in, pard." Bone's voice was low and cold, steel on steel.

For a long minute neither man spoke, though neither did they walk away from each other. It was a sign, they each knew, that they were maturing further into their roles, Regis as owner and chief decision maker, and Bone as trusted lesser partner and relied-upon ranch foreman.

When Regis finally spoke, it was in a cooled-down tone. He

was still steamed, though, and couldn't bring himself to look at Bone yet. He remained gazing out toward the distant river, the Santa Calina, flowing beyond the swaying cottonwood trees that marked the embankment. "What's really eating at you, Bone?"

"All right, you asked. It's that young rancher you strung up. I knew him, Regis Not well, but well enough. You could have asked me, Regis. You and the others could have waited a little longer, listened to the man. Not everyone is out to get you, not everyone is out to take what's yours. Or at least what you think is yours."

Regis's face was tight, like a painted-on mask. "What's that mean?"

"No, no. No changing horses in midstream, man. You know as well as I do that fella was innocent. He was feeding his young family and that beef he cut out didn't even have your brand, nor that of anyone else's in your so-called Consortium, did it?"

Regis said nothing, his jaw muscles and red face doing all the talking for him. Finally, he spoke in a low voice, almost a whisper, "I paid her, dammit."

"I know. But that doesn't bring back her husband, nor a father to those children."

Regis rounded on him, his eyes blazing. "What do you want me to do, Bone?"

"You apologize to her? Tell her you were wrong?"

"How in the hell could that help her?"

"Not her I was thinking of so much as how it would help you."

Regis said nothing, but resumed his stance.

As tensed as his old friend was, Bone wasn't certain if Regis was about to turn on him and take a swing. They'd tussled lightly before, and each man knew the other was his match and would offer no quarter should it come to it. That was something neither man wanted.

Bone sighed again. "Look, Regis, it's ignoring the rule of law that sticks hardest in my craw. If we don't hold onto our laws, as paltry and new as they are, we haven't got a thing. Not a thing left. It's every man for himself, then. Not that it hasn't been, what with everybody rushing around out here, gobbling up cattle and horses before someone else can."

Regis looked about to reply, so Bone kept on. "I'm not pointing fingers—I do it, too. But I'm talking about what makes this land special to us all. Texas isn't a thing without the people who believe in it. And if you don't have a foundation, a layer of bedrock a mile deep of laws and rules and whatever else the fancy politicians care to call it, then you have fools rushing around killing other fools, and that can't end but one way, Regis."

Any scrim of reason and hope he'd seen on Regis's face was gone, replaced with a hardness he'd seen before whenever his old friend was cornered.

"How's that, Bone?"

Bone snorted, reading his friend's mocking tone. "You know that as well as I do. No need for me to spell it out."

"No, by all means, you seem to know so much and I know so little, especially about my business and all, so why don't you go on and tell me how it'll end."

Bone looked at him. "You keep on as you are, you'll find out soon enough." He walked away, feeling Regis's hot gaze burning holes in his back. He didn't think his old pard would jump him, but if he did, Lord help him. For as keyed up as Bone was, he felt as though he could drop Regis with a single blow.

Chapter 6

Ambrose Dalton looked at the group of his fellow Cattlemen's Justice Consortium members, gathered for the second time in the past month, this time at his place. He smacked his quirt lightly against the broad, polished surface of the table.

"Regis Royle has brought up the point that we ought to back off of the lynching the rustlers. Says maybe we ought to let the newly reformed Texas Rangers have at it." He stroked his jowly pink face and looked around the room. "Now, never let it be said that Ambrose Dalton ever told anybody what to think . . ."

A slight chuckle rippled through the small gathering.

"But I say there's no sense in relaxing our vigilance, especially now that we have them on the run. Why, if we don't keep on, we are going to regret being lazy when we had the chance, and for a long time to come."

Ambrose had shoved the table clean at the start of the meeting, and now they waited for his maid to haul in refreshment. The portly rancher had a cook they all envied, a capable fellow who could turn his hand to most any dish a person could think up.

With tasty vittles about to appear, it was tricky to keep their minds on the business at hand—namely, the annoying numbers of rustlers still nibbling away their herds. And now that upstart, Royle, wanting to ease off just when they were starting to get a leg up and over them.

That their herd numbers could be lowered even more in the coming months was something none of them wanted to hear. They had each secretly hoped there might be nothing to the on-going reports Ambrose's new hire, a scout by the name of Tomas, fed them.

"We've been meeting like this for a while now," said Dubber Jones, "and I, for one, have no intention of easing up. Yeah, we already caught a passel of the dirty thieves who've been plaguing us with their constant rustling." He directed his attention straight at Regis. "And that's just the reason to keep on. When something is going full steam, son, you don't stop feeding it fuel."

A few of the other men nodded their agreement, grumbling, "Hear, hear . . ."

Regis nodded. "I appreciate you letting me speak about this earlier. And I knew how you'd feel even before I brought it up, but it doesn't mean I have to agree with you. I just think we ought to give the Rangers a chance at doling out justice in a law-ful way—"

Dubber cut him off. "But you're telling us we got to ease off. Why? Seems to me the more of them owl hoots we can hoist up to swing from branches, the more our warning will be taken that we are as serious as a case of cholera."

"Not ease off on catching and capturing the rustlers, no," said Regis. "Just on the hanging of them. Why not let the law have them?"

Dubber Jones snorted and plunked down hard in his chair, looking away from them all, his disgust unmasked as he stared out the window.

Dubber was the least couth of the half-dozen members and was also the least liked among them. He was barely tolerated in their midst, as the stink of meat grease, flyblown milk gone off in the sun, man sweat, and woodsmoke drifted off him like ripples on a pond surface, traveling outward. None of the ranchers wanted to be the first to show weakness by scooching his chair back or coughing. But, to a man, their eyes watered.

How he got to be owner of a sizable spread, none could figure. At least that's what they leaned on in conversation. But they all knew that Dubber Jones was the most genuine rancher among them. He had come out to Texas some years before—no one could tell how old the man was.

So seamed and puckered was his face, he could have told them he was 102 and none would disagree. Unlike a number of his portly fellow ranch owners, Dubber was whip-lean and moved about the room as he spoke with the grace of a mountain lion.

He'd directed his rant at Regis Royle, youngest ranch owner among them, and certainly the greenest in his knowledge of ranching. But they all knew that Royle was also one of the smartest. At least in a business sense.

Individually, each man envied Royle for his looks—he was tall, regal as befitting his name, princely in his bearing, and a successful businessman, to boot. A couple of the men knew Royle's business partner in a shipping business, Cormac Delany, and respected him. And so, they respected Regis Royle.

Even if it still irked them that a couple of years back he'd had balls enough to ride on into that vast, raw, outlaw-and-vermin-infested border-hugging country—some of it pretty and useful, some of it foul and snakey and godawful—and laid claim to it.

Should have been one of them, they'd thought. But then again, they each had laid claim to a vast empire of land themselves, and had more on their plates than they could handle.

They'd also each had regular, unending troubles with rustlers—vaqueros out of work, gringos with more greed than sense rattling in their gourds, and Apaches and Comanches and half-breeds looking to take anything that wasn't nailed down.

As with the others, Regis came up against such regular depredations to his growing herd—masses of wild-eyed, bawky, corner-me-and-I'll-gore-you, brush poppin' cattle, and the horse equivalent, veritable seas of tangle-mane, hoof-drumming mustangs that would as soon rear up and stomp you to bloody paste as look at you.

Months ago he'd convinced his nearest ranching neighbors, to his northwest Ambrose Dalton, and to his north, Chaw Perkins, that they should form something akin to what he'd heard the cattlemen up north, in Kansas and Oklahoma and Colorado and Nebraska way had, a cattlemen's club, to protect their interests.

At their first meeting, he'd bulled, "Strength in numbers, gentlemen!" pounding a big fist on a tabletop before treating them all to a fine meal and more booze than they'd had in years.

"Don't you all want to make certain when the time comes— and it's coming soon, gentlemen"—he kept throwing out that word and, by gaw, if it didn't suit them—"that we had formed a group where we can not only enjoy such meals on a monthly basis, but we'll have also helped each other, in the spirit of camaraderie, to seek more equitable prices for our beeves? And to protect our hard-won herds from thieves?"

Nobody could argue the point. He'd continued: "The thing to do, of course, is for us to work together instead of fight alone for the same things. If we work together, we can convince the railroads—all we need is one—to run a spur line to Texas. Wouldn't that be preferable to driving our cattle so far north that they end up losing half their worth on the trail?"

The men had grumbled and nodded their agreement. "Together we can get the best prices for our beef. Hell, we can force the railroads to meet our demands, and we can improve our opportunities at the same time. And for years to come. Maybe forever!"

"Strength in numbers," Ambrose had said, nodding his fleshy face.

The others had agreed. After all, they didn't drag their poor suffering families all the way out here to this hot-as-hell place to give their hard-won takings over to others, did they?

"I know I would welcome such a club," continued Royle, sitting down. Before anyone could voice a squeak of protest, he raised his glass. "Gentlemen, to the Cattlemen's Justice Consortium."

And so it had come into being, a rather grand name for a small handful of ranchers looking to make more money and stop the rustling of their beeves. Most of them hoped it would be an excuse for them to drink and chew the gristle, complain about how lazy their hands were, how they couldn't find a decent cook, and how roundup was not as easy as it once had been.

They commiserated without cease on the poor price of beef and how the ranchers to their north had it so much easier, being closer to rail heads and all. By the time the poor Texas rancher drove their head all the way to Abilene or some such cow town railhead, the tallow was walked clean off them.

"Size they are when they get there, might as well be herding damn goats!" Ambrose had shouted. None had disagreed.

That had been many months before. Now, Regis had raised one of the primary points they had all agreed on back then, namely how to deal with rustlers. Except now he was urging them to consider less severe tactics.

He didn't tell them why, of course, but having Jarvis "Bone" McGraw famous Texas Ranger as a friend and, more important, as his ranch manager, had quite a bit to do with it. But the other, larger part was his encounter with the widow and children of the man he'd helped to kill.

Thoughts of the man's begging and struggling blended with the horrified looks and gut-twisting cries of his family, plaguing Regis's wakeful hours, and tormenting his scant sleep, dragging him each night into a morass of nightmare. Since then, he'd awakened each morning, exhausted, dark eyed, and shamed.

He'd promised himself that somehow he'd track down the

fractured family and send them money, and his efforts had proven fruitful, thanks in part to Bone's various connections. It was a small thing, he knew, mostly to soothe his own guilt. It had done little in that regard, but he had to try.

Just like standing before these men, urging them to let the Rangers, and thus the rightful law, not a self-appointed version, handle the suspected thieves. It went over as he knew it might.

He cleared his throat once more. "Judging from the fine smells drifting in here from the kitchen, I think we have just enough time for me to tell you about a letter I received."

"Who from? A sweetie?" Chaw Perkins giggled and a thin drizzle of tobacco juice seeped from his mouth's corner.

"No," said Regis. "If it was, I sure as hell wouldn't share it here." He smiled. "It's from one Mr. De Haviland, owner of the Southern and Coastal Railroad."

Just then a Mexican girl carried in a platter heaped with roasted beef and set it on the sideboard. Other boys and girls did the same with pitchers of gravy, bowls of potato, carrots, and more.

"I think," said Ambrose, shoving up and out of his chair and all but salivating as he eyed the food, "you ought to make it brief and fill us all in on the particulars after the meal, okay, Royle?"

Regis nodded. "In short, Mr. De Haviland has already sent scouts up to the northwest of our state to verify that what our letter to him said was true. He liked what he heard and has sent a crew to begin preliminary work in laying track for a spur line. Gentlemen, the efforts of the Cattlemen's Justice Consortium are beginning to show signs of paying off."

He could see, by the head nods and raised eyebrows among them—with the exception of Dubber Jones, who was still in the midst of one of his protracted snits—that they were pleased with the possibility of having a closer rail head to ship their beef out. "It's early days, yet, but it's a promising sign."

The men were patting each other's backs and smiling as they

tucked into the toothsome spread. All but Dubber Jones, that is. He still scowled as he tucked into the feast with vigor.

Regis sighed and filled his plate. "Can't please everybody," he said to himself.

Ambrose, who'd expended formidable restraint in allowing his guests to load up before him, now stood at Regis's elbow. "Whoever told you you had to please anybody but yourself in life, Royle?" He cackled and heaped food on his plate.

The fat man's words echoed in Regis's ears for long minutes afterward. It dawned on him for the first time that just because he had chosen to work with these men didn't mean he had to like them.

Chapter 7

Tupper MacDonald took a long, hard look at the tangle of rambunctious Longhorns they'd driven down into the long, narrow arroyo. Must have been fifty head of them, all of them snorting and raking the sandy soil with sharp hooves.

You couldn't pay me enough cash money to climb down there and walk amongst them, he thought.

Thankfully, there was little cause to do that. He had eleven other men with him, all of them spread out in various directions, in twos and threes, all slowly looping wide and riding in closer together as they neared the arroyo once more. And each time they brought with them more of the wild, tail-hoisted-high longhorns. Wouldn't take long before they'd all but exhausted the supply of these mangy, rangy critters, at least down here across the Santa Calina and southward.

"Got to be a smarter way to make a wage," Tupper sighed and cut along the edge of the ravine. He yawned and closed his eyes for a second. That's when his horse spooked.

As he toppled from the saddle on the left side, his left boot snagging briefly, then slipping free of the stirrup, between the dancing beast's front hooves he caught sight of the reason he'd been thrown—a rattler, reared and riled and ready.

Had the horse been struck? He wasn't certain, but as it had

danced away and from the looks of it intended to keep running, he'd guess not. Or at least it hadn't yet felt the effects of a bite.

Tupper tumbled, rolling and bouncing off rocks he knew would cause him no end of grief once he reached the bottom. He'd be sore, no doubt. The commotion caused the beeves he'd been watching from on high to scatter. Near the bottom, his right shin smacked down hard into a rock, then his left shoulder hit, and he slopped hard onto it. He felt something inside crunch as he jerked to a stop.

Tupper lay there a moment, waiting for the pain to begin, for reason to settle over him once more. He tried to keep his eyes open, but the sunlight was far too bright. Then he realized he wasn't seeing right anyway.

He was barely aware that the cows had drifted toward him, yet remained parted as if by a magician's hand. They watched from a distance as he wallowed and moaned and tried to suck through his gritted teeth air enough to begin a cursing tirade. But as soon as he pulled in that shallow breath, needles of fire lanced through him.

That can't be good, he thought, his mind skittering from one thought to the next. He'd gone through most of his life without injury, but it looked as though that winning streak was behind him. His shoulder blazed with an agonizing internal fire, and his head buzzed and rang from the blows it had taken. That would account for why I can't see so well, he thought.

Through ringing ears, Tupper heard hoofbeats grow fainter and assumed it was his pesky horse. Should have shot the thing when he'd had the chance. But then again it would not have mattered.

He'd always had piss-poor luck with horse flesh, usually inheriting a flighty, feather-brain mount from some other more experienced cowboy who would say, "Never had trouble with that horse myself," whenever he complained.

Finally, a few years back, a foreman who had no tolerance for anything that wasn't work related told him it wasn't the fault of the horses, but his. He was a nervous person and the horses knew it and he was making them jumpy. Tupper had tried to argue with him, but the seasoned cowboy had stuck a long finger up in the air and shook his head.

That was all it took. Tupper had shut his mouth and kept it shut for the rest of the season. But he'd thought long and hard about what that old foreman had told him. Before Christmas time later that year, Tupper had been one of the men the ranch had cut loose. He couldn't blame them. They only kept the old stove-huggers around since there wasn't much to do about the place all winter anyway.

But before he'd ridden off, he'd thanked that crotchety foreman for being honest with him. Since then he'd worked to be less nervous around horses. Most of the progress he'd made he reckoned just came with age. You live long enough, you'll get used to most anything, and you'll be less nerved up about it, no matter what the "it" is, if you're a baker or a sailor or a cowhand.

All this and more tumbled through Tupper MacDonald's mind as he lay there, face up and sagged, wedged between boulders along the bottom edge of the arroyo. What breaths he could draw were shallow, the barest of sips of the day's hot air. He was aware that he was feeling odd all over, mostly from his neck on down.

There was no way he could seem to get himself up out of there. Arms didn't hurt, nor his legs, but he couldn't make them do his bidding. It was downright annoying. Only things that hurt now were his face and his head.

Even his shoulder, the one he'd landed hard on, the one that had sounded as if it had been crunching apart, like a boulder crushed by a giant's stomping boot, no longer hurt. Maybe that meant he was not as bad off as he thought. Then why couldn't he get up out of there?

Rest, he told himself, take a minute and stop being all nerved up. Think about it. A fleeting vision came to him of that old foreman's face, old Sinny was what they'd called him. Tupper hadn't thought that much about him or anybody from his past for many a day.

The afternoon dissolved like they all do in south Texas, slowly and almost without notice, until suddenly the sky was pink, then crimson, then purple. At least that's what Tupper saw, laying face up in a ditch, unable to move.

Except for the fact that the sun felt as though it were baking his eyeballs, turning them into raisins, that afternoon was the first time he could recall in years that he had paid attention to the waning of the day.

He'd been hired on at the Royle Ranch some months before. He was already used to being in charge of a group of cowboys, and though it was made clear to him when he'd hired on that Jarvis "Bone" McGraw, the famous Texas Ranger-turned-rancher, was the foreman of the outfit, Tupper felt sure that if given enough time he'd be able to show them all what sort of man he was.

He'd been a ranch hand, after all, for nigh onto eighteen years. Not as long as some of the old timers, but then again he wasn't as broken-down as a lot of them, either. He'd always taken care to avoid injuries to either him or his mount, and encouraged his men to do the same.

Not that he'd ever shirked duties when they called for riding hard and fast, or tucking into a sticky situation—a beef bogged in a mire or a mustang thrashing and seized tight in a thorny thicket. But all that had happened before this day.

Now, as he looked up at a purpling sky that indicated the coming night, Tupper began to realize that whatever had happened to him when he fell wasn't going away any time soon. It was with him for a long ol' time. He'd been somehow changed forever.

He guessed that when the men found him, they'd lug him back to the ranch, and he'd heal up as best as he was able, on his cot in the corner of the bunk house. They'd have to bring him his food for a spell, as is always done at any ranch of worth when a man busts a leg, or some such ailment he sustains while on ranch time.

Dusk became full-dark night, and still Tupper heard no hooves clicking on stone, no voices shouting his name, nothing but the skitter of critter claws hurrying across stone, the clatter of dry branches, wind whistling up and around low juts of sandstone. Then coyotes yipped far off. Then closer . . . and closer still. And wolves, too.

"Hey!" he said and coughed. The word was little more than a grunt, a whisper, a wheeze that a man seated next to him would barely be able to hear. Why couldn't he shout like he wanted to? He tried again. Same thing. He'd put all his strength into it and that was all that came out. He sounded as weak as an orphan kitten.

And where were those men of his? They'd surely have seen he wasn't among them by now, wouldn't they? Then Tupper recalled the directives he'd given them all before they'd split up, to make damn sure they returned with a full measure of beeves or stay out all night trying. And land's sake, don't stop every five minutes and hug a coffee pot over a camp fire. He liked a cup of brew as much as the next man, but if they were going to get the task done, they needed to see to it, and he would brook no excuses.

He reckoned now he'd laid it on thick, maybe too much so. But if he had to be honest, he'd wanted to impress Bone, and Regis Royle himself, who he'd only seen on the day he'd been hired. Bring in enough fresh stock as Bone had tasked him to do, along with the handful of men he was loosely in charge of, and word would surely get to Regis Royle that Tupper MacDonald was a man who deserved the consideration of promotion, in due course, naturally. Yes sir, Tupper was a man who could get things done.

He knew the other men thought he was a hardnose, maybe a bit of a seeker of favor, but he didn't much care. He wanted a promotion and, so, he wanted results. Did that mean the men were still out rounding up cattle? Nah, not in the dark, no matter what they'd promised. Then why weren't they here?

That's when Tupper heard other sounds, sounds he knew but hadn't ever heard this close up before. They were low, snuffling, growly sounds. The padding of paws on gravel.

"Hey!" he said again, with as much force as he was able to conjure. By his hearing, it wasn't much. "You there, keep off! Get gone from here . . ."

The sounds stopped. Tupper waited, listening. Soon they began again. They were coming from his left, toward the slope of the bank he'd tumbled down. At least that's where he thought it was.

As embankments went, it wasn't much of one, so since it hadn't been a big tumble, it stood to reason he'd be fine. Something inside him needed to rest up, that's all. Come morning, if not before, he'd be as right as a spring rain.

The snuffling began again. And the paw sounds, slight, but they were there. Could not mistake them for anything else. Coyotes. He growled back at the noise as it drew closer. Then he heard it from the other side, his right. Panting, lots of panting, hoarse breaths, and snuffling. Then he saw the first, a dim shape barely visible in the near-dark. It jerked away when he spoke, doing his best to shout. He tried spitting, but his mouth was so dry, his throat so sore he couldn't work up a gobbet.

The creature's wariness didn't last for long. It was soon joined by other dark shapes that slinked in and out of his view, and this strengthening of their numbers seemed to embolden them all. For some reason that escaped him, Tupper could not move his head. He had to rely on his eyes roving far to either side in their sockets.

He growled—a small, scratchy sound—in frustration. The beasts backed away, but less so with each sound he uttered. Soon they would be on him, and still Tupper heard no hoofbeats, no men shouting his name, searching for him, no sounds beyond the closing-in snuffling and heavy, raw breaths and low growls.

Soon, unless a miracle found him, soon the beasts would be on him. And here I am, thought Tupper. On my back in a ditch in a country that's flat enough that ditches shouldn't even much exist. And I can't do a single damn thing about any of it.

They will be on me, and I will have to let it all happen. He gritted his teeth, or at least that's what he thought he was doing. He opened his eyes wide. "Okay, then, Tupper. Here is that day none of us wants to see, but none of us can avoid. Here's where your story ends."

It had been light for nearly an hour before a man on horse-back, Sol Renard, rode along the upper edge of what looked to be a gully. He saw the horse's tracks, the churned, sandy earth where the horse from the day before had reared and stomped and thrashed in place before digging in and bolting. He halted and studied the tracks.

Then Sol glanced to his left, downslope. And what he saw was something that would haunt his mind for the rest of his long days.

Tupper MacDonald lay face up, staring at the sky, a buzzard standing still as stone four or five feet beyond him, staring alternately at the cowboy up the slope, then back to Tupper. Tupper looked dead. Or at least unmoving. But no, he was dead. Had to be.

Sol could tell by the man's eyes—wide open and staring up. At least one of them was. The other, the right eye, had been plucked from the socket and hung, a halved, bloody mess, from a strip of gristle draped across the bridge of Tupper's nose. What was left of the man's lips were swollen and puckered, but had been mostly nibbled away.

"Tupper?" Sol knew the response he would get was the same he'd just received—nothing at all. Tupper was dead, dead, and dead. But what if he was wrong?

"Hang on there, Tupper. I'm coming down."

Sol slipped from his saddle and ground tied the horse. He scrambled down the dozen feet and slid to a stop beside the prone man.

The buzzard, who was oddly alone, seemed reluctant to give up such a good spot at the table. It squawked and hopped about as if it had never done so before, looking awkward and drunk. Its wings were raised as if it were set to take flight but had decided against it.

"Get out of here!" snarled Sol. He gritted his teeth and squinted down at the dead man, for by now he was most certain of that fact. Tupper was well and truly dead.

The most curious thing about him was that he had tufts of what appeared to be hair sticking out of his mouth. Sol looked closer. Yes, that's what it was, hair. As if he'd bitten something and come away with nothing but a mouthful of hair. Odd.

That's when he saw the paw prints all about the ground around Tupper.

"Coyotes," muttered Sol.

He reached a worn leather-gloved hand to Tupper's shoulder and nudged him. He jerked his hand back, though he knew it was foolish to do so. The man had stiffened, but his head jostled a little. That's when Sol saw that the big rock on the right side of Tupper's head bore stains, blood stains. Likely the earth, too, had absorbed plenty.

Had he laid there unconscious until he'd died? No, couldn't have, otherwise, how to account for the coyote hair in his mouth?

Sol recalled what a hard boot Tupper was, or had been, and with the barest hint of a wry grin, he said, "You gave back what you got, I reckon, Tupper." He looked at the man's hands for signs of bite marks, more hair, broken nails, anything. But of these he found nothing. It was mystifying, that's all there was to it. Strange.

They'd found Tupper's horse ganted and standing near the

corral that morning before dawn. The saddle had drooped until it hung beneath the horse's barrel, the reins were mismatched in length, and puckered where Percy, the cook, had reckoned they'd been trodden on by the horse itself.

"I'd guess that means Tupper got throwed," said a burly man named Dewlap. Most of the men wanted to pass it off as something Tupper deserved. But Bone put a quick stop to their silly chuckles with a quick, barked order and a hard look. "Knock it off."

The inference was plain—it wasn't any laughing matter, and the next time, it could well be any of them that got thrown, crippled, and savaged by night beasts.

Sol and the boys felt doubly bad, for they had been correct. Much as Tupper's big mouth irked them, none of them would wish such an end on any of their fellows, even ones of which they weren't overly fond.

It turned out that the poor man had likely been rendered a paralytic in his body, if not in his mind, when he was thrown. A sad and vicious end to a man. And to find him with wild dog fur in his mouth told them he was as tough and resilient as he, by example, expected them all to be.

Chapter 8

Tupper MacDonald's death had rattled them all enough that Bone gave everyone the remainder of the day of the man's funeral off to spend as they saw fit. For himself, though he had regarded Tupper as a solid hand, he had never taken a shine to the man as a pard. But that didn't mean he wouldn't think back on him, honor him in his own way.

He rode off, leaving Tut in charge for a day or two. He'd been planning on riding off that morning anyway, but the funeral had come up.

It had been a week since he'd been back to his own ranch, the spread left to him by his old employer and longtime pard, Mack Deemworth, and his longer-departed wife, Martha. They were both buried at the ranch, on a low knob behind the house.

It was a small spread in comparison with the Royle Range, but plenty enough for him. Let Regis keep on with his land-buying spree. Bone had all he needed.

At present, his ranch was overseen by Ramon, an old Mexican he'd hired on to keep an eye on things. He'd been considering bringing on another man, or perhaps a boy to help old Ramon out with the chores.

He'd not run much in the way of stock, mostly because the old man wouldn't be able to keep a close eye on them, and Bone was gone much of the time tending to Royle Ranch affairs. That had been a while back. Then everything changed with the arrival of Margaret in his life.

He and the boys had been out gathering beeves down along the southwest corner of the Santa Calina range when they'd come across a slaver. Or rather he'd come across them, making for the border. Bone knew from first glance that the man was a lowly sort.

That had turned into quite a ruckus. They'd ended up killing both the slaver's two outriders, and eventually the foul man himself. They'd heard noises and peeled apart that slaver's odd-looking, closed-in wagon. They found seven women locked away in there, each bound at the wrist and ankle in crate-like spaces no bigger than you'd keep a rogue dog in. All had been alive but one, the youngest, no more than a girl.

Bone found the dead girl in the wagon, locked in a box that the slaver had been using as a bench. A bench, for god's sake! The memory of it still set his teeth hard together.

They'd helped those who wanted to return to their old lives, others they helped ease into new lives. One of them, a black woman, a spitfire by the name of Daisy, had taken up with Lockjaw Hames, a broad-shouldered dock worker who'd come out to the ranch with a batch of sailors and dock hands already in the employ of Regis and Cormac.

They'd been in between cargo loads and coastal shipping trips, so Regis brought them to the ranch to help with various chores. Some of the men were most definitely not accustomed to work on land, away from their beloved ships.

But others, such as Lockjaw, had taken well to ranch life. He'd liked it so well, in fact, that he'd asked to be a full-time employee at the ranch, forsaking life at the docks. And Daisy had settled right into life there at the ranch with him.

Bone didn't mind one bit; they were a formidable pair. As big a man as Lockjaw was, that little woman led him around like a goat on a rope. Bone counted the ranch lucky to have them there.

As for himself and his ranch, he'd also come up aces, in a manner of speaking. One of the women from the slave wagon, Margaret, had emerged as a leader among the women. She was forthright, no-nonsense, quiet, but strong as a steel rod.

At Bone's gentle urging, she'd eased into staying on at his ranch. It seemed she had nowhere to go. He never pressed her about her past life, nor did she offer him any information about such. He figured time would draw it out of her, or not. He didn't much care.

Bone had fallen for her as he'd not done for any other woman in his life. And he believed she was fond of him as well. It had been many months since they'd rescued the women and he'd taken them to his ranch to heal up.

Then the others had moved on, and Margaret was living at the ranch, with old Ramon in the bunk house. Together they ran the place pretty well. She kept a flock of chickens for eggs and meat, and helped Ramon to wrangle the hundred or so head of Longhorns, the dozen horses, and two mules that Ramon insisted they keep to plow and plant, not to mention Ramon's little donkey, Tomatillo.

In addition, there were a few goats and more than a few sheep, beasts that Bone was unfamiliar with, but Margaret and Ramon both liked them for milk and cheese and meat and wool. Made sense, then, to keep them. And helping tend them seemed to make Margaret happy. As long as Bone didn't have to dally with the woollies, he was not opposed to it.

And now here he was, riding the trail northward to his ranch, resolved to talk seriously with Margaret about something he'd been mulling for some time now. It had taken Tupper MacDonald's death and burial to jar Bone enough to do the job. And today is the day, he thought. Today he'd ask Margaret what she might think about becoming his wife. Marrying up with him.

That's something, thought Bone. Him, a freebooting Texas Ranger, settling down. He gigged his horse, Buck, into a jaunty trot to match his mood.

The day was turning off warm. They'd gotten Tupper's grave dug the afternoon before, then the following morning they'd held a sunrise service and buried him. Tut seemed to recall Tupper saying he had a sister and nephew somewhere in Arkansas. Or was it Illinois? At any rate, he'd asked Tut to go through the man's personal things, gather what of value, sentimental and otherwise, there might be. Then he'd get Regis to take the lot back to Brownsville whenever the next supply run was made to town.

Hopefully, Cormac or the bookwormy fellow he hired to help with accounts a few days a week might be able to ship Tupper's goods, along with a letter explaining the man's unfortunate demise and their regret at losing him in this way.

Though the man's personality had been a bit annoying, and he was ambitious, always looking for a way to curry favor with him or Regis, even Shep, for that matter, he'd also been a competent stockman and someone who took every task seriously, which was more than Bone could say for quite a few of the men.

There were a whole lot of saddle warmers in the bunch, belligerent at having to climb down out of the saddle and set to a task. Bone never forgot such behavior, and the ambitious were always rewarded while the shirkers were always heaped with more distasteful tasks until they tightened up, left, or waited to be fired.

His mind returned to the trail. He was still some hours from his ranch house, where Margaret awaited. And then a thought stilled the smile spreading beneath his voluminous moustaches.

Here he was going to tell Margaret about poor Tupper's death by mishap, and then follow that up with why he was asking her to marry him—because the man's death had frightened him?

"Bone," he said to himself, slowing the horse to a walk. "You aren't the sharpest knife in the block, but surely you know better than that." Particularly for such as Margaret, a fine, handsome, intelligent woman his age who he was certain would have suitors all over the range if he hadn't unwittingly holed her up at his ranch.

Now that he knew her, he'd move mountains and rivers, and fight tooth, nail, and claw to hold on to her. He hoped she felt that way about him.

On that score, though, Bone was less certain than he was of his own feelings. Margaret was a curious woman, not prone to smiling, nor showing much in the way of outwardly affection.

But in their infrequent but meaningful conversations, he'd come to believe that when she trusted someone, not something she came to easily, she was steadfast and true, someone to rely on, someone to ride the river with—for the rest of one's life.

Chapter 9

Three hours later, Bone rode through the gate and down the long lane leading to his ranch proper, a tidy little place he'd long admired but had never ever guessed he'd own. He reckoned he was nearly as tired as his horse.

His face was dusted from the trail, his head was hot from the sun, and his back was sore from jouncing in the saddle. All he wanted was to climb down out of the saddle, shake his kinked long legs, rub the feeling back into his rump, and take a good, long pull of water from the sweet well Mack had dug years before.

Then he wanted to see Margaret's handsome face squinting at him from the porch. He could already see her standing there like she always did, as if she'd been born to the place, a towel from the kitchen draped over her shoulder, her sleeves rolled up to her elbows, a little flour dusting her strong arms, those work-reddened hands resting on her fine hips, her chestnut hair caught in a little breeze.

That's what he most wanted to see. Then he'd stride to the porch, not wait this time to ask her permission to kiss her, something that had taken him several months to work up the nerve to do. No sir, this time he'd wrap his arms around about her waist and pull her close and kiss her heartily right on the mouth.

But as with many such moments in life, that flower soon wilted in his mind. When Bone rode up, he saw something he did not expect: An unfamiliar wagon sat parked before the house. A brace of thin, rangy horses looking more suited to trudging before a plow stood hipshot in the traces.

The closer Bone rode the worse the wagon looked. It was in poor upkeep, once painted green, its boards were flaking, puckered, and curled, and from the looks of the neglected wheels, the hubs needed greasing.

"Who in the heck is this?" said Bone to Buck. The horse flicked an ear, and Bone slid down out of the saddle and led the horse to the rail before the house.

He glanced at the bunk house across the yard, with the barn and corral beyond, but of old Ramon, there was no sign.

From the house he heard a man's voice, not deep, but loud, saying a string of words he couldn't make out much of, but they weren't raised in kindness or laughter. A low growl coiled up out of Bone's throat as he mounted the step, then up onto the porch.

A stocky fellow, thick of face and neck, stood in the midst of the dining room. Piggy eyes in a stubbled face stared at Bone.

"I thought I'd surprise you," said Bone glancing at the man, then looking at Margaret full in her shocked face. It was the first time he'd seen her genuinely surprised, and the first time he'd seen her features red from . . . shame?

"Looks as though I have."

She sputtered a word, the man interrupted her, and Bone interrupted them both. He folded his arms over his chest. "Anybody care to tell me what this is all about?"

"Who's this joker?" said the man, flicking a pink thumb in Bone's direction.

Before Margaret could answer him, Bone said, "He's the man who owns this ranch, bub. Who in the hell are you?" Bone took a step closer to the man.

Margaret slid between them and placed a hand toward the

stranger. The other, she placed flat against Bone's broad chest. His heart, despite the oddness of the situation, skipped a quick beat. Any time the woman touched him he felt that way. Even now.

The stranger batted her hand away. That was all Bone needed. He reached over Margaret's shoulder and snatched the man's shirtfront in his big hand and jerked him toward him. "You touch her again and by god it'll be the last thing you ever touch, except when your head hits the floor. You got that, mister?"

Instead of looking frightened, as any sane man would in the grip of a large, rage-fueled man, this slop-gutted stranger grunted and grinned, squirming to get out of Bone's grasp.

"Now look here, sir," said the man who, with a jerk, backed from Bone's grasp.

"What's happening here, Margaret? You know this"—Bone nodded toward the stranger—"man?"

For the second time in mere minutes, he saw for certain a look on her face he'd not seen before. It was indeed shame. She looked down at her red hands and nodded, but did not look at Bone.

"I don't understand."

"You're right, you don't understand, sir," said the stranger, thumbing the lapels on his ratty, ill-fitting brown wool coat. "Because if you did, you'd not be the sort of gent who'd come between another man and his wife."

For a long moment there was silence in the kitchen where they stood. Bone felt his throat closing tight. "What?" he said before his air left him stranded.

The man smiled that dung-eating grin and nodded. "Yes sir, as I said, this fair creature is my wife."

Bone turned a wide-eyed gaze on Margaret, who finally looked up at him. For the first time since he'd known her, this strong woman had tears in her eyes.

"Margaret," said Bone, his voice rasping and quaking all at once. "Tell me it's not true. Tell me there's a mistake . . ."

"Oh, no mistake, man," said the stranger.

Bone turned a hard glare on him. "Shut it."

The man complied, but kept that damnable grin on his stubbled, jowly face.

"Jarvis," she finally said, "Jarvis, it's not what it seems. Believe me, it's not—"

"Oh, but it is, my dear," said the stranger.

Without looking, Bone hauled his left hand up hard and fast, and for that sliver of a moment, he relished the feel of his knuckles backhanding the buffoon's pooched, grinning lips.

The man shrieked and whimpered, bending down and cradling his face in his hands.

Bone kept his gaze on Margaret. "Then tell me how it is, Margaret. Are you married to this man?"

"No, not really. That is to say, he—"

"Not really?" said Bone, sucking in a big breath.

From his bent-over posture, more to keep himself from receiving another backhand than because he was in serious pain, the jowly stranger said, "Don't tell me you didn't mention the children to him, wife . . ."

"Children?" The word escaped Bone's lips as the barest of whispers.

He felt himself shaking all over, as if a temblor had begun beneath his feet and rattled and shimmied its way up the lean, solid trunk of his body, all the way to his face.

She was saying something. He saw her lips move, and she reached toward him, but he heard nothing but the pulsing, pounding in his head, his heartbeat and pumping blood and nothing else.

It was as if he were a great steam engine taxed beyond belief, his steel seams peeling apart and about to explode. He ground his teeth together hard until they ached, nearly powdering them. His big, useless ham fists clenched tight, squeezing as if he might splinter his own bones.

Bone knew only one thing at that moment: He had to get out of there, had to get free of this fresh madness.

With a gush of sound, part animal, part raw disgust and hate, and all rage, he lurched for the open door and somehow made it to his horse. He'd shouted the raw sounds all the way out there and his horse was already on the move even as he jammed the toe of his left boot in the stirrup and swung himself up atop the galloping beast.

If Margaret made any sounds, shouts, screams, if the stranger who was her husband shouted and laughed at his retreating back, Bone never heard them. For he was now a man possessed, possessed by nothing more or less than the brutal, hot anger of betrayal.

Never again, he thought as he pounded out of there. Never again would he let himself fall for anyone else's friendliness and charms, not a friendship with a man such as Regis or a fondness for a woman such as . . . her.

As the horse pounded back up the long lane leading out and away from his ranch, Bone vowed that he would never again utter her name, never dwell on her face, her betraying, pretty face.

It was a good half-mile from the ranch before Bone thought to breathe, to let go a gush of hate and pull in fresh air, then release it once more. Anger still shoved unintelligible words from him in a torrent.

"Married woman!" he shouted, the words streaming behind him in the hot, dry, south Texas air. "Children!"

All that could have been, all that he'd dreamt about, daydreamed about when he should have been working harder, all that had been a lie, the silly dream of a fool with no more right to such notions than a cow has to wear a hat.

And so Jarvis "Bone" McGraw, ranch foreman and Texas Ranger, did the only thing that he knew how to do when life toughened up on him—he rode hard and fast, at first for anywhere and nowhere all at once. Then as the landscape became less blurred in his sight, he made his way for the Santa Calina range, and the Royle Ranch, and back to work.

He and Regis might have disagreements as to how to deal with rustlers and bandits, and the man might of late be rubbing his fur the wrong way, but Regis Royle was a pard, and pards never play each other false knowingly. On that he'd wager his life.

"What have you done?" Margaret looked down at the man at whom she'd spat the words as if they were poison on her tongue. "What have you done?"

The fat man chuckled. "I ain't done nothing a man in my boots ain't got a right to do." He straightened and dragged a grimy cuff across his chaw-stained mouth. "Or have you forgotten our agreement? Huh?"

Margaret sneered at him as a dog might at an unwelcome vermin in the yard. "Filth," she said and turned away.

He chuckled. "Aw, such sweet talk." He walked to her and snatched her upper arm and spun her around, pulling her close to him. "That'll get you just about anywhere." He grinned and mashed his lips against hers. She bucked and shoved away from him. He chuckled once more. "Get you anywhere I say it will, anyway."

His laughter echoed in the ranch house kitchen and rolled out the door, its taint reaching the ears of old Ramon, who stood holding the half-filled egg basket beyond the edge of the porch. He grunted and walked to the bunk house.

Chapter 10

"Ramon."

No response.

"Ramon?" Margaret squinted, leaning in the doorway of the bunk house. She'd only set foot in there once, months before, when she'd first come to the ranch with the other women after Bone and the men rescued them from the slaver.

He'd set them up here at the ranch, no expectation of anything from them. Except, as Margaret came to learn, from her. And from him, there was only a hope of something, something that she might give to him. Something she saw in his eyes that he was ready to give to her—his whole heart.

For Margaret that had not been easy to bear. Yes, Bone was a handsome man, tall, broad of shoulder and muscled in all the ways a man should be. He had a devilish glint in his eye and was quick with a wink when he suspected he'd cracked wise and wanted anyone within earshot to catch on. Proud of himself, he could be.

But he was also a fair man, honest in his dealings, and never had he pushed her to commit herself to him in the least. She'd give him that much. But he was also impulsive, and that is what he'd shown earlier, the absolute end of it, the worst of a quick-tempered judgment. He'd not let her explain.

Maybe there was no explaining, she thought. Maybe she was a fool. No, no maybe about it. She was foolish for not telling him the truth earlier, just as she had been foolish so many times in the past few years. So many times, beginning with answering the *Bingham Gazette* advertisement back in Ohio. Such a fool.

"Ramon? Please, if you're here, I . . . I need to talk with you. I don't have much time."

She glanced at the house once more. She'd made a meal for George and set it before him at the table. He was a pig of a man, shoveling in great grunting spoonfuls of food. That would keep him busy for a few minutes, then he'd said he wanted to go, wanted to get her back "home" he'd said, to "where she belonged."

Margaret's skin goose-fleshed at the thought of going back there. Of tending to this beast's every desire, and those of his children, three repugnant offspring she loathed.

"Sí, sí," said Ramon. The old man shuffled into view within the room.

"May I come in, Ramon? Please, it's important. "

He appeared weary, annoyed, two things she'd never seen on his face before. He was always a cordial, kindly old man, always helping out. Never rude or unpolite. Unlike now. He eyed her. "Okay, what?"

For a moment she seemed to want to say something, then thrust a thrice-folded letter toward him. "This is for Jarvis. Please see that he gets it."

Ramon made no motion to accept it. Finally he squinted at her and said, "I saw you in there. With that man." He looked away.

She sighed. "You, too, Ramon? I thought we were friends."

He looked at her once more and shrugged. "I don't know what to think, Miss Margaret."

She held out the letter once more. "Please, just give this to Jarvis. It explains everything. I . . . you'll find I've been poorly judged."

He looked at her face. She saw his features soften and his old shoulders sag even more than they usually did. He took the letter in a gnarled hand. For a long moment they looked at each other, for theirs, though brief, had been a lasting friendship, and now each knew they were seeing the other for the last time.

Margaret turned and walked to the house. He watched her until the doorframe blocked her from sight. But he knew she was walking back to where that newcomer, that pig of a man, was waiting for her, waiting to take her from here, from his life, from the ranch, from Señor Bone, the only place and the only people to which she truly belonged.

Ramon did not have long to wait before he heard the man's harsh voice, ordering her, urging her to move faster. He moved to the doorway of the bunk house and squinted out. The man climbed aboard the wagon with a grunt, not helping Margaret up, not that she needed or wanted his help.

Why was she going away with him, then? To this, Ramon had no answer. He still held the letter pinched carefully in his left hand. The man cracked the lines across the backs of those two poor beasts in the traces and they jerked the junky wagon forward. The squawking that had heralded the man's arrival at the ranch hours before rose up once more, polluting the air with its metallic shriek.

Margaret had not taken much with her, little more than what she'd had when she arrived. She wore a modest dress she'd made herself, a bonnet on her head, and a small, cloth-wrapped bundle tied and held in her lap. She did not look back.

Ramon watched the wagon depart on up the long entrance lane, watched long after the dust had settled in their wake, long after they were little more than a black speck in the far distance.

Finally, he sighed and turned back to the dark interior of the bunk house. He retrieved a cork-topped, basketed jug and set it on the table. Then he sat down before it, set the letter beside it, and sipped, all the while eyeing the letter. The mescal stung before it soothed, much like a bitter woman's tongue, he thought. Then he unfolded the letter and read it aloud to the little dark room.

My Dearest Jarvis:

I am not a bad woman, let me get that truth out of the way at the start, whether you believe me or not. I am, I believe, a good person. As I do not have much time I will not be able to say in this letter all I meant to ever tell you. All that you have come to mean to me. All that your kind, smiling eyes and that big moustache have come to show me, come to promise me of a future I dared, even for a time, to dream might be mine. Now I see that is not for the likes of me. I hope, Jarvis, for your sake, that you find that future with someone else, someone worthy of you.

As to the man you found when you rode up today, his name is George Tinker, and he is not my husband. Not legally, at any rate. He does have a claim on me, however. A claim I thought I had out-run somehow. I am doubly the fool for thinking such.

I met him little more than two years ago, but I am getting ahead of myself. You see, I grew up and lived, unmarried after my parents died, in the house in which I was raised. I cleaned and cooked and maintained that household for much of my life and on the death of my parents, the house was left to my less-than-deserving brother, James. He married and it was quickly apparent I was to continue my role as housemaid to him, to his wife, and to their growing family. I had to leave then, or I would never have left.

I read an advertisement in the back of the Bingham Gazette *in Ohio, placed by what sounded like a good man, a widower with three small children. He was in a bad way, but with good prospects, if only he could find someone to tend house and consider the possibility of a marriage of convenience for them both. It was to be a trial run, of sorts. In return for six months of such considera-tion, the successful applicant would be provided with her own room, board, and the fare for travel West to northeastern Texas would be paid.*

I wrote, doubting anything would come of it, but I had determined to not spend my life regretting not having at least tried. Imagine my surprise when my letter was chosen by the man who had placed the advertisement. My shock was even greater when tickets were purchased. I left in the night, further adding to the surprises this fledgling venture had been revealing to me. But surprise was not yet through with me.

For when I arrived, after a long and foul journey, I discovered the man I had only briefly corresponded with, turned out to not be the man as represented in the advertisement and letters. He had had much assistance in his writing. I was shocked to discover I had become indebted to this Mr. George Tinker, the man you met. The details of my life with him, I'll not go into, save to say the three "children" were anything but, and more akin to monsters, and well into their teenage years. They were the sad residual efforts from a previous marriage.

From the first, I had no intention of marrying the man, indeed nor had I intended to stay there in northeast Texas, near the town of Cornish, to the depot where I was to be retrieved. But as I indicated, I had fled in the night and owned little more than what I had in my carpetbag. What few dollars I had managed to save had long been spent on the journey West for food. At that, I was nearly starved and had lost much weight on the journey. I did not have the money to pay Mr. Tinker back for the amount he spent on paying my way West. And once I arrived, I saw that I had no prospects of earning money.

As to my life there, I will not go into it. But I received the worst, though not the first, beatings of my life. He regularly set to me with vigor with a leather belt long used to striking flesh. As the farm was located miles from neighbors, and in inhospitable countryside, I was unable to flee. And then a traveling salesman came along. A man you've already met, the slaver himself.

At the time, however, I regarded him through swollen eyes and greeted him through split lips as something of a savior, if only for the duration of a conversation. As Mr. Tinker and his offspring were gone for a few hours, leaving me with the rare sensation of being alone and of the place being quiet about me. That's when this man, a traveling salesman, or so he said, dealing in yard goods, arrived.

I had been starved for conversation, and so I offered him coffee and he unlocked the door in the back of his large enclosed wagon. I should have been more wary than I was. But I was not. I accepted his offer to peruse his wares. I mounted the three steps and once in-side, I found the door slammed shut behind me. No amount of screaming and pounding rescued me.

I heard him rummaging in the house, then whistling as he climbed into his seat at the front of the wagon, then the lines snapped on the backs of his beasts, and the wagon rolled forward. Soon, I heard sobbing sounds from within the wagon and, well, you know the rest of the story. It was some weeks before we were for-tunate enough to have been found by you and your men as the slaver made for Mexico to sell us.

And so you see, Jarvis, that I am unmarried. The children of which he spoke are not mine, nor are they any longer children. And though I don't believe I owe Mr. Tinker a thing, there is part of me that hates that I never paid the man the cash money he spent to bring me West. I have nowhere else to go, and so I tell myself I am still indebted to Mr. Tinker. I will not go through life owing anyone anything.

Anything beyond your saving my very life, of course, which is a debt that can never be repaid. I hope my efforts at your ranch have somewhat balanced the ledger in other matters. Your reaction told me all I needed to know about how you view me, and how it could never be anything but a contentious state of affairs between us.

We are who we are, Jarvis, and so it is with a heart heavy with leaving, but buoyed with hope for your now-freed self, that I take my leave of you and Ramon and the ranch. I wish you well in all

your future endeavors, Jarvis McGraw, and I will think of you
fondly always.
   Kindly,
   Margaret

By the time Ramon finished reading the letter, he had wiped away tears three times from his old, wrinkled cheeks. He sat in the gloaming of the afternoon, then long past dusk, the letter still held pinched between his long, thin fingers.

He pulled in a deep breath, set the pages on the table, and poured himself another drink. He raised it. "I promise you, my friend, I will make certain that foolish man reads your letter." He raised the glass, nodded once toward the northeast, toward where he knew her wagon was bound, and sipped the drink down.

Then he folded the letter with care, tucked it between the folds of his best shirt, which he laid atop the table, too, and ambled outside to tend to the chickens, the sheep, the goats, the mule, and horses and beeves.

"In the morning," he said to the dark coop, shutting the gate behind him, "I will feed you extra, for it will be two, maybe three days before I return."

He wagged a finger at the little feathered creatures, most of them by then roosting, one or two on the ground, pecking at the scant meal of dried grasses and the last of the handful of cornmeal he'd tossed in. "You had better be good while I am gone, or I will lose my temper with you, sí?"

The chickens continued their quiet night noises and Ramon forced a grin. The rest of his nighttime chores, though he was getting to them an hour later than his usual time, did not take him long. He told each group of beasts the same thing and received similar responses, whickers, snorts, and such.

Later he carried a lantern to the ranch house and though he hated to do so, he peeked in, making certain all was well within there. Since Margaret had come, he had been inside, but only as far as the kitchen, where he took one meal a day with her. Had taken, that is.

His breath hitched in his throat as he saw the emptiness of the little, once-happy house. She had left it tidy, and now it would be only for Señor Bone, for he did not doubt that he could truly change the man's mind once he found him. No, Ramon held out very little hope, for Señor Bone was a stubborn man with the mind of a mule.

As he walked back to the bunk house, he said to the quiet night about him, stars winking high and bright far above, "That doesn't mean I will not try."

And come the morrow, he would leave this place and find Señor Bone and force him to read her letter. Somehow. He had to.

Such thoughts chased Ramon to bed and he slept poorly, fit-fully, and woke irritable. So be it, he thought. I will wear this scowling face until I find Señor Bone and force him to come around, back to his senses. And if I fail . . .

"No, Ramon," he said aloud as he finished his chores and did his best to secure the ranch for a few days away. "You will not fail. You cannot break the heart of Margaret. Even though she has given up hope that she will ever see Señor Bone again, I, Ramon, have not. This I swear."

With that, he hefted the flour sack he had filled with tortillas, biscuits, dried fruits, and a cork-stoppered bottle of water from the well, filled after he drank as much as he could hold, his small belly now rounded out and drum tight.

He double-checked that he had tucked in his coat's inner pocket the letter, wrapped in a scrap of cloth from an old shirt and tied with string. Then he cinched his wide-brim straw hat atop his head. He bade the animals goodbye and swung up on his donkey, Tomatillo, and they trudged on up the long entry lane, then walked southward, toward the Royle Ranch.

They would spend many hours on the Royle land before they ever found Señor Bone. If that's where he went. Time would tell, but Ramon knew he did not have all the time in the world. He needed to find the man as quickly as he was able, lest Margaret give up the last of the bit of hope that Ramon was certain was still lodged, like a sliver, deep in her heart.

He was not much for gambling, but he bet the two halves of himself against each other. The one that was small, weaker, but liked to come out now and again and torment him, the one that gave him dark moods and made him sour, sometimes for a day, that part of himself was the one that doubted he would find Señor Bone in time. But the other part, the greater part, felt certain all would be well.

Chapter 11

Bone was in the midst of bawling out a new hire, a young man whose earnestness for the task of cowboying was not matched yet by his ability to rope a Longhorn. Nobody had seen Bone quite act this way before. Ever since he'd come back early from his ranch, he'd been surly and somber. He was normally a man of few words but of decent humor, and would tolerate fits of whimsy among the men. But not since he came back.

"Who hired you, boy?"

The kid, not yet eighteen and looking wide-eyed and clumsy as a day-old colt, said, "You did, sir."

"What?"

"You hired me, sir. I'm sorry."

"What are you sorry for, boy?"

"I . . ."

"Speak up! Daylight's burning and you're standing there tongue-fumbled, and you're a piss-poor rope thrower, too."

"I don't know, sir."

"Don't know what?"

"Why I'm sorry. Why I said I'm sorry, that is."

"You're sorry because you were a poor hire? I'll take the blame for that."

"Now, Bone," said Tut, stepping forward. "It's my fault. I should have checked to see if young Daniel here can throw a loop before I split up the boys and sent them off to fetch—"

"Don't 'now, Bone,' me!" the Texas Ranger barked his words, clipping them off as if they were a mouthful of barbs. "I won't be talked down to. Especially by a ranch hand, you got me, Tut?"

The chubby man, who'd been around the Royle Ranch nearly from the beginning, knew enough to let it roll off his back, or at least he should have. But such things are easier to think than they are to do. Tut did manage to keep his eyes from drifting downward under the harshness of Bone's flinty glare. He did not keep his face from reddening.

Finally, the foreman spat and stalked off. The men all sighed and returned to their tasks, and the kid who'd been bawled out stood rooted in place, shaking and red-faced.

Tut walked over to him. "Don't take it personally, Daniel. Bone, well, he's out of sorts lately. He'll get over it."

The kid nodded but didn't say anything. "Why don't you take a few minutes, get yourself a drink of cool water, then we'll get back to it. Okay?"

Again, Daniel nodded.

Tut forced a smile and walked to the dog trot kitchen. "What do you reckon's going on with Bone?" said Tut to his pal, the range cook, Percy, a few minutes later.

The slim cook shrugged and continued slicing hunks of beef into cubes for a stew. "I don't much care."

"Well, I do. I was about ready to take him on, right there and then."

Percy sighed. "Look, Tut, I am far too busy to listen to your complaining. I'm creating a toothsome repast that will no doubt be wasted on the likes of you and your cowboy hordes."

"Oh, boy," said Tut, sipping water from a barrel hung from the wagon's side. He was trying, not too successfully, to cool down after the set-to with Bone. "I was you, I'd not say that too loud. These hordes are liable to run roughshod right over you."

Again the cook shrugged.

"You forgetting that we came to the Royle Ranch as lowly cowhands ourselves?"

Percy sighed and turned his attention to a pile of dirty potatoes.

"You know, my old Gran used to say that you get more flies with honey than vinegar."

Percy paused, a potato in one hand and a short knife in the other. He looked at Tut. "You are an impediment to progress."

Tut's eyebrows rose and he snorted.

"And what's more, I bet your Aunt Jemmy was, too," said Percy.

Tut turned back to face Percy, eyes narrowed, ready to fight him for his Aunt Jemmy's honor, friend or no. But Percy was grinning, an event that was almost as scarce as was Bone's flare of temper.

"Talk of the devil," muttered the cook.

That's when Bone showed up. Tut walked away from the fire, and Percy ignored the lanky foreman, much as he always did. But he was listening, much as he always did, to everything going on about the camp.

"Tut," said Bone.

The pudgy cowhand stopped but didn't turn to face the boss.

"You have every right to be irked. I'm in a sour mood—"

"You don't say," muttered the cook.

Bone narrowed his eyes and smoothed his moustaches. "You want to crack wise, you say it to my face, damn you."

The cook said nothing else and kept on slicing spuds.

"I thought so. Now"—Bone turned back to Tut—"you might want to head that kid off at the bunk house. I'll wager he's thinking of pulling up stakes. After that tongue lashing I gave him, he was mighty red in the ears. I'll talk to him later."

Tut tilted his head to one side and regarded the foreman. "You know, Bone, I understand things have been hard around here, what with Regis's demands and the railroad worries and the Consortium and all, and I know that Tupper dying put us a man down. But shaking your horns at the youngest won't get us any more reliable hands. I expect you've forgotten more about ranching than I'll ever know, but I'll be damned if I'm going to do your dirty laundry for you."

"Laundry? What in hell are you talking about?"

"I'm talking about making sure that kid don't up and ride off because you bawled him out in front of everybody. I don't know what's eating you, but I'm not the cause, I'm fairly certain of that. And that kid damn sure ain't. He's a good egg, is young Daniel. Don't know half of what he needs to, but then again he isn't being paid anywhere near half of what an old hand is."

For a good twenty seconds, it seemed to Tut that he was about to get a big ol' Bone fist to the face. The rangy foreman's hard gray eyes bored right into him, and Tut felt his face redden once more. But he'd be danged if he was going to back down when he knew beyond measure that he was in the right. Even Percy had stopped monkeying with his infernal potatoes.

Then the hard lines of Bone's face softened, and his eyes lost their flinty glint. He dragged a big hand down his cheek and rubbed his stubbled chin and sighed. "Yeah, I reckon I deserve that. Doesn't mean I want it spread among the men I've gone soft and can be put in my place by the likes of you." He cracked a slight smile.

"Not much danger of that," said Percy, and went back to his slicing. For his part, Tut's ears began to lose their crimson color.

"Now," said Bone, "I best get to the bunk house before that kid packs his traps and makes for the horizon. I know if I yelled at me, I'd be long gone by now. And when I get back, I'd like some fresh coffee made. Okay, Percy?"

The cook set down his knife. "Anything else you'd like while I'm at it?"

"Yeah, matter of fact there is. A new cook with a grateful attitude."

"Not possible with the wages you pay," mumbled Percy as he

fetched the coffee pot. But all three men were smiling now. All was somewhat back to normal. Somewhat. There was still the matter of the cause of Bone's rank attitude of earlier.

Something told Tut it wasn't the last they'd seen of it. Not until the cause of it was taken care of. He sighed and went back to the heat and the dust and the bawling beeves and the tired men.

Later that afternoon, closing in on dusk and grub time, the men were growing slower. They shot sideways glances to see if Tut, as a top hand, showed any inclination toward closing her down for the day and heading in for chuck. Then someone spied a figure in the distance, northward. A dark speck they all knew was too tall to be a lone beef critter drew closer.

Sol, one of the more fidgety fellows, turned to Tut. "Should we get our pieces?"

For a moment, Tut wasn't certain what the man meant. Then he recalled that word was what some of the men used to refer to their sidearms. A few of them carried them on their person all the time, mostly the men from the early days when Comanche and border bandito attacks had been much more common. They still were attacked, though far less often these days.

Word had gotten out that the men on the Royle Range didn't tolerate miscreants and interlopers, as Percy, one of the more book-learned among them, had put it. The rest of them called the stray rustlers "trash" and "rope stretchers."

"No," said Tut, visoring his eyes. "Looks to me to be a single rider, and small at that. Not tall in the saddle. Likely a child or an old man."

"Or a woman?" said Shep, suddenly perkier than he had been all day.

"Well, yeah," said Tut. "I reckon it could well be a woman, too. Not likely, but . . ."

"But it's possible," said Shep.

Tut was reminded once again of how much of a kid Shep still was. Nice enough fellow, and when it came down to it, he would help another, no questions asked. For certain, he had the sand that Regis had, but none of his older brother's moment-to-moment backbone.

Tut couldn't help but smile at the kid's wide-eyed, genuine hopefulness. They might be in the midst of a sour situation and he'd still find something to be chipper about.

Not that Tut would ever have hired the kid had he not been the brother of the ranch's owner. Heck, for that matter, he'd been told by Regis that Shep was a junior partner in the ranch, whatever that meant. Tut reckoned he had as much or more blood and sweat and not a few tears put into this ranch than did Shepley Royle. All but the blood relationship. No chance Tut would ever experience that. He was short on living relatives and long on bruises, bumps, scrapes, and doses of bad coffee and plates of whistleberries. But he did have Miss Belinda Orton, the prettiest school teacher anywhere, stepping out with him.

He looked up again and noted that the lone rider was now within hailing distance. He did not wave an arm, and neither did the lone rider. Then he saw Bone look toward the man, drop the post maul he was lugging, and walk out to meet the rider.

"Good," said Tut. "Let Bone deal with it. We have to get the last of these beeves run through the chute before we knock off for the day."

A groan of disappointment rippled through the gang of dusty, sweat-soaked cow hands.

Chapter 12

"You read the letter?" said Bone, eyes narrowed at ol' Ramon. "Of course I read the letter," said Ramon, not looking away. "She did not say not to, and she did not seal it up with wax or string, did she? Pah." He began turning away, then spun back and raised a gnarled old finger, poking the air between them. "Señor Bone, you are a fool!"

"What?" Now the big man was really getting annoyed. Bad enough he had to deal with wet-nose ranch hands and Ramon calling him out on his attitude. Not to mention the constant din of Shep and Regis and their petty squabbling.

And now this? Bad enough she . . . she had to lie to him all these months, and now his hired man, an old man at that, comes around telling him he's a fool. It was all too much. Too damned much.

Bone walked away, doing his best to get away from him, but for an old man, Ramon was as persistent as a bluebottle on a gut pile. Finally, Bone could take no more. He turned on Ramon and closed the distance between them in one stride. The old man did not back up.

Bone was vaguely aware of several of the men standing within earshot. He ignored them.

"Ramon, what is it you want me to do, huh? You were there—

apparently you think you know more than I do about the matter. But I know what I know, and I believe I don't need to know more. Anything added to what I know would be blather. Smoke from a fire does nothing but make a man cough."

Ramon did not respond, but stood his ground, unblinking, staring up at his employer. Finally he said, "Pretty words, Señor Bone. But I ask you this: In the time you have known me, have I not been true? Have I not been one you could rely on? Huh?" He waited for a reply.

Bone didn't want to, but he finally relented and grunted in the affirmative.

"Then why would I ask you to do something I knew to be wrong? I have been alive on this earth many years longer than you, Señor Bone. I will never ask you for another thing. If you don't like what you read, then you will never see me or hear from me again. I will leave you alone, with your thoughts. You have enough men running around here that you could get one of them to work for you at your ranch, no?"

Bone's gray, haggard face sagged. "What is it about this day that has me turning into some ol' soft-gutted fellow? Okay, okay," he stuck out a big hand. "Give me the letter and I promise I'll read it. But I don't want you to leave the ranch. I need you there, Ramon. Who else'd work so cheap?"

He glanced about, at the backs of the few men who were turning away, having given up on any information from the conversation of ever reaching them. "Besides, most of these fellows couldn't find their backsides with both hands. You aren't an easy man to replace, Ramon."

The old man maintained his rigid posture and glaring look at Bone. "Then we better hope it will not have to come to that, eh, Señor Bone?"

"Well," said Bone. "What about the letter?"

"You will read it while I am here. Or I will read it aloud before you." He glanced to his left. "And your men."

Again, Bone's eyes narrowed. "You're a hard old stick, and no mistake. Fine." Again he held out a big hand. "Give it here. We'll get us a couple of cups of coffee and set in the shade yonder while I read it. That work for you?"

"Sí, that will work, Señor Bone. But first, coffee."

Bone knew the mention of the dark brew would rouse old Ramon's interest. He was an easy keeper as hired hands went. Didn't ask for much, but loved his coffee, and at night, a few sips of liquor. "To ease the bones," as Ramon put it. Bone couldn't argue. He'd been easing his own skeleton for many years in such a manner.

"I can't promise this coffee will be anything like anything you've ever tasted," said Bone when they'd poured two cups. Bone glanced at the cook, who barely looked up from making biscuits, but said, "Don't like it, don't drink it."

Bone shook his head and walked to the long, outdoor eating table under a ramada. The men sat across from each other. "Okay, then, Ramon, let's have the letter. You can watch my lips move while I read the damn thing."

The old man handed Bone the trifolded sheets. Bone left them folded, before him on the table, sipped his coffee, winced, then pulled in a deep breath, opened the letter, and began reading.

As he did so, Ramon watched his boss's face, and within moments knew that what he hoped would happen, suspected would happen, was about to happen. He could tell by Bone's face, the grayness of it, the sadness, the flicker of shock and shame in the man's eyes, that Bone was soon to ride out.

Ramon wanted to go with him, wanted to help this good man find his good woman and make everything as it had been.

But he knew this was not the way it should be. He knew this was something Señor Bone had to do on his own, and even if he did find Margaret, would she have him? Even before then, would she be safe with that beast she went away with?

Bone read the letter through twice, then folded the pages

carefully and set them once more before him. But this time, instead of poorly hidden anger, and annoyance with Ramon, Bone surprised him. "What would you do, Ramon?"

"Me?" said the old man, feeling, for the first time since he left the ranch, surprised and unsure of himself. "Why would you ask me that?"

"Because I value your opinions."

"Oh, I see." It was Ramon's time to breathe deeply. "I cannot tell you what to do, I can only tell you what I would do." He leaned forward, his bony hands flat on the table top. "If I had the love of a woman such as Señora Margaret, I would move all the earth for her. And I would not stop even if I died doing it." He nodded as if that were the final word on the subject.

Bone nodded, then stood. "Okay, I'm off. I'll stop at the ranch on the way northeastward, tend to things there. You can ride back when you're rested. I'll make sure you have a fresh mount, Tomatillo can walk behind."

"Oh no," said Ramon. "I am not staying here. I am going with you. Only so far as the ranch, mind you, but I am going back."

"But you just rode in."

Ramon shrugged. "I did not do the work, Tomatillo did the work."

"Then he'll have to stay here and rest up."

"No, he can walk behind. We will not slow you down. But if you want to ride on ahead, we will catch up."

Bone nodded, knowing that's exactly what would happen. There was no way he was going to wait on a donkey to ride drag. He had to make time. He need only stop at the ranch to feed the animals and water the horse, swap him out for a fresh mount if one was near the stable. He'd decide on the way if he'd bring a second horse for Margaret to ride when he fetched her home. Because that's what he intended to do.

As he read her letter he realized he'd judged her too soon. Better yet, he should not judge her at all. She was who she was, and if he didn't like some part of it, that was his problem, not hers. That went for anyone else, too. There was too much judging lately among the folks he knew.

That began with, Regis and his damned Cattlemen's Justice Consortium. My word, thought Bone. I've done the very thing I've been berating Regis and his cohorts of doing. I judged someone before all the facts were told. I heard what I chose to hear, nothing more.

So how could he have judged her in such haste? Judged her at all, for that matter? Isn't that what he'd been ridiculing Regis for doing? Judging people in haste, then stringing them up, and riding off? And all over something so fleeting and grubbing as a few head of cattle?

He knew with Regis it was deeper than that, that if a man did not defend what was his, he might as well curl up, tuck his knees under his chin, and cry until he died. But did that give him cause enough to take the one most valuable thing that every living thing has, which is its life, the very thing that makes us all who we are?

"No, Bone," he whispered as he and Buck trotted up to the house. "No, it doesn't."

The ride back to the ranch was a hard gallop. He'd let Buck rest up while he saddled Night, a reliable horse that could travel at a decent clip and not let him down.

Before he departed from the ranch, after having been there less than an hour, he saw southward, a far-off black shape that he knew would be ol' Ramon, back at the ranch.

He rode hard, but kept the horse shy of getting played out. He knew he should have taken a second beast but he'd ridden Buck hard back to the ranch and he was so knackered now he'd only slow Bone down. So he saddled up Night, the one fresh mount he could find, a solid black with white stockings, and as he swung out of the ranch yard, he counted on luck to see him through.

Traveling northward, too, along the route he hoped they'd take would lead him through several small towns. With any luck, given the uselessness of the man she was beholden to, he might stop somewhere and get good and drunk, slowing their progress. He had the veined face, red eyes, and sloppy gut of a habitual drinker.

He didn't know exactly where they were headed, but he had his name, the town (was it Cornish?) where he'd picked her up. At any rate, it was some place she'd said had a depot, and he had an ace tucked away—not far up the road was the home of an old friend, former Texas Ranger Monty Jefferson. He was long retired now, but the man maintained his old contacts, knew more people than Noah had critters on his boat, and, most important of all, he owed Bone a favor. Time to call it in. Not that Monty wouldn't offer freely to help, favor or no.

Chapter 13

B one rode into Santo Verde late the next afternoon and asked
directions to Monty's house at a sag-porch cantina at the
northern end of the main street. The little building stood away
from the others along the street, separated by several hundred
feet of dusty earth and broken bottles, and an old, broken-down
wagon.

A man in a serape leaned on a broom, more handle than bris-
tle, and squinted at him. "Afternoon," said Bone. "I'm looking
for Monty Jefferson, a thin man, not too tall, but with hellacious
moustaches and a wicked laugh."

The man nodded. "The Ranger, sí, sí. He comes here every
day. But not for a couple of hours yet."

"You know where I can find him right now?"

Again the man nodded, then pointed. That road, it dips down,
a half-mile from here comes to another road. Travel slower down
an arroyo, follow that, not too far. He has a little place. I go there
sometimes to play cards with Señor Jefferson."

"Sounds like him. He win every time?"

The man nodded and, for the first time, smiled. "When I let
him. He thinks he is better at cards than he is. But he is a fun fellow. What more can we ask in life than to spend time with good
people, eh?"

"Spoken like a true philosopher." Bone was about to thank him and ride on to Monty's house when a thought came to him. "Say, you haven't seen a man, coarse fella, fat, red-faced, nasty piece of work, traveling in a buckboard pulled by two plugs, and a fine woman with him. Long, pretty red-brown hair, not looking like she wanted to be with him all that much. This would have been . . ."

The man nodded again and finished his sentence. "Sí. They came through here yesterday, was it? Before noon time. He bought a bottle of tequila from me. I smiled at the woman but, as you say, she was not happy with him. I remember thinking, especially with the way he treated her, and the way she looked, that she should just leave him alone with himself."

"What do you mean, how she looked?" Bone tensed.

The man shook his head slowly. "Oh, I hope I am wrong, senor. But it looked to me as if he hit her in the face." He touched under his right eye. "Here, it was the color of a storm sky, and puffy. I know the look—my own papa was this way to my mama when he was drunk. Which was all the time. She killed him one night when he slept the sleep of drunkards. Then she was happy. Maybe this woman you seek will do the same, then she will know happiness."

"Not if I get to him first." Bone touched his hat brim and through tight-set teeth he thanked the man. "I am much obliged to you. When I have more time, I'll stop and play a hand of cards with you and ol' Monty. Give him my best. Right now, I have to ride."

"Sí, senor. And good luck to you. And her, too. She will need it."

With the man's sentiments ringing in his hears, Bone gigged Night into a hard lope on the north road out of town. One thought filled his mind. If he was in time, he'd spend the rest of his life working to earn back her trust.

Chapter 14

It took Bone longer than he had expected it might to reach them. And when he did, he wasn't certain he'd found the right place. As slovenly as he recalled the man had been, what came into view ahead shocked him. But it was the only place out this way, the very homestead he'd been directed to by a woman who'd looked on him with suspicion when he asked where he might find such a man as he'd described.

The place was disgusting, the sort he'd seen plenty of before in his travels as a Ranger and otherwise, but to imagine Margaret here, stuck in that godawful mess before him . . . it was too much to bear.

How, he wondered as he freed his revolver's hammer loop and slid his rifle from its scabbard to rest across his thighs, could I have judged her so? The only woman he'd ever felt such a powerful feeling for, the only woman who'd ever seemed like she might feel that way toward his mangy hide, too.

And with that thought blazing hot in his mind, Bone reined up to within a couple of hundred feet of what he assumed was the home of the place.

The abode itself was a jumbled mess of soddy, stick, log, and smeared dung, with junk leaned against it in some attempt to prevent a front wall from splaying out onto the packed, sandy earth before it.

If ever there was a haven for snakes and vile things that craved the dark and dim places, it would be inside that windowless hole before him. Hell, he could barely tell where the door was. Then he saw it, but only because a mangy hound poked its snout out and snuffled the air. As soon as it set its rheumy, yellowed eyes on him, its floppy gray lips rose and it bared browned, stumpy teeth fronting a rattley growl.

"If that's the worst of it, this'll go okay," said Bone, knowing it would not be that easy. Life never was.

The dog pushed its way out the door, and its body was a wobble-walking bone rack covered in stretched, grayed black hair, bald in patches. The door settled back in its accustomed spot in its sagged frame and nothing else moved. The dog advanced on him, its steps slow and unsure, as if it were walking on ground glass or hot coals. Still, the old thing kept up its raspy growl.

Bone had no concern about shooting the beast should it come close enough to pester his horse. The last thing he needed was a crow-hopping mount acting all fiddle-footed because of a dog. That's not what he came here for.

"Best get on with it," he muttered, and swung down, tying his horse to a broken wagon's jutting front wheel. He swiveled his gaze all about him again, but saw no people. Had to be the place, though.

Then from his new vantage point, he spied a quick movement. He paused and waited, the rifle halfway to his shoulder. There it was again, the swish and flick of a tail. He sidestepped to his left, taking care not to blunder into anything that might be shading a coiled rattler.

That's when he spied a sagging lean-to off the back of the house and guessed it must be the place where those two sad horses towing the man's wagon spent the days of their lives.

He walked toward it, taking a half-dozen steps, raising the rifle even higher and glancing about himself once more. He paused, listening, but heard nothing. Then he did—a slight scuffing, dragging sound from within the hovel.

He kept an eye in case a rifle snout should poke at him from the side of the house, but of that he saw no evidence. Indeed, there were no windows, not that the walls facing him were even what you could call walls, nor were they without cracks and puckers, through which he could be spied.

If anyone was in there, that growling old hound would have tipped them off to his presence. The dog had only ventured about fifteen feet from the door and stood his ground, albeit on shaky legs. He was game, though, Bone would give him that. The old beast sniffed and swiveled his head in Bone's general direction. Likely blind, or close to it.

By the time he gained full view of the horse leant-to off the back of the shack, which he did by circling wide, the dog left off the growling. Too tired, thought Bone. He himself was anything but weary, however.

Bone's heart thumped as hard as ever in his wide chest. Soon, once he got a look at the back of the place, it would be time to enter. There was somebody or something in there. He had to know who or what. Thoughts of Margaret drove him onward. Somehow he was more afraid of her reaction than of any fool with a gun.

It took him another few minutes to complete his circle of the hovel, during which he came to learn that there was only one horse in the lean-to. That made him wonder if the man was off somewhere with the other horse. Or given their state of ill use, perhaps one of them had died since he'd seen them.

It would not do to blunder in with some odd assumption in mind, only to have the bastard open up on him. He could well be in there, choking the life out of Margaret right now, thought Bone. And with a grim sneer, he chucked the last of whatever caution had accompanied him as he'd surveyed the yard, and came upon the house from the side.

At the last moment, he jerked close to the front wall. He hugged it, though didn't lean against the flimsy thing, and sidestepped over old posts and two rusted rods from some odd implement. They were wedged at an angle and looked to be holding the wall upright, and slid closer to the door. Of the dog he saw no sign.

He reached the door and, pulling in a quick breath, stepped out, stuck the rifle barrel between the door and the frame, and jerked the door wide.

There, inside the dim, dark space, stood the dog, growling. Bone leveled on him, but a voice from within the dark space croaked, "Don't shoot him, please . . ."

It was a hoarse whisper, not much of one at that. "Show yourself!" he barked, glancing back over his right shoulder once. Still clear. The only thing back there that moved was his horse's flicked ear.

"Go . . . go away . . ." The voice said, but it was weak, barely a whisper now, and not as threatening as the words wanted to be. A thought stung Bone. Not enough of one to lower the rifle snout from ending the miserable dog's life, but still it quivered like a fresh-sunk arrow in his mind.

"Margaret?" he whispered.

In response, he heard a hoarse sob that tailed off in a cough. And he knew, somehow, though it was as far from her voice as he could imagine, that it was her, his Margaret.

Recklessness of the sort that he'd never allowed in all his days as a Ranger shoved aside any abiding caution he carried with him. It forced him past the growling old dog and into the hovel. He half thought to boot the old thing out the open door and close it, but the dog beat him to it, cowed and tail-tucked as it wobbled outside. A beaten dog, he thought fleetingly. A man who will beat a dog is no man. He's a base creature at best.

He said her name again and as his eyes adjusted to the dark and his nose to the stink—unwashed man, human filth, badly cooked meat, uncured hides greening, woodsmoke—he caught sight of something shift and move in the far-right corner.

"Margaret?" he said again, still keeping the rifle pointed, though lowered. That jerk who'd dragged her off might be waiting for him, could be a trap. He had no idea how many of them there were. Margaret had said there were children. Had she said how many? Their ages? Weren't they now grown? He couldn't recall.

"Oh no, no, Jarvis, go away . . ."

If any doubt had remained in him, it scattered and blew away. It was Margaret, but what had that man done to her? Thank the Lord she was still alive, but how badly hurt?

"Margaret, it's me, hold still, stop moving so," he reached out, covered the few feet that took him into the darkest recesses of the windowless, light-deprived space. He barked a knee on what felt like a stump and bit back a shout of pain, then failed to duck his head and smacked into a sag in the roof. Something up there shifted and he jerked his head down out of instinct. Might be a snake ready to drop.

And then he heard a solid thud on the soil floor to his right and a hissing rattle. Yep, snake. He jerked to his left and kept moving. Finally, she'd stopped scrambling as if trying to avoid him, trying to get as far back in the foul space as she might. Light appeared ahead, cracking open, accompanied with a squawk. It was a back door being opened.

Bone raised the rifle once more, expecting it to be the jerk who'd stolen her, but he saw in the light, a hunched form, dragging away from him, forcing itself through the door, trying to get away. It was Margaret.

He kept low and covered the last two paces in one, snatched at the rickety door, and yanked it open. The force he used ripped it from whatever feeble hinges it had been secured with. The planks, covered with scraps of critter hide that looked like rat hair, wobbled and splintered as he whipped the door past himself and into the space he'd just walked through.

Then there she was, sagged even more, leaning against the doorframe, sobbing, her shoulder and back half to him, her hands to her face. She looked to be half the woman he'd come to know, in height and muscle.

Margaret was no bone rack, but a solid woman that was as much fierceness and determination as she was muscle. But no longer. Her shoulder was bare and whatever had been left of the dress, something he barely recognized as a garment she'd made for herself from cloth left behind at the ranch house from the old woman and her husband who'd left the place to him. But now that pretty dress was a shredded thing, matted with dirt and blood and hair and who knew what else.

"Oh Lord, Margaret, honey, what has he done? What has he done?" Bone closed the short distance between them and tried to stand before her, but she turned farther away. He leaned the rifle against the wall and took her shoulders in his hands.

She winced and jerked away, but he held firm and gently turned her to face him. She did not look up. Still, he saw the mess that was her face. Both eyes were puffed, the left buttoned up so she wasn't able to see out of it.

Her lips were split, her cheeks purpled and puffed, her nose didn't look broken, but leaked blood, as if a fresh round of pain had been delivered to her not long before he arrived.

But it was her neck that shocked him the most. Each side of her downturned jaws and chin was crimson with blood and purple with handprints. The man had choked her. It looked as if he'd nearly crushed her windpipe, until she was passed out or near death.

Visions of what he'd witnessed as a Ranger in the past by the vilest of men and what they'd done to women, often prostitutes, curdled inside him. He would kill the man who did this to her. He knew that as certainly as he knew he would spend the rest of his life working for this woman's forgiveness.

"Oh, Margaret," he said, his voice lost, fighting between trembling rage and bald-faced sorrow. "What did he do to you . . ."

She sobbed once, kept her face down. And he pulled her to

him. She remained with her hands up, stiff in his arms, and he hugged her tight, but not so much he'd hurt her any worse. "Forgive me, woman, please. I will never let you go again," he said. "Never."

She weakened then. Her stiffness dropped away like a shed cloak, and she sobbed against him.

Chapter 15

Never had Bone felt such a war within himself, a tearing apart of something in him that he guessed the preachers would call his soul. Whatever it was, two mighty forces were peeling it apart while he stood holding his sobbing Margaret.

It was ironic that he must save this woman, who was stronger than any person he had ever met. By doing that, he would address the other side of the fight within: a bone-deep need to kill the man who'd done this. Then he would take her away from there and bring her back to a good life, her life, at the ranch.

That was when Bone heard a guttural, snorting growl from behind, past where the lone, dejected horse stood. He spun, his hands still on Margaret's shoulders, and saw the fat man looking bigger, meaner, harder somehow than he had looked at Bone's ranch.

He also looked dirtier, his unshaven face begrimed. Gore, long dried, streaked his clothes and face, his filthy hands hung at his sides. His short brown wool coat, looking as though a smaller, younger version of himself had worn it years before, seemed more hole than coat, and rode on his fat frame comically, his arms protruding from it as if he were about to pantomime a part in a comic play.

Past him, the missing horse now stood, though standing was

something it seemed nearly incapable of. It also did not look much like the paltry horse it had been. The trembling beast's long, bony face was criss-crossed with fresh lacerations welling hot, red blood that ran in long strings and pooled on the ground. The top half of one of its ears had been sliced off and from what Bone could see, the rest of the beast's body had fared no better than its head.

The fat man regarded them each through heavy lids, fat eyes that though only half open, took in everything before him, assessed it, then moved on to the next thing.

A bluebottle fly circled the man's bare, greasy, half-haired head. It landed on the side of the man's sweaty, bristled face and he didn't move. He stood staring at them, his chest moving like a slow-worked bellows. His pooched lips stretched wide and he smiled.

"Now then, I didn't expect company. Been dealing with an insolent horse. Fixing to do the same to my woman, but I reckon that can wait."

Before Bone could react, the man's furthermost hand, the right, partially tucked behind his angled body, whipped up, holding a revolver. The barrel furrowed to a stop just behind the horse's near eye. With no hesitation, the fat man pulled the trigger. The horse waggled side to side a moment, then the last of its stretched abilities gave way and it crashed to the hot earth.

The shock of such a fast action, coupled with the long, hellish, sleepless journey there, caught Bone unprepared, and the fat man swung the revolver on him before Bone's own revolver had cleared his holster.

The fat man shook his head, still smiling. "No, no, see, that's not the way. This here's the way," he jerked the barrel of his revolver to his left and nodded his head. "Both of you git on in there."

Neither Bone nor Margaret moved.

"Now!" barked the man. His evil grin had disappeared and in its place a grim, downturned mouth, as if painted there by a blind man, sneered. His lips parted to reveal blackened, stumpy teeth within.

Bone stepped to his right and stood before Margaret. She walked backward into the doorway. Bone followed, facing Tinker, as the fat man walked toward them.

"Yonder," he said, nodding toward where Bone had first seen the dim, moving shape that had turned out to be Margaret. They all were in the hovel now, darkness making sight tricky while their eyes adjusted. In the sunlit doorway, Bone saw the old, crotchety hound gimp slowly up behind the fat man.

It tried to nose between the man and the doorframe, but the side of its head touched the fat man's leg and he glanced down, saw the dog, and brought the butt of the revolver down hard on the old dog's head. A quick yelp was all the beast was capable of before it dropped, lolling, its head spouting blood on the hardpan floor. Its tremblings ceased within moments.

Bone took advantage of the dog's distraction and peeled his revolver clean out of the holster. In the same motion he thumbed back the hammer, then squeezed the trigger.

His bullet, delivered in haste, drove lower than he intended and caught him in the side of his paunch. The man squealed like a pig being tortured to death as he spun in a dervish dance.

The fat man lurched into the room, within feet of them, the revolver still in his left hand, but he looked far too distracted to return fire. Instead, he knocked into things, squealing and spitting and snotting on himself.

Bone thumbed the hammer once more and pulled the shocked Margaret past him and out toward the open door, following her backward. The fat man came to his senses then and locked a wide-eye gaze on the retreating Bone. The men each moved toward the door. Once Bone was certain Margaret was out, he raised the revolver to the position he wanted and touched the trigger.

The last bullet cored the prairie rat's forehead and tore its way out the back of the greasy, fat head, its exit much sloppier than its entry. A high-pitched sound like air squeaking out of a pig's bladder whistled from George Tinker's pooched lips, below his wide, heavy-lidded eyes, and pinched off with a drawn-out sigh.

The squealing fat man folded as if his bones had dissolved, and he collapsed in the doorway of his filthy hovel. His revolver, still clutched in his filthy left hand, twitched.

Bone thought the trigger finger might reflexively pull hard enough to deliver a round after death. He'd seen it before.

They were too close to do much of anything to save themselves, but Bone managed to step before Margaret and raise his revolver, knowing in that hair of a second it would do no good, but it mattered not. That last, reflex-driven shot never came.

The fat man was dead, already leaking out whatever glistening gray filth had filled the bone bucket that was his head. It was not a pretty sight and he spun, urging Margaret away. She shook her head slowly, pushed past him, and stood looking down on the dead mess that had been her tormentor for so long.

She'd been the one to deliver the shot that had killed the raping slaver so long before, a shot that likely had saved Bone's life. Now, for a fleeting moment, Bone wondered if he had wronged her by robbing her of the opportunity to exact vengeance on this rascal, too. But no, she only looked down at the dead man, shook her head, then walked past Bone toward the remaining horse.

Bone retrieved his rifle from where he'd leaned it. It had fallen back into the darkness of the house. As he stood, he saw a tin oil lamp without a globe standing on a propped-up table. He hefted the lamp and it felt half-full. Not far from it a low can lay upended, its contents, wooden matches, lying around scattered.

With no more thought than that, Bone unscrewed the top of

the lamp, drizzled the contents atop the dead dog, and tossed the rest about him, spraying the room. He tossed the lamp to the floor and snatched up a handful of matches.

Careful to not touch his hand to the back of the fat man's sagged, exposed head, Bone grabbed the man's collar and dragged him a half-dozen feet backward into the room. He stepped over the fat man's feet and thumbed two matches together. They flared and he tossed them back into the room. One landed atop the fat man, looked to be extinguished, then a jutting fold of greasy shirt cloth took flame and danced.

The other match needed no invitation to the ball and bloomed bright on a puddle of oil it found particularly toothsome. Its offspring, tiny licking flames greedy for life, raced from spot to tempting spot. Black smoke built, boiled upward, hit the close ceiling, and rolled toward him. Bone stepped backward out the door, then turned.

He saw Margaret, but not as he had expected. She was now some yards away from the house, astride the remaining bony horse, seated on a ratty saddle blanket. A crude hackamore had been fitted about the beast's head.

Margaret's features were swollen, battered, crusted, and bloodied, her clothes torn, and she didn't look as if she cared.

For a long moment as she looked down at Bone, their eyes met, locked together, and a lifetime of possibility, of all the things intimates share, of loves and losses, and children and hardships and happinesses all passed between them.

Then Margaret spoke in a voice that was once more hers, though hoarse and strained. "Thank you for this, Jarvis. I am forever indebted to you, but you owe me nothing, if ever you felt such. We'll part here and that will be for the best, I think."

If what she was saying were true, all those things and more that had just passed between them would never come to be.

Bone could utter no words. He staggered closer, to the horse, and still no sound came from him. The light in his eyes turned to fear. Panic seized him from within and he threw his arms about the neck of the tired beast and held tight.

"No!" he shouted, a demand, a command, and a begging sound all at once. He didn't care, he would not, could not let this happen.

"There is no way you are leaving here without me, Margaret. I . . ." He recalled the hundreds, thousands of things he had thought of on the ride to this place, things he wished to tell her. But they all sugared down to the one thing—he was sorry, painfully, woefully, eternally sorry for thinking so poorly of her, for being so wrongheaded.

But all he could say was, "No, Margaret, no." He felt wearier than he'd ever been in his life. He leaned his head against the horse's neck. His hat fell off. "Margaret, I love you, woman. More than you could ever know."

For long moments nothing changed. Nothing moved except smoke and flame behind them. Under the last of the day's vicious, skin-frying heat. They were surrounded by sand and dirt and rock, by the stink of the rank little hole of a place.

Bone did not look up from leaning against the horse's neck, even when he heard a soft sliding sound. What would anything matter now, sounds, no sounds. In the pit of his weariness, nothing mattered and to hell with it all, he thought.

Then he felt a hand on his right shoulder, and the hand patted him, reached up and smoothed his sweaty, unwashed hair, and rested there.

He looked up at her, his forehead resting on the sweating horse's skin, at Margaret. His Margaret, and she looked at him once more. They held like that, as if time had slowed, then reversed. All those wonderful things he'd felt when they looked at each other moments before suddenly bubbled back and passed between them. And they were within grasp, and were his, theirs, once again.

The man and the woman walked their mounts, side by side, southward, away from the black, smoking fire fed by the greasy meat of man, horse, dog, and snake.

From a distance, the mounded mess on the flat land resembled a volcano spewing the last of its pain and hate, with smoke and flame reaching into the darkening sky. They did not look back.

Chapter 16

"You mean to tell me you haven't done that yet?" Regis shoved upright so hard his chair flipped and the table before him shuddered forward on the wood puncheons. Spoons and forks rattled and cups slopped coffee and a platter of flapjacks skidded, loosing its load onto the tabletop.

Bone regarded Regis as one might an unreasonable, unruly child. "I've been busy."

"Busy? Too busy to tend to the things I ordered you to do?"

Bone ground his teeth, but held his place. He hated that his face had hotted up, hated that Regis chose to air this grievance before the men.

"It's that damn woman, isn't it? She's got you all fouled up."

That was all Bone could take. He did the opposite of what any other man would do when confronting an angry Regis Royle. He crossed the room, closing the gap between them in two strides, and met Regis face to face.

The men were evenly matched in size, in broadness of shoulder, and in musculature. Where they differed was a bit in age—Bone being the older in years and in grim experiences in gritty, low-down, serious scraps.

The Ranger had tangled hand-to-hand with Apache and Comanche warriors out for vengeance and fueled by raw hate of the grubbing whites. These warriors were men who fought without rule, but with pure conviction that they would win. Bone had nearly lost his life to such a number of times over the years.

Other brutes had crossed his path as a Texas Ranger, too, men who came by their money by stealing and pillaging and ruining anything good. They sold men, women, and children as slaves, butchering the innocent along the way because they were filled with too much liquor and not nearly enough sense.

They were, largely, border-hopping trash on a constant, self-serving spree. Then there was the war with Mexico. He'd put in his time in that mess as well. Nobody had been more relieved than Bone when the 1848 Treaty of Guadalupe Hidalgo was signed.

Regis Royle had had his own ample experiences brawling onboard his and other men's vessels, at the docks, repelling coastal pirates, and the like. What Regis Royle did not have was the burning passion for a woman in his life. He felt much the same for his precious ranch, but both men knew this was no substitute.

Only Bone felt such fire and now that he'd been granted a last and lasting opportunity with it, he would stop at nothing to protect it. Both men knew this. And yet they still came to blows.

Regis was unwilling to let anything interfere with his plans for his ranch, and Bone was not about to let anything interfere with his plans for a life with Margaret.

He was about to say so when Regis launched himself at his friend, his best friend, barring his close companionship with Cormac, who had filled the role of father figure for far too long to be considered solely as friend.

Bone ducked low, but Regis's wide right fist barreled through the air faster than Bone expected, and caromed off his left shoulder before connecting with the side of Bone's head. It set up a buzzing inside, and his vision blurred, then righted itself.

He countered from his crouched position with a steel-hard upswinging right of his own that caught the exposed belly of Regis square, hard, and fast.

No amount of muscled midsection could withstand such a

blow, and a deep whoosh of breath pushed from Regis's mouth. The sound ended in a gasp as Royle folded in half, one hand reflexively clamping to his midsection.

"I will take a whole lot of things in life, Regis Royle, including being ordered about for months as if I was a wet-eared kid, but I will not tolerate, ever, anyone maligning her. I don't need a damn thing from you or any other man. Least of all a man whose head is so far up his own backside he'll never see the light of sun again. Bone turned and stalked to the door, pausing in the doorway only when Regis's forced voice reached him.

"Pull in your horns, man! Think about it!"

"We're done, Regis. For good."

"You're a partner here—you can't just walk off!"

"Watch me."

And he did.

Percy the cook, and the other two hands in the grub house, Sol and Dewlap, said nothing, made no moves. After a few moments, Regis groaned and pushed up to his feet.

"Hell," he said, and, raking a big hand through his hair, he snatched up his hat from where it had toppled off the table to the floor, and walked stiffly to the door, then out.

"Well," said Percy. "That there was something." He slid a fry pan off the stove's hot spot. "Yep, that was something else."

Chapter 17

Shepley Royle was mired deep in a fine slumber in which he had convinced the lovely—and somehow, thanks to the oddness of dreams, now the same age as him, eighteen as of that very day—Marietta to ride on out some miles southwest of the ranch proper to that pretty rise covered with waving grasses and no snaky rock outcrops.

There he had produced from somewhere, in a dream one of the more suspicious happenings was that required items would somehow just turn up, no explanation as to where they came from—a fine, bulging picnic basket with a blue-and-white checkered cloth and napkins.

He spread the cloth and had her sit while he pulled out all manner of toothsome treats, and even a bottle of grape wine. This was not something he usually went for, but it was a dream after all, and the folks who control such things must know what they are up to.

Well, sir, he set it all out and uncorked that wine and poured them each a glass and looked at her and smiled and she smiled back and they leaned toward each other—hadn't even tasted the ruby-red wine yet, and he felt her soft breath on his face and he closed his eyes and leaned closer to her and she to him and—

Something, he wasn't certain what it was, rapped him on the

foot. Lordy, was it a snake? And in a dream? How could that happen?

It happened again. He looked down, or tried to, but it was a dream after all, and no matter how hard he tried he couldn't seem to see much anymore. He looked back to where Marietta was seated beside him on the pretty blue-and-white tablecloth, and she wasn't there. And neither was the cloth. Nor the wine nor the grasses nor the pretty blue sky . . .

"Shep."

Again, something touched his foot.

"Shep, wake up."

Then he knew for sure the dream was gone. And the one thing he didn't want to think about was what replaced it. His big-headed brother, Regis.

"What?" Shep figured he'd start with a question. It might buy him a few more winks. Trouble was, he thought maybe he said it into his pillow.

Regis hit him in the foot again.

"Uh."

Shep heard a sigh, then: "Okay, I guess I'll eat this tasty birthday breakfast all by my lonesome."

He heard boots on the floorboards, on the short trip to the front of the small ranch house. Slowly, what his brother said leached into his drowsy head, and Shep shoved up and rolled over onto his elbows. Birthday? Hey . . .

"Hey!" he said to the empty room. "That's right—I'm eighteen today!" He shoved up out of the bed and stood, naked as on that day, eighteen years before, that he'd been born. "I'm a man!" he shouted.

"Not hardly!" he heard a voice from the front of the house shout back.

Regis. Wet, wool-blanket Regis. But he did say there was a special breakfast. And Regis wasn't a half-bad cook at that.

Shep jammed his legs into the soiled, smelly clothes he'd

worn the day before and hopped out of the room, tugging on one sock, then getting the second halfway onto his foot by the time he reached the front room. It also served as the kitchen, dining room, repository of soiled clothes and piles of gear, as well as the ranch office, which consisted of a table cobbled together from old wagon planking atop a rickety base of leaning wooden legs.

A carpenter Regis wasn't. Shep had thought this several times as he eyed the sagged, swaying contraption, laden as it always was with papers and books and account ledgers.

Of course, Regis had only resorted to building the thing himself after Shep had failed to remember to build him a suitable table for working on "the books," as he called them. He'd given Shep two weeks to do the job, the average number of days he was away from the ranch when he was back in Brownsville, tending to his business concerns there with Cormac.

But Shep had been kept fairly busy by Bone and the rest of the men, who failed to treat him with the respect he felt a junior partner in the ranch deserved. They worked him like a wrung-out dog, day after day. That didn't leave a fellow much time to tackle a project as challenging as a table. It was possible, too, that he might have found more time if he skipped the nightly poker games he and the boys got up to after dinner.

"About time you dragged your sorry self out of that bed, kid brother!" Similar such words greeted Shep nearly every morning when Regis was back at the ranch after less-frequent trips to town, much to Shep's annoyance.

The words had the daily effect of turning Shep's face and ears red, as they did on this day. But when he turned to face Regis, with slitted eyes and tight-set teeth, ready for a scuffle, he instead saw Regis smiling. This was not a sight he was used to.

"Have yourself a seat, Shep." Regis waved a big hand at the table with a flourish. "I'll serve up your hot meal in a couple of minutes. Until then, why don't you have yourself a cup of coffee?"

Shep could hardly believe what he was seeing or hearing. He

sat, slowly, and surveyed the table. It was set with what passed as the best crockery they had, which was also the only stuff they had, but it was strange looking. He picked up the cup. "What'd you do to the dishes?"

Regis snorted. "I washed them. Figured it was time, being your birthday and all, plus, we ought to try to not live like hogs at the trough anymore."

"Huh," said Shep, sipping the coffee. "This coffee's good."

"Glad you like it," said Regis over his shoulder, as he shoved around sizzling meats in the frying pan atop the small woodburning stove they sometimes cooked meals on instead of eating with the men all the time.

It was usually only used as such when Regis was too busy with bookwork to stop for a meal break. Other than that, the stove was used as a heat source.

"You know what would make this coffee even better?" said Shep, sipping once more. "A splash of whiskey." He tried to say it as though he'd heard it was a solemn truth, a trusted remedy they would be fools not to try.

Regis canted his head and gave Shep that long, slow head shake, then went back to dishing up sizzling bacon, two yellow-eye eggs, thick-slice potatoes, and beefsteak.

As he set a plate before Shep, he said, "You'll note that steak is a fancy tender cut, something you'll look back on with a smile."

As he sat down himself across from Shep, the younger brother said, "Well, that's good. 'Cause holed up in this place, it'll be the only thing I will smile about for years."

Regis's smile slid from his face like an egg off a greased plate. "Let it go, Shep. Not today."

"Like you always do, huh?" Shep knew he should shut up. Smile, make it a joke. But he couldn't. He looked over at Regis and saw his brother's jaw muscles flexing. "Aw, I'm just digging and you know it."

Regis set his fork down. "No, I don't know that, Shep. And I tell you that nearly every day. And now today, of all days, your eighteenth birthday, when I thought we might for once not squabble like a pair of old biddies, might get up to a few brotherly hours of fun. Ha."

Regis shut up and shoveled in a couple of quick mouthfuls of eggs and potatoes, then savaged his own slab of rare steak with his knife and fork. He ate as if he were in a hurry to get somewhere, anywhere.

"You always tell me when I eat like that I'm going to end up fat and old before my time."

Without looking up, between bites Regis said, "Yeah, well, maybe I'm in a rush to get there. My presence here sure as hell isn't welcome."

Shep's face reddened deeper. "I don't know what you're getting all worked up about, Regis. I was only funning you. I—"

"That's all right, Shep." Regis stood, squawking back his chair. "You enjoy the food and, yeah, there's a present for you over there. I'm headed back to town today, and I might as well get started. I'll be out of your hair again and you can get back to your life." He plunked his hat on his head and yanked open the door. "Happy birthday, Shep. Many more." He left, the plank door rattling in the frame behind him.

For a long moment, the kid at the table didn't move, then a slow smile spread across his face. A dark, slow smile. He was a man now, after all, he thought. Why not celebrate how he wanted to? Regis wanted to pout and huff and puff, well, then he could, too.

By the time he finished his breakfast, Shep had worked himself up into a fine lather. This was just another example of how Regis was always angry, never able to take a joke.

"Well, I'm good and tired of it," said Shep to the empty little house. "And I'm done with it, too. I'm a man now, after all. Eighteen years old, and the law says I can take care of myself, even though I was doing just fine before I ever made the mistake of coming down here on my own and getting stuck with the original old biddy himself, Regis Royle."

He was halfway to the back door where they kept the wash stand and bucket of water with his dirty dishes when Shep realized what he was talking about, truly talking about. He looked down at the dirty dishes in his hands. "What am I doing?"

He walked back to the table, resisting the urge to toss the dishes on the floor, and instead strode to his bedroom. He didn't have all that much he intended to take, but since he wasn't planning on coming back, he figured he ought to do it up.

Under his bed he found the leather saddlebags Regis had given him for Christmas and filled them with a spare couple of shirts, socks, and his good striped trousers. Then he checked his gun belt with the holstered six-shooter, made sure the loops were filled, and patted his front pocket for his Barlow folder.

The last thing he took was his money pouch, heavy with coins and folding money. Not a lot of it, but plenty to get him somewhere, especially if he headed inland. He was strong, and he had a good horse. He could work, he damn sure knew ranch work, Regis and Bone had made sure of that.

Shep tugged on his tall, black stovepipe boots, pulled on his vest, settled his fawn hat on his head, and, with a last look, was set to walk outside. That's when he remembered that Regis had said there was a present for him over there. He'd gestured to the desk.

Shep chewed the inside of his cheek for a moment, then said, "Aw hell," and walked over to the desk. There on top sat a parcel a foot or so long, and wide as a wrist, wrapped in brown paper and tied with twine. Atop it rested a tightly curled scroll of paper, also nearly a foot wide. It was tied with a length of string as well.

Shep held it up, peered into one hollow end through to the other, saw that it was just paper, and grunted.

Then he unwrapped the parcel and, with the brown paper unfolded, sat a stunning belt knife, brass bolster and pommel, and rich, walnut grips. It rested in a beautiful, dark-brown sheath of oiled leather, and smelling as only good leather can.

Shep grasped the handle and slid the knife out. A gleaming wide blade emerged. It was a couple of inches wide, serrated along the top and bore as keen an edge as he'd ever seen on a knife, about ten inches long before tapering to a drop point.

"Whoa," he whispered, hefting it. A sudden urge to find Regis and thank him and, what's more, to hug him, overwhelmed Shep and he reddened again. He was a man now, dammit, such thoughts would not do.

He bit back the buddings of hot tears and shook his head, sliding the blade back into the sheath. It was then he noticed small lettering ringing the handle at the base, close by the bolster. He looked closer and read his name there in fine script.

It was a knife custom made for him, with his name and all, this was no ordinary smith's job. Must have cost Regis a pretty packet. He always did have good taste in gifts.

"Damn you, Regis," Shep muttered, fighting back a fresh volley of hot tears and redness in his face and ears.

He picked up the knife and stuffed it in his saddlebag, then once more sat at his spot at the small eating table. He shoved the dishes aside, got up, crossed to the desk, and returned to the table with a pencil and scrap of paper and wrote a brief note.

He set the corner of it under the oil lamp and laid the pencil across it. Then he grabbed his bags, walked out the door, and made for the stable, muttering curses directed at his brother and hating himself for doing so the whole time.

Nobody was in the small building that served as the tack shed, and his favorite mount, Scouter, a mustang, wasn't far. He and the horse got along pretty well. That's because you're both headstrong, Bone had told him.

With Bone, he was never certain where he stood, though he expected the Texas Ranger liked him well enough. Or at least tolerated him because he was Regis's little brother, something the other men did, too.

Shep hated that feeling, knowing he was there only because he was born into it, there by relation, not by choice or earning. Now, he was about to fulfill the promise he'd made to himself over and over again since he'd been forced into life at the ranch.

He was going to strike out on his own, live his own life. Only this time, there was nothing anybody could do to stop him. Regis could shout and bellow and throw things and order him around all he wanted, but it was going to be to an empty little house on a big mess of a ranch that, as far as Shep could see, at this point was still more dream than ranch, and more Regis's dream than anyone else's.

He saddled the mustang and rummaged in the tack shed for useful gear. There was plenty of it, as hands regularly used such things when they were working far from the ranch proper for more than a day.

He rolled together a slicker and a bedroll, then tied them behind the cantle. Then, into a sack he stuffed a tin cup, and a small pan for cooking and boiling water, plus a sack of coffee beans. He looped the sack's drawstring to hang off the saddle horn.

At the last, he let the horse drink its fill from the trough by the corral he helped Bone build more than a year before. He filled a water skin from a bucket of fresh water for the men, mounted up, and heeled the horse northward.

The last thing he wanted to do was cut across the trail of anybody he knew from the ranch, especially Regis, though he was headed back to town, southeast of the ranch.

The damn spread was so big it would take Shep the better part of the day to get across, or at least that's how Regis liked to describe it.

"Let him describe it all he wants, eh, Scouter?" Shep patted the horse's neck and chuckled. He'd ride northward for a while, then cut east, maybe hug the coast. Why not? There was way more excitement along the waterfront than there was riding through days of hot sun and sand. He knew this from previous experience. And he had no interest in feeling that wrung-out ever again, if he could help it.

Then, as so often happens on one's birthday, it occurred to Shep all at once, one more time, that it was his birthday. But not just any old birthday. This one was his eighteenth birthday.

"Hoo-whee!" he shouted to the high, blue sky and far-off, purple horizon.

With that fresh thought pulling a smile on his face, and earlier than he intended to, Shepley Royle guided the horse eastward.

For he knew now where he was going to celebrate his special day, and it wasn't in the midst of the sun and sand and snakes. Plenty of time for that. But today? Today he was headed to the little port town of Corpus Christi.

And he had just the fellow in mind to help him paint that town bright red—himself. And if he felt like it, heck who was he kidding, if luck was with him, he might find a young lady who was willing to help him celebrate his big day in fine style. What a way to cap it all off.

Chapter 18

There were a whole lot of things in Regis Royle's life these days that he was beyond frustrated with. But his little brother, Shepley, took the top spot on the pile. Regis knew he could be a prickly pear at times, but Shep was the one person of anybody he'd ever known who could twist his crank and make him angry with no warning.

All they did was fight, with short, sweet moments of genuine brotherly affection. But even those moments had become fewer and further apart than when Shep had tracked him down two years ago.

The kid had ridden in, looking for him, and ended up saving his neck in the midst of the Santa Calina range. He'd been pinned down by a band of killers they later found out were brutes in the employ of Tomasina Valdez, the witch whose family once owned the range.

Her attempts to win back the land had become more unscrupulous with each week that passed, culminating in a brutal kidnapping of Shep in some misguided notion of blackmailing Regis for the land. He'd called her bluff, though, and rode in under cover of night with the help of Tut, an impressive young man and one who had the makings of a foreman one day. (That day might come around sooner than later, should Bone keep on the lone wolf path he was running.)

They'd ridden in to that rocky hideaway where Tomasina Valdez had holed up with her gang, keeping Shep barely conscious and shackled in a cave. But he and Tut had killed most of the gang. Regis's one regret was that they'd let that devil woman escape. She was not the sort to give up on a thing, but he hadn't heard from her since. He had begun to hope she might have somehow met a fate only an evil creature such as she so richly deserved.

She'd had Shep shackled deep in a cave in her rocky desert hole. After that, whatever tensions had been between the two brothers had nearly dissolved. For some time following, Shep had become dependent on Regis to such a degree that he had to think of ways to get the kid back on his own feet.

It had worked for a spell, and then Shep began to revert back to his old, independent self. And then, as time passed, he seemed to go beyond that, to become even more self-serving and unruly.

Regis sighed and adjusted his hat. The trail to Brownsville was more than familiar by now, but it wouldn't do to let his attention drift, even if the region had undergone a whole lot of change, and much of it for the better, mostly because of the efforts of his men.

They were as solid a team of ranch hands and brush fighters as he'd ever seen. That was Bone's doing, himself a longtime fighter, as well as a rancher and a leader of men.

The rest of his trip to town passed as such, with Regis paying half as much attention to his surroundings as he should, and thinking of how he was going to talk with Cormac about the two new, vast swaths of acreage he'd spoken for.

Knowing Cormac, he'd say they don't have the money, so don't go trying to buy more land. But to Regis's way of thinking, a man could never go wrong amassing land, especially range that bordered the Royle Ranch ranges.

He rode King to his old friend Cotton's stable and out front, he slid down out of the saddle and stretched his back, musing that if anybody needed to stretch out the kinks after a ride like that, it was probably the buckskin. He was a fine horse, had been with him since the ranch's beginning, and had carried him through a good many scrapes.

Regis hoped like hell such shenanigans were behind them. He was so close to his dream of building up the biggest ranch in the state—and beyond. He intended to become a somebody, a wealthy man to whom gentry would look and say, "Now there rides a fine cut of a man in his custom barouche. And look at that woman beside him, he landed a prize catch when she agreed to marry him." Then they'd wink and say, "Or maybe the other way around."

With such thoughts dancing in his mind, Regis led King through the open double doors of the stable. "Cotton? Where you at, friend?"

"Hey? Hey? What's that now?" An old man of indistinct age shuffled out from an open side door that led to a lean-to off the back of the place, which served as Cotton's office and home, all in one.

Regis had been in there more than once, sharing stories and gossip and warming hands by the small woodstove when the season demanded, with an occasional nip from the bottle of decent whiskey that Regis took care to keep the old man supplied with.

He didn't need to, as in most ways he was no more to the old man than Cotton was to him, a customer and a merchant, engaging in transaction. Cotton's trade was that of stable owner and keeper, and though his accommodations were spartan, they were clean. Best of all, though, was that Cotton knew horses.

The same could not be said of Brownsville's other stables, which varied in quality from downright appalling places a fellow wouldn't leave a rat to fend in, let alone pay for, on up to a seemingly sumptuous accommodation for horses at the King's Arms Livery.

The latter was anything but the case—Regis had heard tales of horse abuse when wealthy owners were away dallying at the games tables or some other lofty pursuit. But Cotton's place, which had come quietly bubbling up to him in the form of recommendations from several friends, including Cormac and Bone, had been at once welcoming and comfortable.

And his horse, and Shep's, too, when the kid was in town, were always relaxed, brushed to a gleam, well fed, exercised if need be, and their tack always cleaned. None of this had been part of the agreement to shelter and feed horses whilst under Cotton's care. But they'd been provided anyway.

Regis appreciated this sort of person, this kindness, this outlook, this way of being and doing and carrying himself. It was all wrapped up in this old, bent, white-haired, nut-brown-skinned old man with clear brown eyes and slow-to-smile way about him.

But it was Cotton's razor-sharp wit that always challenged Regis and forced him to consider each conversation they had, either for a moment, should Regis be in a rush, or for an hour or two, of an evening, when both men had completed their day's travails.

Though their ages were far apart, Regis found a kindness that marked Cotton right away as a friend for life. He guessed Cotton felt the same about him.

"Regis Royle," said Cotton. A slight smile and a quick eye wink let Regis know he was glad to be seen. Then he shuffled over to King and rubbed the big horse along the neck, ran a gnarled hand up into the horse's mane. The horse bowed his head and gently nuzzled the old man in the side, his mouth searching for something toothsome in an inner coat pocket.

Cotton chuckled. "Yeah, you know where old Cotton keeps the goods, huh?" He helped the horse and withdrew a couple of slices of dried apple and fed them to the horse.

"So that's your secret," said Regis. "I'll have to keep it in mind."

"Yeah, you do that. You'll do all right. Some folks, though. They got mean right through them, and to a horse, that type of thing shines off them. Like you can see dirt on a kid's face? Well, a horse can see mean on a man. And that horse won't go rubbing on a fellow who's mean even if he had pockets filled with lump sugar." Cotton shook his head. "No sir, he won't."

Regis reached in his saddle bag and tugged out a cloth sack. "I found myself stopping off at Tilbert's place, thought you might be getting low on that rheumatism medicine."

He handed the parcel to Cotton and the old man's sharp eyes narrowed as he smiled. "Oh," he drew out the contents enough to gaze down at it. "That's fine, that's fine. I sure do appreciate it, Mr. Royle. My bones ain't what they used to be, no sir." He peeked further in the sack.

Regis nodded. "Somehow I realized a sack of horehound boiled sweets made their way in as well. I don't suppose you'd be able to put them to use?"

"As it happens, I am partial to a taste of such sweeties now and again myself. I reckon I'll make do with them." He winked at the tall man and set the parcel carefully atop the grain bin by his left side. "Now, let's us see what we need to do to get ol' Mr. King more comfortable. I expect you'll be in town for the day?"

Regis nodded. "Yep, a couple, at least. Cormac wants to talk. I think it's accounts time."

Cotton whistled. "I don't envy you that conversation. Ol' Cormac, when he gets going on about high finance, ain't nobody safe. If I can offer advice?"

Regis finished stripping off the saddle. He never left it for Cotton and couldn't imagine how the old fellow managed to do so with other horses. Or saddle up a beast, for that matter, even with the step-stool contraption he'd built for himself. But he did it, and that's what kept him moving.

"Always, Cotton. I'd appreciate it."

"Okay, then. I was you—and I'd not want to be because you are chewing on a mighty wad of steak and I prefer tiny bites in life—I'd consider what's behind the words he's saying. Where they come from, why he's saying them, why he's not saying others. You understand?"

Regis rasped a hand across his chin. "Yeah." He nodded his head. "Yeah, I think so. But I have a few things I need to say to him, too."

"Mm hmm, yeah, I bet you do." He sighed and looked away.

Regis thought that was odd, almost as if his old friend was disappointed in what Regis had said. Oh well. Doesn't much matter. He's him and I'm me.

They chatted a few minutes longer, then Regis said, "Okay, I've put it off long enough, Cotton. I best get to the office and see what sort of trouble I'm in with Cormac."

Both men knew he was only half-kidding. But Regis alone knew how rough the conversation was likely to be. He'd been ignoring his partner's advice and warnings for months now, and had intentionally withheld certain recent agreements and transactions he'd made on the financial behalf of their shared shipping firm. Items that Regis was certain by now Cormac knew all about.

In the senior partner's weighty opinion, there was no more egregious affront to a relationship, be it with a business partner, a friend, or worse, both, than to operate behind the back of the partner and conduct business.

And then to neglect to reveal this breach of trust was unheard of. And yet Regis had done so. Because land was all. Cormac would come around one day and realize he'd been right.

Cotton's stable was but a two-minute walk from the offices of Delany and Royle Shipping on Beecher Street. He didn't bother to knock, though it had been weeks since he'd logged any time behind his desk. As he walked in, he saw the desk had grown to resemble his makeshift desk back at the ranch—a jumbled sprawl of papers.

"Cormac?" Regis peered around the large, cluttered room. No Cormac. Not unusual, as their days at the office were often peppered with visits to the warehouse at the dock, about a block from the office. They used to have offices at the docks, but Cormac long ago figured that if they filled the space they used for two desks and chairs with freight, they could increase their monthly haul. He'd been right, of course.

Just then the back door of the office, behind Cormac's desk chair, swung inward with a squeak. The senior partner looked up, across the office. "Regis. Good, you're here." He sat at his desk and rummaged in papers. "We have some talking to do."

Regis walked over, smiling. "That's it? No hello? No questions about the ranch? Not curious how your investment's doing?"

That stopped Cormac cold. He let his paper-filled fingers collapse to the desktop and looked up. "You have some nerve to say that to me."

"What? Cormac, what's got into you?"

"Look, Regis. I'm overworked, carrying the load of this place so you can go off and play rancher."

Regis felt himself bristling, and tried to interrupt, but Cormac plowed ahead.

"And I say 'play' because it's not really a ranch yet, is it, Regis? No, now don't answer. I don't want to hear your answers. I want to hear something magical, such as how you expect to have the place pay for itself in, say, six months. Now that would be magic."

"Cormac, you know yourself buying raw land and building up a herd takes time."

"Course I do, dammit!" Cormac stood. "I've been around a time or two myself, you know. Don't forget who taught you about risk and opportunity, man." His finger jabbed at the air between them.

"But the thing I am not hearing and I have about given up on expecting to hear from you is a plan, an actual plan as to how you're going to pay that money back. You recall? The money we borrowed on our good names, on the name of our business. Huh? I don't argue that I was all-in on this deal, but that was for the Santa Calina range, Regis. Eighteen thousand acres of prime country." He nodded. "Good land, too. I saw it for myself with my own eyes. You were right, it's got promise, real promise. And your initial plans were just right for risking an investment on."

"So? What's the matter now, Cormac? It's a little late in the game for cold feet, don't you think?"

"You bet it is. It's also a little late in the game to start taking on mountains of new debt."

Regis lost whatever was left of his hopefulness. Oh boy, Cormac already knew. He'd hoped to break it to him himself. Damn.

"Yes, Regis," said Cormac, seeing the surprise on his younger partner's face. "I know all right. I know about the two large parcels you've spoken for. I even know about that little wedge of land, oh, only a thousand acres in size you've committed us to. Trouble is, Regis, how are you planning on paying for that land?

"And when were you going to tell me about it? You used my good name, my good name, not saying a thing about the firm's, to barter and wheedle and cajole and make deals with bankers and other businessmen and who knows who else. Some of them men I wouldn't dare deal with in all my years in business! You did this to us? To me? Dammit, man, how much land is enough for you? Maybe you'd like to enter into negotiations with all of Mexico? I bet you could get a whole lot of it pretty damn cheap!"

"It's not like that, Cormac." Regis looked down. "I know, I know. It's unforgiveable." He folded his big arms across his chest. He didn't know what else to do with them.

"No, dammit! Don't put words in my mouth. What I was going to say is that it's downright malicious, that's what it is!"

"Mal—now hang on just a minute, Cormac. I know I should have told you, I know I should have done a whole lot of things lately, but malicious? That's too far."

"Is it? Is it?" Cormac spat the words, his head shaking in rage. The two men stared at each other for long moments over Cormac's cluttered desk.

Finally, Regis cleared his throat and was about to speak when

Cormac held up a hand. "I don't want to hear your excuses any-more, Regis. I'm not saying I'm done with you, because we're far too knotted up in business just now. I'll figure out how to untan-gle my own finances from yours. I'll look into buying you out of the freighting business and you can do the same with me and the ranch. That sound fair to you?"

Regis stood before the desk, staring across at Cormac, unable to speak. He owed this man, this red-faced, rage-filled Irishman, everything. A man who'd found him years before as a skinny stowaway.

But instead of tossing him out onto the nearest pier, he'd kept him on, fed him, worked him, sure, but also educated him, paid for schooling, then took him on as a junior partner, and finally a full partner. In short, Cormac Delany had treated him like a son and what had Regis done?

Oh my God, thought the big man. What have I done?

Then he said it aloud, and for one of the few times in his life, Regis felt the stink of raw fear tickle his nostrils. Felt it knot and twist in his gut.

Cormac, a man he'd known well for years, a man he knew bet-ter than he knew most anybody else, save his own sorry self, stood poised behind his cluttered desk, staring him down, anger flexing his nostrils.

For the first time in a long time, Regis saw how the man had aged. How unkempt his usually tidy self was. He saw his ink-stained fingers, the crumbs littering his shirt, the stubble on his face, the circles beneath his eyes, the red veins lacing the whites of his eyes. Cormac's now-thinned hair, usually kept brushed, neat and short, now looked as grizzled as the rest of him. What have I done to him?

"I'll make it up to you, Cormac. I promise you." Regis did not recognize his own voice, a thin, trembling thing. It could have come from the kid Cormac had found huddling belowdecks in the damp hold of that old steamer all those years before.

"Too late, Regis. You crossed a line I don't think we can ever step back from."

"But Cormac, I'm telling you—"

Again his old friend held up an ink-dappled hand. "Not now, Regis. Not now." He sank back into his chair and picked up a folded sheaf of papers.

"On top of everything else you've put us through financially these past months, this arrived earlier today." He tossed the papers across the desk. "Read that, then tell me how everything's going to be okay, Regis. See if you are able to do that then."

He poured himself a glass of whiskey and did not offer Regis one.

Regis sat down and read the papers.

Chapter 19

The top sheet was a letter, which Regis held in shaking fingertips—shaking, as he read, out of a mounting rage. It was from Robt. Haskellet and Son, attorneys at law. They were a local firm there in Brownsville, one that Regis and Cormac knew well.

They'd used the firm several times when a legal point came up about which they were uncertain, something they had perceived as a threat to their business. They'd been successful a number of times in defending their holdings from scurvy dogs out for little more than an easy pay day and ill intent.

They were using them at present, in verifying to whatever extent was possible, the various land grants, titles, and such of the parcels of land they, which meant Regis, had been pursuing in an effort to solidify ownership of the lands that made up the Royle Ranch.

But this time, as the letter told him, he and Cormac were the ones being called on the carpet. Or rather their company was. And Regis found he didn't much like that thought.

What he most wanted to do was to read it aloud and then sit down with Cormac and consider it from all angles. But his partner was more steamed with him than Regis had ever seen. He finished reading the letter, then began once more, at the top.

To Whom It May Concern:

In our ongoing efforts on your firm's behalf to investigate the origination and current legal status and ownership of the Santa Calina Range, and to secure all legal rights to that parcel of range land, we regret to inform you that our efforts turned up heretofore unknown information regarding ownership of the parcel of land in question.

This discovery coincided with the arrival of a letter to our offices, delivered in person, by a legal representative of the Valdez family, whom you may recall as the original possessors of the Spanish Land Grant for the entirety of the Santa Calina Range.

The letter, a copy of which I have enclosed, states in short that there is a newly discovered and rightful heir to the original land grant. This heir was unlawfully circumvented by one Señor Valdez, patriarch of the family and the man who sold the parcel to Don Mallarmoza, from whom you bought, in good faith, as did he from Sr. Valdez, the Santa Calina Range.

The wording, it seems, referred specifically to the fact that the eldest surviving child of each successive generation of the Valdez family was the sole and rightful heir, and thus owner of the land contained within the Spanish Land Grant.

Your assumption, as was Don Mallarmoza's, as well as ours, was that since Sr. Valdez sold the land to Don Mallarmoza, he was at the time the rightful heir and thus the owner. However, he was technically not the owner. That distinction transferred not to his daughter Tomasina Valdez, with whom you are by now well acquainted, but to her older sibling.

In short, gentlemen, it seems that your ownership of the Santa Calina Range, is in serious doubt, and thus, in serious jeopardy.

Given that you have invested an extraordinary amount of time and effort and money in the Santa Calina range with the intention of building up a most singular ranch, I suggest you visit our offices at your earliest convenience so that we may all confer and together devise a strategy to address this, shall we say, interesting turn of events.

Regis scratched his chin and continued to stare at the letter. "I . . . I don't understand."

Cormac sighed. "What's not understandable about that? There's a legitimate owner to the land and it isn't us. And considering we don't want this to fall apart in our hands, which it may well do anyway, it appears that we have to do as the man says and meet with him to figure out what we're going to do."

"But . . . this is impossible. We took care of Tomasina Valdez, paid for the land fair and square. This is Don Mallarmoza's problem, not ours."

"Don Mallarmoza will be obliging, I'm sure, but he's a Mexican, and legally he doesn't have to do a damn thing on our behalf. And if I know him, which I do and have for a long time now, he will smile and shrug and say something like, 'business is business, eh, boys?'"

"But . . ."

"But nothing! If this is a legitimate claim to ownership of the land, it might well supersede any deals subsequent to it. You know that as well as I do."

"No," said Regis, shaking his head. "No way."

"Look, Regis. I don't like it any more than you do. Especially in light of the chicanery you've been up to lately."

"Chicanery? What do you mean by that?"

"Everything we talked about before you read the damned letter, boy. You've been playing me false, and I don't tolerate that from anyone. Least of all someone I've treated as a . . ."

The word he was about to utter hung in the air between them like acrid smoke in a rain storm. It hung and stung the eyes and tightened the throats of the two men. Finally, Regis broke the moment wide open.

He strode to the door, crushing the lawyer's letter in his big hand.

"Where in hell do you think you're going? We have to go to Haskellet's office!"

"You go," said Regis. "I'm in no mood for all that thick talk right now."

"No way," said Cormac, rounding the desk. "You landed us in this mess, you're helping to dig us out of the hole!"

"A wise man once told me that when you find yourself in a hole, the first thing you do is stop digging." Regis looked at his partner a moment longer, then left, clunking the door shut behind himself.

The words Cormac had told a younger Regis many years before echoed within each of them.

Chapter 20

It wasn't until Regis had ridden for an hour northwest of town, once more toward his beloved Santa Calina range—Ha! he thought, how much longer can I consider it mine?—that he realized how short and snappy he'd been with ol' Cotton when he'd showed up at the stable to retrieve King.

Even the horse had seemed shocked, as Cotton was in the midst of brushing him down and talk-singing to him in that peculiar way he had with the beasts in his charge.

Regis had all but demanded the horse and tack, then had all but shoved Cotton out of the way as he went about the task of saddling the horse himself, faster and sloppier than Cotton would have, but he didn't care.

"What's wrong, boy?" the old man had said. And at that moment, Regis had almost stopped, almost held off from slamming through saddling the big horse.

He'd wanted at that moment more than anything to sit in Cotton's room and tell the old man everything that was happening in his life, how everything was falling apart, how he and Bone had had a falling out, how his brother, Shepley, had left him.

He wanted to tell him how his oldest friend, and a man who was so much like a father to him, didn't trust him any longer, and what's more seemed to want to sever ties with him. And how the ranch land that he'd staked everything on, the large centerpiece of all his holdings that were leveraged to a ridiculous level, might well not be his and likely never had been.

How the ranch was far from a profitable business, how he'd taken responsibility for all those Mexican families, hell, entire villages, buying up the livestock that were their livelihoods. How he'd convinced them to relocate to his ranch, all with the promise of good, paying work, and a whole new life here in Texas on the Royle Range. How all of it was falling apart, all because of him and his freakish greed, all dusting away like sun-dry sand out of a clawed hand.

Regis wanted to tell Cotton all of this. He wanted his old friend's opinion. For Cotton's judgment, he knew, was sound, if at times buried in meaning, layers of words and winks and pauses and chin scratches and long silences that were as telling and as important to the man who chose to pay attention, as any he might encounter in his life.

But instead, he had done what he always did when he was angry and desperate, the same thing Shep did all his days, Regis saw that now. He lashed out at the person closest to him at the time.

He'd tried to bite back the bile rising in his gorge, but hot stinging words flew out of him, stabbing straight at the wide-eyed stable man, his old friend, Cotton.

"Mind your own damn business for once, will you, old man?" He shoved by him, knocking Cotton backward into the grain bin before he could right himself. Even then, Regis could only look on the man with a scowl.

Throwing a leg up and over King's saddle, he snapped the long tag ends of the reins against the horse and thundered out of the stable, nearly into the path of a slow-moving team carrying a spiffed farmer, his bonneted wife, and their brood. He'd lobbed a few choice words their way, too, then pounded up the street toward the west end, then out, thundering toward the ranch once more.

Each hoof fall brought Regis closer to the Santa Calina and farther from the headaches his visit to town had visited on him. As the hours trickled by, he grew wearier and thirstier, as did King. As they walked along, he thought and thought and mused on his foolish behavior. He did not want to return to the ranch. He was not ready to go back there and lose himself in work. That was no solution. Not yet. He had some thinking to do.

He had scant provisions, but he had a rifle and a knife and a revolver, all if need be. He had a way to make fire and he had a bedroll and a slicker. And the free-flowing Santa Calina was not too far ahead. He'd make for it and think things through.

On Regis rode, the faintest glimmer of hope sparking deep in his breast, the hope that, as Cormac had once told him, when he hits bottom, there's only one direction a man can go.

"Up," he said, his voice cracking in the still, hot air. King's ears twitched.

But, he wondered as he rode toward the river, had he hit bottom yet?

Chapter 21

Shep's first intended stop in the little burg of Corpus Christi was a place where his horse might get attended to. Not too spendy, but enough that he'd not have to worry about it. He also planned on keeping his valuables with him—coin pouch, which he'd need, six-gun and cartridge belt, now also balanced nicely with the fine knife Regis had given him.

He still lumped a little in the throat when he thought about their parting, but decided there was nothing to be done beyond the note he'd left. He was a man now, after all, and sometimes a man had to make difficult choices.

He quickly changed into his best shirt and trousers, and rolled up the old ones—after snapping the trail dust off them. He stuffed them into his saddlebags and decided he'd risk leaving the rest of the gear in the livery as well. From the looks of it, two others had done just the same. He didn't see anybody about beyond the old Mexican man who tended the place.

He seemed trustworthy enough. Besides, other than the too-fancy saddlebags, also a gift from Regis, the rest of his traps weren't of much value. Didn't mean he didn't want to keep them. So he balled it all up beneath his slicker, and tucked it behind the hay near his horse, who was feasting on oats.

Whistling a jaunty tune he made up as he went, Shep strode

out of the stable and along a short, dusty track that led to what he assumed was the main street of town. Mostly he saw people moving in all directions, lots of dust raised, and between the people, lots of horse teams, irate drivers shouting at people walking, and, to either side, tents and plank-fronted buildings. The signs tacked or hanging from most read "saloon" or "bar." Others bore the usual "guns," "eat," "bath," "shave," and "laundry." And one that made Shep laugh—"signs." Judging from the terse vocabulary on display, he guessed that was the shop that had made the signs for the whole strip.

He did not need a shave or a bath. And his clothes were clean enough—he couldn't smell himself through them, so they must be doing their job. What he really wanted was a celebratory glass of beer, but what he knew he needed was what his horse was getting—food.

"Where to get some food, where . . ." Although Shep said this to himself, a habit he had picked up while working often alone at the ranch, a woman in a flop-topped bonnet and wiry red hair scowled at him down her long, pointed nose. She looked so sour and pleased with herself that he stuck out his tongue and grunted, "Gaah!"

She gasped, "Oh my!" and recoiled as if he'd tried to bite her. Shep laughed and continued on his way, swinging up onto a length of wood-topped boardwalk alongside the buildings on the right side of the street. Nothing could touch him this day. He felt as though he was floating and that his boots weren't touching the ground at all.

He made his way toward a promising looking, board-fronted place with a low-pitch roof and a sign atop its ramada that read "Joe's Cantina," thinking maybe he could get both food and drink for a reasonable price.

The front-door was open and a wide-shouldered, bald man with short, clipped moustaches gently escorted a tail-tucked black-and-white cur out. He used a grimy, once-white towel and flicked at it as it walked away from him. "You have been told, little one."

The bald man retreated back into the cantina.

He took that as an encouraging sign and walked up the two steps. He stopped before the little, sad-looking cur who now sat outside the door, one ear up, one down, looking into the dim interior of the cantina as if he might still be welcomed back inside.

"Hmm," said Shep to the dog. "I can't abide anyone beating a dog, and as he was good enough to scoot you out of there without kicking up a fuss, I'll drink to his good health, and yours—and mine, too."

He hadn't gone more than a foot or two inside when the fat bald man appeared with a wooden bowl filled with scrumptious-smelling beans and a hunk of bread.

"Ah, hello, hello," said the man. "Sit anywhere. I'll be with you in a minute. Just feeding another of my customers." He chuckled and, as Shep watched, the man set the bowl down before the little dog. He grunted down on one knee and broke up the bread into little hunks and spread them atop the beans in the bowl.

The bald man patted the waiting little dog, said, "Okay, then," and the patient dog tucked into the bowl of food with the single-minded vigor only a dog can truly muster.

The smiling man stood, grunting again, and saw Shep watching him. He blushed a little and shrugged. "He's a daily visitor. If he paid, I'd be a wealthy man."

He chuckled and wiped his hands on his grimy white apron as he walked by Shep. "What can I do for you, sir, on this fine day?"

Shep followed him a dozen feet up to a bar along the back. Behind that was an open door that led to a kitchen. Steam and succulent smells drifted toward him.

"I tell you, sir. If you have a bowl of something that smells half as good as what you fed that little dog out there, I'd be obliged."

The man nodded. "I think we can figure out something that will feed a growing fellow like yourself."

For a second Shep wasn't certain how to take that. He didn't take himself to be doing much growing anymore. He was a man, after all. "Well, maybe you could pour me a beer, too, while I'm waiting."

He settled himself on a wobbly-looking stool, rested his hands on the bar top, and looked around the cool, darkened interior. He saw only one other person, a fellow in what looked to be an army uniform, though it was difficult to tell. That was interesting. Maybe he'd chat with the fellow. Heck, maybe he could get the man to buy him a drink.

Shep sighed and looked back toward the fat, bald proprietor who was busy hacking a loaf of bread into thick slices. The bread steamed its fresh warmth into the hot air.

"After all," said Shep in a raised voice, "I am celebrating."

"Oh?" said the man, glancing over his shoulder at Shep. "And why is that?"

"Well sir, since you asked, it's my birthday."

"Well, a happy birthday to you." He set a pewter tankard filled with beer on the counter and raised his eyebrows. "And how old today?"

Shep looked from the tankard up to the man's face. The man hadn't released his grip on the beer. "I am, as it happens, eighteen years of age on this very day."

"And not a whisker younger, eh?" The man slid the tankard toward Shep on the smooth plank bar top. "That is my present to you, then. To your good health."

"Why, thank you, sir. I appreciate it." Without waiting, lest the man change his mind, and because he realized he'd worked up a powerful thirst, Shep hoisted the tankard and wet his whistle. He didn't stop until he'd drained the glass. He lowered it and smacked his lips. "Ahhh. That's just what the trail told me I needed."

But the bald man had disappeared into the kitchen before he could ask for a refill.

"Happy birthday."

Shep turned to see the uniformed fellow standing beside him. The man set his own pewter mug on the bar top. Next round's my treat. He stuck out his hand. "Name's Pinski. Friends call me Pin."

Shep shook his hand. "That mean if I call you Pin, you won't take a swing at me?"

The man smiled and nodded. "Yep."

"I'm Shep." He straightened on his stool. "Shepley Royle."

"Well, pleased to meet you, Shep."

"Pull up a stool."

"Better yet, how about we share a table? Mine's in a cool corner, away from the kitchen smells."

"Don't mind if I do," said Shep. "But I'm partial to kitchen smells. I'm also hungry and waiting on my food."

"No worries, I won't take it from you."

"You just try."

The two men walked back to the table, though Shep had been looking forward to chatting with the owner some more. Any man who fed stray dogs was okay with him. He looked out the door on his way by, but though the wooden bowl was there—licked spotless—the dog was nowhere in sight.

"So," said Pin when they were seated. "Eighteen today, eh?"

"Yep, that's about it."

"You mind me asking—oh, just a second." He motioned behind Shep, who turned to see the bald man once more behind the bar with a plate of food. "We've moved back here, barkeep. And two more beers, if you please."

"Okay," said the fat man. Shep thought maybe he looked a little disappointed, as if he might have wanted a chat, too. Oh well, he thought. The day's young and I have nowhere else to be. The thought warmed him almost as much as the first beer did.

"Where was I?" said Pin once the bald man had brought the food and beers. "Oh, yes, you say you're eighteen now, and that sets me to wondering if you have any attachments."

Shep paused, a mouthful of some of the tastiest frijoles he'd ever had the pleasure to spoon in. He swallowed them down. "Attachments?"

"Yes, in other words, are you married or, oh, wanted by the law or employed somewhere, that sort of thing?"

Shep nearly sprayed another spoonful of beans at the man. He managed to keep them in his mouth, but he snorted in laughter. "No to all of them. But if I did, I'm not so sure I'd tell you, now would I?"

"True enough." Pin sipped his beer and smiled.

Much of an hour and another beer later, Shep had moved back to the counter to settle up with the owner.

"Oh, well." The bald man wiped at the bartop slowly. "If you're sure." Then he smiled and looked at Shep again. "Say, how about another beer? My treat. I'll even join you."

Shep looked from him to the doorway, where Pin was standing, hands on his hips, waiting for him. "Well, what time do you close? I could come back before then. Round out the day with you."

"Oh, sure, that's fine. We're open late, no trouble. Come on back. But hey," he lowered his voice and nodded toward the door. "That one? Be careful, huh?"

"What do you mean?" said Shep.

The bald man shrugged. "I dunno. Just a feeling. I get them sometimes about folks."

"All right. Well, thanks. I'll bear it in mind." He turned, walked to the front, and over his shoulder said, "Thanks again for the beer. See you later."

"Okay."

But what Shep really wanted to say was why didn't the man mind his own business? Everybody was trying to tell him what to do, how to behave, how to act, what to say, what not to say, do this, don't do that, drink, don't drink. Too damn much, that's what it was.

Pin said, "All right, Mr. Birthday. Being the young, single fellow I am, I have enough pay in my pocket to choke a horse, and two days of leave before I go back to my soft job. For which I get paid a lot of money. Did I mention that?" He had leaned toward Shep when he said that, then winked. "So, first whiskey's on me. You pick the place. I'm new here."

"Me, too," said Shep, not minding one bit that he'd already made a friend here in Corpus Christi, and one who wasn't covered in sweat and dung and prickle-burrs. Pin sounded as if he had his life figured out. And to boot, he didn't seem too much older than he was.

Shep fell into line beside the man, who, he couldn't help notice, folks gave sideways glances to and offered courteous nods to. Some even sidestepped to let Pin, and by association, Shep, pass. But most impressive of all were the smiling women, from girls on up to two middle-age ladies in very fine dresses who made no attempt to hide their glances of approval at Pin.

Shep glanced at Pin himself. Sure, he was tall, but Shep noted with pride that he was just about the same height. Where they differed was in clothing.

Shep wore his best white shirt, which, now that he saw it, had yellowed a bit under the arms. He kept his wings down and wished he'd thought to bring a coat, too. But it was too hot and the one he owned was a brown wool affair with moth holes.

Shep did notice, too, and not without a little pride that puffed his chest, that he was wider at the shoulder and appeared to have thicker arms and legs than Pin did. Not to take anything from the soldier, but Shep had a sudden sense he was on an even field as Pin, and in a few ways, well, he was . . . a man. Damn, but it felt good to know that.

"Shep, how about this place?"

Pin broke Shep's reverie. He stopped beside the soldier and

looked up at a two-story building with the barest hint of gilding on a sign that read, "House of Secrets," and beneath that, "Ales, whiskeys, good times."

Pin whistled and before Shep could say a word, the soldier had pinched his shirt sleeve and led him around a pair of men chatting drunkenly. They walked up the steps, shoved through the batwing doors, and into the darkened interior.

Chapter 22

The warm feeling riding low in his belly from the mugs of beer at Joe's Cantina had all but left him when Shep smiled and nodded his head at Pin's offer of a glass of whiskey. Now this was more like it for a fellow on his birthday. And not just any birthday.

As if reading his mind, Pin topped up a fresh squat glass with the first of a new bottle of whiskey and said, "Nothing but the best—or nearly so, anyway—for my new friend on his natal day."

"Natal day? Huh, never heard it called that before. But I like it." He raised his drink, and the two men clinked glasses.

That drink followed another, and the third was the last one Shep was aware of. After that, the afternoon blurred by. He joined his newfound bar comrades several times out back at the open trough latrine and jostled and joked and went back in for more of a grand old time.

Some hours after they arrived, Pin corralled Shep over to a wobbly table in a corner and talked his ear off about how great being a member of the US Army was.

Shep told him about how awful being a little brother was, and one who had so much expected of him, one who was treated harsher than anybody else at the ranch, his ranch, well, along with his brother and a few others. And how he was, by Jove, fed up with it.

"Ain't I a man of my own now, after all? Huh?"

Pin nodded, a long, slow gesture accompanied with a sloppy hand dropping on Shep's shoulder. "Look." He leaned closer. "I am your friend, ain't that right?"

"Sure you are. We're as close as pards can be, I reckon," said Shep. "You seem to be the only person I've ever met who understands what-all I have to put up with in life."

"That's right, so I'm going to tell you a secret." Pin nodded.

Shep's eyes widened. Here was a friend among friends. Willing to divulge something meaningful to him, something from deep down inside.

"You have my word I won't tell anyone."

"Okay. You know how I told you before that I am making all sorts of money . . ." he looked about them.

Shep did the same. ". . . as a military man?"

Pin nodded.

"Sure, I recall. You should be right proud."

"I am, you bet. And I am in a position to help you feel that proud, too."

"Huh? What's that mean?"

"Means that one of my duties is to share with only a select few men, just a very few, mind you, the secret of becoming a military officer in the United States Army."

Here his voice trembled a little, and he looked away.

Shep looked at him with mouth sagged and eyes wide. "You . . . you'd do that for me?"

"Why, of course I would. I tell you true right now, Shep. In all my travels, and for the Army, I get up to some mighty traveling. Seeing all sorts of country and all manner of folks, including lots of ladies." He nudged Shep on the arm. "If you know what I mean."

In truth, Shep wasn't exactly certain what the remark meant, but he had a pretty good idea, and it was an idea he liked hearing a whole lot. Shep nodded in solemnity and in a low voice, said,

"How would a fellow go about signing up? I'd hate to let you down and all."

"You know, of all the wise things you have said all day, Shep, I do believe that is the wisest yet. And it will prove to be one of the smartest, maybe the absolute smartest, thing you have ever done in all your life." His vigorous nodding had the effect on Shep of all but sealing the deal.

Before the younger man could speak, Pin reached into his blue tunic. "I happen to have the very papers right here with me—which tells you just how serious the United States Army is about employing good men. I have not found anyone in all my long travels I deem to be a worthy to wear the uniform as you, Shep, and that's a fact. I don't say it lightly, as my duties are important to me."

The man pulled out two sheets of somewhat yellowed paper, slightly bent at the edges, and creased in four. He unfolded them and smoothed them on the table top between them. A small puddle of spilled whiskey soaked into the paper from beneath, but neither man seemed to notice.

The top of the page bore an official, printed symbol of an eagle below an address. Below that sat two or three handwritten lines that though Shep tried, proved to be nearly impossible for him to take in. Not that he didn't try. He squinted and squinted and held the sheet closer to his face, then closed one eye. No luck. He was drunker than he thought he was.

"No worries about what it says, friend," said Pin, tapping a long finger on the sheet. "I wouldn't play you false, would I? Now, what you want to do is sign it here and there. Too many people wait, say they'd like to think on it once they've gotten out of the rain."

"I don't have a pencil or some such to make my mark," said Shep, rubbing his fingers up and over his thin-whiskered face.

"You can read and write, I take it?" said Pin, a look of confusion on his face.

"Oh sure, no worries there."

Pin smiled and reached once more into his tunic. This time he pulled out a short, much-blackened quill. It, too, looked worse for the riding in his coat. "Ink," he said. Both men stared at the quill in his fingers as if it were about to speak to them. Finally Shep stood. "I'll ask the bartender."

"Good idea. And while you're there, how about a beer to seal the deal?"

"Sure," said Shep. "But beer's not anything to drink on such an occasion. Whiskey."

"Whiskey it is." Pin nodded.

He watched as Shep smoothed his sleeves and walked with caution toward the bar. The army man's lopsided grin dropped away and his eyes seemed to sharpen. Then a slow, wry grin pulled at his mouth.

"Got another one, Pin, old boy," he said to himself. "That makes"—he looked to the ceiling—"six this week alone. That bonus money is stacking up. Yes sir, it surely is."

Before long, Shep made his way back to the table, one measured step at a time. With much care, he set down a small cork-stoppered bottle of black ink and a fresh bottle of whiskey.

"Now then," said Pin. "Where were we?"

"Secrets," said Shep, plunking down in his chair and holding a finger to his lips.

"That's right. Before we get into that bottle, I think we ought to make it official. What do you think?"

"Why sure, pard." Shep reached for the quill laying on the table. He missed it the first two times, but his fingers pinched down on it the third. "Okay, where do I sign?"

"Right there." He pointed to the bottom half of the page. "Anywhere there is fine."

"Wait," said Shep. "Regis may not know much, but I think he'd tell me to make certain I get a copy for myself."

Pin smiled and lifted the sheet. "That's what that there is for." He pointed to the second sheet, a duplicate of the first.

Shep smiled. "I should have known you'd watch out for a pard's best interests."

"You bet I will . . . pard."

Shep once again set to the task of writing his name on the sheet.

Pin watched him with no trace of his smile, but with narrow-eyed concern, nodding when Shep finished.

"Okay, now you'll want to do the same to the second sheet." Pin slid the first sheet out of the way, clear to the other side of the table and held it down with his far elbow. When Shep had finished, he whisked that sheet away, too, then took the quill and ink and dated each sheet and countersigned. Then he blew on the pages and wagged them in the air a moment, then handed one to Shep. The other, along with the little, sullied quill, he tucked back into some pocket in his tunic.

"Okay then, Mr. Shepley Royle. You have given yourself the best birthday gift a man could ever want. Welcome to the US Army."

"Well now, that's mighty fine sounding to me." Shep's eyelids were at half-mast, but his smile was running at full-bore. "Mighty fine."

Pin poured them each a shot of whiskey, making certain to top Shep's to the rim, and they toasted.

"You know what?" said Shep, tucking the poorly folded paper into his own trouser pocket, at Pin's urging. "I find I need to visit the alleyway again. Hold my seat, will you?"

"Surely, pard."

Shep pushed up out of his chair and smiled, weaving in place. "Pard. Ha. Take that, Regis. And Bone . . ." He kept mumbling to himself as he weaved his way through the busy bar to the back and out the latrine door once more.

At the table, Pinski ran a tongue over his teeth and a hand over his face. He stood, with near-normal ability, and leaving his untouched drink on the table, he brought the bottle of ink back to the bar and thanked the barman. Then he exited through the batwing doors and down the steps.

If I hurry, he thought, I might catch the lieutenant in his office at the garrison. Then I'll tell him where the men can find the newest recruit. His smile widened as he thought of all that bonus money he'd just earned.

Chapter 23

Regis rode on, and eventually the harsh, unceasing sunlight succumbed to the orange glow of late afternoon. Still, he rode on. Only when the purpling light of coming dusk lost its quiet daily war with the sun, and the gentler light and the cooling temperature, however slight, surrounded him, did Regis feel the beginnings of the calm that had eluded him all day.

He'd stopped some time before along the river. He and the horse drank their fill, Regis topped up his water skins, and they lazed a while in the scant shade of a yucca. But it was not right, not yet.

Sure, it might have been the sunlight blazing down, baking his poor head and the horse's hide. But something inside told Regis to move on. He had much to ponder, and the same thing that urged him into motion once more prodded at his mind and sent his thoughts circling and swirling.

With the cooling temperature came a gradual peace in his mind, and with that, a weariness. And what's more, he was surprised to find himself sensing a familiarity, however vague, with the landscape in which he now found himself.

The earth in this southerly direction was familiar—was he still on his ranch? He did not know. And for the first time, perhaps since he assumed he owned the Santa Calina range, he did not care to know the answer, did not feel the swell of pride in his chest. He took that not as an omen but as another step in his strange, unexpected little journey on which he found himself.

Then there it was—a rising, rocky landscape before him. And now that he paid more attention, the waning day's shadows gave the rocky land before him a broader, darker look, not without a tinge of menace, too. But something told him this place was where he should camp for the night.

He cut to the southeast of the rocky mass, and as he walked, he thought perhaps he saw a faint trail. Not uncommon out here, as horses, coyotes, cattle, bush pigs, and the like were forever cutting through, relying on trusted routes of their forebears since time began. But this trail smacked of familiarity. What might it mean?

Stacks of sandstone jutted nearly horizontally to the left, and the trail on which he rode angled down, though not by much. He rounded a knob of wind-blunted stone, and the sun halved on the distant skyline, casting a brilliant last wash of color, fading even as he watched.

Regis caught sight of a vast rocky bowl to his left, half-darkened, yet lit enough to reveal it for what it was—a place of caves and shadow, canyonlike and raw. And he knew where he was.

This was the former hideout of Tomasina Valdez and her murderous gang. She of the Valdez family, she, the heir—or so all had thought—to the Santa Calina range, land her father sold to Don Mallarmoza. Land that the Don sold to Regis and Cormac. Land that was now owned by . . . ? Who?

Here was the rocky, craggy place where he and Tut had blasted their way in in a fight they should have lost, a fight the young cowboy who'd barely been in Regis's employ for but hours had nonetheless volunteered for. It had been a rescue mission to free Regis's young brother, who Regis refused to believe had already been killed.

Regis sat his horse and watched the shadows grow over this

hellish place. The intervening time hadn't done much to smooth the jagged memories he'd garnered here.

That witch had imprisoned the boy, really just a kid, younger in many ways than his teenage years. But she was shrewd and had not killed the boy, for she needed him alive, at least for a time, to use as a poker chip in her gamble to force Regis to give up the range.

She had not much expected him to ride straight into her sticky web, crawling with her hired spiders. But they had. And they had delivered death in many forms, with guns and knives.

He shuddered, despite the warmth of the evening. And yet, as he surveyed the scene, the rocky grotto below, the maze of up-thrust gray-red fingers of stone before him, he realized he felt not revulsion at being there, only at the harsh memories it evoked. The place itself somehow he found welcoming.

He nudged King forward, a step at a time, along the winding path. This, he recalled, had been a route out, a backdoor entrance and exit for Valdez and her gang. Soon he came to the place where he freed the gang's mounts. Even in the growing gloom of dark, he could tell little had changed. This place, he felt in his bones, no longer served an evil purpose.

Was it on his ranch? And as quickly as he thought that, he then thought: Who cares? And for the first time since the morning, he smiled. Who cares, indeed.

The faint scent of heat-soaked sand greeted him, and with it a light breeze touched his burned face, cooling with the gentlest of touches. Here is where he would spend the night, here is where he needed to spend the night.

"Okay, boy, let's get down there and explore before the last of the light leaves us."

They continued threading their way through, and Regis found a passage wide enough for him to lead the horse, who'd become balky as the tall stone walls drew closer. There was no room to turn the beast, so they had two choices, keep going or back the horse out and find a different way in.

He was about to try the latter, least desirable option when, around a sharp curve in the stone passage, the sandy-floored trail widened and a cool breeze wafted against Regis's face. Even King nickered and sniffed.

"Yeah, boy, feels good, doesn't it?"

They walked on, Regis leading the horse with a double-wrap of the reins about his big right hand. Another dozen feet and the passage ended and there they were, smack in the low grotto where Tomasina Valdez had holed up with her gang of killers and thieves.

A thought came to Regis that caused him to doubt his choice of campsites. Men had died here, not but yards from where he stood. And some of them by his hand.

He had never found the notion of specters and malicious ghosts of the slightest interest, nor were they believable to him. Nonetheless, if ever there was a place tailor-made to be haunted by ill portents, it was this.

He double-looped the big horse's reins on a jag of stone, then he explored. One by one he visited the spots where the men he and Tut had fought had died their last.

He had expected to see tatters of cloth draped about the cages of their bones. In this he was surprised. There was no evidence of death. It was as if nothing had ever happened there, no brutal fight, none of it.

Someone must have retrieved them, perhaps loved ones or friends, though he had a difficult time imagining any of those leering brutes had much in the way of family or chums.

The only sign of humans having visited the place was the large, charred spot where they had had their central campfire. It was but a few yards from the entrance of the cave where Valdez had holed up, and deep within which she had held Shep, bound, gagged, and shackled to a ring in the rock.

Regis squinted into the dark of the cave. The last of the sun's rays began its final shuddering, winking out, and Regis decided, far later than he should have, to kindle flame and consider a meager repast for himself and his horse.

He had never been afraid of the dark, of the emergence of sound and pinching out of sight as darkness grew complete. But on this night he would prefer not to have a cold camp. He worked quickly, scouting for any scraps of wood the gang might have left to feed their long-ago fire. In this, he was rewarded with an ample pile just inside the cave's entrance.

As he ferried a quick armload of wood to the stony fire pit some feet away, he wondered if Shep would think him crazy for being there. The ordeal the kid had gone through had left him as close to death as Regis hoped to ever see anybody for whom he cared.

For weeks, months even, afterward, Shep was a hollow-eyed nervous kid who said little, clung close by Regis's side, and spooked at sights and sounds most men barely noticed.

It was short work to kindle a small but promising blaze, and he was glad he'd long ago taken Bone's sage advice and carried a standard traveling kit in his bags—a small tin pot in which he could make a stew, heat water, and even fry up meat or cook small batter cakes.

Just then he had a hankering for coffee. Nothing went better at the tail end of a long day, no matter the weather, hot or cold, than a steaming cup of coffee. The other accoutrement he carried, squirreled in the small pan, was a squat tin cup.

He fed King from the nosebag and settled down to wait out the coffee, seated with a big boulder to his back and the larger wall behind that, and so was relatively assured of some scrap of protection from ambush he doubted would present itself.

Still, he was aware that the fire, though he kept it reined in, would reflect its dancing, happy self and cast a noticeable glow visible for some distance should anyone be out and about in this direction.

He'd been avoiding giving serious thought to the matters that pressed in on him, it seemed, from all sides, within his mind and without. Though they were troubles, mostly self-made, that dogged his trail for many days before today.

Eventually, with a cup of hot coffee in hand, and ample wood to keep his small fire fed and satisfied (was a fire ever really satisfied, he wondered), Regis let his mind untether from shore once more and drift.

Faces floated into view, drifted away again, and he settled on Cormac. Other than Shepley, the Irishman was the one who meant the most to him in this life. He'd wronged the man terribly, and the wonder of it was that he hadn't taken note of it, hadn't admitted to himself that he was betraying his partner and friend, and to such a degree that he was crippling their friendship forever.

Could it be possible that that stray, distasteful thought that had sneaked into his mind earlier on his ride, like a rat in the night, telling him that buying all the land he might, raking it in like a man on a winning poker spree at the baize goddess, might not that lust, that greed, and the resulting debt, might that not be the root of all his troubles?

Regis groaned and King flicked an ear. There was so much to think through.

Suddenly the horse raised his head from where he'd stood, head hanging and hipshot. Ears were perked. Regis froze, letting his own ears do their job, looking away from the firelight so his eyes might accustom to the surrounding darkness. He heard nothing, smelled nothing save woodsmoke and the night scents of evening in the desert—dryness and an overriding sweetness rising off the earth, as if it were breathing once more after being suppressed and baked by the sun all day.

But there was something different, something all around them that hadn't been there moments before. The presence of something. But what?

Whatever it was, Regis felt different. He looked at King and saw that the horse, too, though not threatened, was alert. His ears were perked forward, he stared into the night, though he stood hipshot, somewhat at ease.

The stars had begun winking as full darkness draped itself finally over the land. Regis shifted his eyes skyward, not watching the night but listening, straining to detect whatever it was that had changed.

Maybe it was just a night creature, a snake, mouse, rat, even a curious coyote. He saw no eyes dancing in the darkness about him, nothing had changed in sight or sound, just in feel. And yet his neck hairs had not prickled, he felt no threat, certainly not the sort that warrants the rise of instinct within a man.

The cave entrance, to his right, sat black in the dark night. He'd ventured in only as far as he needed to in his quest for wood. Once he had been rewarded, he had not ventured farther, thinking at the time that perhaps he'd light a brand and venture in. This seemed a good idea now. It was not fear or caution that drove him to thrust into the fire an arm-length stick for use as a torch, but curiosity.

He knew that the cave emptied out again through the mass of rock, as he had followed it when he'd freed Shep, but even then he'd had the sense there were other tunnels to either side.

How had such caves formed? And how long ago? Mother Nature was a curious crone, creating beguiling shapes and mysterious entities that man in his yearning for new and different experiences could never get enough of.

Regis rotated the stick a few times and lifted it free of the fire experimentally. It had caught well and now a small, tight blaze flickered from it. The tip was a tight knot, pitch locked within, for it sizzled and popped slightly.

He rose to his feet, eyeing King once more, but the horse was hobbled, and within this stony bowl could go nowhere but in circles.

Though he felt no call to arm himself, Regis nonetheless unholstered his revolver and held it firmly in his left hand. He reached the entrance to the cave and, feeling foolish with the gun in hand, he reholstered it, though he left the hammer thong loose should he need to snatch the gun out quickly. Bending low, Regis walked into the cave.

Chapter 24

Torch light danced and skittered, leering small shadows into larger ones as Regis advanced. The cave floor's dust rose in light, powdery bursts as he stepped. He slowed his pace and regarded the walls. He shoved back the memory of the last time he had been here—rescuing Shep.

Sooner than he expected, he came to the spot where he'd found his strength-sapped brother. He knelt and held the guttering torch low, scanning the spot, running his free hand over the stone.

There was the bit of chain, the odd steel ring pounded into the cold, grooved stone. And here, thought Regis, here is where Shepley sat, bereft of hope, waiting to die.

He'd let slip once that he'd been convinced that Regis, his only brother, a brother Shep had all-but worshipped as a child, and who he'd only recently come to know once more, would not bargain for him. Would never come to look for him.

Here the kid sat, chained and starved, barely watered, treated like an unwanted dog, convinced that his captor, the vile Valdez desert witch, had no intention of using him as a bargaining chip with his brother, but rather that she intended to let him wither and die a slow, pathetic death there in the cave. For her amusement.

Had Shep become convinced that he, Regis, was so bent on clinging to the ranch at all costs that he would not negotiate with the woman for his only brother's life?

"Oh god," he whispered, for it was true. Hadn't he, after all, wanted both the ranch and his brother? And because of that, because of his no-quarter attitude, he had stormed the place, risking his brother's life, and all-but dared the world to defy him in his righteous wrath. And it had worked. Yes, it had worked as he had intended. No, as he had hoped it might. But . . . what if it had not? The thought shuddered him there in the cool, dark cave.

But it had worked, and they were all alive, and the vile ones who caused it, well, some of them, most of them, were dead.

Regis stood, looking into the depths of the inky blackness beyond. It would wait for morning. But he would explore it.

As he turned toward the cave's entrance once more, he felt a chill breeze play at his back, and a memory of his brother, delirious, he'd thought at the time, telling him, no, insisting to him that he'd survived only because of a woman's help. The help of a veiled woman somewhere in the cave.

Of course, that had been foolishness, even now Regis realized it was little more than the scattered, water-, sleep-, and food-deprived ravings of a failing mind. Yet in his weakness, Shep had struggled, babbling that they couldn't leave the veiled woman behind, that she had saved his life.

Regis had soothed him as best he could, told him he would feel better once they got home. Still, the kid had been insistent, even when weeks later he'd recovered his strength and his mind, he swore it was not Tomasina Valdez he'd been talking about.

It was curious that these thoughts should come back to Regis now.

He walked back toward the cave's entrance, guided by the increasing glow of his meager campfire ahead and the dwindling flame atop his torch.

The fire was a welcome thing, and as he sipped the last of the coffee, gone tepid in his cup, he relished the view of the light-pricked night sky above, the warm scent of the desert about him, and, closer in, the relaxed posture of his dozing horse.

No longer did he feel there was some presence about, at least nothing more than the night itself. The place felt oddly welcoming, as if it had been that way long before Tomasina Valdez and her trail trash had sullied it. And if he could help it, he vowed to ensure it would remain so long after.

With that scrap of conviction still in his mind, Regis Royle unrolled his wool blanket, and for added warmth, tugged on the only other clothes he brought—the slicker, and he swapped his socks for the extra pair he always carried with him.

He recalled his mother telling him long ago that if he was cold, he was to change his socks, and it would go a long way to making him feel better. He'd always remembered that and followed the advice, because it worked.

He settled in for a doze, not covering his face with his hat, but letting himself slip into sleep while watching the winking stars so very far away.

Chapter 25

"Hey, kid."

Somehow, even in his whiskey-fueled fog, Shep knew the man off to his left by the stacked crates was calling to him. He turned, jaw stuck out, and fists balled at his sides. "Who you callin' 'kid'?"

The man ambled closer, weaving and buttoning the front of his trousers. The closer he walked the more Shep thought maybe the man wasn't angling for a tussle. He was rather well dressed and, in fact, he did not look all that unfriendly. He looked kindly, and not a little drunk. Me, too, thought Shep. Wonder if Pin would mind a third pard at the table?

"I only wanted to tell you there's a filly back yonder who's got something a fellow such as yourself might find of interest." He winked and staggered a little, then elbowed Shep on his way toward the back door of the bar. "If you know what I mean."

That was the second time he'd heard that phrase today. Today, today . . . yes, it was his birthday! And by Jove, he did indeed know for certain this time just what the man meant. What both of them had meant, in fact.

He gazed toward the left, in the shadows, where the man had come from. Was there a door there? Looked to be just crates stacked atop one another. And none too carefully, either.

He smiled. "Bone would have himself a right fit if he saw such sloppy work," he said and giggled as he walked toward the leaning boxes.

"Hello? Hello . . . somebody back there?"

He heard movement. Likely a rat, he decided, and was about to turn around when he heard something else, and a whole lot more human. A sigh, he thought it was. Then a voice said, "Yeah, yeah, I am still here." A woman's voice.

Shep stopped and squinted, looking toward the darker space behind the boxes. He saw now that there was some sort of space back there. Almost like a little room, but it was open to the heavens. Sort of like a fortress a child might build.

"Hello?"

Another sigh reached his ears, then the voice said, "I told you I am here. Come on if you are coming."

He squared his shoulders, knowing full well what this meant. And the importance of the day and of all the things he'd been doing since he awoke at the ranch, came back to him. Why not top off the day with another fine accomplishment? He had promised himself that he'd make the most this day had to offer, hadn't he?

Shep tugged his hat down low over his brow, and, puffing his chest, he walked forward and peered into the odd space behind the boxes. There was a shuck-topped mattress, and standing before it, with her back half-turned to him, stood a woman with a veil covering part but not all of her long, black hair. It was shadowy enough that he couldn't make out her features too well, even when she turned to face him.

She had a bedraggled look and was obviously older than him. But she was still a comely woman, he could tell by the shape of her body through the few layers of dress she wore.

"Well?" she said, sighing once again. "You got money?"

"Uh, yeah," he said, and before thinking about it he reached for his coin purse tucked into his trouser pocket.

"You don't die so well, huh?" said the woman.

He looked up again and leaned forward. "What? What did you say?"

A laugh scraped up out of her throat and her face smiled in the dim light.

The laugh sounded somehow familiar, but how could that be? "I know you?" he said, taking a step forward.

"You should," she said, staring at him.

She made no move, but stood facing him, her arms folded on her chest.

He leaned closer, confused, and looked at her face. He saw dark eyes, black eyes. The woman smiled slowly, her lips pulled back to reveal staining teeth in a too-thin, but once-pretty face. But it was the eyes that told Shep all he needed to know.

Even in his drunken state, they were eyes he had not forgotten. Eyes that woke him in a sweat, night on night for months after . . . the cave.

"You . . . you!"

This could not be. He jerked back as if she'd slapped him in the face.

Still, the woman didn't move. She did laugh, however. A long, low, throaty sound that sent him stepping backward.

She advanced on him, stepping slowly to his right. "Yes, it is me, baby boy. You see what you have caused in my life, no? You see how I am forced to live?"

"I . . ."

"I say again, you don't die so well, pretty boy."

Shep straightened and pulled in a deep breath. "I . . . I'm not a boy."

"Oh?" she stepped close.

Somehow, without him noticing how, she had managed to cut around him and he was now standing where she had been when he found her, his back to the cot.

Shep shook his head and forced his eyes open wide. What the hell was she doing here?

As if she were reading his mind, in a low, catlike voice, Tomasina Valdez said, "I want to apologize to you, Shep. After all, this is no way for neighbors to behave."

Shep squinted at her. "Huh?" He didn't know what she was talking about. This was all so confusing.

"Sí, Señor Royle. I and only I truly own the Santa Calina range. You know this and I know this. This is why I wanted the Santa Calina back. It is mine by birthright, but..." She shrugged, but didn't take her eyes from his. "Maybe what will be will be, huh?"

Shep snorted. "If you own the Santa Calina, then what are you doing here?"

She smiled, but her eyes were hard, the smile thin. "I am, how do you say, an heiress, yes? This?" She waved a hand. "Bah! This is temporary."

"So you're telling me you're rich."

She nodded. "Sí, soon . . . again." She laid a hand on his chest. "And you and me, Shep, we could be rich together, eh?"

He liked that feeling of her hand on his shirt, then shook his head. "No, no, no. Regis is right. You're a game player. You . . . you tried to kill me!" He stepped back once, and his legs bumped her cot. "Lady, I can't figure you . . ." He squinted hard at her. Man, he wished he wasn't so drunk. "I . . . I don't trust you, as Bone would say, as far as I can throw you."

She moved her body closer than ever to him.

Shep flinched. She smelled of grime, of sweat, but also a thin scrim of something sweet. Sickly sweet, like rosewater. Oh, but she was stunning, and there was something else there, too, something exciting, something animal-like about her, all musky and wild at the edges. And dangerous all the time.

She pressed herself hard into him, slid her leg up his. He noticed her blouse had somehow come undone, as if the buttons surrendered their meager lives for this opportunity.

"Señor Shep, I cannot stop thinking about you. Since your brother pulled us apart, I cannot stop, I tell you. Please don't leave me again." She rested her forehead on his chest and he felt her shudder and shake, as if she were sobbing.

Damn, thought Shep. This is more than a man can handle.

But something inside, a voice that sounded a whole lot like that of his big brother, sounded within him. It began as a whisper and grew louder and louder in his head until he could swear Regis was right behind him.

Shep pushed her away from him. He tried to speak, choked, then tried again. "Woman," his voice was low, husky. "How much is enough? You kidnapped me, tried to kill me. Then you got away when you should have been locked up! When is enough enough?"

Her reply was a low, churlish laugh as she shoved herself back into him, her face nearly even with his. She was timeworn, from hard living, to be sure, but there was something about her that was difficult to turn away from.

Even when she had kidnapped him to blackmail Regis out of his ownership of the Santa Calina range, even when she had tortured him, bound him and left him to rot in the cave, let her men beat him, even then, she would come close, rub her chest, barely, against his arm, and he would nearly forget everything vile and foul she had done to him. Nearly forget it, anyway.

And there in the alleyway behind the saloon, he did the same once more. All thoughts of Pin and his birthday and whiskey and Regis and the ranch, all of it gone because this once-pretty woman still held him in her gaze. His strength had gone away, somewhere, and he stood limply staring at her.

At the cave, Regis had ridden in and saved him. It came to Shep that he would always be one of those fools who needed saving. Even as he thought this she moved closer and though her breath was rank, he could not flinch. Her mouth so close to his.

He felt her hand then, sliding down his arm, off his fingertips, touching his trousers, over, over . . .

He did not feel the knife as it slid into his gut. Not right away, anyway. And then he did. At the same time as he saw Tomasina Valdez's once-luscious lips, now cracked and thin, parting to reveal stained and blackened teeth in a wide, wide, cackling laugh.

He felt every one of the following jabs she delivered to him, and then he felt himself slide away from her. Somehow his legs had gone away, and he dropped to the earth, his head smacking something on the way down, then hitting the ground and bouncing. And still she laughed.

As the early evening's glow shone high up in the sky, high above the rank little alley, he thought maybe she was close to him once more, leaning over him, so kind, perhaps she was helping him. Something must have happened to him. Maybe it was the whiskey. Yes, the whiskey that would be the cause.

And then he remembered his new pard, Pin, then his thoughts skittered backward, through the long day to his horse, the dusty trail, Regis, the ranch, his birthday . . .

He thought, "It's my birthday. Happy birthday, Shep, ol' boy."

And then he knew no more.

Chapter 26

The morning sun didn't bother Regis until it had made a full appearance. Then it felt as though someone was tapping him on the shoulder. He popped open his eyes, felt the new day's warmth on his face, and remembered where he was.

A glance around the rocky bowl told him not much had changed in the night. King stood nearby, looking bored but rested. Regis stood, stretched, and, instead of feeling stiff and knotted as he usually did when he'd spent the night on the ground outdoors, he felt pleasantly fit and rested. "Time for a drizzle, then a fire and coffee, eh, boy?"

The horse flicked an ear and kept nosing the already-nibbled sparse brown tufts of grass wedged and struggling at the base of a boulder.

"I'll tend to you in a minute," said Regis, fiddling with building a fire.

Soon he had coffee bubbling and a ragged hunk of jerky in his fist. The horse was tended, and as he looked about the rocky place, now in full light, he realized that the night before he'd seen as much of it as he was likely to see, certainly as much as he needed to see. He wasn't certain why the place had beckoned to him or why he felt no fear while here, only a calmness.

A gift, take it as a gift, you lunk, he told himself. But a gift, he knew, usually required something having been deserving to receive it. And he knew that in his case, it meant something in his life, in the way he had been treating his friends, had to change. Toward Cormac, Shep, Bone, all the men at the ranch, and certainly to Cotton, who he had treated so poorly. Time to make amends, repair where he could, and trust it would, in time, be enough.

As he mused on this, he strolled over to the cave's entrance once again, and peered in.

The morning sun's easterly angle slanted in such that the first dozen feet or so of the quiet, rocky grotto was lit. He saw something he'd not seen before, along the left side wall, some sort of crude pictures painted on or chipped into the somewhat smooth sandstone wall.

He walked over, sipping his coffee. It could well be a trick of the light, his mind playing at something fanciful. But no, once he drew closer and squinted, angling himself with his back toward the dark depths of the cave so as not to block the light, he saw distinct renderings of large beasts with horns, buffalo, perhaps. And angular men in various poses, as if built of sticks. Other shapes looked like wavy lines, perhaps mountain shapes, rivers, and something round, sun-like.

He traced them with his work-hardened fingertips, imagining the real hunts these carefully depicted shapes represented. Huge beasts, likely buffalo, with lances wagging from their great neck humps, and the darting shapes of wolves or coyotes, low doglike shapes slinking around the others. The men, now that he looked up and down the wall, appeared in multitudes, waving weapons.

Regis closed his eyes a moment, fingertips still resting on the wall's artful depictions, and pictured the hunts, the boiling clouds of dust, the great sun, the bellowing, the stink of sweat and dung and blood, the screams of trampled warriors, the thunderous pounding of hooves . . .

"They are interesting, no?"

Regis spun, the coffee in his cup slopping down his leg and over his left boot. He had no time to do much else than spin and stare . . . at a stranger half-hidden in the shadowy blackness of the cave.

"Who are you?" he said, his hand inching down toward his revolver.

The figure moved half a step into the light. It was shrouded in black, but he could see it was a woman. Yes, the voice was soft enough that it could well be a woman.

"Nobody who needs to be shot today," said the figure.

Regis thought perhaps there was a tinge of humor in the comment. He kept his hand on the gun's grip, but did not draw it out of the holster.

"Who . . ." was all he could get out before the figure leaned once more to its right and out of the angle of sunlight. But it did not turn and flee from him. Regis stood fully, the cave's arched ceiling tall in that particular spot.

"The drawings," said the voice.

It was indeed a woman's voice, now he was certain of it.

"They are of interest to you?"

Still, Regis stared at the shape, afraid to take his eyes from it, so mysterious did it—she—appear. "I . . ."

"You are not much for talk," she said.

Again, he thought perhaps he detected humor behind the words, as if he were being regarded by someone who was also judging him, assessing him.

"No," he said finally. "I mean, yes . . ." He was inclined to look down at the wall, where he'd been hunkered, but he knew somehow that she would disappear like smoke.

Oddly, he did not feel all that surprised by her, certainly not worried that he needed to defend himself. And then because he felt this, much the same feeling he had the night before, he relaxed a little bit.

"You're wearing a veil," he said, sudden understanding giving his statement the feel of a discovery.

She nodded. He could not see her face, but her voice had been level, sweet somehow. And from what he could see of her body, which was not much at all, she was tall, perhaps thin. From the tone and timbre of her voice, he guessed she might be his age, perhaps older.

He could not see her hands. But that she did exist, he was now convinced. So Shep had been telling the truth after all.

"You helped my brother."

"Yes."

"You saved his life."

"Are not all lives worth saving?"

He nodded, but sensed the question was not one expecting an answer.

"Thank you," he said.

"You are here for a reason," she said, still not moving.

Regis figured he could rush to her, be at her side in two, perhaps three strides, yet he knew he would never do so. "Yes, I . . ." and then what had been troubling him for so long came to his mind easily, as if the notion to reveal it had been there all along.

The words began to flow from this man who never spoke more than a handful of polite words to strangers, who loathed revealing anything about his life to anyone, especially to a woman. Yet here he was, talking and talking.

"It will sound odd to you . . ." he began.

She merely shook her head no. Now that more light angled in, he could see there was a face beneath the black veil, perhaps s cheekbone? A jawline, part of an ear?

"I was riding last night, trying to . . . thinking about some things I have done lately, things I knew weren't the things I should have done. Yet I had no choice, or so I thought."

"There always are choices, Señor."

The voice reminded him of someone, though who, he could not say at that moment. He nodded and continued. "Friends all. I've wronged them in ways and I do not know if I can make amends."

"No one knows such things. The task ahead for you is to think about them, then work them through in your head, get to know them as you would your own self. Only then can you tell the truth to those people you feel you have wronged. If they are your friends, then they still will be."

"Mend my fences, then," he said.

Again, she responded with a nod of her head. "Not with force and cruelty. An open hand holds so much more than a closed fist."

He nodded. "Thank you."

At that moment, a sunbeam fingered through the opening on a long, angling shaft and backlit the woman. For the briefest of moments, her face was more visible to him than it had been. And what he saw convinced him that he wanted to see more of her.

He saw the line of her jaw, a cheekbone, a long nose, dark hair. Perhaps a smile? He got the sense that she allowed him this briefest of moments, then she stepped backward, deeper into shadow and, at that moment, King whickered.

Regis glanced briefly toward the horse, just in view beyond the curving arch of the cave entrance.

He looked back and the woman was gone, no longer a shadow against shadows. Nothing there. He'd heard nothing, no soft sounds of footsteps shuffling, nothing.

"Hello?" he said. "Are you there?"

Nothing.

He felt compelled to make for the dimness back in the cave, but no, he stifled the impulse. Somehow, something told him that would be wrong.

Questions dogged him while he walked back to the meager campsite. He poured himself the last of the coffee, turning his head now and again, hoping but not expecting to see the woman standing there, in full sunlight, in her startling black veil and night-black dress, so tall, so like a wraith.

Once again, he doubted what he'd seen. Did she exist? If so, he wondered as he saddled King, what was she doing so far out here? Living in the cave? But that was impossible. How could someone do that? And it had been more than a year and a half since she had saved Shep. Who could live there amid the rocks and snakes and bats and cactus and heat?

"Well, Regis, plenty of critters live out here," he said, leading King toward the narrow passage they'd come in by. "And have forever, I expect." He looked back toward the cave one last time. But a woman? Alone, out here?

Why not? he thought. The more time he spent in this life, the stranger much of it seemed to him. Strange, yes, but fascinating.

Such thoughts occupied him as he rode toward the headquarters of the Royle Ranch. He now knew what he had to do. He had to talk with Bone, then he had to talk with Cormac, and Cotton, too. Trickiest of all, though, was going to be Shep.

He had no idea where the kid had gone off to, or in which direction to renew his search. The kid could be most anywhere.

Most of all, thought Regis, I hope you're happy, Shep. And I'm sorry for doubting you about the veiled woman in the cave.

Though in his mind, she was more wisp than woman, Regis felt certain she was as real as anyone he'd ever met. Perhaps more so.

Chapter 27

Regis stood for a long time in the little cabin, a ragged scrap of paper in his hand, looking out the open door into the afternoon's heat. After a while, he looked down at the paper and held it up and read it once again.

> *Regis,*
> *When you find this note, I won't be here. I'm 18 now and that means I'm a man and I can make my own decisions about my own life. I know you're going to want to come after me and drag me back to your ranch, but don't. Just do us both a favor and let me find my own way, even if the world is, as you said, a hard place. I expect I know that already. Don't forget that before I tracked you down in Texas, I was on my own. I'll come back some time. I don't know when. But when I do, we'll have some of those good, brotherly times together. Until then, thank you for everything. I do appreciate it.*
> *Your loving brother,*
> *Shepley*
> *PS: Thanks for the knife. It's something else. So are you.*

Regis wagged the note as if to air it, then tossed it on the messy table. "Fool kid," he said, his breath at last leaving him in a rush and a sigh. He sat down at his makeshift desk, and his gaze fell on the scrolled paper he'd left as part of Shep's gift. It wasn't where he'd left it, and Shep would have had to move it to get at the knife.

Regis grunted and picked up the scroll. Not even tampered with. Would it have mattered if Shep had read it? Would it have mattered to Shep that Regis had had a lawyer draw up a simple document stating that Shepley Royle was now an official owner of a share of the Royle Ranch?

Regis tossed it back on the desk, and stood up slowly, his knees popping. He stretched his back and looked about the dismal little cabin. No wonder the kid didn't want to stay, he thought. He walked over to the woodstove and laid in a few twigs and small splits of mesquite, teepee style. Then he looked about for the matches, saw the box of them atop the desk, and as he retrieved them, he picked up the rolled paper once more. Then he laid it in the stove atop the wood and set fire to the lot.

"Have it your way, Shep. If being left alone is what you want, you'll not find me dogging your trail." He said it, but it hurt to do so. He whispered a curse and hefted the coffee pot.

He'd been so confident on his ride back to the ranch after talking with that intriguing woman in the cave, so certain he could work things out that he couldn't wait to see Shep, to tell him he'd met the mystical veiled woman the kid had sworn he'd seen, the one who'd tended to him. But now all her words seemed like campfire smoke lost in an afternoon breeze.

As he filled the coffee pot from the small water keg out front, he paused. Maybe somehow this is what she was talking about, maybe he had to just let the kid go. He couldn't control him, couldn't save him from troubles in life any more than he could save himself from them. That certainly hadn't worked so well lately, had it?

He walked back indoors and set the pot on the stove, then chucked in more wood. He had a whole lot of thinking to do, and come tomorrow, he'd do some of it while he rode up to Bone's spread. It was time to make amends. He'd been a fool. They both had.

Chapter 28

"Bone!" Regis stood in the ranch yard beside King, holding the reins in his right hand, his left visoring his eyes under the broad brim of his hat. He was looking toward the tidy little ranch house. "Bone. You home?"

He held like that another long moment, then the summer-slat door under the low porch roof opened and a woman walked out a few feet, wiping work-red hands on an apron. She walked to the edge of the porch, at the top of the two steps. She regarded him while she wiped her hands.

"It's Regis. Regis Royle, ma'am."

"I know who you are, Mr. Royle. Jarvis isn't here just now. He and Ramon rode off at sunup for the northwest boundary to tend to a few things." She let that hang.

"I see." He waited a moment, wondering if she was going to invite him in. He didn't really want to, but he didn't want to appear rude to depart quickly, either.

"You're welcome to water your horse," she said. "There's a dipper at the well for yourself." Then she turned and walked back into the house.

So, she really is part of his life, thought Regis. He'd no idea it went that far. The last Bone had mentioned of her, before their dust-up, she'd stayed on at this place even after the other women they'd rescued from the slaver had moved on.

Well, good for him, he thought. Just now his concern was not that, but rather to make amends with Bone. He needed him, and though it was a tough seed to swallow, there it was. He needed his old pard's help.

But first he had to find him. And this woman had been of some help. He tugged the reins and led King to the trough over between the stable and the bunk house. "Northwest, pal. That's all I know. But first some cool water."

As King sipped at the trough, Regis admired the handsome set of buildings. The house was a low affair, single-story, with a long shade porch along the front, upright board-and-batten siding. Though the planking was unpainted, the storm shutters were green and the flower boxes were all painted red. The windows wore white trimwork. The bunk house bore the same treatment, along with its own tidy shade porch.

The barn was taller, broader, and sported a solid corral with a worn snubbing post in the middle. He saw cattle in the distance, to the southwest, and for a moment wondered if some of his own cattle were somehow mixed in with the little herd. He bit back the thought, cursing himself for thinking such things about a man such as Bone. Man was a Ranger, after all. More than that, he was a friend. Or had been, anyway. With any luck, he might be once again.

He refreshed himself with a couple of dippers of cool water, then topped up his water skin and mounted. As he guided the horse around in a half-circle, he glanced once more toward the house, but the door remained shut and he saw no one. It had been an odd encounter and he was inclined to think Bone had shared with her the news that they had argued and parted ways. It was the only thing he could think of to excuse the fact she had acted so abrupt with him.

They clopped out of the yard and followed a direct trail leading northwest. It bore fresh tracks in the sandy dirt, and before long he was rewarded with the sight of a fresh dumping of horse dung. How far they were he had no idea. He had provisions, of course, for himself and the horse, but he hoped to take care of his business with the man and be headed back toward his own ranch house well before the sun quit on him that day. It was becoming obvious to him that he'd likely not be welcome under Bone's roof that evening.

As Regis rode, he admired the land, though he chided himself for smug thinking. But he couldn't help it—the land wasn't any better than the most middling of his own land. Then his smile slipped.

He didn't have ownership of anything, technically. He had ownership of a handful of bank drafts, thick wads of papers with complex wording that added up to the fact that he did not really own his ranch. Might never at the rate his life was unrolling.

But that damned Bone, now he actually owned his entire ranch. Fellow like him gets such a thing left to him. Regis knew it was petty of him to feel envy. He knew he should keep in mind the words of that mysterious wraith woman at the cave. He knew he should do that and a whole passel of things.

But there was a whole wide river betwixt knowing a thing and doing a thing. And by god, Bone's gifted ranch still rankled Regis to no end.

He sighed and shook his head as if to dispel the irksome thoughts. "Horse," he muttered, "I am wrong-headed about this, I know, but it's a hard thing to swallow when everything you've got came from your own hard work."

Even as he said it, he knew that was not quite the case with him. He'd been lucky in his life, as lucky as Bone, maybe luckier. He owed so much to Cormac Delany. So no, he hadn't done it all himself, and neither had Bone. He knew the story behind the little ranch. He knew that Bone had been a good and true friend to the aging couple who'd lived there.

They'd built up the place from raw land many years before. And knowing Bone, he'd done all manner of tasks about the place, and more as they aged, whenever he rode by. And Regis knew the ranger had made more frequent passings of the ranch the older the couple grew. Just because he was a good man, with no thought to inheriting the place.

Was the old man a father type to Bone? He knew Bone's upbringing had been less than pleasant.

Heck, maybe that was the root of the problem between him and Shep. He knew the boy had not grown up with a father. At least not in the years of a boy's life when it mattered. Their father had been a useless laggard who'd died early, and their mother was a mother, a darn good one, but not a father.

Regis blamed himself, even though he'd been just a kid himself. He'd run away to sea and, by the time he'd begun to make money, he tried to make up for his absence in their lives by sending money to his mother, some of it for an education of Shep at that Quaker school in Connecticut.

That had been too late, though. Not only had the kid bailed out on the schooling, but he'd taken the money and instead lived a life of foolishness and debauchery. After their mother had died, he'd up and ridden West in search of his older brother. Now he was eighteen years old and a man, legally, if not by thought and deed. And where he was, who knew?

"Exhausting," said Regis to his horse as they topped a low rise. "That's what the kid is."

His words clipped off there as he took in the full vista before him, spreading toward the northwest. He was looking at a wide flow of a river, what he thought might be the Nueces, or maybe something that fed to it.

No matter, it was a pretty sight. Made even prettier because of the long, wide silvering ripple of wind-kissed grasses, the fringe of scrub along the water, and dotting the plain hundreds of cattle, some clustered but most spread out, grazing in contentedness on the lush grass.

It was a range in its own right as pretty as the Santa Calina, and he found himself first enjoying the sight of it all as much as he always did the prettiest sections of his own river range. Then he felt the first nibblings of envy.

This was a land that begged to be ranched and ranched properly, not run with a few paltry head such as this. Regis felt he was a rancher with a vision after all, a man who could justify this range, much as he was doing to the Santa Calina.

In certain times, when the day was pleasant and he was alone, walking through the grasses, he thought that the Santa Calina and the other ranges about it he was purchasing, speaking for, or had bought, had been waiting for him since time began, waiting for a man such as himself.

No, that's not right, he believed in those sweet brief moments that he was the one and only man who could justify such grandeur. And justify it with a ranch the world had never known. The biggest and the best. And he was making it happen.

And now this range had hooked him, too. What if he could convince Bone to sell to him? Regis breathed deeply. It might well be best for all. But first, he needed to reconcile with Bone, his old friend.

With such bold yet conflicting thoughts in mind, Regis Royle rode downslope toward the river, toward a thin string of blue smoke, and beside it two busy figures.

Chapter 29

Working out on his own range, on his own land, with Margaret back home where he hoped she felt she belonged forever and for good, felt so right to Bone. Right as anything he'd ever felt. Even if he was out here with Ramon, which meant Bone was doing most of the work.

He discovered that though the old man was useful, very much so at the home ranch, as an extra pair of hands out on the range, repairing gathering corrals or castrating and branding, he was not as helpful as Bone would like in a ranch hand.

Bone knew it wasn't fair to ask him to do the heavy work anymore, and Margaret, at his urging, had offered her opinion on the matter. She told him what he already knew. Ramon was an old man and while he was great to have around the house and barns, he was too old to be dragging all over the countryside on the muscle chores.

It bothered Bone that he had to ask Margaret to share her thoughts on the matter, because he wanted her to offer them freely. If they were to be married, to spend their lives together at this very ranch, perhaps even raise children, then she needed to feel free to speak up. He wanted a partner in everything, not just someone who agreed or disagreed and did his bidding and tended to ranch chores.

He knew this was unfair of him. It was early days yet. They'd only returned from bringing her home. It would take time, even old Ramon had said so.

"How come it is that you aren't afraid to offer me your opinions freely, whereas Margaret takes her own sweet time about it?"

The old man shrugged and repositioned the end of his stick so that he might lean more comfortably. He was supposed to be prodding the fire so their lunch wouldn't burn. Then he looked up at the blue sky and rubbed his bearded chin. "It is that way with women, Señor Bone. As it has always been, so it shall always be."

"That's it? So you're telling me I have no say in the matter?" Bone paused and dragged the back of his hand across his brow, knocking his sweat-rimed straw hat farther back on his head.

The old man nodded slowly, but did not reply.

They were widening a cattle and horse trail that led down to the river. Every time Bone had driven cattle across here, from either the north side or up from the south to cross, the cattle had clotted up, then they'd wander up and downstream, splashing and stomping away like unruly children.

It annoyed him enough that he decided to do something about it. He needed a way to haze them across but keep them from scattering. A couple of runs of temporary fencing was one idea he'd come up with. One on the upstream side and one down, maybe twenty feet apart, a chute of sorts to guide them through. It'd take a lot of corral poles and rope, he reckoned, but it might work.

He'd shared the notion with Ramon, more as a way to tell him they'd need to tally up whatever poles they might have on hand.

The old man had said, "You know, Señor Bone, I think I know a different way."

Bone had not been in a particularly good mood, covered in grime, sweat sliding into is eyes. "Huh?" he'd said.

"Yeh, how about you just clear back some of the bramble on either side of the river, both sides, that way they don't fight so much. The only reason they do what you do not want them to do is because the riverbank is doing its job."

The more Bone looked at the river crossing, the more Ramon's notion made sense to him. Bone nibbled his moustaches a moment.

He was pleased with the old fellow's idea and told him so. Even shook hands on it. And to think he'd not really wanted to listen to the old man's subtle complaints about how he always had to work so hard whenever Bone was at the ranch. Served Bone right for keeping his ears closed, anyway. He vowed to avoid being like that, especially with Margaret.

He'd almost laughed as Ramon's face drooped when he'd told him they'd tackle the job together. After all, he told him, he was going to be around the ranch on a more permanent basis, though he didn't tell anyone but Margaret that he'd had hot words with Regis.

Margaret had taken it as he hoped. She didn't question him, though he wouldn't have minded if she had, as he'd wanted to talk about it with someone. She eventually surprised him a few hours later, once he'd eaten and they were sitting on the porch.

He'd sat down heavily and grunted when she offered to help him tug off his boots. As soon as he'd made that dismissive sound, he regretted it and looked at her. Their eyes met. "I didn't mean that," he said.

She'd surprised him by offering him one of her rarest gifts, a smile—a small one to be sure, but it was there.

"It bothers you, then," she'd said.

He knew what she meant, and nodded. "It does. Especially when we've been partners for quite a while. And friends longer. I never even wanted to be a partner in his damned ranch in the first place!"

He'd made a funny noise with his nose and was only vaguely aware of it when he got worked up. She'd laughed at him, a magical sound like how bells should sound, he thought at the time.

"You think it's funny, do you?" he'd said, smiling back, and that had ended with them chasing each other around the house, him with one boot on, one off, her making little gleeful shouts whenever he drew close. It had ended well enough, with Margaret in his arms, both of them breathing hard.

"Señor Bone."

"Sí, Ramon." Bone did not look up when the old man spoke. He'd been enjoying his daydream.

Ramon spoke again, then nudged him in the arm.

Bone looked up and saw a rider approaching from the direction of the ranch. He bristled, and his deep fear of leaving Margaret alone at the ranch bloomed hot and fast in him. He reached for his gun belt, which he'd taken off and hung on a nubbed branch.

"I think you know him," said Ramon. Bone trusted the old man's sight. And a couple of seconds later, he saw that he was correct. It was Regis.

"Man's got a nerve," muttered Bone.

They stood waiting for Regis to draw closer.

Within a couple of minutes, Regis dismounted and led his horse over to within a couple of yards of the two men.

Bone folded his arms over his chest and eyed Regis, but said nothing.

The old man, Regis saw, eyed them both without shame, taking in the situation. He almost seemed on the verge of a smile. Odd, that.

Finally, Regis cleared his throat. "Look busy," he said, knowing it sounded stupid even as he said it.

Bone nodded. "Yep."

Another long, painful silence stretched on and on. The old man cleared his throat and Regis spoke. "Look, Bone . . . I came here to . . . look, I don't like how we ended things. I know you need to do what you need to, here. I understand. It's your ranch. I see that now, and with her." He gestured southeastward, in the direction of the tidy little ranch.

"Oh, well, that's big of you, Mr. Royle. I was worried you didn't approve of my life here on my ranch."

Regis leaned forward, having an inch of height on the Ranger, and pulled in a breath as if he were about to shout. Then he closed his eyes, squinched them tight, and shook his head. "No, no, that's not the way." He opened his eyes.

"Ah, look . . ." He ran a hand over his neck and looked at Bone again, but saw only a hard-set jaw and harder glinting eyes. "Forget it."

"I reckon you came here because something's gone off at the ranch and you need help." It was a low punch, and Bone felt bad about it as soon as he saw the wince on his old friend's face.

"No," said Regis, his cheek muscles bunching and hardening. "Not hardly." He jerked the reins and climbed aboard his saddle. As he turned the horse, he did his best to not look at Bone again, but he couldn't help it. And he saw the man's sweat-matted blue chambray shirt, stuck to his back, as he set to work again with the mattock, clearing brush from the bankside. Hard as stone, thought Regis. Now I know what it's like.

The old Mexican fellow looked at Regis not with anger, as he expected any loyal hand might, but with an odd look of pity. Not unlike the look he'd heard in the voice of the woman in the cave.

He sighed and gigged the horse southward, back toward the Royle Ranch. It was his concern now, his and his alone. Well, his and Cormac's. But the running of it now sat hard and square on his shoulders.

It also told him what he needed to do with Cormac. They had to come to some sort of agreement. He'd have to tend to the ranch while Cormac tended to the shipping business. That's what had been happening anyway. They'd both have to tend to any further legal matters that might come up as they fought the possible challenges to their ownership of the Santa Calina range.

And now, instead of feeling guilty about leaving Cormac to shoulder so much, Regis would have to work like the devil to make the ranch pay sooner than they hoped it might. He'd already decided to back away from his other land-buying commitments. He couldn't afford to take on more debt. The ranch, as it was now, could barely carry itself.

The first goal would be to meet the debts, and the second would be to pay off Cormac so Regis could own the place all to himself.

He didn't know how Bone had left things regarding the orders Regis had given him to buy up cattle, at any cost. Regis groaned. "I've been a fool, King," he said to the horse. The horse did not reply. Just as well, thought Regis. The last thing he needed to hear right now was somebody else telling him off.

But fool or no, he had to make the ranch pay, and the surest way to do that was with the railroad. If they could get that railhead established by the time the drives rolled around, he might save some money, enough to carry them through the thin winter. Hell, he might even make some cash, enough to keep the creditors from tearing him apart.

Maybe.

It was a tall order.

Chapter 30

It was late in the day when Regis and King rode back into what his men still called "camp," though he preferred they use the term "ranch proper." It irked him.

Just because most of them had been there since the early days when the Royle Ranch was little more than raw wildlands and a hatful of hopes on his part, didn't mean it wasn't now a proper ranch with a barn, stables, corrals, reservoirs, a smithy, a swelling village, a schoolhouse coming along. Hell, it was everything he'd hoped it might be.

His mixed thoughts of pride and annoyance were nipped off when he spied a familiar fellow peel away from a knot of others conversing at the near corral.

It was Marshal Corbin from Brownsville. That might mean nothing, but then again, given the way Regis's world felt to him just now, Corbin's presence at the Royle was likely for tainted reasons.

"Regis," said the lawman as Regis swung down out of the saddle and walked, stiff-legged, over.

"Marshal Corbin." The men shook hands and Regis handed his reins willingly to a young hand whose name he'd been told but couldn't recall. He gave the youth a nod and a quick smile, then turned his attention back to the lawman. "What brings you out to the ranch, marshal?"

"Well," Corbin toed the dirt and looked away, then folded his arms over his chest.

"Can't be good. As I recall you like talking as well as the next man."

"It's about Shep."

Regis felt something in his chest, in his heart, everything in his mind drop away like the floor of a hangman's scaffolding. "Shep?" His voice came out as a thin, strained version of itself. "Is he . . ."

"No! No, no, he's alive, Regis. He's alive. He's been hurt bad, though. The poor kid's been knifed in an alley up Corpus Christi way."

"Knifed?"

Corbin nodded. "Hell of a thing. I got word from one of my deputies who'd escorted a thief who was wanted there. Anyway, he heard the name 'Royle,' and poked his nose in, knowing you and Cormac and all. You know my deputy, that Rogers kid. Good fella. Anyway—"

Regis cut him off. "What was he doing in Corpus Christi?"

"I just told you . . . oh, you mean Shepley. Well, that I don't know."

Regis still felt hollow, but something was filling him back up. Now that he knew his brother was alive, and maybe okay, he felt a bitterness building in him. "That damnable kid!" He growled it, his big fists clenching and straining, groping for a fight that didn't exist. "Who did it?"

Before Corbin could answer, Regis cut him off again. "That damn kid. Should have never let him go."

"Hell, I know how you feel, Regis. A little bit, anyway. The kid's, well, he's a kid. Bull headed and all. But there's something about him I like. We all do. He's had a rough run of it since he showed up out here, and he doesn't make life any easier on him-self."

Oddly, the marshal's words cut through the bitter murk clouding his thinking. Regis pulled in a deep breath, let it out, and said, "Thanks, Corbin. I appreciate it. You're certain he's all right?"

"Yeah. It's early days yet, but the doc there says he'll pull through."

A long moment passed, then a thought came to Regis. "The men know?" At the same time, he was doing his best to remember all the questions he needed to before the man headed out.

As if reading his mind, Corbin said, "Got a couple of deputies keeping a lid on doings in Brownsville. Thought I might bunk the night here, ride along with you in the morning, if that's all right."

"What?" Regis looked at him, the words just making sense to him. "Oh, of course. Yeah, but I have to get going. Long ride to Corpus Christi."

"Well, it'll be dark soon, Regis. Not safe to ride at night. Hell, you know that."

"Yeah, yeah. But Shep . . ."

"As I said, he's being tended by the town's best doc and a nurse. Nothing you can do by showing up in the wee hours all wrung out. Best wait 'til dawn."

"Okay, yeah, you're right, of course. You can bunk with me. There's room. Shep's digs . . . if that'll do."

"Only if it won't put you out."

"Nope. Then we can hit the trail early."

"Okay."

As they walked to Regis's cabin, Corbin said, "Regis, there's something else. Most of the reason I am riding along."

"What's that?" Regis was listening, but a hundred thoughts skittered in his mind at the same time, mostly about that damn kid and how he could not seem to keep himself out of trouble. And to think he'd fallen for that note, agreed in his own mind to leave the kid be, let him go off on his own and live his life. Adult now. Ha. More like a fool.

"Regis." Marshal Corbin stopped.

Regis walked ahead by a pace, two, then paused, "What's wrong?"

"You're not listening to me, Regis. I said there was something else. Something Shep told the nurse. Well, more like he said it sort of raving in his sleep."

Regis nodded. "He does that, yeah, thrashes in his sleep, shouting and all. Usually it sounds like he's having a grand old time."

"Regis, he said the name Tomasina. Over and over, Tomasina Valdez. Said her name a lot, then said it was the devil herself who attacked him."

"What?"

Corbin nodded. "Yeah. If it's her, and it might well be, I have to find her. Not just you and Shep, but she's left a whole lot of folks down this way in bad straits. She and her men. Then when you broke up her gang, she disappeared. I'd hoped she went off somewhere and died."

"I never got a shot at her," said Regis, regret clenching his teeth. He covered the last stretch of trail to his cabin, the older lawman hustling behind.

"We ride before first light, marshal."

"Yep," said Corbin, biting back his own hunk of regret. More and more of late he was beginning to think this lawdogging was a young man's game. Maybe he could capture that she-devil, Tomasina Valdez, and call it a day. That'd be a hell of a way to top off a career.

Chapter 31

"Can't seem to keep you out of dark alleyways, can I, kid?" Shep flinched. Surely whoever that was—Regis? Sounded like his annoying voice—should know enough to leave a sleeping man alone.

He drifted once more. An eternity of time passed before he heard words again. This time he recognized that it was, without doubt, Regis.

"That puts the damper on your fool army plans, and yes, I read your enrollment papers when you went to relieve yourself. Good thing, too. Childish . . ."

There was that edge to his brother's voice that he hated. So smart, knows better than anyone else. Wait a minute, what did he say about the army? Then some of what he'd done dribbled back to him. That fellow in the uniform . . . Pin, that was his name. He'd been in the army. Is that what Regis meant?

Then the intent of his brother's words came around again, as if on a whirlpool of water, drifting in a circle. He'd said "your army plans." Then Shep recalled the paper, signing the paper. He'd . . . he'd joined the army?

That thought drifted away, but Regis's words clung to him and set his teeth tight. Regis hated the thought that Shep had done something, anything, without telling him. Shep smiled. And cracked his eyes open. "Don't count on it," he whispered.

Saying it took all the strength Shep could muster. He was spent, wiped, wrung out, but it had felt good to say that to his brother's smug face. Just now, he couldn't even keep his eyes open, let alone speak any hot words.

Regis flinched at the hard-flung response. The kid wasn't serious, couldn't be. He stared at his sleeping brother. It was all he could do to not slap the damn fool kid across the face. Finally, in a low voice, he said, "We'll talk later, once you're home."

As Shep slid back into sleep, sorting through what scraps of memory he had, he knew one thing for certain: He was damn sure going to follow through with that army business once he woke up.

Late on his first day in town, Regis stormed his way to the local army stockade, where he bulled past a weak-kneed simp in an outer office and slammed the paper on the desk of someone with authority.

"What's this all about?" said the man, calmly removing the arms of wire-frame spectacles from his ears and placing them on the desk before him.

"My brother, a kid, that's what it's about." Regis pointed to the paper.

The man lifted the much-creased, ratty paper, one corner of which bore red-brown stains. "This all seems to be in order," said the man. "A bit worn and abused, but in order."

"Well then take it out of order. My brother signed that when he was drunk. Likely coerced into it. He'd never do such a fool thing sober."

"I'm sorry you feel that the United States Army is a 'fool thing,' sir." The man leaned back in his chair. "Won't you have a seat?"

"No, thank you. I won't be here but a minute. Long enough for you to take him off your list of new recruits."

"Why should I do that? He signed it, did he not? And was he of age?"

"Eighteen, just that day."

"Plenty old enough. Plenty. Why, I joined when I was—"

"I don't care how old you were, mister. My brother's laid up at the Covington House, under the doctor's care. He was knifed in an alley, and nearly died. Not long after signing that foolish paper."

"I'm sorry to hear that about the young man." He looked at the sheet again. "Shepley Royle, is his name?"

"Yep. And he may or may not be out of the woods yet."

The man let out a deep breath. "I see. And these injuries he sustained, am I to assume they may prove a hindrance to him for some time to come?"

"Likely for the rest of his days."

"Naturally," said the man. "All right," he sighed. "Leave this with me and I'll tend to it."

"Nope. You'll tend to it now, while I wait. And a letter from you should seal the deal."

The man behind the desk looked at Regis for long moments. "You know, my sainted mother once told me that you catch more flies with honey than with vinegar."

"And my sainted mother said never suffer fools."

Instead of taking offense, the man smiled. "It seems our mothers were cut from the same cloth, sir. Give me a few minutes. But please take a seat." The man shuffled a few papers, looking for a clean sheet. "And while you wait, you might consider joining up yourself. The Army has need of bold men such as yourself."

For the first time since he stormed into the office, Regis smiled. "I always suspected as much, but now I know the Army serves loco weed at mealtime."

Ten minutes later, Regis walked back to the hotel to check on Shep. Nothing had changed, and the woman tending him said the doctor had given the kid something that would make him sleep deeply for a good long while.

He needed it, she'd said, what with all the screaming and

shouting he'd gotten up to in his sleep. Repeating that woman's name, over and over.

Regis intended to depart Corpus Christi two days after arriving. He'd made certain Shep was well tended and would want for nothing, and the kid, when he was awake, barely looked at him and hardly spoke at all. Regis could hardly blame him. The doctor said he was as close to dying as anybody he'd ever tended, and he'd been a field surgeon in the war with Mexico.

On the morning he was to leave, he talked with the doctor and was told Shep would be well tended. Then he paid two weeks' worth of hotel bills in advance, and visited with Shep a last time. The kid was asleep, but Regis spoke to him anyway.

"I have to go, Shep, but I'll be back in a week or so. The doc says that you're young enough you should heal pretty quickly. Then you can travel, if we take it easy. We'll get home and safe where you can get well. All right, then."

He lightly squeezed Shep's foot through the sheet. "Take 'er easy, brother. I'll be back. Oh, and don't worry about that army mess. I took care of it. You're a free bird once more."

He nodded to the older woman they'd hired to sit with him, then crossed the room and left, closing the door quietly behind him.

As soon as the door clunked shut, Shep's eyes flickered open the tiniest bit, then they narrowed and he frowned before sliding back into sleep.

After saying goodbye, Regis checked in with Marshal Corbin over breakfast. The two men conferred about the events of their last two days over coffee, eggs, ham steaks, and bread and jam.

Their first day in town, the two men had visited the alley where Shep had been knifed, but there was little evidence anything had happened save some darkness on the ground that may have been where the kid's blood had seeped. But they had seen the makeshift bed, and an old drunk taking a leak up the alley confirmed that it was a whore's crib.

So that was what the kid had been doing out there. Regis consulted with the doctor and was told that Shep had been so boozed up he had no idea what had happened to him for a full day. Hadn't even required morphine when the doc sewed him up.

On his own, Corbin had come up with nothing in his quest for Tomasina Valdez. His descriptions of the sultry, vicious woman, oddly dredged up no one who could, or would, help. It seemed she had made a few friends in town, and none of them, if they knew who the lawman sought, wished to give her up.

"I've about had it with searching," said Corbin, tossing his balled napkin on his empty plate. "Wish I could stay longer, boy do I, but work beckons and as much as I trusty my deputies, I don't trust some of the shall we say spicier characters in Brownsville."

"Well, I'm heading out to Brownsville myself after we finish here. You're welcome to join me."

Marshal Corbin smiled. "Maybe it's you who'll be joining me, you whippersnapper."

"That works for me . . . old timer."

Chapter 32

The two Royle brothers hadn't talked in some miles. Finally, Regis said, "Are you cold? I have another blanket—"

"I'm not cold." Even as he said it Shep pulled the wool blanket tighter about him.

It was turning out to be a warm day, but Regis didn't shed his own coat. He could only guess how Shep might take that. He'd been more prickly than usual the last few days since Regis showed up in Corpus Christi and got the okay from the doctor to bring Shep home.

"As long as it's in something that isn't horseback and that doesn't move at a breakneck speed," the grizzled doc had told him. "Can't risk his wounds opening."

"I've already arranged to rent a barouche. And I'll take 'er easy, I promise," said Regis.

Shep had not received the news well. It had surprised Regis a little bit to learn that the kid had assumed he'd continue to convalesce in the comfort of the Covington House for an indefinite time. Regis had other ideas.

"Oh no," said Regis, gathering Shep's few possessions—he'd told Regis at what stable he'd find his horse and gear. That had taken some doing, as Shep's memory of the hours leading to his attack was gappy.

In the end, Regis found the horse and most of the kid's gear, though he didn't have the heart to take the cooking goods from the little Mexican fellow who ran the place. He paid him as generously as he was able, keeping a mental tally of all the money the kid's escapade had so far cost him. Someday, he'd make him reimburse what Regis had begun to think of as "the fool's fund."

"Why can't I just stay in Corpus Christi?"

"And live on what? Your charm, your intelligence?" Regis shook his head. "Nope. I can't afford it. And if I can't, then you surely can't."

"What about taking me to Brownsville, then?"

"Where would you stay?" said Regis.

Shep shrugged, half knowing the gesture annoyed Regis. "Cormac's place, I guess."

"Not a possibility. He never takes in guests and we're on less-than-cozy terms at present."

"What did you do to Cormac, Regis?"

The kid had overstepped a line assuming he'd done something to cause a rift. But Regis knew he was right. "Nothing that concerns you," he'd said, thinking back to the birthday gift the kid never bothered to look at—the offer of official partnership in the ranch. The one Regis had burned in the stove.

"A cheap place in Brownsville, then. Heck, maybe I could set up in your warehouse down at the dock."

Regis had stopped fiddling with Shep's goods and stared at the kid, sitting up in bed, looking a whole lot better than he had a couple of days before. "You really hate the ranch that much, Shep?"

He'd not returned the glance, but shrugged.

There were lots of things Regis knew he could have, maybe should have, said then. But he didn't feel like it. He was tired. Life of late hadn't been working out according to his plan.

Falling out with Bone, losing patience with the ranchers in the Consortium, risking too much and likely losing his friendship with Cormac, the odd new threat to his ownership of the Santa Calina range—the crucial jewel in the Royle Ranch crown, all of this and more had all taken its toll on Regis. And then there was Shep.

And now they found themselves bumping along together to the Royle Ranch, neither of them making an effort to talk.

Finally, Regis spoke once more. "What is it you want, Shep?"

The kid had shrugged, but kept looking at the horizon.

"Moving your shoulders isn't much of an answer."

"I dunno."

"Well, when you figure it out, you be sure to let me know."

They spent the rest of the long ride in silence, hearing only the steady clunk of the wheels on the rough road, the hoofbeats of the two-horse team pulling them, the hoofbeats of their own two horses trailing along on lead lines behind the barouche.

"You don't know anything." Shep spoke to the tiny, empty room he thought he'd left behind. He tried to rise, but grunted in pain as he attempted the simplest thing he could think of, which was to shove himself up on one elbow. His belly twinged with the exertion. Would he ever heal? It had been weeks now. Three? Four? He'd lost count. At least a month.

He'd been knifed and left for dead by her, that she-devil he thought he'd left behind nearly two years before, back in the cave. He wished Regis had shot her then. And yet, as evil as she was, as old and aged and pinched as she'd become since those days in the cave, despite all that, she was also . . . something else.

Shep couldn't stop from feeling her soft breath on his face, her touch, how close she'd been to him, rubbing against him . . .

But as the days ground on, he remembered more about that night. The drunk who'd admitted he had been robbing Shep, initially thinking him a passed-out fool—he'd been partially right, thought Shep, with a groan. Then the drunk had felt the blood, seen the mess, and had staggered back into the bar and said aloud, "Hey, I think there's somebody dead out back!"

His words had created what the drunk had hoped for—it had made him a center of attention, if only for a few minutes. He wandered back out there, buoyed up by the grasping crowd, desperate for blood.

"By God," somebody shouted, "ol' Nedley's right! Look at that!"

It took someone else, an English barmaid who never drank alcohol but did swill copious amounts of tea, to shove through the clot of drunks and kneel down and find that Shep was still alive.

All this Shep had been told by her at his bedside. He'd awakened days later to feel her dabbing his hot forehead with a cloth. The doc had allowed her to be one of the three women who'd tended him.

She'd talked a lot to him, but he'd only heard some of what she said, and remembered little of it. She'd been pretty once, he bet, he remembered her chubby face, gray strands of hair blended in amongst the blond, and her lined but kind eyes. By the time he had been able to speak more than a wheezy whisper, she'd gone back to work. He'd never really thanked her and vowed, from his bed in the little depressing cabin on his brother's Royle Ranch, that he'd make it up to her somehow, someday. Maybe take her to a fine eatery or a picnic. Maybe she was not so old as he remembered.

Then some cowboy would shout or the cattle would bawl and moan and he'd be snapped from his reverie. Or worse, thoughts of Tomasina Valdez, her now-wizened, leering face standing over him, a long, thin knife in her hand, dripping his blood, and then she would laugh, long and loud, her head thrown back as her cackle echoed in his mind, even awake she would not let him be.

Through all the thoughts that came to Shep awake or in the long nights, he knew one thing above all others: He wasn't long for the Royle Ranch. He might not be much of a man, but he reckoned that under his bandages there was enough to him that he had to find out if he could stand on his own, away from Regis's constant pestering, always telling him what he should and shouldn't be doing. Shep knew he'd messed up badly, but isn't that what young men were supposed to do? Make a few mistakes and . . .

Shep sighed. He knew he was fooling himself. Not now anyway. But when he'd healed, when he felt pretty good again, he was gone from here.

Who knows, he thought, wincing as he folded his hands behind his head and leaned back in bed. Maybe he'd give the army another go. "See what those folks know," he said to the little room. He laughed, but it sounded thin and hollow to him. Not at all like the big, booming, confident laugh a man should make.

Chapter 33

Tullis Robicheaux, known by his associates, and by the law, as "Tull," did not mind one bit, never did in all his thirty-six years, that other men clammed up around him and refused to look into his eyes. He could hardly blame them. One of his eyes was glazed and milky, the other was a peculiar shade of ice blue.

The blind one came about when he was a child. He'd been playing a game he and the neighbor girl called "kill or be killed," and Rina, the neighbor girl, had taken the notion to heart.

She was a headstrong little thing, and she said she'd had enough of his bullying, so she'd smacked off the heavy bottom of a tincture bottle. She held the green-glass neck, pinned him in place with a sweet smile, then ground the jagged tool in his eye.

What he still recalled the most was how worked up this normally quiet girl had become, and all because of him. He'd made her so angry she attacked him. That was some power he'd wielded over her, and he hadn't even known he was doing it.

The other thing he recalled about the event was that he'd not believed it was happening, so very odd was it to see Rina acting such. He didn't move until the damage was well inflicted.

Oddly, there hadn't been much pain. He couldn't say the same about blood, and he could still see for a few weeks afterward, then his sight diminished in that eye, pinched out gradually like daylight will do before you notice it at the tag-end of a hot day. The center of the eyeball itself turned color from blue to milk-gray.

But it hadn't slowed him down much. He compensated for his size and strength for a few years, then he grew. And he grew, then grew some more. He didn't slow down until he was in his early twenties. By then he was wide at the shoulder, wider than most men by half again.

His arms bunched beneath his shirts and coats, and he was able to put them to good use time and again when he was challenged, simply because he was quiet, large, and, because of that milky eye, odd looking.

He was also used to being beaten, since his father was a drunkard and took after young Tull for most everything, from the way he looked to the way he looked at the old man. Mostly it was because the old man was smaller than him and afraid. Once Tull figured that out, he stood his ground and finally threatened the old man with a promise of a head-to-toe beating if he didn't let well enough alone.

The old man couldn't help himself, though, and he buttoned up Tull's mother's eyes one too many times after a long toot on the bottle. Tull intervened, the old man didn't back down, and the younger man delivered a hard left fist to the old man's chest. The old man never rose again.

His mother set the law on him. Tull, only fifteen, took to the road, lived as an outlaw and fugitive. Then, after several years, he found himself in the West and finally managed after several years of living like a hounded cur, to outdistance the law.

Tull grew bigger and thicker and meaner. Men gravitated toward him and followed him because he wasn't stupid and could express himself. And life, he came to believe, was there for the taking.

If you weren't bold enough to take, you were to be peeled apart and trod upon by him and his followers. That was some years before. Tull, at well north of six feet tall and in his physical prime, now had a gang, as he called it. He led the curly wolves from job to job, hired by powerful, quiet men who wanted much, who controlled much, and who would tolerate nothing less than full success. Tull felt the same and wanted the same.

Three months before, he had hired on to deal with a certain problem foreseen by someone he'd never met, but who had much money and power and who wanted them to stop the advance of the rail lines deep into Texas. Tull didn't much care who or why, just the when and the how much.

This whole deal, though, had become little more than an annoyance, and a debacle from the first day. He should have known better, but he'd been swayed by the money offered, a thousand dollars to not only disrupt the Southern and Coastal Railroad's progress into southern Texas. It was a spur line of some sort that promised great things for the folks whose settlements and ranches were along its path or in its way—rumor has it the railroad had been paying handsomely to buy out nesters and such so it might not have to alter its intended route.

As was his custom, Tull had not openly questioned the prudence of such a venture, though to himself he wondered about it. He'd studied the map supplied him by his new employer's representative, a moodless, somber man who only shook his head when Tull had asked him what to call him.

The grim man mostly pointed and grunted, nodded, and sighed depending on the questions Tull fired at him.

In the end, Tull got what he'd requested, half the money up front in gold coins. It made for a hefty little buckskin sack and he immediately wanted the second half. He'd also been told by the somber gent that there could be more, much more cash in the offing should his services prove of use, should they live up to the hype and promise, or, as the somber man put it, "Should your efforts live up to your reputations."

For some reason, that comment more than any other made

Tull want to twist the snake's head clean off his neck stalk, bony throat apple and all. But he held his temper and glared at the man a long ol' time with his good eye.

Usually that sort of fierce look, could with his height, width, and big, shaggy mane of wild brown hair and beard, which he'd never bothered to trim, let alone shave, usually made grown men quake and women and children wet themselves. Not that bastard.

It wasn't until later that Tull wondered if maybe that goober had been the employer himself. Could well be. In the end, he didn't much care one way or the other. Within a week of the date he'd promised to begin disrupting the rail line, some sort of creeping illness had skittered through his home base, a blockade-type of compound he'd built, tucked in the hill country of Arkansas.

They had themselves a decent set-up there, but he wasn't idiot enough to assume the law didn't know about it. He had guards patrolling the outskirts of his land, legally bought and paid for by him over the years, enough guards anyway that he didn't think the law dared move in.

Maybe they'd send a passel of cavalrymen on up there with cannons and whatnot. He hoped if he was ever caught in a situation that he couldn't climb out of, that he was caught with his trousers off, his bed filled with him and a woman or two, and a half-filled jug of pappy's best corn squeezings dangling from his finger. He reckoned that might be the way to go out.

But not just yet.

He never figured on a sickness so rascally that it laid low more than half his men, not just ill but dying off within two, three weeks of it first being noticed in camp.

First, it leveled off three babies and two camp whores, then several men came down with it. Open sores popped out on their faces and they heaved back up every single thing they tried to take in. That was bad enough, but then the sores started to stink and their hair came out in clumps and they leaked from every place possible on their unwashed damn bodies.

It was all he could do to go around the camp and shoot the sick in the head. The stink was so bad he had to wear three layers of rags over his mouth. Then he had to shoot old Miguel, a perfectly healthy fellow he'd known for years, and all because he refused to muckle onto the dead and drag them out to the burn pile.

Miguel's death was a lesson not lost on the other men. There were only nine of them left, but they snapped to and got those sick leavings heaped up and doused them all with coal oil. Tull himself set match to the stack.

Unfortunately, the day had been a tad breezy and, like all fires, no matter where you stood the smoke and the stink followed. Tull finally rode off with a jug and told the men that the mess had better be dealt with by the time he came back. He returned the next morning and the pile was but a smoldering heap of ash and bone rubble.

But that greasy stink of burnt flesh and sickness still hung in the air. He didn't know if his beloved mountain hidey-hole would ever be the same again. The next morning, they rode out, him and eight men—he'd lost another to sickness in the night—southward for Texas and the railroad job. He had to hire men along the way, making two side trips to hole-ups and rat-dens he knew of to recruit men.

In the end he got himself an even two dozen men, not counting himself, among them some deadeye, arrow-shooting Apaches, and one recalcitrant buffalo hunter.

Chapter 34

"Boss! Boss?"

Regis roused himself from his nap, awake right away. He glanced about—he was in his little bedroom at the ranch. He often found himself confused on waking these days, because he spent so much time riding between the ranch and Brownsville.

It took him but a moment to recall all he had been in the midst of, all he needed to accomplish that day at the ranch. There were the ledgers to tally, then he had to make certain the surveyor had been busy while he had been back in town. And Bone, he needed to talk with Bone about—then he remembered they were on the outs.

Somebody banged on the cabin door again. Whoever it was needed him. Someone who sounded familiar, one of the ranch hands. Whichever it was, he sounded worked up.

"Coming." Regis hated that the man would know he'd been snoozing in the middle of the day, but he'd tried functioning, vowing to get though the rest of the ledgers by noontime, but he kept nodding off. He tried coffee. Too much of it, then he tried dunking his head in the water trough, all of it. Nothing worked.

He had to admit that getting up early the day before, riding to the ranch, then working with Bone—their differences notwithstanding—and the boys for the rest of the day had worn him down to a nub. They'd cleared a space for the new schoolhouse, then dug a perimeter ditch for the foundation. That should have been enough for him, but he had the books to tend to.

"Sleep when you're dead, Regis," he'd mumbled and put on another pot of coffee to boil while he burned through the midnight oil on the ledgers.

Well, it had all gotten to him. And now here he was. According to his pocket watch, he'd gained little more than an hour of sleep.

"Tut," said Regis, nodding at the red-faced young man leaning in the doorway. "Come on in quick, don't let the snakes out."

Tut's eyebrows rose.

"I'm joshing you. Come on in and have a chair. I need to warm this awful coffee."

"Sorry to bother you, boss, but one of Ambrose Dalton's men rode up in a lather a few minutes ago. They need you."

"Who needs me for what?" said Regis, concern for the first time since waking drawing his brows together.

"Ambrose Dalton. The rancher."

"Yeah, I know who Ambrose is and what he does, Tut, thanks. What's he want?"

"Fella wouldn't say. Said he had orders just to tell you. I heard him say something about a gang of rustlers, though."

"Oh hell, that sounds ominous." Regis knocked back several gulps of cold coffee, then grabbed his hat. "Where's this man at?"

"Not far, hung back by the barn to water his horse."

Regis pushed past Tut and scissored his legs fast toward the barn. He saw the stranger and made for him. "What's this all about . . ."

"I'm Scott Jeffers."

"Okay, Scott. What's this about?"

"Mr. Dalton sent me."

"Yep, I know."

"Well, a new fella, Tomas, he says he knows where that big gang of rustlers that's been hitting everybody lately is at, says if we act now we can get them all at once instead of going about it one at a time."

"I suppose I don't have to ask if he's sent anybody for the Rangers."

The kid nodded. "He said you'd say that, Mr. Royle, sir. That's why he also told me to tell you he sent a man to Brownsville to round up a few Rangers."

Regis thought a moment more. This was the last thing he wanted to do today. If he didn't go along, Ambrose was more likely to string up anybody he came across. At least he might be able to prevent some sort of massacre. "Did Ambrose say how many of us he wants along, or where it is we're headed?"

"Oh, he didn't say. I should have asked."

"No, that's fine, Scott. Give me a few minutes to round up some men."

Tired but ready for whatever shenanigans Ambrose had in store, Regis and three men—Tut, Sol, and Gregor—lit out for the northeast. They followed the young cowhand, Scott Jeffers, who knew where they hoped to meet up with Ambrose.

Turned out it wasn't that far up the trail, as Ambrose had left his place later than he'd expected. And so, Regis found himself riding alongside Ambrose Dalton, once again, scouting up rustlers. This time, however, he vowed to keep them alive—unless they fought back.

Nine outriders, including his three men, flanked them ahead and behind, bristling with guns. Regis was aware that most of them were more experienced in ranch life than in life riding the owl hoot trail. The others, though, he didn't know, though their employer vouched for them.

The one among them Regis was most curious about, though, was that fellow Ambrose recently hired, who went by the name of Tomas. There was something about the man and this foray that made Regis nervous. How well did Ambrose know this man? Enough to trust all their lives to his convenient bit of information?

He wished he could have left the entire affair up to the Rangers. Maybe the Consortium had grown too big for its boots. Maybe Bone was right, maybe the doling out of punishment was best left to the law. Problem was, there were too few lawmen, Rangers or no, and too many damnable rustlers. Back to where we began, thought Regis.

And here he was, once more chasing thieves on a day when he'd expected to be helping Tut and the boys expand the big holding reservoir north of the ranch house and buildings. They had to get that task finished so they could accommodate the cattle he planned to add to the herd. It would also provide water to the growing village of relocated Mexican families.

Overall, they were lucky at the Royle Ranch. They had found a couple of rich seeps they'd widened into springs, and were building, with the help of ox and man power, with many shovels and much grumbling, a modest reservoir any tiny Texas town might beg for.

Hard as the work was, Regis wanted to be there, working his muscles, sweating in the sun and at the end of the day standing back to admire their efforts, after cooling off in the very water they'd dredged. And he wanted to be there the next day to do it again, and the next after that, until they'd built what he had in mind in the first place.

That was what work at the Royle Ranch was about, he'd decided. Feeling the satisfaction that comes with work well done. That was what paid the debt down. Not chasing after rustlers who may or may not be there. At least not like they were doing it.

Chasing after rustlers, on the tip of a recently hired vaquero who had the look of a shady fellow to Regis. But Ambrose had vouched for his new man, and they'd agreed as part of the Cattlemen's group to help each other when one or more of their fellows asked for it.

Tomas, the vaquero, had said he knew where a big camp of rustlers was located. Regis wanted to ask him how he knew. And where he'd worked before he'd showed up at Ambrose's western-edge cow camp. But he didn't get the chance, and Ambrose wasn't a man who liked to be second guessed, one of the many things Regis had learned in the past few months getting to better know his fellow ranchers.

"Tomas tells me the rustler's camp is over by that big gully I took to calling Schick's Ravine some years back, on account of it's a nasty piece of work. I had me an uncle name of Schick, same thing. Just an awful man. Anyway, that ravine, if they're there, is a-crawl with snakes and prickers and things that live under rocks that eat the snakes themselves. I don't know what they're called, but I know I would not choose to visit there if I didn't have the chance to kill me some rustlers, no sir."

Ambrose nodded his head at his own sage words.

Finally, Regis could not keep to himself what was on his mind. "You trust your man, this Tomas fellow?" he said, not really expecting an answer.

Flint for a brief moment sparked in Ambrose's eyes. Then he simmered.

Regis supposed he should be grateful that a surly look is all that came of it. He and Ambrose, as chummy as they'd gotten, had their share of horn-knocking. Dalton was a hard man who didn't take kindly to anyone questioning him or his ways. He'd earned the right to be that way, too, reckoned Regis, being in the region there as long as he'd been. But that didn't mean Regis had to put up with it.

The afternoon wore on. Dust rose up in clouds and at times, with no blessed breeze to accompany them, it clogged noses and throats and reddened eyes. They wore bandannas and tugged hats low, but it was slow, hard going.

About three hours in, Ollie rode up beside Regis and kept pace for a few moments. "We're getting close," he said.

Regis nodded. He trusted this man's judgment about the land hereabouts above the rest, mostly because Ollie knew this country inside and out. He was born and raised in it. He preferred to spend his own time off riding the range, exploring. Regis sensed the kid loved the place as much as he did, maybe more so.

Bone had hired the kid on, sensing a fellow cattleman. Indeed, Ollie had had his own little ranching operation for a spell, but it was meager, and eventually he reckoned it wasn't his time yet. So, for the promise of a steady stream of coins and steadier food, the young man had hired on with Bone. And for that, Regis was pleased.

He was a good kid. All bone and muscle and teeth and squint, with the swarthy look to him of part Mexican, which some men looked down on, but Regis admired. Kid was a worker. Just what he hoped his own brother, Shep, would have become.

In fact, he'd had Bone pair Shep with Ollie on a number of tasks. He was a couple of years older than Shep, but Ollie didn't mind Shep's incessant chatter and Shep hadn't minded Ollie's lack of inclination to talk much. They seemed to get along fine.

But Shep hadn't stuck with it. And then he'd turned eighteen.

A few minutes later, Ambrose dropped back. "About time we spread out and go slower. Also have to keep an eye for guards. Tomas says they shoot first, then feed anything they shoot to pigs."

"There's a cheery thought," said Regis.

Ambrose glanced at him, the sarcasm in Regis's reply lost on him. "Ain't nothin' cheery about it. Them sidewinders are killers and thieves who'll do for us if we don't do for them."

He nodded as if agreeing with himself. "Before this day is done, I aim to get me a handful of them bastards, hoist 'em high and watch them toe dance their way to the hereafter."

"I'd prefer we tie them up and deliver the lot of them to the Rangers."

"Rangers?" Ambrose shook his head. "My god, Royle. Spending time with ol' Bone has got you soft on that group of miscreants. I'll tie 'em, all right—right around the neck! Why, if the Rangers was here, they'd do the very same thing."

"Maybe," said Regis. "But the Texas Rangers have the law on their side, the legal right to make such a decision."

"So do we, Royle. Look here, you catch a man on your property slinging lead in your direction, and at the same time his compadres are driving off a sizable bunch of your own stock, what are you going to do about it?"

Regis nodded. "Okay, I get your point. But I'd still rather take them alive and let the law play out if we can."

"Sure, sure," said Ambrose.

But Regis saw the wink the fat rancher gave to one of his men.

"Any of them still alive after this deal plays out, why, we'll truss them up like bawling calves and drag them on back and let Marshal Corbin deal with them. Sure thing."

That was all the chatter they had time for. From ahead to the right, a man's scream burst out, then clipped off.

Every man among them surrendered to instinct and jerked down. Their weapons drawn, they slid from their saddles and kept their horses between them and the southern side of the trail, from where the gruesome sound had come.

All about him Regis heard nothing but the hurry of horses snorting, stomping, being urged along by low whispers and the muttered words of men.

Did it mean one of their number had been ambushed? And while they were yammering away about foolishness? Their men had been ranged far before and aft of them. They'd all ridden into this mess, full of themselves, assuming, somehow, they'd take the day.

"You think we're surrounded?"

It was Ambrose's thick voice, close by. Regis heard the fat man's hard breathing. With the excitement and the effort the fat rancher had spent getting down off his horse, Regis wondered, for the briefest of moments, how the man ever managed to climb into his own saddle? Regis had never seen him on horseback before tonight. It had always been in town or at somebody's ranch house, and he'd always showed up in a two-man carriage.

"I don't know," said Regis. "Hope not. But we can't stay here. It's still light enough that we'll be picked off. Follow their lead," Regis jerked his chin toward a handful of Ambrose's men. "Get yourself over there with your protectors," he said, unable to resist the dig at the fat rancher.

Regis was annoyed enough for letting himself get talked into yet another fool's errand with Ambrose. One of these ventures was bound to end in headache. It might well be this one.

They had no more time for small talk. A high, sharp whistle sounded from west of them, another closer, lower in pitch, but equally strident, picked up the call. It rang out, then, too, faded as another, closer, sounded.

As the second whistle pinched out, Regis knew them for what they were—a signal. From the sounds, they were surrounded. They'd ridden into a trap. He wanted to choke Tomas, for it was plain to him it was that lying bastard's doing.

Instead, he uttered a low, hard growl and hastened his horse into a lateral move that took him a dozen yards westward. It was closer to the source of the whistles, but also closer to a knob of boulders.

He didn't doubt he'd find cover there, and maybe a killer or two.

Sure enough, as he drew near, he spied movement ahead, past a boulder that seemed to lean its reddish bulk against a girthy trunked mesquite. He had unholstered his revolver and now, at risk of sending his horse bolting, leaned the gun across his right arm, which gripped the reins.

He led from the left side of the saddle, still guiding the horse westward and keeping its muscled girth between him and what he assumed were most of the awaiting rustlers. He pictured dozens of them, guns drawn, waiting for him in the darkening day ahead. But all he needed was a clear path for the bullet to whistle along and find the man ahead.

Regis laid the revolver over his arm bone, cocked back, and hoped his bullet would beat the waiting killer.

His gun barked, its raw sound matched by others near and far off. He thought perhaps he saw the figure in the shadows whip forward, too quickly and too awkwardly to be intentional. At the same time, Regis's horse thrashed and nearly took off his right hand at the wrist.

He wanted to growl, "Settle down!" but he opted for a hard, tight jerk of the reins, and it helped steady the horse. The animal's instincts prodded it to bolt hard and fast from there.

He felt bad about having to do that, but not bad enough to stop and talk with the beast about it. Life was life and death was close, all the time. Closer for some creatures than others, particularly if it was down to humans and non-humans. The non-humans would end up on the losing end of the stick every time.

Two yards more and he'd make it to the relative safety of the oasis of stone and wood. Then he spied movement to his left, far left, somebody running. It was dark enough he couldn't tell if the figure was coming toward him or fleeing. It was unlikely their scouts would act as such, and he didn't think any of their men would have had the time to get over there.

As Regis dithered, his decision was made for him. A burst of quick, bright light, like seeing a struck match flare in an ink-black room, appeared along with a booming sound. He flinched and heard a buzzing, whistling sound above his head. They'd missed.

He fired back and was rewarded with a clipped scream and a

grunt. The shape he'd seen had pitched forward, similar to the one he'd seen but seconds before. He couldn't believe he'd been lucky enough to get two of the devils.

Regis continued his advance and, keeping low, crept closer to the stilled form.

Chapter 35

His revolver he held out before him, ready to bark. He toed the man, a long, skinny drink, face down, head toward Regis. The man's right arm lay outstretched, a hand gun a couple of feet from it in the dirt. Regis kicked the man again. He felt nothing but yielding flesh and saw the man's plaid shirt rock slightly with the effort.

Regis knelt, revolver still held before the man, aware that the fellow's left hand lay beneath him, trapped—or holding a deadly surprise.

He loosened his grip on the horse's reins and unwound them, all but one wrap. With the freed slack he reached down and shoved the man by the shoulder up and over onto his back. His face, pulled forever in a rictus of pain and confusion, was not familiar to Regis.

The man's chest had been shot, and there was another puckered hole below that, off to one side, but still in the cut. Had Regis laced him with both shots he'd fired? Unless the idiot had shot himself somehow.

All the while, behind him, from the south, and to the right of him, the west, he heard shots, not steady, but telling—they had been expected, he'd bet a whole lot on it. And his men—and Ambrose's—though good at being nimble and keeping ahead of trouble, might not be so good at such in an ambush situation. Volleys of several shots, fired quick, rattled through, sometimes the bullets whistling close by.

"Come on, King," he whispered to his horse, wondering if the man was alone in this little copse. That in itself might be the answer. It was too small to be of use to more than a couple of people.

Regis led the horse close to the far edge of the sparse stand of trees, barking his knee on a jut of rock and biting back a curse. He tied the reins low to a wrist-size tree trunk and peered farther westward.

That's where Ambrose said the gulch lay. Regis had only ever seen the spot from a distance while riding by a year or so back, and wasn't as familiar with it as Ambrose had assumed.

He had an awful tickle in his throat and wanted to cough it out in the worst way, but he heard a voice, no, make that two, dead ahead. The murmuring voices were too far to be intelligible. Yet as far as he could tell, nothing about them sounded familiar.

They drew closer, he heard their footfalls, slow and cautious, their talk, not whispered but low, even, one deeper than the other.

Then one of them paused. Regis held motionless, stifling back a raw tickle in his throat that itched and scratched like a mouse in his windpipe and threatened to get him killed. His eyes watered.

"You see that?" said one of the men. Regis had crouched low. The dusky light was darkening, but enough? Could they have seen him? He had his revolver at the ready, aimed toward them. His hand was a sweaty mess. Off to his right he heard more intermittent shouts, a couple of shots, no shrieks. He wished again he hadn't agreed to accompany Ambrose on this foolish ride.

One of the men spoke: "It's a horse."

"I know it's a horse, but it ain't one of ours."

"How can you tell?"

All ours are in the corral, fool."

"Don't take to calling me names, Rupert. You know how I get. Liable to—"

"Shut it, Wass." The man's voice was low, but as they talked, they advanced. Now they were within a dozen feet of Regis.

"I tell you, it's not one of ours. And what's more, I sense something."

The other man, the one Regis thought might be Wass, began to speak, then the one called Rupert must have clamped a hand on his pard's mouth, because there was a stifled, sputtering sound, then silence as Rupert whispered, "Shhhh!"

Regis held, but the cough was clawing its way up his throat. He was doing his level best to breathe through his nose, shallow breaths, without making a sound. But the damn mouse in his throat had other ideas.

At the same time he was realizing he was about to lose the fight with his cough, the two men advanced on him. He saw the one on his left side, the larger of the two, poke the air to Regis's right with a meaty finger. It was a silent directive, and the smaller man responded by cutting off into the shadows.

Regis was amazed they hadn't seen him yet. Or if they had, their plan was to step on him. He watched the larger of the two, the one to his left, angle farther away. They were cutting wide around him, one to each side. He'd frittered valuable moments crouching, suppressing his cough, and so lost his opportunity to shoot them both at once, side by side.

He figured he still had the advantage of being hidden. And from the looks of it, the big man had cut wide of him and appeared to be making for the horse. That's when Regis made his second mistake.

"Hey!" said a voice behind him. "Who are you?"

Regis's eyes widened and his cough clawed its way up and out of his throat at the same time. He wheezed, "It's me." Hoping the fool would think he was his pard.

The man leaned closer, a rifle held across his chest. "I know you?"

"Yep," said Regis as he leveled on the man's chest and pulled the trigger. "I'm Death."

The man whipped sideways from the power of the barreling bullet. It jerked him nearly in a circle before he pitched backward onto a rock. Regis heard the man's screech stop with the sound of something heavy and moving smack into something hard and unmoving. Wass flopped to the earth.

All this happened in the time it takes to pull in and push out a breath. A third wasn't possible because a sound, perhaps boot on gravel, spun him from his crouched position. He was on one knee, and instinct forced him to lurch to his right, slamming his own revolver into a boulder. He didn't drop it but fumbled it in his grip, barely retaining hold of it with his fingertips.

He glanced up in time to see a big man, he of the name Rupert, so Regis assumed, wide of shoulder, and of gut and face, standing over him, revolver aiming downward at him. A growl boiled up out of the brute's chest.

But Regis was no wilting flower himself. He'd been in enough dockside brawls to know if he didn't get the upper hand, he would die where he knelt.

He thrust himself even farther off-balance, but as he did so he snaked outward with his left leg and hooked his boot behind the big man's own tree stump of an ankle. Regis kept moving to his right, jerking at the same time as hard as he could with his left leg.

It did the trick in upsetting the man's stance. As Rupert stumbled sideways, he bellowed, and the raw, animal sound mingled with Regis's ragged coughs. Rupert went down on one knee, his gun hand slamming as did Regis's moments before, against a boulder. But his other hand, the left, was already clawing at his foe.

Regis jerked his head in time to avoid much of the impact of the big hand, but the thumb caught him in the cheek and it felt as though the man had a dagger for a thumbnail. Worry about it later, he told himself. If there is a later.

Already the big man had regained control of his gun hand and swung it toward Regis.

Regis pulled his up an eyeblink sooner and pulled the trigger. Nothing happened.

Rupert grinned and Regis had no time to thumb back the hammer. He did the only thing that came to him—he dove forward toward the attacker, the man's gun between them, seconds from opening his chest as he had done to Wass.

As he shoved, he whipped his own gun hand wide in a backhand, with all the force he could muster. He succeeded in slamming his knuckles into the big man's gun, which fired, right beside Regis's right ear. The inside of his head felt as though it had been a bag that burst, blowing his skull apart with it. His vision sliced apart in bright colors—orange and yellow and blood red flashed in counterpoint with the instant gonging and clanging of bells in his skull.

He didn't waste time thinking about it because Rupert was far from finished.

Regis growled and kept shoving his full stature and weight against the now-stumbling Rupert. Regis felt the man's arm collide with his, felt his gun hand shudder, and his grip on the gun loosened. The revolver spun away into the dusky light.

Any second, thought Regis, that man's going to jam the death-dealing end of his gun into my guts and jerk the trigger. But he wasn't about to wait for it.

Regis kept ramming, and now, with both hands free, lashed downward hard with his right. He found no purchase there, but his left swung in from the side and collided with the meaty, growling face before him.

Rupert's head was as solid as rock. So is mine, thought Regis.

And he jerked his head back, then slammed it forward into Rupert's homely, bearded maw.

Regis's forehead connected with the man's big long nose. It kept going and Regis felt something crack and snap just north of his eyes. But it wasn't his head. It was the big brute's nose.

Rupert screamed and staggered backward, wobbling to one side. His meaty hands, neither holding a gun, as Regis saw through bleary wet eyes, grabbed at his face. Sounds as though a bull was being savaged with a hammer came bubbling and bellowing up from his bent-over form.

Dusk was coming in fast, but Regis saw something that looked slick and wet pouring from between the man's clenched fingers.

He wasted no more time. Though he was dizzy and half-deafened from the gunshot, he clasped his own two meaty hands together, tight, lacing the fingers as if he were about to pray hard for something.

As Rupert, from his crouched position below Regis, began to raise his shaggy, black-haired head, Regis raised his own hands, locked together, high. He drove them downward with all his formidable strength.

Regis felt something pop in his little fingers, but the reward of seeing the big brute sag beneath the blow as if he'd just had a sack of stones dropped on him from on high was reward enough.

Regis looked about for his gun. He couldn't see it, but he did see Rupert's in the dirt before his right boot.

Regis reached down for it, and a big hand snagged his wrist. The fingers tightened and pulled, hard and fast. He pitched forward and smacked his ribs into a rock. His breath abandoned him, and the left side of his head caromed off the solid surface.

This man will not die, Regis thought as he scrambled, dizzy and blinking back tears or blood, he knew not, nor did he care. In the near-dark, he was fighting for his life with a man who was doing the same, causes and right and wrong did not matter.

They were two beasts with claws out, snarling and lashing for supremacy—to the victor all, and to the vanquished, nothing.

The grim thoughts came and went in finger snap speed as Regis struggled, barely aware the man was still below him, worming his big body, trying to rise, to buck him off. But Regis, no small man himself, was having none of it.

Even dizzied, he was able to slam the roiling brute with a knee, perhaps to the throat. He could not see where it landed, but it did not matter, for it had a helpful effect. The big man, this Rupert, did not quit his struggle, but lost something with the knee blow. He seemed to weaken, sag a little beneath Regis. So Regis delivered another, at the same time punching at what he hoped was the man's gut.

His knee blow landed and his fist did as well, but he realized it had driven lower on the man's body than the gut, though it brought the same result: Rupert's breath left him in a great whoosh.

Still the brute's grip on Regis was as tight as forged steel. Even in his twin agonies of neck and crotch, in a final bellowing heave upward, the bull of a man managed to unseat Regis and gain the top position.

There was light enough about them that Regis saw the shaggy bastard's face close up once more and it bore the makings of nightmare. His thick, curly hair, dark as wet earth, hung matted and dripping with sweat and blood, blood that oozed and ran and dripped from the man's eyes. His mashed, pulped smear of a nose and the flesh about his eyes swelled, giving the bloated face a piggish look.

"Gaaah!" the beast man gasped, his crushed throat offering the sound as a raspy burble through split, bloodied lips ringed with more wet hair, a raggedy beard on a face aflame with rage.

"Youuu!" The beast howled, raising high a meaty broken fist. From beneath, it looked to Regis as if it were three fists, so confused in dizziness was his mind. His eyesight blurred and pulsed. He'd be damned if he was going to let that brute fool pummel him any longer.

"Yes," he wheezed. "Me."

And with that small word, representing the single most precious thing of all to Regis, he snatched free his bone-handle sheath knife and jerked his head to the left as the fist descended on his face.

At the same time, Regis drove his right arm up, arcing in, the knife's gleaming steel blade flashing, the bone handle gripped as tight as his enfeebled fingers were able. The wide, polished blade plunged inward, seeking blood and sinew and bone. And it found it, to the hilt.

The big man began another of his wheezing screams, then as Regis rammed the blade as hard as he could once more into what felt like the middle of the man, deep in his gut, the big beast's voice rose high and his last breath wheezed out. He stiffened and crashed to the earth.

From somewhere ahead, in the dark, the east, he thought, there came more shouts, increased in frequency and frenzy. Gunshots, too, echoed in the descending night sky. What have we done? thought Regis.

He did the only thing he knew to do—he walked forward, for he was near enough that his horse would only be a hindrance in getting close to the action. All he could think was that he was glad Shep wasn't around tonight. If he had been at the ranch, healed enough by now to ride, Regis would surely have insisted the young man go along on this trip, to toughen him up.

The thought of that led him to other thoughts of how he had behaved toward his brother, and toward others. Too bullheaded, he thought. And now here I am, in the midst of foolishness that could prevent me from doing right by those I care for.

Bone was likely right, should have left it for the Rangers. Admitting it was too late for such thoughts, Regis pushed on, his head still ringing, his arms sticky with Rupert's blood, despite wiping what of it he could on the man's shirt.

He'd clawed up the man's dropped revolver, not bothering to rummage on the man's belt for other bullets. He'd found his own gun, so having Rupert's was a bonus. He carried one in each hand, each thumbed back, snakes poised to strike. He wasn't certain if either gun would shoot, but he had no way of finding out until he was within range of needing it to do so.

The voices rose and fell in pitch, stepped on each other, and irregular shouts burst out with venom. He began to make out the words, and they weren't kind, a blend of curses in English and Spanish. Then he heard a whip crack and he thought of Ambrose. Did that mean the portly rancher made it through to the encampment? If so, did he do it as captain of the victorious raiders or as a prisoner of the rustlers?

Regis stepped and stopped, stepped and stopped, with each step glancing with caution all about him. He was surrounded with shadows, and his head throbbed with each footfall, careful as he was. He wasn't concerned with the mass of men he heard ahead, but with those who were still about the perimeter. There had to be others, patrolling, waiting their opportunity to kill a rancher or two.

What possesses a man to seek out crime? Is the good feeling of setting about a task and seeing it through, with all the sweat and muscle-challenging effort, not enough? Perhaps they never knew the value of a job done well, were unaware of the satisfaction and feeling of deep pride a man could feel doing such. Making something for his family, something that would last for the whole of his life and beyond.

These men, the rustlers, were parasites suckling off the work of others. "Verminous snake," muttered Regis, once more feeling that urge to stop the thievery and be done with it, put it behind them all so they could concentrate on the challenges of the present and the promise of the future.

"Yeah," said a hoarse voice ahead. "You think you can ride in here like you own the land or something?"

"That's because I do, you dumb son of a—"

A whip cracked and a man's voice squealed, then tailed off in a quick sob.

"Mind how you talk now, fat man. If I thought you were going to say something bad about my mama, oh, that would be bad for you."

Two or three other voices chuckled.

The other voice burst out: "You're thieves, nothing more!"

Yes, thought Regis. That's Ambrose, all right. Not good. That means he's been captured. And that might mean other of our men are also with him, trussed and waiting to die. Or they've run off, which didn't seem likely, given how much Regis felt he knew about their various ranch hands.

Another possibility was likely: That their men had killed, as Regis had done to the two, no, three men behind him.

He had to do something before whoever was talking, sounded like a boss man—lashed out at Ambrose with a knife or gun next.

Regis began to hear, beyond the men's voices, something familiar—the random lowing of cattle. It was far off, farther from him than the men. How many and whose were they? With any luck he'd find out soon.

Acting alone, with no way of knowing if any of his men lived to make it this far, other than Ambrose, Regis figured the only thing he could count on was luck at this point, no matter how thin the threads holding it.

He stepped again and gravel ground beneath his boot. The voices ahead continued with their halting, sometimes laughing, sounds. Like a dog stalking a rabbit, he waited until the distraction of a babble of voices rose once more, then Regis scrambled forward, using the noise as cover, keeping low and doing his best to not trip over something he couldn't see in the near-darkness.

All the while a line of light ahead, and slightly raised, grew

brighter. He realized before long that it was what he'd guessed—
the glow from a large campfire. But what had confused him until
now was that it looked raised because it was hidden partially behind a long berm of land running north-south.

That would be the lip of the gulch in which the rustlers had
settled in. A slight rise in the earth on which he walked bore out
this suspicion. Regis crept up to it, closer to the source of light
and sounds.

Chapter 36

Regis switchbacked his way up the rise, hearing more clearly with each step the shouts and cries from the other side, where the light bloomed. By then he was convinced that one of the two primary voices was that of Ambrose, his friend and fellow rancher. Others, those in obvious pain anyway, he was unsure of. Likely they were some of Ambrose's ranch hands, who outnumbered his three men. None of those voices sounded familiar.

It was obvious that the louder of the voices belonged to someone in a post of authority among the rustlers. The cattle noises, too, grew louder, still beyond the group of men ahead. He smelled cattle, though, as the pungent, dry scent of powdered dung wafted down to him now and again. He crept upward.

He estimated the top of the rise was only about twenty or so feet higher than the flat from which he'd climbed, but once he gained the top of it, it would hopefully afford him a solid view of the proceedings. He also hoped he wouldn't arrive too late to save whoever was being abused.

Five feet more to go when he heard the rustler shout, "Enough, I've had enough of this crap!" He smacked his hands together and shouted, "Jojo, shoot the fat one. Then do the same to the rest."

Immediately, a voice, presumably Jojo, said, a bit muffled to

Regis's hearing, "You want I should take them out of here so as not to sully the camp?"

"No! We're done here anyway. These fools know we're here, others will come sniffing for them. We get gone tonight."

He said something else but Regis couldn't make it out. He also didn't much care to hear any more. They were going to commence shooting his friends.

Emboldened by not seeing anyone else who wanted to stop him, Regis heaved his throbbing body the last few feet and landed prone with a dust-stirring thud. He held there, half-raised on his elbows, eyes squinting downward, taking in the scene. Nobody looked up at him, no one seemed to notice the mild, dusty stir he caused but thirty feet from them—a surprise, given that there were a fair number of people below.

To his left stood a small, thin fellow, neatly dressed and standing, eyeing the rest of them, rocking back on his heels. He had one hand tucked in a trouser pocket, the other held a chipped gray enamel cup that steamed in the firelight. He wore a sand-color hat tipped back on his forehead. Below an outsize nose rode trim, close-clipped black moustaches.

"Jojo, what did I tell you to do, boy?" said the dapper, coffee-sipping man.

"Yes, sir, I would, 'cept I knowed one of them, is all." The man who spoke, Jojo, was if possible half the weight of Regis, though a couple of inches taller. When he spoke his Adam's apple rode up and down in his neck like a pump handle.

"Oh, you knowed one? Well, which one is that?"

"Yonder," said Jojo, nodding toward a bound fellow Regis, too, recognized. Tomas, Ambrose's man who'd tipped them off about the location of this place. Perhaps he wasn't as guilty as Regis had suspected of leading them into a trap. He'd see about that later.

The dapper man strode forward, stepping over something large. As he did so, the men blocking this from Regis's view shuffled somewhat. Between them Regis glimpsed a figure on the ground, but whoever it was, he was large, and he was moving. And not dead.

Then Regis knew who that was—Ambrose.

The dapper man still held his coffee. He stopped before Tomas and eyed him up and down. "I remember you. Came to us wanting work, and we gave you that, and then some. Now you are back here, with these . . ." He waved his free hand about him at the scatter of standing and prone men. "Your fellow men, seems to me, ought to be sufficient judges of a fellow like you. What say you, men? You ready to set to on the fellow who caused all this ruckus?"

Nobody said much, though there were roughly a dozen of them. Regis guessed they were too afraid, fearing the little man. His big mouth had them all buffaloed.

"No? Oh, what a shame."

And then as Regis watched, deciding on a best course of action, the dapper leader pulled a derringer from within his jacket. In one smooth motion, thumbing back the tiny hammer as he raised his fist, he placed the business end of the derringer against Tomas's forehead, direction between but slightly above, his eyes.

Before the gagged man could do much more than widen his unbelieving eyes, the dapper leader pulled the trigger.

"No!" whispered Regis, and he wasn't the only one. Nearly everyone down there flinched and stepped backward or to the side, unsure of what was coming next.

Regis vowed not to keep them waiting.

The dapper man spun. "Should have known better than to delegate the important tasks." He bent at the knee and took aim downward, toward Ambrose.

Regis grunted, eyed down the barrel of his revolver. At this distance, he might well miss, but at least he'd distract him.

Regis pulled the trigger before the dapper man did the same.

For a moment, despite the roar from his revolver, Regis thought nothing had happened. Then the dapper man looked skyward with a jerking motion, as if he were about to pray to the heavens. His clean, sandy hat popped backward off his head, and his gleaming, back-combed hair shone in the firelight. It glistened almost as much as did the third eye he'd grown in the last few moments, nearly a twin in appearance to the one he'd given Tomas.

The dapper man's derringer, still clutched in the whipped-up arm, snapped and cracked. Jojo screamed, clutching his ribs where a tiny bullet had just been delivered into him by his beloved boss.

The confusion wrought by Regis's bullet afforded him enough time to shove fast backward, dragging his belly on the graveled slope. He did so right away, but he thought for certain some of the men standing down there had turned their gaze upward.

It occurred to him maybe they, being close to the light of the blazing campfire, couldn't see so well. Maybe they thought they were under siege. He had to somehow save his friends. How?

First things first, he told himself. Stay low and get the hell away from where they might look. It won't take long before the confusion gives way to logical thinking. They'll fan out and look everywhere for him.

And here I am, thought Regis, shoving sideways, doing his best to ignore the sand and grit peppering into the top of his trousers, half-lame by my fight with that bull of a man, Rupert. But I'm still alive, and what's more, I'm the only chance my friends have at living.

He hurried southward along the berm, keeping low, wincing at the twinges of pain in his right leg, his right hand ached, and the sharpish stabs in his chest, his right side, evidence of damage to a rib bone, perhaps more than one.

No matter, he thought. There must be a solution here somewhere, somehow. Of all the people to call to mind, his rascally, impetuous brother, Shepley, appeared, smiling, shaking his head as if viewing an amusing exploit from afar.

What would the kid do in such a fix? He had a remarkable way of surviving dire situations.

He'd wait for somebody to haul him out of there, that's what he'd do. Regis bit down a grim smile and angled along the berm. He was doing his best to evade notice before the men below boiled up and over the edge, searching for the deliverer of their boss man's death.

He rammed into a stunty mesquite, unseen before him and paused, rubbing his shoulder. He did not hear a lick of what he had been convinced was to follow his gunfire. No shouts chased him from enraged men bent on revenge, no boots shoving up and over the berm, sliding on scree. Why was that? He struggled to keep his breath quiet, but other than shouts and commotion from the men, there was no sound of agitation, or of pursuit.

Regis climbed upward again and risked another look. Of the ten or so men unfamiliar to him, most were clustered in two groups, with several of the men walking back and forth between the two. They were hard-looking characters, grizzled, unshaven, soiled clothes stained with meat grease and trail dust. To a man they looked hard worked and tired. Ill-used is how Regis would describe them.

He heard snatches of conversation, heated at times, but overall, he was surprised to see the men were not interested in trailing him, nor were they apparently all that keen on killing the strangers in their midst. But there were three, no, four who stood apart from the others, their rifles and revolvers drawn and held at the ready.

These men scanned the top of the berm, ears cocked. They were the guards for the group, posted knowing someone, maybe more than one, was up there, someone who had shot their leader and maybe Jojo, too.

"Don't want no more killin' . . ."

"But they know us now . . ."

After a few seconds of this, Regis understood. These were all the hired fools, desperate men who'd chosen for their own twisted reasons to take to the owl hoot trail and rustle the cattle of others than work a life of honesty and integrity.

From their talk and their actions, and the fact that they left their dead boss where he fell, Regis guessed they'd grown weary of being mistreated for little gain and a whole lot of risk. And a possible end jerking and gagging at the end of a tight rope. They also did little to ease the plight of twitching, bleeding Jojo.

Regis's eyes settled on the prone bodies of his friends—he called them that, but other than his own men and Ambrose, who was more of an acquaintance and a damned annoyance, these men were not friends to him.

They were dependent on him, though, and as far as he knew, they were honest men asked to ride the river with him or with Ambrose, part of this growing headache that was the Cattlemen's Justice Consortium.

Were there more of them? He'd not given much thought to how many more of their number were out there.

They'd ridden into an ambush in which the now-dead Tomas might or might not have played a role—not that it mattered—so Regis had assumed that the others besides the men below, including the unmoving bulk of Ambrose, had been slain or driven off.

Was Ambrose wounded, unconscious, or good at playing dead? And the others—his men—had been trussed up by the very men they'd been intent on hanging. He didn't need any distractions while he was thinking through his slim list of possibilities.

One of the outlaws tossed a couple of wood chunks on the fire. Sparks rose and blue smoke pulsed outward before rising up into the still night air once more.

"Attract attention with that fire."

"Naw, we got 'em all . . ."

"Then who shot the boss, huh?" The man who said this, one of the guards with a cradled rifle, spat a stream of chaw juice a yard from his boots, shaking his head at the poor logic of his fellows.

Regis couldn't disagree with the spitting man.

He eyed the group again and decided he could wait for the decision. These men looked tuckered and played out, and spooked enough that they might well lean toward leaving without further gunplay.

He'd give them a few minutes more, then if it looked to go against him, he'd open up on them and take as many with him as he could. He figured he was alone, so his options were as limited as they could be, short of being down there, trussed, with his compadres.

He rechecked his revolver, and that of Rupert, found the big man's gun only had one bullet left. He'd use that last and set it beside his knee, ready to be grabbed.

Raising his head slowly, lest his movements attract attention from one of the guards below, Regis eyed the group as a whole once more. In the wavering light cast by the revived blaze, movement in the shadows pulled his gaze here and there.

As he listened to the weary arguments of the men below, he looked at an angle across the ridge's rim. Perhaps fifty feet from him he saw a face looking back at him.

Regis tensed, his left hand gripping his revolver tighter. He cursed himself for not paying more attention, and for thinking he was alone up here. Surely there were other outlaws roving the compound. There had to be others tending the stolen cattle, too.

The face angled, observing to the side as if it might help him to see Regis better. Regis dared not move. Then a hand appeared by the man's face and the man looked downward toward the outlaws and their prisoners, then looked back to Regis and the hand waved once, twice, thrice, and held there, palm out as if in friendly greeting.

What was the man up to? Then Regis felt a twinge of hope. The face looked familiar. Could it be Tut? He squinted back, stretching his neck forward a couple of inches, as if that might help him to see better across the fifty feet that separated them.

It surely looked like the ruddy young man.

The man pulled his hand back in and Regis nibbled the frayed ends of his moustaches. If it was Tut, how could they work together? As if the man had heard him ask that question, he held up his hand again, then paused it. Regis glanced downward and saw one of the guards turning slowly, eyeing the dim dark above, along the rim that roughly surrounded the camp.

Had he been an outlaw, he'd only have chosen such a spot in which to camp if he was confident he had plenty of men scattered along the outer edges of the place, patrolling, guarding.

The thought made Regis nervous, and he turtled his head back, looked about himself once more. It was a fruitless thing to do, as the dark was close now and his eyes had lost a little of their keenness given that he'd been looking down at the glowing camp below. Didn't mean there weren't others out there waiting to sink a blade in his back or drive a bullet into his skull.

It had only been a few seconds since the man across the way, a man Regis hoped was Tut, had motioned to him again. The guard looked away and the man waved a hand once more, caught Regis's eye, and nodded.

Regis didn't know how they could work together, but they had to try.

Tut waved to him once more and pointed at Regis, then pointed at the men below. Pointed again at Regis, then down below. Did that mean he wanted Regis to open the ball? It's what he was considering anyway. If so, there would be two guns drawing down on the outlaws instead of one.

That meant they'd live a little longer. But with all those guns below . . . Unless he could convince the rustlers they were surrounded. A slim shot, nearly a death warrant, but there was no other option.

He glanced at Tut once more and nodded, glanced at the guards, saw they were not looking his way, and held up his revolver, then pointed to his face.

Tut nodded. It was the best they could do.

Regis stayed low, pulled in a deep breath, and though he had never been a praying man, invoked words from his mother. They were stronger words than his usual "in for a penny, in for a pound," also words from his mother. This time, he whispered, "Lord, guide me through this day."

That it was night didn't much matter to him. He'd take all the power his dear, dead mother might pass to him by way of memory and time.

"Hold steady down there!" He bellowed in as deep and big a voice as he could. "You are surrounded! We are the Texas Rangers! I repeat, you are surrounded!" Forgive me, Bone, thought Regis. But I need the help.

His words caused a ripple of jerking, spinning confusion in the little gang. Even the prisoners moved, drawing themselves into tighter balls, as if to avoid being trampled.

Two of the outlaws hotfooted along a worn trail that he assumed led toward the cattle and freedom. Good riddance, he thought. Unless they decide to act brave, double back, and save their fellows. Not likely, though. There was no spine among the mewling, thieving class.

One of the outlaws jerked his rifle to his shoulder and fired a wild shot toward where Regis lay. The bullet sizzled through the darkness a good dozen feet to his left.

He was set to return fire when a bullet ripped into the shooter's neck from his left. It came, Regis saw the puff of smoke, from Tut, across the way.

"Hold your fire!" Regis bellowed at the confused mess of men below, each with a gun drawn. "Or we'll kill you where you stand!"

Silence draped over the remaining men like a wet, wool blanket. None of them spoke or moved. Regis figured he'd better make his intentions plain, and fast, or they'd grow bold once more and do something foolish.

"You get the one chance, right now, to toss those guns on the ground, away from you, toward the edges. Do it now or die where you stand!"

Another man with a revolver bent low, as if to lob his rifle away, but as he pulled it from his body, he spun from knee height, ready to shoot, once more toward Regis.

Regis delivered the shot this time, one that blew apart the closer of the man's knees. The shot spun him and he triggered his rifle, screaming high and wild, a banshee's chilling howl of agony, before collapsing on his back and grabbing at his smashed leg.

That stalled the rest of them in their tracks—that left seven of them, if Regis had counted right and they'd begun with eleven. Two fled on foot, one was shot in the neck by Tut, and he'd just shot the knee out from under another.

And the remaining seven looked too stunned to move. Good. "Throw down those guns! Now!"

That did it; each man slowly bent and tossed their guns to the sides. Then they stood and in the widely accepted show of submission, raised their hands.

"Tut!" he shouted. "You there?"

"Yep!"

"Go on down, collect those guns. We'll cover you!" Regis's heart pounded. He'd nearly said "I'll" and not "We'll."

The young cowboy did as Regis bade him. He hustled about it, though Regis could see the lad's leg had bled and he dragged it, the right one, a little behind, afraid to put full weight on it. They'd all come out of this with a whole lot of misery. But with any luck, they'd be alive. Most of them, anyway.

Chapter 37

The man whose knee he'd shot moaned once more, capping off a long, low wave of howling, and flopped backward to the ground, unconscious or dead. Regis didn't care which.

One of the men, a tall drink of water with long, dragoon moustaches and a face-wide sneer, began to lower his hands. "You done kilt Charlie!"

"Maybe," said Tut. "Though something tells me he's not smart enough to die. Yet! Now keep those hands up!"

The tall man said, "I don't think you got the Rangers up there at all!"

Regis cranked off a shot near the man's feet. "And I don't think you know what the hell you're talking about!"

Other than forcing the man to hop a bit when he fired that round, Tut did pretty well, making quick work of retrieving the guns away from the seven captives. Regis wanted to search each man for hidden weapons, but that would have to wait.

"All right—you men with your hands up, stand two by two, back-to-back. Hurry up now or I'll start shooting again!"

The seven men bumped into each other and for a minute couldn't seem to figure out just how they were supposed to stand. Regis sighed. As soon as the men had figured out what they were doing, he shouted again: "Lay down face forward, arms out in front of you! Do it now!"

They flopped forward, arms out, a fat one broke wind and giggled, and one of the others cursed him. Another one, a gray-haired man with no teeth and a patchy beard and a bald head, had a tricky time of getting down on the ground. He looked to be afflicted with rheumatism. Good, thought Regis. Might make him think twice about being a thief.

"Tut."

"Yeah?"

"We're coming down. You cut our men loose, see if any need tending to. We'll deal with these six. Shouldn't take more than six bullets. Maybe three, if I aim right."

"What?" It was the tall man again.

Another of them, the stiff old man with no teeth, began blubbering. Yet another started yammering, making all manner of promises Regis doubted highly he had any intention of keeping.

"Hands out, like I said!" shouted Regis, twinging even himself at the rage in his voice.

His captives, at least those conscious, complied. Regis finished switchbacking and sliding down the slope and stood in their midst.

As he rummaged for something, anything to bind them, finally slashing loose reins from a sloppy sprawl of tack leaning off to the side, the tall, dragoon-wearer said, "'Twas only cattle."

"What?" barked Regis.

"Your cows for our lives? That ain't a fair trade."

Regis said nothing for long moments as he lashed wrists together tight behind the back of the first man he came to.

"You should have thought about that before you stole them."

As he came to the tall man and began tying his wrists behind his back, the man said, "There ain't Rangers up there, nor I'd wager within a hunnert mile of here."

Regis said nothing.

"You'd not have taken us if we wasn't so run down and all."

Again, Regis said nothing as he moved on to the next man.

The thin man kept talking. "I tell you we'd have fought like tigers."

"And you would have died like kittens."

"Harsh words come easy to a man in charge."

Regis heard a rougher edge to the man's speech. He had plucked a nerve. Good. Try another, he thought. "Your boss man—was he a big talker?"

"Yeah, sure," said the man. "That's all it takes in life to be the boss. You ride hard over anybody in front of you. I see you are cut from the same bolt of cloth."

He'd had enough of the man's niggling and needling. "Close your mouth."

Regis was doing his level best to keep in mind, if not the words of the woman in the cave, then her meaning, the weight of the intention behind those sage words.

He knew it would be important to him in some inexplicable way, sometime down the road. It would come to him in the small hours when he woke to cold sweats, the damning, tolling bells of guilt clanging in his mind, to have thought kinder somehow of these men, to act toward them out of a sense of mutual regard, one man to another. He knew all this . . . but damn, if it wasn't difficult.

He did not doubt that these rascals, to a man, would gut him with a dull knife as soon as look at him, then pick his corpse clean of anything they thought of value before moving on to new pickings, the blood on their hands as little concern to them as the blood on their minds.

Tut had freed the other of their own men, including Ambrose, who apparently had dropped into a swoon of some sort when the shooting began. Regis decided his fat friend was not made of bold stuff.

All counted, there were six of them, an even match for the remaining rustlers. Tut pointed this out as he tipped water onto a rag and bathed the head of one of Ambrose's cowhands. He'd taken a foul knock to the temple, and an ugly, blood-filled welt had risen there, as if a crimson egg were emerging from the man's skull. Despite that, he looked to be awake and responsive to Tut's questions.

"But," Regis noted, "we don't appear to be in as good a condition as those heathens."

That raised a cackle from the toothless, bald man. "You ain't a-gonna kill us, are you?"

Regis ignored him and helped Tut to get the men over by the south end of the campsite. It was the most protected spot. Should other of the rustlers return, they would be able to defend themselves, particularly with the guns they'd confiscated.

Regis didn't yet dare ask what had happened to the rest of the men. He didn't want yet to hear how many of their men, including the other two of his own, who'd ridden with him from the Royle Ranch, had been laid low. The story would come out. Just now they had to fortify their position, then wait out the night.

Regis, Tut, and two more men of Ambrose's crew, made haste as they moved the fire toward their end of the site. They even found half-grilled hunks of beef and a crock of water, which they also relocated.

All the while, Ambrose himself remained oddly quiet, pale, and sat shaking his head as if he'd seen something that simply could not have happened.

Without being asked, Tut hobbled about the camp, rummaging in the rustler's gear, and came up with ropes that he cut to short lengths and bound the feet of the prisoners. They had become emboldened and mocked him, kicked at him, and threatened him.

Regis kept an ear and eye on the proceedings, but Tut was as unflappable as he'd ever been, and went about his chosen task as solidly as if he'd been building a corral back at the ranch or digging in the reservoir or breaking mustangs.

By quiet strength and determination, he'd led by example, particularly the younger cowhands. Regis had noticed, mostly after Bone had pointed it out to him, that Tut was looked up to and deferred to among all the hands.

"Hey!" said the toothless man. "You don't have to yank down so hard on them ropes! My bones is old and brittle, by gum."

Regis noticed that Tut smiled as he bound the whining man's ankles even tighter.

They arranged the prisoners far enough apart that they couldn't be of use in untying each other. Any movement would be seen from the fifteen feet away where their now-crackling fire was broiling hunks of the sizzling beef. Stolen or no, it was going to taste good, decided Regis. And likely it was either Ambrose's or his, anyway.

They'd been at it for about fifteen minutes and had about done all they needed to in the rough-made camp. Regis knelt beside Ambrose. "Hey," he said, poking the fat man in the arm. Ambrose blinked, shook his fat face, and looked at Regis. "Huh?"

"I said, 'Hey.'"

"Oh. So . . . we're okay now."

The statement set Regis's teeth together. "No thanks to you, yeah" is what he wanted to say, but what he said was, "Yep." Then he stood, stiff and sore.

"Could use a hand scouting out their entrance. See who else is out there, what the cattle are up to." He'd heard them, not too far away, since they'd claimed the camp and were trussing up prisoners.

"Yeah," said Ambrose, already sliding back into his glazed look.

Regis shoved him hard in the arm. "I mean it, Ambrose. Time you get up and help us. We need your help, man."

"Oh, yeah, okay. I'll get the men to help out."

But he just sat there, staring at the fire.

Regis sighed and went for one of the other men, one of Ambrose's who didn't appear too badly wounded. "How about you come with me. We need to check on things."

The man's eyes widened in fear, but he swallowed and nodded.

"Good," said Regis and clapped the younger man on the shoulder. "Grab that rifle and let's go."

He gave thought to tracking down his horse, but it was so dark, and the distance was too great at night in strange country. He didn't fancy risking it when other thieving fiends could be out there, so he said nothing of it. He hoped the horse would fare well for a few hours.

From the looks of it, all the other men were in the same boat. Horseless. Could be worse, he thought. And it damn nearly was. With any luck, they'd be able to use the rustlers' corralled mounts.

The two of them followed the same route the two rustlers who'd run took. There was little light, save for what the slivered moon offered from on high. But once they were away from the fire's scant glow, their eyes adjusted to the dark about them.

"I think the cattle are off there aways," whispered the younger man. He gestured with the rifle, held at the ready before his chest. Regis had noticed the man wore a bloodied bandanna about his right arm but was able to use it well enough.

"What's your name?" he asked the man, also in a whisper.

"Joseph. Joseph McCready. I work for Mr. Dalton."

Regis nodded, realized that was a useless gesture in the dark, and said, "Good to know you, Joseph." He took the lead and they walked toward the intermittent rustling and lowing of cattle.

"Friends call me Joe," said the other man.

"That include me?" said Regis.

"You bet, Mr. Royle. Sir."

"Friends call me Regis."

A pause, then he heard Joe say, "That include me, sir?"

"You bet."

They walked with caution, each eyeing their side, Joe glancing back now and again. The scent of cattle—dung and musky sweat—grew more pungent, as did the sound of them. Still, no sign of other men. Thankfully, the cattle were still here, and not scattered. How many were there?

Of course, once they drew closer, the cattle nearest them spooked and rambled away a few yards, but they were not nearly as spooky or as wild as Regis had expected. That was good, as they would be able to work them better come daylight. How they would do so was another matter. Living through the night without being jumped by the unaccounted-for rustlers was yet another.

"Hold," whispered Regis. The younger man seized in place. Both men searched the dark about them.

Finally, Regis whispered, "Just making certain. It pays to stop and listen without warning now and again." Beside him, he could see Joe nodding.

"Let's cut south, trail along the perimeter of the gully."

Again, the younger man nodded once and fell into line behind Regis. They walked on, slowly, the night nearly all about them now. To their right, above the rim of the gully, they saw the dull glow of the campfire.

It could be noticeable from a distance, but likely the only ones who would be looking were the very men Regis and his men didn't want to see, especially not in their worn-down state and with their paltry numbers.

By keeping the campfire's glow always to their right they were able, in step-and-stop fashion, to pick their slow trail around the ravine, where everybody waited for them.

Eventually they came once more to their point of beginning. They'd been able at any time to climb up and over the low berm walls, but that would not have eased Regis's mind about who may still be lurking. They found no one, nor sign of anyone.

Tomorrow would be a different story, he suspected. A number of dead men, some of their own among them.

Regis knew who was definitely out there, stiffening in the night.

He'd personally killed three outside of the berm, and there were another four, no five, counting Tomas, dead within. He had not wanted to make mention of it, but the one they called Charlie, the man whose knee he'd shot, was dead, Regis was pretty certain.

He likely had died of the strain of the grievous wound. The loss of blood hadn't helped, but it must have been the pain, raw and hot, that had finally overwhelmed him. Regis swallowed down rising bile in his gorge and forced himself to think of immediate tasks. Like living through the night.

All was as they had left it, save for the succulent smell of broiling beef as he drew close to the campfire.

"Hey!" shouted the tall prisoner with the dragoon moustaches. "We need water and food over here! You're taking all our food!"

Regis stopped midway between them and the campfire where his compadres sat and leaned against rocks, backed up close by the berm. He turned and walked to the man and looked down at him. After that slow, nervous-making patrol with Joseph, he was in no mood for a loudmouth to sully the night any more than it already was.

Death, all about the place. He'd been forced to kill too many people on this day alone. One was one too many, and yet . . . When had he turned into a killer of men?

He walked up to the man's boots and stared down at him. And when, thought Regis, did I begin to care so little for the lives of others? All others? No, no, just the ones he deemed deserving of his ire.

And who deemed you worthy of such pronouncements, Regis Royle?

"You . . . you heard me," said the tall men, snapping Regis from his reverie.

"I expect everyone here heard you. The cattle you stole, too, likely heard your big mouth." He drew his revolver. The men behind him, his men and Ambrose's men who had been murmuring, quieted. Everyone did.

The fire cracked, a knot, perhaps, giving way to flame.

The tall man gulped.

"I have had a long day, I don't want it to be any longer than it has to be. I also don't want to have to kill another man today. I have killed a good many on this day. One more really won't matter. Not really."

The man's face looked old, older than it had moments before. His thin cheeks sagged and took on an ashen hue.

Regis turned, but kept the revolver in his hand as he continued on toward the fire. Tut handed him a tin cup of coffee. "Not enough cups to go around, but we've been sharing just fine."

The coffee was good, hot and thick and bracing. He followed it with a couple of cups of water, making certain everyone else had had their share. Joseph had his while Regis had been talking to the prisoner.

"How's the meat, Ambrose?" Regis said.

The fat rancher still was not in a chatting mood.

Just as well, neither was he. Regis sought a seat by Tut.

He noted that the young man had set three guards and had already worked out a rotation of men patrolling the encampment such that they might all get some sorely needed shuteye.

Chapter 38

The morning came far too soon. Regis popped his eyes open. Nearly light. The horrors of the previous day dropped into his mind unbidden, each memory more raw than the one before. They ended with him sitting down to eat a few bites of roasted beef . . . and that's all he recalled.

He looked about him and saw several men asleep, two more crouched before the campfire, a promising sunrise glow already conjured from the gray ash.

He was sore all over, his ribs, his head, his right hand. Regis shoved up onto his elbows and dragged a big hand down his face. Even that hurt, but not as much as he bet the prisoners felt. They were all still asleep, bound wrist and ankle, and leaned against each other's shoulders, though he'd asked the boys to keep them far enough apart they could prevent chicanery.

Tut walked over and with a grimace plunked down beside Regis. "Sleep well, did you, boss?" He spoke in a low voice.

Regis nodded. "I would have preferred that you woke me so I could do my share."

"Naw, wasn't too bad. Enough of us to stretch it out just right so we all got some shut eye. Any more would have spoilt it."

Regis gestured with his chin. "Ambrose lend a hand, did he?" He already knew the answer.

"Well . . ." Tut looked down at his feet. "Like I say, any others and it would have knocked us off-kilter."

"Tut, you're a genuine politician."

The younger man's eyebrows rose. "I don't know if I take that as a compliment or not."

Regis smiled. "Well, nothing harsh intended. I appreciate your dedication to the task at hand, though."

In response, Tut nodded and with a slight groan stood. "Coffee'll be ready soon." He ambled back to the fire.

Regis allowed himself a groan or two, then limped toward where he'd seen young Joseph emerge. He assumed he'd been urinating back behind that snag of dead standing brush. Yep.

It was a relief. When he, too, had finished, he walked to the fire. And it was a fine feeling to begin the day still able to walk, talk, and see and hear. He spoke a morning greeting to Ambrose, who looked up at him and nodded, barely smiling.

Still trouble, thought Regis. Good. Might be it will give him pause before he rides off hell-for-leather on another of these half-hatched goose hunts.

Once they'd all passed around the couple of cups of coffee, sipping and grimacing at the harsh taste and hotness of the brew, Regis looked at Tut.

"Before we figure out what we're facing today, that is, before the sun makes a full visit, why don't you tell me what happened once we all became separated."

The young man nodded. "Sure thing. As you remember, we were all walking along, talking too loud, I see now, but we didn't know it then. Tomas, rest him, never warned us until we were too close. That makes me wonder."

"Me, too."

Tut nodded again. "First thing I noticed that something was off was that shot. Then the others. Same as you, I recall. But you peeled off to our left and the rest of us melted off the trail to the right. The only thing that saved us was the coming dusk, otherwise I fear we'd all of us have been lost. As it was, we lost track of a passel of the men. I believe there were more."

"We'll look soon. It's almost light."

"I hope some of them are still alive, holed up and waiting out the night. Nothing we could have done any sooner." Regis sipped again when the cup came to him, then filled it and passed it on.

"Most of us lost our horses, bolted when we tried to yank them where they didn't want to go. I can't blame them. All that gunfire, most of it from hidden guns. I didn't think I'd live through it."

"We were unprepared."

"We were sold down the river is what we were," said Regis. He glanced quickly over at the laid-out body of Tomas.

"You think it was him?"

"Nobody else it could have been, Tut. How about you, Ambrose, what do you think?"

They looked, but the man was not where he'd been sitting, a dozen feet away, nestled up to a boulder.

"Ambrose?"

At the same time Regis said the man's name, a shout from behind him spun Regis, hand already reaching for his sidearm.

It was one of the prisoners, the toothless, bald man. He was shoving his feet against the earth, pushing himself backward.

There stood big, fat Ambrose, looming over the prisoners, his broad back halfway turned toward them. Regis walked over and laid a hand on Ambrose's shoulder.

The burly rancher angrily shook him off and snarled and turned a rage-shaking face at him.

That's when Regis saw the cocked pistol in Ambrose's hand.

Through gritted teeth he said, "Keep the hell away, Royle. I been hearing you well enough. I started it, fine. Strike me down for wanting to keep what's mine, earned by hard work and all. But I'll be damned if I'm going to let these killers and thieves live when good men died because of them!"

"Ambrose, I understand how you feel, believe me. But shooting these men when they're trussed up isn't right. They'll pay for their part in these crimes, believe me. They'll pay and I'll make certain of it. But this is not the way. Not like this."

He saw the fat man's face soften, the angry creases above his eyes, the sneer on his mouth, all relax. "No, no. Your way, Regis?" The man shook his head. "It's too nice, see? It just doesn't work. You have to learn the ways out here. I'm talking the ranching ways, man."

As he spoke, still staring at Regis with a look of pity, he squeezed the trigger. There were screams and shouts from everywhere in the camp, mostly from the thrashing, rolling, bucking, bound prisoners.

Regis staggered backward. "Ambrose! What have you done?"

"What you should have last night!"

Before Regis could regain his stance, his ranching friend peeled the hammer and squeezed out another bullet, into the forehead of the man seated next to the now-dead toothless, bald man.

The tall man with the dragoon moustaches died screaming.

Regis slammed into Ambrose and knocked the big-gutted rancher sprawling sideways. The revolver flew from his hand and landed smack dab in the crotch of one of the prisoners. He saw it at the same time as Joseph did.

The young ranch hand darted in between the bleeding prisoners and grabbed for his employer's revolver. He had it in hand when the thrashing prisoner hooked a boot around the kid's ankles and upended him. The revolver, held in a loose grip in Joe's hand, spun from his grasp. It landed in the dust, and the young man righted himself with the agility of a cat and leapt at the captive.

He pulled back a muscled arm and delivered a quick snap to the man's stubbled jaw. The prisoner's head whipped sideways and swung back, his face leering, his teeth rimmed with blood.

"Enough!" Tut grabbed Joe about the waist and flung him backward. The younger man staggered, fell to his backside, and sprawled, then leaned back on an elbow, chest heaving, and wiped at his face. "Okay. Sorry."

"It's all right. An honest reaction never needs apologizing for. Unless you shoot somebody."

They turned to see Regis straddling the big, sagged form of Ambrose. He held the man by the shirtfront, but Ambrose, though awake, did not even look at Regis or the other men. He was back in his memory hole, or wherever it was the chunky man descended to.

Regis was so steamed he couldn't reason straight. "Somebody keep an eye on this damn fool, will you?"

One of Ambrose's men walked over.

"Good," said Regis. "Time we get this day rolling. Now, we need to think about burying the dead."

Another of Ambrose's men hustled over. Regis was certain he didn't know the man, but it didn't matter. They were all in it together. He and Ambrose had always gotten along, in part because Ambrose had supported Regis in his quest to form the Consortium, and in part because they were neighbors. Other than that, Regis doubted they would be friends should they have met in other circumstances.

Now all he wanted to do was beat the fat man's pooched, pious face with a couple of fists until one of them fell away, exhausted. Instead, he checked the unmoving Ambrose over for other weapons, found none, then helped tend the living prisoners.

There wasn't much talking for the next twenty minutes. They all pitched in, using a bunged-up shovel the rustlers had. They a dug a shallow trench of a grave and laid the dead outlaws in it.

They were going to free the remaining rustlers and make them dig the graves, but nobody much trusted them, so in the end they decided it would be faster to do it on their own. They discussed the fate of the corpse of Tomas and decided that the obvious evidence pointed toward him being in cahoots with the gang.

They buried him there, too. At the insistence of Ambrose's men who'd worked with him and who liked him, despite the possibility he'd played them false, they dug Tomas a separate grave and covered him over well with stones.

One of the men cobbled together a crude cross with two lengths of leftover firewood and a scrap of rawhide binding them at the center. He spoke quick, low words in Spanish over the grave.

On the insistence of one of the rustlers, they retrieved what valuables they could find from the dead. Tut made a quick tally and matched names to them. They'd pass the goods and information along to the law. Maybe their relations, if any existed, would get cold comfort knowing their kinsmen were dead, and where, roughly, they were laid to rest.

"Now," said Regis. "The cattle. We have to find them, see what we can see by way of herding them back to Ambrose's place. The rustlers' horses should be in their corral, hereabouts somewhere. Once we get a sense of the state of the cattle, how many, where they are, we'll go back out toward where we were set upon and see if we can find any of our horses. Most of all, we need to find any of our own men who might still be alive and needing help. And our dead . . . well, they'll come home with us."

The men nodded, but no one gave voice to what they were all thinking: There was slim chance any of them would be alive.

The next few hours were gnawed away by doing just what Regis had intended, and they found seven more dead rustlers, including the three Regis had laid low. The scene of which, in daylight, nauseated the big rancher as well as the rest of the men. It was by far the bloodiest, grimmest mess any of them had left.

Tut rubbed his mouth and shook his head. "No wonder you were so tired, boss. Lord Almighty, it's a wonder you're still walking."

"I feel as though I'm getting around on wishes and hide glue." He nodded toward movement north of them by a few hundred feet. Whoever it was was partially hidden by a knob of sandstone. Three of them cut wide, two circling to the east side, Regis taking the west. As they rounded the sandstone jag, they sighed and relaxed.

It was King, Regis's horse, looking as sagged and unimpressed with his lot in life as Regis felt. The saddle had slumped until it hung to the side of the beast's barrel, and the reins had been stomped a good many times.

The horse had looked for what scant shade it could find— away from the place where all that blood and stink and awful noise of the day before had taken place.

"Good to see you, boy. Good to see you." Regis patted him, then led him down the long slope and met up with the rest, giving the shaky horse a few decent pulls of water. Until they came to the Chollo Stream on their way home, they'd need to ration their water.

They all pitched in and dug another trench of a grave for the newfound dead rustlers and rolled them in and covered them with what grit they could, mounding it up before topping it, as they had with the other grave, with stones.

Neither grave looked able to withstand an assault by a pack of dedicated coyotes, but they could at least say they did what they could, should the time come when they were called on to defend their actions to the law.

As to their own dead, they prepared to bring them back, draped and strapped over mounts, to their home ranches, Ambrose's and the Royle.

They had found plenty of extra mounts, having located the outlaws' remuda, not far from that northeastward mouth of the gulley where they'd spent the night. The herd, such as it was, consisted of roughly thirty-five head of beeves, most from Ambrose's herd. The rest, about a dozen, were from the Royle Ranch.

With the prisoners mounted, and the several extra horses saddled and lead lined, the haggard group drove the herd southward for a few miles, then cut west.

With each mile covered, Ambrose grew more like his old, complaining self. He even tried twice to justify his actions to Regis, who rode away the first time, then reined over the second, halting them both. He stuck a long finger in the fat man's face. "You listen to me, you wretched rat. I've had enough of your foolishness. This whole damn mess came about because of you and your greed."

"My greed? What are you talking about, Royle?"

"Your foolish need to kill, kill, kill to protect and then retrieve what's yours."

"What's so wrong with that?"

"A lot, when there's no plan. More the fool I am for trotting along with you, and bringing my men into it, too. And now men are dead, Ambrose. These are men's lives! Doesn't that give you pause?"

"You bet. All the more reason we should have strung up the rest of those outlaws when we had the chance! Now they'll be coddled by your bosom friends, the spineless Rangers!"

"Yep," Regis turned his horse and trotted off. Over his shoulder, he said, "And you better hope they coddle you, too. Because you'll be right there with them!"

"Me? Hold on a minute there, Regis Damn Royle! A man doesn't threaten Ambrose Dalton and then ride off!"

"Get used to it, Ambrose."

The rest of the trip was a long, frosty one that found them reaching Dalton's ranch an hour or so before dusk. Without much palaver between them, Regis and Tut cut out their head from the paltry herd of stolen beeves and kept driving them toward the Royle Ranch.

They'd spend the night in a lean camp, he knew, halfway home, but he'd be damned if he was going to assume there would be such a thing as Ambrose's hospitality offered to him any longer. Tut went along with him on it.

An hour down the trail, they heard a horse coming up behind

at a steady clip. Regis was on drag duty, and Tut had circled back to make sure all was well. Each man pulled a gun.

A rider jogged into view and as Regis was about to say "halt yourself!" the rider did it himself.

"Mr. Royle?"

"Yeah?"

"It's me. Joseph McCready. Joe to my friends."

Regis exchanged a look with Tut, though both men kept their revolvers raised.

"What do you want?"

"I figured since you're down a couple of men that you might be hiring."

"Aren't you in the employ of Ambrose Dalton?"

"Well sir, I was. We had words not long after you left. Me and him, we haven't seen eye to eye on much, and I don't see that changing any time soon."

"Clean break with him, then?"

"Yes, sir. If you can call him telling me I had ten minutes to clear off his range as a clean break."

Regis sighed and glanced at Tut, who nodded and in a low voice said, "I like the kid. He's solid."

Regis nodded in agreement. "Okay then, welcome to the Royle Ranch crew, Joe-To-Your-Friends. Now, get on over here and eat some dust. I'm heading up front of this enormous cattle operation of ours."

It took Joe less than a minute of comfortable chatter with Tut to let him know he'd made the right choice, a lucky choice. Joe had heard good, if cautious things, about the Royle Ranch. Sure, the owner was green, but Regis Royle was a businessman and he had genuine investors.

And best of all, he'd heard that he had Jarvis "Bone" McGraw as ranch foreman, and everybody who knew cattle or knew of the Texas Rangers—usually if you knew one you knew the other in Texas—knew of Bone. None finer to work for, or with.

As for Regis, he felt awful about the two Royle Ranch men draped over their horses, tied down and trailing behind Tut at the rear. They were men who had families, Gregor Woolery back in Kansas City, if he remembered right, and Sol Renard, who lived at the Royle with his pretty wife and a small baby daughter.

He'd see that they were treated right. But no matter what he could do for them, it would never be enough for those families.

The only spot of hope he'd found in the entire ordeal had been in meeting the kid, Joe McCready. And now the kid was working for him. The more level-headed hands he had at the Royle, the less the sting of losing Bone would be for them all.

Regis told himself that, and tried to believe it, but he knew it wouldn't be as simple as that. Not by a long shot.

Chapter 39

They came down to the south Texas country from the north-east, a dust-boiling mass of men on horses, riding steady, neither fast nor slow. But no one seeing them could mistake them for anything but men on a mission.

At their head rode a huge fellow, wide of shoulder and shaggy of mane. Atop his head sat a black, dusty, dent-crowned bowler with a lone feather jammed in the brim along one side, and a wooden spoon in the other.

His horse, surprisingly graceful given its burden, was, out of obvious necessity, also a brute beast, a mottle of black and white patches and ragged-chopped mane and forelock. Its head-size hooves stomped forward as though its master weighed little more than a sack of meal.

The man who rode at the head of his gang was named Tull. He had long ago given up on the notion that he might at any time be shot in the back, stabbed in the back, or gashed open from be-hind, by any of his followers. He'd lost whatever scrim of fear he might have had back in those early days because he realized they were afraid of him, all of them. Too afraid to do him harm.

So deep and wide had he driven his fear before them, among them, within them, that all they dared do was follow along and offer supplicating gestures now and again when he turned on a whim to eye them.

They brought him food, the choicest takings from their unfortunate victims, the best spots about a campfire, all of it because they feared him. He rarely ever had to exert his power over others. Tull owed this fear to his size. And to his milky eye.

And now here he was, once again riding toward the madness of violence and destruction. And he couldn't be happier. In fact, it was one of the few times in his life that Tull allowed himself to smile.

He'd studied the maps well, maps only he and the railroad officials possessed. And those men in the field of course, but they hardly mattered. They would soon be dead.

Tull indulged in another smile. It was, after all, going to be one hell of a day.

Jasper Saliers wondered aloud for the hundredth time that day, and here it was not even nine of the clock in the morning, how he could have gotten himself roped into this debacle. A "fact-finding trek" was what Mr. De Haviland had called it, nothing more.

Hadn't they, as the Southern and Coastal Railroad, already done that for a year and more before? They had learned everything they needed to and had determined that yes, the vast volume of ranches and beef animals to the south could justify a spur line to which the ranchers might drive their beef animals, enabling them to get their beasts to market sooner.

It had already been determined that the venture could well be most profitable. All the contracts with the two other rail lines had been hammered into place. These would enable the Southern and Coastal to establish a rail head in that part of Texas. The beef animals, or beeves, as Jasper had been informed the Texans called them, would then be hauled north- and eastward to slaughterhouses, thence on to the dining tables of a public with a growing hunger for beef.

Mr. De Haviland's logic was, of course, far shrewder and more involved than that. He had foreseen great potential to exploit a vast and largely unpeopled land by being the first railroad company to make such an excursion.

"Trail blazers!" he'd thundered to the board room full of men puffing eagerly on cigars and pipes and not taking care in the least to hide the glint of greed in their rheumy eyes.

As Mr. De Haviland's junior assistant, Jasper Saliers had been present in the board room that day, and the experience had both thrilled and emboldened him. So much so that he'd asked Mr. De Haviland for his daughter's hand in marriage.

The look in the tycoon's eyes had alarmed Jasper. There was a sudden rage there, quickly veiled with something Jasper had not seen on the great man's face before, something . . . unsettling. And then Mr. De Haviland had smiled and told Jasper about how he was going to prove himself worthy of the fair Esther's hand by spearheading the expedition.

And now here he was, in Texas, as he had been for some three weeks. All about him were the crews of working men he had been sent forth to "assess and manage." This was a directive Jasper was as uncertain of as he was of the terrain of this place, it being as different from Boston as he assumed the moon's landscape was from that of earth.

Still, if he were to ever hope of achieving that ultimate prize, of having once and for all the hand of the fair Esther De Haviland in marriage, he reasoned he had better do something, anything in order that he might report back to Mr. De Haviland that all was proceeding apace.

And that is what he had done for these three weeks, filing reports that he had sent via a dispatch rider to have telegraphed back east, one detailed report every four days. But now they were too far to indulge in such civilized niceties, so the sending of his updates would have to wait.

The project's real overseer, Zola, a rough-and-rowdy character, proudly Greek in origin, sneered at everyone and cracked a literal whip at any worker who dared slow his pace.

Jasper kept to his side of the tent, rarely spoke with the frightening man, and did his best to avoid him altogether, no matter the time of day, even at meal time. Especially at meal times, as it turned out, because the man was possessed of the most appalling of dining habits.

Jasper assessed, and did his best to imagine what "managing" might possibly be required of him. Mostly, he stayed out of the way. Zola sneered at him at least two dozen times a day, when he wasn't snapping his whip and bellowing at the rock-breaking crews, the ground dragging crews, and the men who hauled supplies from the seemingly endless lines of ox-pulled freighting wagons.

His presence, it soon became apparent to Jasper, was not necessary. He assumed, however, that since he would be in short order, one of the family, as it were, Mr. De Haviland was likely testing him to see how he might fare should he have to take over the running of the family business one day.

The thought heartened Jasper and buoyed him during the frequent times in camp when he found himself at a loss as to what he should be doing, or even why he was there in the first place.

On that particular morning, with a cup of piping hot tea in his hand, Jasper had been standing outside the closed flaps of the canvas wall tent he had been forced to share with Zola, the surly Greek overseer.

A mass of dust in the northeastern distance boiled closer, moving toward them from the northeast, and Jasper paid it little attention, assuming it was another freighting outfit ferrying timbers and other supplies they seemed never to have enough of.

He knew little of the mechanics of the undertaking, but he had understood enough, he felt, to assume an air of judgment and superiority about the project itself, if not about the day-to-day running of the camp.

He had learned that De Haviland himself didn't dare risk fronting the money wholly for this venture, preferring instead to spread out the risk among a number of investors, men of his acquaintance who could afford to risk part of a grand sum in such speculation.

The entire promising venture was underwritten by a consortium of three insurance companies whose stock in trade was speculating on bold maneuvers such as whaling, foreign trade and goods, and slave-trading expeditions.

As the dust cloud drew closer, Zola himself walked over and stood beside Jasper and pointed a thick finger outward. "Who is this?"

Jasper looked at the man, who did not look back. If he thought Jasper knew who they were, they would all soon be disappointed. Jasper had hoped Zola knew who the newcomers might be. Nonetheless, as Jasper felt that since he was the one likely to have been addressed, he did not want word getting back to Mr. De Haviland that he had failed to perform, in any way, his duties.

"Likely it is more supplies," Jasper had said, with as much authority in his voice as he could muster.

"No." The Greek shook his head. "Not yet. Too early." Then he turned to face Jasper. "You tell me."

"What? But I have no idea who it might be." He turned to look northeastward once more. "Whoever it is, they are in a rush. Perhaps they are merely traveling this way, and it is coincidence that they shall cross our path."

He didn't believe it even as he said it. Hearing the Greek's snort of unbelief, Jasper sighed. "Well, there's nothing we can do about it until they arrive."

The Greek looked at him. "Don't count on it, fancy man. There is something not right about them." He smacked the whip against his palm. "We shall see. But I will be ready. Help me to tell the others."

Jasper nodded, surprised at how much the man had said to him, all without sneering, and also at the measured tone of the man's voice and the calm demeanor in which he said it. It told Jasper that something was amiss. Or would soon be.

He wanted to ask Zola what he meant by that, but the surly Greek was already gone, striding toward the knot of black men whose task it was to unload and place the track timbers.

Jasper followed the man's example and hustled toward the lay-down yard to spread the word among the other laborers.

As soon as he walked into sight, two men who had been talking as they worked stopped and looked to their tasks. Jasper felt a deep twinge of guilt. He had never imagined himself as the sort of man others would be cowed by. Even though he knew the workers resented him for nothing more than his presence among them.

Some of it he suspected had to do with the fact that he wore a dapper, back-East suit and wielded the hollow power authority gives a person. He had vowed from his first day there that he would not give up until he formed at least one friendship among them. It hadn't yet happened, but neither had he given up on trying.

Dust from the approaching riders began to be the only thing any of them could see of the newcomers. By then, they were a half-mile away and closing the gap fast. They weren't moving at an all-out clip, but they were giving it hell, as Jasper had heard men out there in the West call making haste. And they were.

Another phrase he'd heard several times since the train, then stagecoach, then freight wagon had deposited him in the midst of sand and sun and scorpions and snakes and lord knew what else, was "hell for leather," and it meant the very same as the other phrase. Both were appropriate and neither reassured him that the strangers were intent on good.

"Now, now," he muttered to himself as he sought the nearest laborer. "They might well be in trouble and need our assistance. Yes, that's it."

Jasper found he had no time to explain what little he knew to the four men he knew spoke in English. Two of them were black men, the Greek had said they were free men. One was Chinese and one looked to be of native descent.

He turned to mark the progress of the thundering newcomers and saw they were now barely a few hundred feet away.

Chapter 40

J asper's eyes went wide and he could not move. They were so close, closer with each second. At any moment their raised dust would soon be choking and blinding, he was certain of it. Still he could not move from the spot, could not seem to figure out how to flee from their path, to warn the others, to save himself from a trampling.

They thundered up, though just before reaching the camp the rear of the mass of men and horses teased apart. Through the dust, Jasper saw riders scatter left and right. Those who scattered looked to be cutting wide and circling the camp.

The half-dozen or so others rode straight for him. They reined up when still a dozen feet away.

As the dust parted, Jasper coughed and saw that in the lead was a mammoth horse on which sat a mammoth man. He was easily the largest man Jasper had ever seen, from afar or up close. Jasper looked up and up and still wasn't certain he was taking in the full measure of the man.

He looked not unlike a wide, thick tree topped with a crown of hair, from beard to topknot, long and radiating outward like branches. Atop all this mass sat a bowler hat that looked a tad comical on such a big brute. Jasper was not about to grin.

The horse looked to have been ridden straight from the gates of hell. Its great rubbery snout quivered, the nostrils flexing and snorting. Steam or dust or perhaps smoke rose from the brute's quivering black-and-white flanks and shoulders. Its mane was curiously cropped and gave the thick neck an even beastlier, snakelike look.

The big man urged the horse forward a few paces until it stood but five feet from Jasper. His near boot, the left, was big enough that Jasper thought he might be able to fit both his legs in the dusty black thing.

The man looked down at him through a part in the mass of hair. He reached up with a leather-wrapped hand—gloves without fingers, begrimed where the leather ended and skin began—and, as if he were holding up the hand to his face to pray, used the thick fingers to part the hair wider.

Jasper saw the gap in the hair reveal a long wide nose, then higher up sat the eyes, and above those, thick, furred brows. The eyes shifted, opened wide, the man canted his head to each side. That's when Jasper saw one eye glare at him. It appeared to be black, and the other, its opposite.

The eye looked to Jasper as if the whole of the world had been drained of color. But this was not so, for it was a gray-milk mass, unswiveling, a dead, wet thing that chilled Jasper to a core within him of which he had never before been aware.

"What do you think, huh?"

At first Jasper didn't know that the voice had come from somewhere beneath that mass of hair. He glanced beyond the brute, to either side, but saw no other person, the man was so close and looming.

"What do you think?" bellowed the mammoth man.

It was then that Jasper noted he was staring right at him. Jasper stammered, then Zola strode into view from behind the nearest pile of timber. Jasper had not seen the swarthy boss man

step from behind the timbers. He held a rifle at waist height and
levered a round as he walked forward, raising the weapon.

"What is it you want here?" he said, that characteristic sneer
on his moustachioed, shaved, yet swarthy face.

The Greek's voice sounded a bit shaky to Jasper, as if it had
caught a shiver. As if the man were afraid. But that could not be,
for somehow in Jasper's mind, the Greek had become the patriarch of them all, the boss man who knew best for everyone in his
camp.

Jasper suspected the man had enjoyed this role, strutting about
the camp, exuding superiority, daring each of them to differ with
him. None had, not even the two biggest men in the work crew,
two muscled black men who worked in near-silence, save for
grunts and low bellows when a timber or a maul did or didn't do
their bidding.

But not even those powerful men, whose muscles were knotted and as hard looking as thick wood, not even those men had
ever taken the Greek to task for snapping his whip—which now
that Jasper thought about it, he never did with those two men—
or stomping about the camp and growling his directives.

And so, it was unnerving to hear the Greek's voice quaver as if
it were, for the first time, unsure of itself.

Jasper was aware, too, that other men of the camp stood off to
his sides, back a few paces. They rested with their limp, work-
swollen hands hanging useless without their accustomed tasks to
attend to. No one spoke.

For a long moment the only sound were horse snorts, the
stamping of a hoof, the flick of a head. Once a man smacked at
his own face, annoyed perhaps by a drop of sweat sliding and
tickling.

The big man swung his bovine countenance toward the
Greek. The stranger raised a huge hand from his saddle's horn,
where it had rested. Every movement the man made radiated

through his largeness and sent out subtle sounds into the still, hot air—the soft ratchetings of leather creaking and popping, as the body adjusted itself to each slight movement.

A mammoth brass-and-wood-and-steel revolver appeared in that hand. The gun looked to Jasper to be far too large for any man to hold aloft, any man save this one. The big brute thumbed back the hammer and, holding the gun leveled on the Greek, said, "Where's your guards at?"

Jasper tried to swallow, but it was as if his gorge had been packed with powdery sand. He wanted to shout, to scream, to run from there, straight back East to Boston, to his beloved Esther, never to see the West of this huge land ever again.

He knew at that moment he need never again feel the vicious, skin-blistering sun, never hear the incredible nothingness of the place, a land devoid of sound and kindness, a land peopled with unsavory beasts on two legs as unkind as the sun itself.

Jasper wanted to be anywhere but where he was. And yet . . . here he was. For Esther. Always for Esther. She would be there when he returned, whenever that may be, and he would have such tales to tell her. Oh such tales.

"Go to hell," said the Greek, his thick fingers tightening on his gun, his infernal whip looped at his waist.

The boom of the mammoth man's gun startled everyone except for the big brute and his gang. The one who moved the most was the Greek.

The bullet punched square into his chest, slamming him backward to the dry, sandy earth. It seemed to pin him there, his legs snapping at the knee as if he were trying to kick at a bee. His arms flailed, those thick fingers that had so recently gripped the braided leather handle of the whip now clawed at the earth as if he were looking for a dropped coin.

From his mouth, high, tight sounds of agony or ecstasy pinched out from between his stretched lips. Jasper watched the man's dark eyes flicker left, right, left again, seeing nothing that might help him.

A gunshot sounded behind them, not close, and forced Jasper to turn. Another followed. There, he saw blue smoke and a stranger on horseback wheeling a horse, circling on the axis of a pistol raised skyward. Another burst of smoke rose from it, followed by the popping sound.

Beneath the man prone on the earth, two people lay, unmoving, stretched as if floating on a pond. From their white clothes, Jasper thought they might be Chinese, maybe two of the Mexican laborers. Perhaps one of each. Not that it would much matter now, he thought, sudden raw fear mixed with weariness shoving down on him harder than the sun's heat ever had. What was happening?

"No sir. I won't."

The words tugged Jasper back to where he was standing. There was the big man atop his big horse, there was the Greek, on his back and now stilled. His arms lay at his sides, upturned palms filled with loose earth, chest blackened, reddening outward from the center of the wound.

But it was one of the two large black men, the quietest and hardest-working men in camp, who had spoken. He stood beside the other, to Jasper's left, looking up at one of the strangers, a horseman in buckskins. Tull.

The wide, big-armed black man shook his head slowly and stared at a buckskin-clad man atop the horse before him.

"You say 'no, sir' to me? Now that's too bad for you. Ain't nobody tells me no, no matter they attach a sir to it or not. Leastwise not a man whose skin looks to have been too long in the sun."

This struck the man as humorous and he began laughing at his own joke. A couple other of the riders back in the pack chuckled, none as heartily as the buckskin man. He'd barely finished guffawing when he slid from the ragged red sash about his waist a long-barrel revolver.

He worked the hammer with his thumb before squinting one eye closed. Then he leveled down on the black man before him. "Say it again."

Silence once more. Then the mammoth man sighed and that broke the spell.

"No, sir," said the black man.

The buckskin man's pistol boomed, easily one of the loudest sounds Jasper had ever heard. The bullet hit the black man in the center of his uncovered chest.

As if he had been jerked by hidden ropes, the man's body whipped backward a half-dozen feet before slamming to the earth shoulder blades first. His legs, clad only in their grimy cotton duck trousers, kicked upward in counterpoint to each other, then his booted heels drummed the earth and stilled.

Already the second black man, with whom the shot man had worked closely each day, side by side, task for task, had dropped to his knees beside him and had screamed.

The sound startled Jasper, so thin and high a sound to come from so large and muscled a man. He cradled the shot man's head in his lap, smoothing the man's cheeks with his pink palms, saying, "Joshua? Joshua?"

Joshua, Jasper saw, would never again respond to that or any other name.

"You!" shouted the bereft black man looking up at the buckskin man.

The killer stared down with a half smile at what he had wrought. "You look like you want a taste of the same."

"You killed my brother!"

"Oh, that's who it was?" said the buckskin man, cranking back on the gun's hammer once more.

"Stop it! Stop it now!" said Jasper. He had no idea he'd said it or how he'd been able to. He also suspected, as the words ripped from between his lips, that he was about to be shot, too.

His throat felt thickened, filled with his very own heart, a heart that had seized and now clogged his neck, cutting off his wind. Sound came to him as if stretched thin and taut, and his vision speckled with bright dots of light.

The buckskin man held his revolver aimed at the grieving, sobbing man who now rocked and moaned as he held his dead brother's head, hunched over it as if protecting it.

Tull looked down at Jasper. "Is it that you want a taste, too? I can oblige. Got me the bullets."

"Nope," said Jasper.

Tull had almost forgotten him. "Any such gets done, it's me, less I tell you to."

The words fell on them with the finality of a rock slide. In response, the buckskin man eased the hammer back to sleep on his gun and slid it once more beneath the sash about his waist.

Jasper noticed that the shooter wore moccasins on his feet, odd husks of skin that looked misshapen and odd as they hung limp to either side of the horse's belly.

He looked back to Tull, who had once more parted his hair with a long finger and was regarding Jasper with that black eye.

Without taking his gaze from Jasper, he produced from beneath the patchy flap of coat the revolver he had used on the Greek. It was as if he were doing little more than pointing a long finger at the softly moaning man cradling his dead brother on the ground. Then he shot him in the head.

"Brotherly grief's the worst of all."

Magically, the revolver, still smoking, disappeared beneath the big coat.

No one spoke. The big man sat his horse, his grimy hands, each as big as a ham, rested on the saddle horn. His head jerked a little right, then left.

As if beckoned, one of the men back behind him stepped his horse a couple of feet to the side. The fellow wore a top hat with remnant strips of a faded lavender band fluttering atop a chewed-away brim. The man was gawky, long yellow teeth rested on his bottom lip, and that pooched atop a chin that did not entirely exist. The look was unsettling. The man probed a nostril with a grubby, long, pinky finger.

"The rest," said the mammoth man.

The top-hatted man nodded once and, still reaming in his nose with the pinky, gently guided his horse to the right, jerked his own head in a motion similar to his boss's, and three men followed him.

It was then that Jasper caught movement to his right. He looked, and saw other of the riders, the ones who had broken off to that side when they'd first ridden up. They fanned out a dozen yards apart from each other. He saw three, four of them, there may have been more. What did they want? Were they all going to die?

"See, first off, yon pilgrim"—Tull nodded at no one else but Jasper, a thin smile pulling his bearded face wider—"You started off with me in an awful way. You ought really to have said kinder things to me from the start."

Jasper knew he was in trouble, because the man was a killer, and in Jasper's experience, anyone who had such a coarse attitude was highly unlikely to be capable of involved thought, let alone reasoning. And so, the notion of the brute letting Jasper survive was fast becoming a grim and fading thought.

Tull leaned forward and fixed him with that lone black eye. "You the one they call Jasper?"

Jasper nodded, his eyebrows rising.

"Good. You're the bonus. The rest, they was the work itself."

As a boom thundered, time slowed. Jasper saw something burrowing its way through the hot day's thickness, peeling apart the strands of the air. It made straight for him, as if it were hunting him and only him.

Then Jasper knew it for what it was—a bullet, his and his alone. He would carry it forever, he guessed. He also knew with all the surety one can know such a thing that he would never again set eyes on his darling Esther.

And then, just before the bullet cored his forehead and bloomed out the back of his until-then whole and healthy head—a head filled with dreams and kindness and love and faith in his fellows, a head with ideas that he had known could have well changed the lives of thousands, perhaps more, with notions of justice and invention and goodness—Jasper knew his dreams would never come to be.

He also knew who had set that bullet in motion. It was not the mammoth hairy man atop the mammoth black-and-white horse. It was Mr. De Haviland, his beloved Esther's father. He had not wanted him in his life, had not considered him anything more than an impending headache, and so he had conveniently had him dealt with.

And the rest of the men in the camp? The "work itself," as the man had said? They were the last impediment between Mr. De Haviland and a massive payout from the underwriters of what the cranky tycoon had called a "foolhardy venture."

So Esther's father hadn't intended this fact-finding foray to be anything at all, hence the inexplicable work for laying track for a spur line from nowhere to nowhere. All to have him excised from Mr. De Haviland's life. And so, from Esther's life.

And all these other men? The Greek and the Chinese and the big black men and the rest? All to die because of him?

That was it, then. And this, thought Jasper, was something few, perhaps no one, would ever know. He would take this vicious news, and an abiding image of his sweet Esther, with him into eternity.

The bullet passed through his head and out the back, sending meat and hair and blood and bone spraying like a hideous flower from Hell itself, blooming at last.

"Lop off his head, cinch it in the sack." The mammoth man circled his big horse. "I'll make one last pass for whimpers. Rest of you jackasses gather wood, build a fire, then go through their goods. We'll camp here tonight."

Chapter 41

"Who are you?" Bone eyed the young man on horseback who rode in and reined up hard, not twenty feet from the house. "And what's your hurry?"

Although Bone stood on his porch in his stocking feet, trousers, and unbuttoned shirt hanging loose, he had taken the few extra seconds to cinch on his gun belt. Strangers were strangers, after all.

Who knew? Might be some of the stunty offspring of that rascal who'd beat Margaret so. He was them, he'd consider a slice of revenge pie, too, he reckoned, for leaving their daddy, as useless as he was, dead.

"Mind if I climb down?"

Bone let his fingers curl around his holstered revolver's walnut grips. "Not at all . . . as soon as you've answered my questions."

The young man, a thin fellow wearing a sweat-stained straw sombrero, gulped.

Bone saw his Adam's apple ride up and down.

"Yes, sir. I'm Howard. Howard Strickland. I'm a Texas Ranger." After he said that, the young man sat up straighter in the saddle.

Margaret walked up behind Bone, wiping her hands on her apron. "Who's our company?" she said, eyeing the young man.

"That's what we're figuring out right now," said Bone. To the rider, he said, "Well, Howard Strickland, Texas Ranger, what's your hurry?"

Strickland nodded. "Captain Sam Fiedler sent me. Said you'd recognize the name."

Bone nodded. "He's right. Water your mount yonder at the barn. You'll find a shady stall and feed. You get him situated, come on to the house, we'll chinwag."

Strickland nodded, tipped his hat to Margaret. "Ma'am."

Bone waited until the young Ranger made for the barn before he followed Margaret back into the house.

"What do you think he wants?" she said, hefting the coffee pot.

"Something to do with the Rangers, no doubt." Bone rubbed his whisker stubble. He stared up at the ceiling, mired in thought, Margaret left him alone and busied herself with brewing coffee and slicing up a pan of fresh cornbread.

A few minutes later, they heard boots cross the porch, then a knock on the door. "Come on in," said Margaret, surprising—but pleasing—Bone.

He stood, noting she was becoming more at home and at ease since they'd come back to the ranch after her hellish adventure than she'd been before George Tinker had taken her away from here.

Bone guessed it might be because that man was well and truly dead and gone and out of her life forever. She'd even become more open with him, more affectionate and even playful. These were good days, and if what he guessed the young Ranger was about to tell him was true, he'd not risk a moment of his new-found happiness with Margaret, Rangers be damned.

"Hang your gun belt on that hook by the door there, then take a seat," said Bone, nodding to the chair across the table from where he'd been sitting. He waited for the young man to do his bidding, then as Margaret served them each coffee, he introduced her.

"Mr. Strickland, this is Margaret. She'll be joining us." Bone caught her glance. She began to object, and he shook his head. "Anything this young man has to say concerns you, too."

"Pleased to meet you, ma'am."

The kid had left his hat on the porch and hand taken pains to rid his shirt and trousers of dust, Bone had seen that when he'd walked in.

He'd also washed his face and hands and slicked his hair back, revealing the typical half-sunburned face of a man who wore a wide-brim hat most of the time. He was young, Bone guessed early twenties, if that, but he rode well and had the callused hands of a fellow unafraid of hard work.

Once they were served and Margaret had joined them, Bone nodded. "Okay, Mr. Strickland, let's have it." He was trying not to sound too stern, but an unreasonable annoyance was gnawing at him.

"Well, sir. Captain Fiedler, he sent me, as I said. He's . . . this is very good coffee, ma'am."

"Thank you, Howard," said Margaret, smiling at him.

Bone grunted. "You were saying?"

"Yes, sir. Uncle Sam, that is, Captain Fiedler—"

"Sammy's your uncle?"

The kid reddened. "Yes, sir."

Bone leaned forward. "That would make you Tina's boy?"

"Yes, sir. My father was Clarence Strickland. He was killed when I was just a kid. An accident with a wagon."

"Oh, I'm sorry to hear that," said Bone. "Huh. Last time I saw you, you were . . ." Bone held his big hands a couple of feet apart. "Not very big. But your mouth was, as I recall. Cleared the room with that wailing of yours."

"Yes, sir," said Howard, his cheeks and ears reddening even more.

"Jarvis, you're embarrassing the young man," said Margaret.

She rested a hand on Bone's arm. Lord, but that felt nice, he thought.

"Go on, Howard," said Bone. "You were about to tell me why ol' Sammy needs me."

"Oh." The kid looked surprised. "Yes, sir, he does. That is to say, that's why I'm here. As you know, the Rangers are reforming and there's ample need. What, with the Comanche raising Cain with the homesteaders, not to mention all the rustlers, why, we're spread thin."

Bone nodded. "So where do I figure into this?"

Howard smiled. "Uncle Sam said you were not one to dilly dally."

"Oh, he did, huh? Wonder what else he told you . . ."

The kid begin to speak, but Bone cut him off. "Maybe later."

"Right, yes. Well." The young man pulled a paper folded in quarters from within his vest and laid it on the table, then spun it so that it faced the older Ranger.

"A map." Bone looked it over and his eyes settled on a spot circled with blue ink. "What's that?"

"That's where we, or rather I and I hope you, too, are headed. It's the location of a proposed train line. A spur off a bigger line, actually."

"Up by the Louisiana border?" Bone leaned closer. "I don't recall any lines up that way, nor anything that something might spur off of."

"That's the trouble. It's a little odd. But Uncle Sam's caught in a rough spot. He was hoping to recruit you to help a group of Rangers riding southwest to deal with Comanches, but ranchers all over the state are having trouble with rustlers and they're calling for more help. At the same time, the railroads are starting to sniff around—"

"At the request of the ranchers. Yeah, I know all about it, Howard. Can't say I blame them. Why drive cattle to Kansas or worse when you can get them to a train in your own state? It's a good plan and the time has come for it."

Strickland nodded. "So that's where this spur line comes in. To be honest, sir, it's all a little confusing."

"What part?"

"Well, Uncle Sam, he got a telegram or some such passed to him from somebody he knows, somebody who doesn't get their boots dirty, if you know what I mean. The letter was from a woman back east, claims she's the daughter of the man who owns the railroad. She says there's a scouting party out there." He tapped the spot on the map circled in blue. "And she's not heard from them in some time."

"How long?"

Strickland shrugged. "Nobody knows."

"Why would she hear from them and not her father, the owner of the railroad?" Margaret asked.

Bone nodded. "Good question."

"I wish I knew. But Uncle Sam, he promised my mother he'd not send me into a Comanche situation without letting me get my feet wet first. It's embarrassing, but well, Mama's always been a little protective of me." He reddened and looked at his empty coffee cup. Margaret got up and biting back a smile, filled his cup.

"Thank you, ma'am."

"So, while we find out what's what with this spur line nobody knows anything about, I'm supposed to babysit you?"

"Jarvis." Margaret's voice was quiet but sharp.

Bone had not heard her speak that way to him before and it shocked him. He cleared his throat. "I reckon I was a little harsh."

"No," said the kid. "It's true. I'm capable, I promise you that, but Uncle Sam was told that the owner of the railroad has plans of spending a whole lot of money here and if we let this scouting party come to harm, the politicians say no railroads will touch us in a hundred years.'"

Bone smiled. "Your uncle has a bit of the politician in him, too, as I recall."

The kid nodded and sipped his coffee.

"Be the two of us? Nobody else?"

"That's right, sir," said the kid.

Bone sighed and leaned back in his chair. "I'll have to think on this. In the meantime, why don't you go introduce yourself to ol' Ramon in the bunk house. He'll fix you up a spot to spend the night. Take care if he breaks out that jug of his, though. He's partial to a few swigs of an evening."

"Yes, sir."

"And come on back in about an hour," said Margaret. "We're having chicken and dumplings for supper."

"Aww," said Bone, standing and stretching. "Ol' Howard ain't hungry, are you, boy? He's a Texas Ranger. He can live for weeks on cactus squeezings and a handful of coffee beans."

The red-eared kid's eyebrows rose. "Yes, sir," he nodded. "You bet." He backed out the door, nodding. "Ma'am."

Bone and Margaret waited until he was halfway across the yard before they could not contain their laughter any longer.

A little while later, Margaret and Bone sat on the edge of their bed, and he held her hand. "Funny that he came out this way today of all days. You know that letter Sammy sent me a few weeks back asking me to join back up, that there was need of somebody such as me, 'seasoned' he called me."

He shook his head, smiling. "Well, I'd all but decided I was going to send Sammy my official 'no thanks' letter. Planned on writing it tonight, in fact, as you and Ramon are headed to town soon."

Bone looked at her. "It's what I want, Margaret. I've been a

Texas Ranger. I know all about that, all about the danger involved, the long days in the saddle, the lousy food, the lousier
pay, all of it. I have a ranch here, and most important, I have you.
That's all I want now. Besides, that Ranger business, that's a
young man's game."

"Since when did you become an old man?" She rubbed a hand
on his chest.

"Who said I was old? Not me. I'll show you old!" He tipped
her back on the bed, and they laughed.

"Jarvis," she said. "If it's as quiet as it sounds like it'll be,
you'd be doing your friend, Sam, a favor. His mother, too." She
looked at him with those pretty eyes. "And Howard, he's just a
boy, really."

Bone sat up and stared at the wall. "I guess one last ride as a
Ranger. Only if you think it'd be a good idea. I hate to leave you,
though. I'd rather not."

"It would help the ranchers."

Margaret sat up and held him. "I'm not trying to talk you into
it. I want you to make certain you're leaving the Rangers for the
right reason."

"You are a smart one, aren't you?"

"Somebody has to be around here." She giggled.

"Saucy, too!" he said, and tipped her back on the bed once
more.

The young Ranger and the older Ranger had traveled northeastward for an hour, the morning sun just beginning to warm the
land about them. Neither man had talked much. Finally, Howard
broke the silence. "Is . . . Margaret . . . is she your wife?"

Bone didn't reply for a moment, then, reining in a smile, said,
"In a manner of speaking."

Strickland didn't respond right away, then he said, "I apologize for being so forward. It's none of my business."

"Not a worry. If you ask me anything I don't care to answer, I won't."

Strickland nodded.

"Let me ask you something," said Bone a few minutes later. "Why rangering?"

"You mean why did I join up?"

"Yeah."

The kid looked aside for a moment and Bone saw him turning red. Hell, maybe I'm the one who'd asked a rude question.

Then the kid said, "You."

"Beg pardon?"

"You, sir. Oh, and my uncle. Growing up, I heard all about the adventures you and my uncle have had."

"Uh-huh." But Bone was thinking about how very old that made him feel. "Well, your uncle's a good fella, known him a long time, but he has a habit of telling a windy now and again."

Strickland laughed. "I know that for certain. He told me once when I was just a kid that he likes to ride horses backwards so he can see where he's been."

Bone shook his head. "That sounds like ol' Sammy."

"He also said you saved his life."

Bone lost his smile. "I guess that part's true. But he paid me in kind. Anyway, that's not the sort of thing pards keep track of."

"Tell me again what you know about this railroad deal we're riding out to meet."

"Okay. Let's see. Uncle got a request from somebody back East, a woman, he said, daughter of the man who owns the railroad. Anyway, she wanted to know if he could spare some men to check on the encampment of this scouting and work crew exploring terrain for a spur line. Said they were also doing early work for the track while they're out there."

"Sounds odd. And it's up toward the Louisiana border?"

"Yes, sir. But not too near the coast."

"Can I see that map again?"

"Sure thing, sir. Here you go."

"Thanks. And my friends call me Bone. That means you."

"Yes, sir. Bone, sir. Thank you . . . sir."

Bone sighed and unfolded the map as they rode, side by side, toward something odd, something Bone knew little about. And something about it didn't sit right.

Chapter 42

As so often happened, they saw the buzzards before they saw the dead. Bone grimaced at the sight of them. He knew what they meant.

"Howard, would you say we're close to whatever it is that blue circle on the map is supposed to show us?"

The kid unfolded the map once more and squinted down at the crease-worn paper. "Yeah, I'd say. It's not terribly detailed, but . . . yeah, looks like were about there."

That's what Bone was afraid of. "You see those buzzards over there?"

"Mmm, oh yeah, now I do."

"Well, I don't like the look of them."

"Why? They're just . . . oh. You think . . . ?"

"Maybe, maybe not. But keep your eyes open and your head low and your rifle ready."

"Okay."

Until then, Bone had only mild cause to regret saying yes to this fool's errand. He should have figured out some way to keep the kid from riding out here, should have kept him at the ranch and sent for more Rangers to help them. Should have done a whole lot of things, Bone, he told himself. But you didn't do a one, and now you're stuck with a wet-nose kid and the possibility that something's wrong up ahead.

"Buzzards don't usually come together for the fun of it."

The kid, if he heard, was too enrapt by the sight to do much more than stare. Moment by moment they rode closer. Neither man spoke as they covered ground.

Within fifteen minutes, there they were, staring ahead at a mess of a camp. Bone drew his revolver and glanced about slowly.

Howard saw him and did the same.

Three canvas campaign tents were visible, though one stood off by itself. The contents of each had been flung out, as if the tents themselves had sickened and disgorged cots, a chair, bedding, a leather portmanteau, and many articles of clothing, mostly raglike garments that sat strewn and balled on the hot earth or snagged in a cactus.

A blackened, much-used fire pit sat in the midst of the camp, with rocks and planking for seating surrounding it. But it was the other things tossed about the spot that gave them pause and caused each man to raise their eyebrows and hold their breaths.

Singly and in heaps of twos and threes, the bodies of men, their bellies and chests and heads bloody black and a-crawl with bluebottles, were strewn about the camp. They had begun to swell with the day's heat.

Bone rode forward, startling a few brave buzzards who'd been surveying the scene themselves. The big, lopsided, winged beasts walked as if they were hopping from rock to rock in a river. They squawked low and throaty sounds and did not like the arrival of newcomers to their potential meals.

"Git! Psssst . . ." Bone whispered his commands as he walked Buck forward. Howard rode close behind. And then he got a closer-up look of one of the dead.

Young Strickland had seen dead people before, some he had known, his father among them, though he was young enough that the sight had been, while jarring, more confusing than sickening. His mother's reaction had startled him worse. But seeing this mass of dead, slumped, and flopped bodies overwhelmed him, and without warning he leaned to his right and vomited, a quick, harsh retching that trembled him. He felt the flush of embarrassment in the midst of it and tried to hurry it, spitting the last out and dragging his cuff across his mouth. "I'm sorry, sir. Sorry."

"You don't need to be," said Bone through tight lips, doing his best to keep his own gorge from rising. "This is grim. Grim." He motioned to the kid. "Pull that bandanna up over your nose and tuck the bottom in your shirt collar. It won't do much, but it'll help. These boys are going to be ripe."

One of the first they came across was a man dressed in clothes different from the rest: the coat, vest, and trousers of fine-spun blue wool, and on his feet well-tended brogans, not the togs of a man engaged in physical labor.

But the startling thing about this dead man, who lay on his back, was that he had no head. Just a black-red, fly-crusted stump, with ragged bits of meat and a glistening bone stalk where the head had been hacked away.

"Why his head and not the others?" said Bone, as much to himself as to Howard.

Nearby lay two large black men, both shot at close range, one slumped atop the other. Another man lay on his back, off to the side.

It went on like that, with other bodies close by the camp proper, still more farther out, ten in all, though Bone hinted there may be others, nodding toward lines of tracks leading off away from the camp.

"Howard, help me keep an eye at all times. We don't know if those who did this are lingering, watching us. And we have work to do." Bone dismounted and tied his horse to a work wagon away from the bodies. The young man did the same.

Bone gave the entire site a thorough look, beginning at the center, where most of the dead were clustered. Howard walked by his side and Bone pointed out tracks, fresh dung, the fact that the campfire was not yet dead cold. They circled wider and wider, making certain they didn't miss any tracks or other sign. Some distance to the west they found more dead, this time three Chinese men, but no others beyond.

The entire time they kept at least one set of eyes up and swiveling. "We don't want surprises," said Bone.

"You see these tracks, not just from horses, but men, moccasins and boots, and look at those there, what do they tell you?"

He pointed to a set of prints in the soft earth before him.

"They are huge," said Howard.

"Yeah, they are. Man must be twice the size of a normal fellow. I've rarely seen the like. And what's more, these men have been dead, I'm guessing, two days. That's why they're ripe. What's that tell you?"

Howard scrunched his brow. "Well, since you say a lot of these tracks are new . . ." He looked up at Bone. "They stayed around after they killed them?"

Bone nodded. "Looks like it. And judging from the lingering trace of heat, barely any but it's there, plus the smells off the campfire, I'd say they spent the night, pillaged the goods of the dead, likely ransacked their bodies—you see the way their clothes are tugged and mussed up?"

Howard nodded.

"Then they lit out today. And in no hurry, either." Bone shook his head. "Oh, this is grim. From the looks, we're talking more than a dozen men. Maybe closer to twenty." He rasped a hand across his bandanna-covered chin.

"I'm torn," he said slowly, looking past young Strickland to the horizon to the northwest, the direction the killers rode. "Head back for more Rangers."

Howard said nothing but Bone glanced at him and saw a shadow of disappointment cross his face.

"Thing is," said Bone. "The trail's fresh. Fresh as it's going to get, anyway. I've a mind to tail them, scout it a bit to see if we can learn something of them. Then go back for help."

"That doesn't sound very Ranger-like."

Bone looked at Howard, his eyebrows raised. "Maybe not, but that's how you live to fight another day."

"I reckon."

Bone didn't want to take the kid with him, but he didn't want to leave him behind, or worse, send him back alone for help. Who knew if they were out there right now, backtrailing them? All in all, he'd feel safer having the kid where he could see him.

They walked back to the camp and Bone made to mount up.

"But shouldn't we bury them?" said Howard.

Bone nodded. "Yeah, we should. But if I'm right, those who did this aren't but half a day ahead. If we stopped to bury these poor souls right now, we'll lose the rest of the day in tracking the killers."

The young Ranger, staring at the bodies, nodded.

"Don't worry—we'll come back and tend to them. They won't get any deader, son."

Chapter 43

When he'd returned from the mess with the rustlers, as he'd come to think of it, Regis had been sore, annoyed, and exhausted. It hadn't been the cattle the men had taken from him, but their attitudes of somehow having deserved whatever they might grab in life, as if the hard work that begets ownership didn't apply to them.

Well, they'd find out how the law applied to them. They were all going to be hauled to Brownsville tomorrow and turned over to Marshal Corbin.

Mostly, it had been the raw violence and killing that he'd been forced to partake in that troubled Regis beyond measure. That and Ambrose's possessive lust and what it had driven him to do.

It had been shocking to witness, but it had helped Regis to see that he had been much the same. Land and his greed for it had blinded him to so much, had made him abuse his friendships and to feel as if he had somehow gained the right to have others serve him and his whims.

It was with these thoughts that he trudged into the cabin, weary and wiped out, and said, "Shep? We're back. It took longer than we expected, but we're back. Some of us in better shape than others."

He crossed the room and plunked down in the chair before the work table stacked with papers and books and maps. What he wanted most was a hot bath and a long night's sleep. Smiling at the thought, he almost slipped into a doze, but realized he'd not heard a sound from his brother's room.

"Shep?"

He shoved up out of the chair and walked with slow, tired steps across the cabin and rapped on the closed door. No response. "Shep?" Nothing.

He thumbed open the latch and the door swung inward. He peeked around it. There was no Shep in bed, no Shep standing at the small mirror, there was No Shep. But the bed was made and the room had been tidied. He looked over to the wooden peg on the wall and there were no saddlebags. He glanced behind him toward the front door. There was no fawn hat on the rack, no boots on the floor.

And he knew what it meant. The kid wasn't out for a ride, he was gone. For good. There would be no note this time, nor did he need one. The bed, the room told him all he needed.

His first thought was to send men after him. To track him. Then what? What if they found him? They'd somehow drag him back here to a place he did not want to be. What was the use? The kid didn't want, no, not quite right, Shep, the man, didn't want to be there any longer. He had a life of his own that he had to find and to build, and it didn't involve the Royle Ranch.

Regis sighed long and low, the past days' travails leaking out of him. "Good luck, Shepley. I'll miss you, and I'll worry for you, that can't be helped. But I'll not seek you out."

He walked a few steps to his left, into his own small room, and with his boots still on, Regis lay down on his bed and slept like a dead man.

Regis rubbed at the soreness of his ribcage, one of the lasting traces of his fight with the rustlers, and stood straight, squared his shoulders, and said, "In for a penny, Regis Royle," and opened the door to Delany and Royle Shipping, the very firm of which he owned half share, the very firm he'd put in jeopardy, and what's more, the firm built on the back of his dearest friendship.

There sat Cormac, much as Regis knew—or hoped—he'd find him. Much as he had two weeks before, when they'd had their big dust-up and Regis had stormed out.

Cormac looked up from the eternal columns of figures in the ledger book before him. In the full afternoon light slanting in from the side window, Cormac looked old. Better certainly than he had at their last meeting, but not as robust as he should, or could.

Regis felt a sharp twinge of guilt deep in his gut. But he could not let sentiment pollute his visit.

"Regis," said Cormac, annoyance at having been interrupted giving way to a flash, however brief, of genuine happiness at seeing him. Of that Regis was confident.

Then that happy look was wiped away and replaced with that serious, level gaze only Cormac could throw at a man and make the receiver wither in fear. "What brings you here?"

"Cormac," Regis smiled. "Good to see you. I . . ." He cursed himself. He was never at a loss for words or backbone when he was at the ranch. He knew what he was about there, knew what needed doing, and everybody there, the ranch hands, the Mexican villagers, and even Bone, too, depended on him to make not only decisions, but the right ones. But with Cormac, he always felt like a fool kid.

Cormac looked at him with raised eyebrows, waiting for him to continue.

Regis sighed. "Look, Cormac, that last visit. Our argument—you were right and I was a fool. I've let my greed for land cloud all my good judgment and it's harmed us pretty badly."

The senior partner nodded, but said nothing.

"I'd like to make amends. But honestly, Cormac, I'm not certain how. And I can't do it without your help."

Regis let out the rest of the pent-up breath and marveled at how much clearer, lighter he felt. He'd fretted and gnawed over having to say this to Cormac.

The woman in the cave had helped him to think more evenly about it all. Even if Cormac were to rush at him swinging a branding iron, he could somehow sustain it, though he hoped that would not be the case.

"Regis." Cormac leaned forward and folded his fingers and rested his chin on them.

It was a gesture the younger man had seen so many times he'd almost forgotten it. Now, he found it endearing, and a relief.

"It's good to hear you say all this, though I daresay it's a little late for it. As to amends, I just don't know how. Not yet anyway. You remember that letter from the lawyer?"

Regis nodded. "How could I forget? It might mean the Santa Calina's not mine. Ours."

Cormac smiled at the slip. "Well, after you . . . left that day, I visited the lawyer on my own. Turns out they discovered something you might find of interest."

Regis leaned forward, resting his hands on the chair back.

"Take a seat, son. I'm in no mood to stare up at your big ol' face."

Regis did so and waited.

"It seems that the newly discovered Valdez heir is none other than a woman."

Cormac waited to see the reaction on Regis's face. "Yes," he nodded. "But not Tomasina. An older sister. Her name isn't known to us yet, but we know a little—very little—about her. She was disfigured somehow in an accident, something about a horse kick to the face, of all things.

"For reasons we may never know, her family regarded this disfigurement as a disgrace and sent this child, their oldest, away to be educated at a convent. Not unusual in itself, but their motives were plain enough.

"The family had little to do with her after that. Out of sight, out of mind, apparently. It was assumed she became a nun, for nobody heard from her after sending her away. Since discovering she was the sole legitimate heir to the once-mighty, now-squandered and torn-apart Valdez fortune, people have tried to track her down. But she's not at the convent, and if the sisters there are to be believed—and who would accuse a nun of the sin of lying— nobody knows where this disfigured Valdez woman ended up. Or if she's even all right in her head." Cormac tapped his temple with a finger. "Or even alive, for that matter."

Regis thought for a long moment, then half smiled. "I think she's alive. And I think I know where she is. And if I'm right, she's all there." He tapped his own temple.

He stood. "Look, Cormac, I can't tell you any more than that. Not yet, anyway. I need to see if I can find her. Maybe I can talk with her about all this. I'll tell you how it goes. Do you still trust me?"

The older man scowled. "I shouldn't. You know that, right?"

Regis nodded. "But?"

"Oh . . . all right. Do what you need to. But don't go running away from here just yet. If you're serious about making amends, as you said, we have some hash to settle."

Regis nodded. "Okay, I'm ready."

"Good. First thing, you can make some fresh coffee. We're going to need it. And wash my cup while you're at it." Cormac nudged his grimy coffee mug and shoved papers out of the way, dragging a fresh stack of others before him.

"Anything else I can do for you?" said Regis, trying not to smile.

"Yeah," Cormac looked at him. "You can hurry up about it, you whelp."

Regis thought for sure his old friend might have been smiling.

For three hours the business partners plowed through book work, tallying, disagreeing, sputtering, tapping fingers to numbers, and drinking too much coffee. Finally, they figured out a way that they might, just might—with a shovelful of luck and with no business missteps for at least six months—be able to emerge once again with their heads above water.

Regis felt the weight of the problem pressing down on his shoulders mightily. It was far too late to do anything but ride Cormac's plan to the finish line. At least they had a plan. He vowed to himself he would see it through, and successfully, with no excuses.

It was too late in the day to head back to the ranch, but he felt a growing urge to visit the mysterious woman in the cave. He'd kept it tamped down in order to concentrate on the task at hand, so that he might show Cormac his intentions were serious. Nothing could be done about it that day, anyway, he thought.

Nightfall came and finally the men knocked off, secure in the knowledge that their plan was going to succeed. That it had to succeed. They retired to Hazel's Hash House, and Regis treated them both to a big feed—steamed greens, turnips and potatoes, mashed and drizzled with thick, steaming hot gravy the color of river mud, and nearly as thick.

But the steak won them over. Both men sliced into their tender, juicy, pink-in-the-center-yet-charred-all-over beefsteaks. They dipped that first forkful into the pooled hot gravy, and chewed in bliss, their eyes closed and smiles spreading wide on their faces.

They followed this with more hot coffee—decidedly better than the tarlike swill Regis had poured down them all afternoon. Ample slices of pie accompanied it—cherry and peach, drizzled with fresh cream.

At the end, they patted their drum-tight bellies, uncertain if they could walk to their respective abodes, Cormac to his house, and Regis to the King's Arms, where he always took a double room when he was in town.

The next morning, they went over a few more items, then Regis touched his hat, said once again, "Trust me. I'll be back in a few days," and departed town, though not until he'd spent time with Cotton.

He was a wise old gent and tallied the insults and uncharacteristic behavior of Regis's last visit as "something a man goes through now and again." He'd graciously accepted the sack of gifts—whiskey and horehound sweets—in the spirit they were given, as an apology and peace offering between the two friends. "Trick is to keep such goings-on from happening much, elsewise you're likely to lose friends."

It was a kind warning from a man who Regis counted among his small cluster of true friends. When he took his leave an hour later, he felt once again that he was on, if not great, at least better footing with Cotton, much the same as he felt on leaving Cormac.

Now he rode away from Brownsville, hoping to solve the conundrum that had been dropped into his life. And she was mysterious, annoying, and alluring.

Chapter 44

It was earlier in the day this time, when Regis sought out the once-spooky rock canyon where Tomasina Valdez had kept Shep prisoner. Much had happened lately to him and to those he knew, and he felt different somehow.

During the weeks since meeting the woman in the cave, he'd half-convinced himself she had been little more than a ghostly figment. And then with Cormac's news about a disfigured woman, she took on a more solid presence in his mind, and her identity made sense. Why appear at Tomasina's old hideaway? And why else wear a veil?

He hobbled his horse once more, unloaded his scant gear, much the same kit as before, and kindled a late-afternoon blaze with some of the same scraps of firewood he'd left by the firepit. Once he'd made coffee and snacked on biscuits and jerky, he glanced again toward the cave. "Okay, Regis. Time to test your guess. Is she or isn't she?"

He strode into the cave, once more carrying a burning brand to light the way, for he intended to venture deeper in. He passed the spot where Shep had been chained, and kept walking, trying not to knock his head on the low ceiling. At one point he had to crouch down and angle his wide shoulders, but he was able to pass through a narrowed gap.

He'd made his way to the outside once more, to a small clearing at the end that the bandits had used as a corral. He was there
on the rescue mission, but he hadn't seen sign of her then. Doubt
nibbled at his resolve.

Was she actually real? If so, was she living here? Where did the
cave tunnel fork away from this one? And how could anyone live
here, all alone?

He spent another minute or so of slow groping and squinting
into the dim, near-darkness about him, all the while hearing
rustlings above, and the occasional flutter of a disturbed bat.
Then his left hand, which he'd been feeling along the right wall
with, suddenly felt nothing beneath it where the moment before
there had been solid rock. He paused and brought the torch
around.

Regis bent low and swept the torch ahead, verifying that there
was indeed a floor there, and not some awful, bottomless chasm.
He felt hopeful and nerved-up about what lay ahead. This spur
of a passage narrowed but he kept walking, one slow step at a
time.

In a minute or so, he thought there might be a glow of some
sort up ahead and suspected it was daylight. Good thing, he
thought, as he wanted to be shed of the cave, wanted to feel the
fresh air on his face and get his bearings once more. Being inside
had fouled his sense of direction.

He walked forward slightly faster, more confident with each
step that he was nearer to the outdoors. The closer he drew to
the light, though, the more doubt he felt. There was no welcoming coolness of fresh air, and the glow was mellower somehow,
and wavering.

Then, before he expected to, he emerged into a candle-lit
grotto. There had to be two dozen candles flickering in the
space. The ceiling domed up at about a dozen feet, and the
room itself was rough-walled, but appearing hewn by tools, as

the walls bore a regularity in their patterning. Candles flickered and smoked, perched in little scooped shelves at random heights. Despite the candles, the air was fresh. Well, fresher than he expected it to be.

"Hello?"

There was no answer. He stepped farther into the space and noticed more about it. Off to the far left, hidden in a curve of the wall, sat a simple wooden rope-and-timber bed with a ticking mattress and bedding folded neatly atop.

Beside this sat a simple wooden table holding yet another candle, this time unlit and sitting in a brass candlestick, and by that, a Holy Bible.

Beside the table, on the floor, sat a small wooden trunk, no taller than his knee and no more than a foot-and-a-half wide, with the same rough dimension front to back. The thought of lifting the lid flitted through his mind and he felt instant shame at the thought of indulging in such a violation.

Instead, he looked about for other clues as to who lived here, though he had begun to form a pretty solid idea. "Hello?" he repeated. Again, there was no answer.

He noticed that the candle flames, now and again, wavered and leaned slightly toward where he'd come from. Which meant air had moved them, which meant there must be another opening at the far side of the room.

He approached that end with continuing caution, and discovered another narrow passage hidden in shadow. He looked in and saw more of a glow, this time the light was brighter, bolder, and he walked toward it. Soon, after two sharp bends, the light increasing beyond each, he emerged once more into a scene that was as surprising as discovering the candle-filled room in the cave.

Regis found himself in another rocky grotto, but this time it was open to the sky above. There was greenery about, and the distinctive smell of moisture, which, as he listened, came from somewhere to his left.

He walked forward another pace and saw a lively little stream trickling down out of a gap in the rock, no more than three or four feet from the earth. It trickled and spattered and splashed into a smooth-worn rocky basin.

It must have been doing exactly what it was doing for a good many years, hundreds, perhaps thousands, because the rock was as smooth as if it had been scraped and rubbed by a craftsman's hands.

Vines and little yellow and purple flowers grew about the basin, nurtured by the odd source of moisture in this place. More vines grew about the walls of the grotto, which, he guessed, measured roughly fifteen feet in diameter. Even the earth of the intimate space was not rocky and harsh but soft, smooth and welcoming somehow.

Close by the basin of clear water sat a plain wooden chair. Atop the caned seat, another book. He could not make out the gilded lettering, but judging by the plain crucifix on the cover, it was a religious tome.

When he looked up, something drew his gaze to the right, toward the shadowed far wall. Where he would have sworn nothing had been moments before now stood a woman in a black dress and veil. The same woman he'd met on his previous visit.

"I thought you might come."

Before he replied, he had the sudden thought that she was a peaceful creature, all soft and kind, and highly intelligent. All the things I fear I am not, he mused. And as suddenly, he found he did not know what to say.

All of this had been so clear, so obvious and certain in his mind as he rode out here. Now, he did not know how to begin.

"You helped my younger brother, Shep, when he was kept here by . . . your sister."

He thought perhaps he saw her stiffen then. As quickly, she softened. "Then you know who I am."

"Yes, ma'am. At least I think so."

"And I believe I know who you are . . . Mr. Royle."

Though she stood in shadow and though she was veiled, Regis knew she was staring at him. They stood this way for some time, neither speaking, but he sensed a stirring of something between them. It was undeniable. He wondered if she felt it, too.

Finally, he recalled one of the many things he'd wanted to say to her. "What you said to me, before . . ." He gestured behind him, nearly turned his head, but then caught himself. She might well disappear from his view.

"Back there, in the cave's entrance. They helped me. It took me a while to mull them over, but they helped me very much. I want to thank you for that."

She nodded. "I am pleased I was of help to you, but I cannot claim credit for something you have done on your own."

"Ma'am," he said, fiddling with the stick that was his now-extinguished torch. "As you know who I am, you know I'm . . . that I believe I am . . . that is to say, I thought I was until recently the rightful, legal owner of the Santa Calina range."

He let the words hang a moment. She merely nodded. It was unnerving, not seeing any more than the mere outline of her face. He wanted to look across the dozen feet that separated them and see her face, her eyes.

She sighed, then surprised him by leaning against the rock wall to her right side, and crossing her arms. It seemed so casual and human a pose that it disarmed him for a moment. It also served to accentuate the trim womanly form of her body.

"You want me to tell you I believe you are the owner of what was, and may still be, my family's land. You want to hear that I believe I have no legal right to the land. That I give you the blessing to own the land. That I will sign some document and make it so."

Her voice, in contrast with the hard-edged words, was still soft, warm, and kind.

When she didn't go on, Regis nodded. "Well, yes, that's about the long and short of it, yes, ma'am."

"Well, I cannot do that."

Regis felt a twinge high up in his gut. That wasn't what he'd wanted to hear, but it wasn't much of a surprise. "May I ask why not, ma'am?"

She pushed away from the wall and walked three paces, then turned and walked the other way, then over again. At one point, a shaft of light, as had happened back in the cave on his first visit, lit her face beneath the veil. He caught a glimpse of what he'd seen then, a strong, high cheekbone, perhaps a long, pretty nose.

"Mr. Royle."

"Yes, ma'am?"

"Have you given thought to who was there first?"

"On the land? Well, your people, ma'am?"

"No, before them. I'll tell you. Before them, the animals and the plants and the water was there, Mr. Royle. The very things you are working so hard to exploit to your own means, to benefit from."

"I . . ."

She held up a hand. "What was it that you saw when you first came upon the place, Mr. Royle? What was it you felt?"

He thought back to that day and an unbidden smile spread across his face. "It's beauty." He looked at her. "It's still the most beautiful place I've ever seen. I don't know why I feel that way, to be honest with you, but I do." He shrugged. "Can't help it, I guess."

She nodded. "That is what I hoped you would say."

When she didn't go on, Regis thought perhaps he was on shaky ground. He tried to guess what it was she wanted him to say next. "I can assure you, ma'am, I want the same thing for the Santa Calina range that you do."

"Oh, and what is that, Mr. Royle?"

Regis froze. How could he answer that? He waited, uncertain of what to say.

She laughed then, a soft, fluttering sound. "Relax, Mr. Royle. The truth shouldn't be so painful. It is possible I have no more right to the place than do you. But I ask you, regardless of how this situation may evolve, that you keep in mind"—she waved an arm, and he saw her long slender fingers sweep through the air—"that the land is not only beautiful, but it is an ancestral home to many, long before my people laid their claim on it. And it must be honored. Always."

He knew then what she meant, for he felt the same. He hadn't known it in as many words until that moment, but he felt it, deep down, within him. "The Santa Calina range is special, ma'am. I would never do anything to bring about its ruin."

She regarded him a long time then. Finally, she spoke, in a low, grave voice. "Do not ever forget the animals, the plants, the water that was there first. Do not forget the people who came there later. For though they be poor, they are rich in spirit and will gladly work their hearts out for the person who treats them well. They only want what we all want."

"What's that, ma'am?"

"Why, Mr. Royle, they are the simplest of things in life. They are love, compassion, kindness. The want good, honest work to do, food without want, education for their children, and homes for their families. They deserve this, Mr. Royle. And with it comes respect. We are all God's creatures, and we all deserve that same thing. Do unto others, Mr. Royle . . ."

"As you would have them do unto you. Yes, I'm familiar with that. I think I know what you mean, and I agree with you."

She stood leaning against the wall. They stared at each other a long time, the only sound the tickling, burbling of the spring as it splashed into the basin.

Finally, she spoke. "I believe you, Mr. Royle."

He felt relief sweep down over him like an unexpected but welcome breeze. He had a faint idea that he would have to get her to sign documents to make this legal, but he dismissed it. Later, he told himself. There will be time for such later.

"I guess I should be going." He fussed with the stick in his hand. "Will you be okay here? Alone, ma'am?"

"But Mr. Royle, I'm not alone."

"No?" Regis looked around, startled that he might be jumped or caught by surprise somehow, in this moment of calm.

"No. I have my books, the birds, the water, the flowers, this fine day. I have so much, Mr. Royle. So much to be thankful for."

"I see." He nodded. "Ma'am, will you be here?" He cleared his throat. "I mean, I was wondering if I might . . . Would you mind if . . ."

"I should like, Mr. Royle, if you would call on me again. I would enjoy the company. I suspect we will have much to discuss, you and I, in the coming months."

He thought perhaps he detected a smile in her voice.

"Yes, ma'am." He nodded. "Until then, ma'am."

As Regis threaded his way back through the caves to where he began, he felt once more that the thing he'd just experienced was not quite real. As if it were a conjuring of some sort. And yet he knew the grotto was as real, that she was as real, as anything or anybody he'd ever met.

All the while he rode the long trail back to the ranch, he wondered about her, this mysterious woman in the cave. He wanted to believe that what she had said, though not in so many words, was true, that she would not prevent him from owning the Santa Calina range.

Yet something deep within him nibbled and gnawed away at her words. What did it all mean? He hated that he had introduced a thin sliver of the sinister feeling of doubt.

Regis cursed himself and shook his head, trying to get the veiled woman out of his mind. It did not work.

Chapter 45

Bone and Howard had been tracking the killers for two hours when a rifle shot cracked somewhere to the east, sounding like little more than a quirt snap. Another followed it.

The two Rangers pulled their heads down and hugged their saddle horns.

"Dang it!" growled Bone. He looked over at the kid. "Keep low, boy!"

"You think they know we're trailing them?"

"Not certain. Might not even be them, though I'd bet wages it is. Could be they're hunting."

"Or killing each other off," said Howard, offering a thin grin.

"We should be so lucky," said Bone. Since they left the grim death camp, he'd become pretty well convinced that the group they were tracking were all headed in the same direction, and so the risk of sending the kid back wasn't too bad.

But now that shots had been heard, he knew they'd closed the gap between them, which meant the killers were traveling slow, likely not aware they were being followed. It also meant he might be able to get a look at them, then they'd turn tail and make for civilization and a fresh batch of Rangers.

Captain Sam would just have to find them. This was too brutal a crime to go cheap on.

He turned to Howard. "I need to ride on ahead aways, not too far, see what we're facing. My guess is they've encamped for the day."

"Let's go," said Howard, shifting in his saddle.

"Nope, not you. This is a one-man job."

"Aw, now, Bone, I'm a full-bore Texas Ranger. It's time I—"

"And I have seniority here, and I don't like my decisions questioned, got it?"

Howard looked away, his mouth scrunched as if he were chewing the inside of his cheeks.

"Got it?"

"Yes, sir."

"Good. Now, keep over there behind that little berm. Stay low and armed. I'll be back as soon as I'm able. Not too long, is my guess."

They rode over and Bone nodded. "This should do. Keep your revolver and your rifle to hand. And look in all directions all the time. It's possible and it's necessary. Ask any Ranger who's ever fought Comanches."

"Okay, I will, Bone. Good luck."

"Thanks. You, too, kid." He wheeled the horse and looked down once more. "See you soon." Then Bone rode northeast at a lope, keeping low in the saddle and sliding his rifle out of its boot.

Howard waited until he was certain Bone was well and gone—noting the man's direction as northwest of the little berm. Then he mounted up himself.

What was the point, he wondered, in having two full-bore Texas Rangers (and if he really wanted to be picky, he thought, he was technically the only Texas Ranger here. Bone hadn't yet officially re-upped) out here on this mission if the skills of only one was being used?

"No sir," whispered Howard to his horse as he nudged the beast eastward. "Two of us out here, might as well cover twice the ground. I'll scout out this direction and meet him back here, and he won't be the wiser for it."

His uncle Sam had said over and over again that a Ranger had to be resourceful. Well, he was about to do that very thing. Howard smiled and thought of how proud—and still nervous, reckon she'd always be that way—his mama will be when she hears that her son, one half of a two-Ranger team, captured a band of murderous outlaws.

As he moved over the rolling landscape, he kept a sharp eye, as Bone had said. But he slid his rifle back in its scabbard, as it was cumbersome to ride and hold the thing. He'd tug his revolver free soon.

Crest that next rise and see what he could see . . .

Chapter 46

Howard Strickland never felt the arrow as it slid, neat as you please, into his breadbasket. Then he felt a prickle, a quick, lancing needle of heat in his chest. He looked down and saw the oddest thing he'd ever seen in all his young days—the wooden shaft of an arrow, the fletching but inches from his sweat-soaked blue chambray shirt.

He said the thing he always said, even when he was happy: "What in the heck?" It would be the last time he ever said it.

As he spoke, in a strange, slurred whisper, a second arrow appeared, as if conjured, right beside the first, to the left of the first, in fact, and Howard's eyes snapped open wide. He pulled in a deep breath, smelled sun-baked sand, horse sweat, his own stink, and he heard a shout, then another.

The warm, spoiled taste of bitterness he knew to be blood filled his mouth, then gushed up and out his nose. As it flowed, he stiffened, then sagged, flopping sideways to his right, out of the saddle. His right boot fouled in the stirrup.

His horse, Nick, had sensed something odd was in the offing. After the first arrow, the gelding had slowed to a halt. He moved again moments later when the second arrow whistled in and buried itself in Howard's chest, inches to the side of the first.

The horse didn't know that the second arrow did what the first failed to do, at least not right away. The second arrow punctured Howard's heart, and as he flopped from the saddle to the ground, his boot and leg still connected to the horse, Nick did what any lathered, annoyed, and spooked horse would do in such a situation, he bolted.

The whomping, pounding, thrashing ride that Howard received as his body caromed off rocks and cactus and furrowed through the loose-packed earth didn't matter a whit to the young Texas Ranger, because he was dead. The bloody arrows had snapped off, front and back, those bits lost in his sloppy trail.

His right foot slipped from the boot that had wedged between the horse and stirrup, and still the horse thundered on, gray wool sock flopping like a loose tongue from the boot top. Another few strides and the boot, too, dropped away.

As if freed finally from encumbrance, despite the jerking, flopping saddle on his back, Nick the horse beelined for some unseen point far to the southeast.

Howard Strickland lay oddly humped, half resting on his right shoulder, his neck bent at an angle no breathing human could muster. Grit and dust caked his wide-open eyes, nose and mouth, and his hands were drawn, knuckles down, as if he were about to shove back from a dining table.

His legs, one ending sockless and bootless, pointed straight out, at odds with the trail his slamming body had left behind. He had ended up in a declivity that even from a distance of a dozen feet away could easily be overlooked.

It was likely that his stringy body would not be discovered by anyone save for buzzards and coyotes and other range beasts. The bones would be of little use once they'd been cracked open, sucked, and licked clean.

The sun would bake what was left, puckering and curling the man's leather accoutrements—his vest, his hat band, his gun belt, his last boot, and his own skin, what would be left of it after the critters removed their share.

Then the sun would bleach and dry and crack the bones until all that remained was a grinning death's head. But that, too, would end up somewhere not too distant from his death place, dragged and wedged deep into a den, one more secret kept by the desert.

Chapter 47

The man's horse had been seen and was valued by the leader of the men from the rag-tag gang of killers that the Rangers had been following.

Tull chose two among his men, Apaches, to bring it to him.

With his brass spyglass, Tull had tracked the two riders—he thought one might be wearing a badge—then sent one rifleman, the mangy old buffalo hunter with a Sharps rifle that could, as the hunter said, shoot the pecker off a gnat at a mile and a half, after the northerly rider.

Since the Apaches chose to use arrows, which Tull found amusing, he sent them after the southerly rider. He didn't much care how the men dealt with their prey, just that they did.

If either the buffalo hunter or the Apaches failed him, he would kill them. They knew this and he knew this. Nothing to take personally, it was an agreement everyone accepted when they came to work for him. It was rare that one of his men failed him.

It took the two Apaches about ten minutes to show back up in camp. They were still on foot.

Tull gave them the hard eye. "Where's his horse?"

They looked at each other, then at their moccasins, off to the campfire, anywhere but at him.

It was tricky for Tull to tell if they were turning red from shame since they were of a dark skin hue. They were also covered in dust and trail grime, same as the rest of the men, Tull included. But he knew they both spoke English well enough.

He kept staring at them.

One of them finally spoke. "It ran off."

Tull didn't know which one said it. He'd been looking past them, toward the plain beyond. He couldn't easily tell them apart, nor could he be bothered to learn their names. For that matter, he never put effort into learning any of the names of the vermin he hired.

Why bother when they were all going to die off at some point? If he remembered any of them, it was because they lived longer than the others. After a time, their names would stick in his head like a seed 'twixt his teeth.

"Well, did you give chase?"

Again, one of them spoke. This time Tull saw it was the one on the left.

"We tried."

Tull shifted on the rock against which he leaned and stretched out his left leg, massaging is knee cap. He'd taken a knife point to it some years before in a scuffle over a chicken, of all things.

He'd been hungry and the emigrants he'd come upon didn't want to give it up. Claimed they needed all six of their hens for when they got to the "promised land" of Oregon Territory.

Tull had considered this, then decided that his desire to eat was more important than their need to have a half-dozen chickens. Five should do them when they go to where they were bound.

But no, the farmer wouldn't let up. So they scuffled, the man sunk his spindly little knife in Tull's knee cap. At that point, Tull decided he had no choice but to shoot the peckerwood.

Then the man's wife and two kids got all riled about poor, bleeding Papa, so he shot them, too. No choice.

He took the one chicken, left their bodies and all their possessions right there. Ordinarily he would have rummaged through
their goods. Maybe if he was feeling kindly, he'd have lined up
their bodies and set the horses adrift, chickens, too. But he hadn't
been feeling too damn kindly, just sore in his bleeding knee.

So he took the one chicken, wrenched its head from its body,
and lugged it with him as he limped along on his way.

Turned out that bird was one of the worst meals he'd ever had.
Didn't know what they had been feeding that chicken, but it
tasted like dirt somehow. Never even finished it, and as hungry
as he'd been, that was saying something. That's how he came to
be rubbing his knee years later when those Apaches stood there,
trying to weasel out of their duties.

"I don't think so," said Tull.

They said nothing, but that chatty one on the left looked like
he was fixing to sputter some more words at him.

Tull said, "Reason I don't think you tried to track that horse is
that you are Injuns and it's bred into you to give chase and steal
things and whatnot. Must be you two got some white in you,
elsewise this would not have happened."

Tull stood and stretched, letting loose a big yawn. He noticed
out of his good eye that other of the men, those who'd been with
him a while, had begun to pretend they needed to do something
farther away from the tiny campfire one of them had kindled for
coffee.

"Besides, you two ain't hardly popped a sweat, and you damn
sure ain't breathing hard."

The other Apache, not the one who'd spoke, moved his right
hand up to his waist. He was angled away from Tull, but the big
man knew the rascal had a beaded knife sheath hanging off that
belt. And he knew that sheath held a vicious blade, because he'd
seen the man honing it two nights back.

Tull sighed and, faster than any man had a right to, his own hand whipped down fast as a snake strike and plucked his revolver from its holster. He thumbed back the hammer as he raised it and, in the same motion, delivered a round, neat smoking hole to the middle of the would-be knifer's bronze, sweat-stippled forehead.

The man's mouth widened, formed an "O" of surprise, and with his wet eyes still staring straight at Tull, he collapsed as if someone had axed him at the knees.

The second Apache, the one who'd done the talking, said, "No! No!"

He turned to face his dropped friend, then glanced quickly back to Tull, his eyes narrowed in anger, in hatred.

"Yes! Yes!" said Tull, and sent a second bullet out into the world. This one drove straight into the man's face, a pinch lower than he'd done on the first Apache. The bullet bored in at the top of the man's long, arched nose, smack between the eyes.

As with the first, Tull saw part of the back of this man's head burst away. Blood, bone, and some sort of vile goo slopped outward, leaving a dark trail for six feet or so, visible after the man joined his chum in collapsing to the earth.

Tull grunted and stuffed his revolver into its holster, then walked to the men, looked down at their still bodies, and grunted again.

He stepped around them and scuffed dirt over the gunk that burst out of the man's head.

"Now, let's hope that old hairy cur with the Sharps fetched back a mount."

"He did," said the buckskin-clad mountain man Tull had sent out to lay low the other spying scout.

Tull turned to see the man sitting astride his own dun, and leading a brown. The man was smiling. "I think that other fella got spooked, but I managed to intercept the horse them Apaches neglected to catch."

"Good," said Tull. "Don't ever sneak up on me again."

The man shifted in his saddle. "Didn't think I was sneaking. Just rode up, is all."

Tull sighed. Once more, with no warning, he shucked his pistol.

The horsed rider began to lower his big buffalo gun, and had it nearly leveled on Tull when the big man's revolver barked. The buckskin-clad man pitched backward in his saddle, and fell away to the right.

His Sharps, aimed skyward, boomed. His dun reared, thrashed side to side, and bolted. The brown he was leading, now freed of the mountain man's grasp, spun in the opposite direction.

Tull smiled, though no one could see so behind his beard. "I'll take that Sharps," he said to the group of not-so-startled men. "And somebody best fetch those mounts."

Only reason he'd hired that surly old smart-mouth mountain man had been because of his rifle. Tull had always admired such a gun and when he took the man on for this job, he figured his time to own one had finally come.

A skinny whip of a man, whose ears looked to have been made out of teacup saucers, brought up the Sharps and held it out to Tull. "Here's your gun, Tull."

The big man grunted his thanks. He relieved the kid of the massive rifle and hefted it. The kid stood there looking at him.

"What?" said Tull.

"Oh, I . . . aah . . ."

"Don't give me that crap, kid. Get away from me before you taste my boot."

The kid skedaddled. Tull normally would have trotted him off gleefully with a couple of rounds set to his heels to make him dance for it, but he was busy eyeing the rifle.

At long last he had himself a Sharps. He'd had opportunity to possess one in the past, but none were quite what he wanted.

This one was used but well cared for. He'd have to rummage on the old man's body for his possibles bag, see what else he could acquire for the maintenance and upkeep of the rifle.

Men such as that buckskin wearer always carried it around as if it were a baby. He had no intention of doing such. He wanted it as a toy, something to shoot bottles and rats with back at camp. It was an impractical thing to have on the trail. But he'd make damn sure it was lugged through this railroad escapade and on back home.

"Hell," he muttered to himself. "Might need it today if we get in a set-to with that last one still trailing us."

He gave it thought, then said, "I'm gonna backtrack that horse's trail, see if those Apaches really did lay him low." Really, the only thing he wanted was to shoot the big buffalo gun. Hell, he was downright looking forward to it.

Chapter 48

Regis felt a twinge of relief mix with the gut flutters as the entrance to Bone's ranch came once more into view. The last time he'd left here he would have bet he'd never again set foot on the property. But here he was.

He credited the notions that woman in the cave had set to rolling around in his head. He'd been thinking of a whole lot of things since he'd seen that spectral creature, but foremost on his mind had been making amends with Bone, with Shep, and with Cormac. Then it had all gone to pot on him.

Still, once he'd faced down death on that foolish escapade with the gang of rustlers, and found himself surprised to have lived through it, Regis found himself more convinced than ever that he had to make things right in his life.

And since Shep was still surly and withdrawn, he'd decided to try, once again, to talk with Bone. He had to at least leave it better than they had between them, even if Bone never again took on the duties of ranch manager of the Royle.

As he rode into the ranch yard proper, he caught movement to his left and saw that old Mexican fellow (Ramon was his name?) walking from the barn toward the water trough lugging two wooden buckets. The man saw Regis at the same time and paused, then he looked toward the house and motioned that way with a nod of his head.

Regis returned the nod and rode toward the house. He stopped at the hitch rail before the bunk house and left his horse there, then walked toward the little ranch house.

He was still a couple of dozen feet from the porch when the woman, Margaret, emerged from around the far side of the house, carrying a wicker basket of line-dried laundry, from the looks of it. She paused and visored her eyes with a free hand.

He walked closer. "Hello, ma'am. It's Regis Royle."

"You're persistent, Mr. Royle."

"Yes, ma'am." He offered her a hopeful smile and to his surprise, she returned it with a brief one of her own. She walked up onto the porch. "Come on in. I expect you're dry, riding all that way."

"Thank you, ma'am. I should tend my horse first."

She looked past him. "Ramon is taking care of it."

Regis turned and sure enough the old man had led his horse to the trough. He waved and nodded, and the old man nodded back.

This is a far cry from the last reception I got here, thought Regis, following Margaret into the house. He could not help but notice she was a handsome woman.

He took off his hat and stood inside the door.

"There's a hook beside the door for your hat, and you're welcome to take a seat at the table. I was about to pour coffee. It's fresh. She set down a clay pitcher and a drinking glass on the table and he sat and filled the glass. The water was good and cold.

He looked about the room. It was small but tidy, neat as a pin, as he'd heard someone once say of a clean home.

"Thank you, that hit the spot."

"Glad to hear it."

"You'll be wanting to talk with Jarvis."

The comment caught him off guard but a moment. He still had a difficult time thinking of Bone as a Jarvis. "Yes, ma'am. That is, I'd like to try." He knew she was savvy to all the rough dealings between the two men.

She set down two cups, poured black steaming coffee, and set one cup before him. Then she sat down opposite him at the table. She sipped her coffee, then fixed him with an unnerving steady gaze. "Jarvis is not here, Mr. Royle."

"Regis. Please call me Regis."

"Very well, then you may call me Margaret."

"Thank you. Do you know when he'll be back?"

She shook her head. "No, actually."

For the first time, he saw something alter the forthright features of this strong woman. He knew it at once as doubt, perhaps a little fear, as well. "Is he all right, ma'am?"

She looked down at her cup. "He's off Rangering."

Oh, he thought. So that's it. Bone, that devil, couldn't keep from taking up his old adventuring ways.

As if she'd read his thoughts, Margaret said, "He didn't want to, but his old captain, a man by the name of Sam Fiedler, he asked him to attend to this matter himself. It has to do with a rail line, a spur line, actually, something about being of benefit to the ranchers, well, such as yourself."

"Hm. Well, that sounds harmless enough." But Regis was wondering if this meant that Mr. De Haviland's crew was out there, exploring.

"That's what I thought. He had with him a young Ranger, the nephew of this Sam Fiedler. Bone felt obliged to see to this matter. But he was adamant that this would be it, he'd only do it as a favor, then he was done with Rangering for good. He said he wanted to be here, with me, to run the ranch. I believe him, Mr. Royle, but . . ."

"But?" Regis sipped his coffee, if only to somehow tamp down the rising nib of worry he was feeling. Something was off about this.

She looked in his eyes once more. "I'm afraid I pushed him to do this. He didn't want to go."

"Can you tell me anything else about this spur line?"

"Not much. It's up heading toward Louisiana. There was a scouting crew of some sort, exploring the region . . ."

She went on to explain all she knew, including the location, the mention of the letter from the woman back east, and she ended with the fact that the spur sounded as if it went from nowhere in particular and would end the same.

"That sounds . . . odd," he said. Why would De Haviland do something like that?

"Jarvis said the same thing."

He looked at her and saw a pleading look in her eyes, as if this strong woman was asking him for help, somehow. But not certain how to do so or if she should. But he saw in that moment that she loved Bone very much, that was obvious.

Regis nodded. "You know what? I have some time to myself. I'm going to go out after them. Can't hurt and even if he'll talk with me"—he smiled—"it's unlikely he'll need my help. Bone, or Jarvis, is the most capable fellow I've ever known, in most any situation."

He stood, noting the relief on her face. As he lifted his hat down off the hook by the door, he said, "You never know, he might just need an extra hand." He smiled to show more confidence than he felt, and nodded. "Thank you, Margaret, for the water and the coffee and the conversation."

They moved out to the porch and she said, "I'm obliged, Mr. Royle. I know I'm being silly, but . . ."

"No, I understand. It can't hurt, and it might help, as somebody smart once said." He plunked his hat atop his head, then turned to her and said, "One thing, though."

"What's that?"

"It's Regis. Not Mr. Royle."

"Yes, of course. Thank you, Regis."

As he stepped down off the porch, he said, "We'll be back soon, you'll see."

Neither of them believed that, though they could not say why.

Chapter 49

On hearing the second shot, Bone cut the horse southwestward, back toward where he'd left the kid. His unsheathed rifle, laid across his thighs, was ready to raise and fire at the slightest movement.

Not for the first time that day did he question his decision to trail these killers, nor of his decision to leave the kid back there and scout on his own. He wanted to keep the kid safe, sure, but the nasty little truth was he'd given in to his urge, that old Ranger itch, to pursue his prey before the trail grew cold. Just for a few minutes, he'd told himself.

As he rode, chastising himself, two more gunshots, on top of each other, cracked the sky. But one of them was louder, deeper, bigger than the other.

"Fool," he said in a grim voice, tucking low and spurring the horse into a run. "I'm a damn fool." Doubly so for even agreeing to go along on this silly errand. A trip that had become something far more foul than he ever dreamed it might.

Once I get back to the kid, we're breaking off, heading home. This whole thing turned into something bigger than two men could be expected to wrangle.

He rode for ten minutes or so, following his own tracks back and looking ahead for the kid. Before he expected to, he came upon the slight berm where he'd left Howard, but the kid was not there. Bone's moustaches twitched in anger. "Dammit, kid," he said, trying to believe that the kid had merely disobeyed him and not something worse.

It was simple tracking to follow the kid's trail around the far side of the berm, then southeast. What was the kid thinking and where in the hell did he think he was going?

They rode a good few minutes, Bone half paying attention to the trail the kid's horse's hooves left in the hard pan, and half eyeing the skyline for sign of danger. They topped a slight rise, and the tracks changed.

The horse had halted suddenly, as if it had been surprised, the denting deeper than it had been. Then it had dug in, hard, and bolted northwestward. Bone looked ahead and his eyes saw an odd furrowing, a ragged line of bent and snapped yucca and dug up earth, as if something had been dragged.

"Oh no . . ." He jerked the reins and spurred his horse in that direction. It didn't take much effort to follow the haphazard trail. Then, with no warning, his horse's ears flicked forward at the same time he jerked to a halt.

There not twenty feet before them, lay Howard Strickland, back to Regis, hunched on his side, as if he were about to roll over in bed and yawn. Yet this was no pose a napping man would ever undertake.

The back of his fawn leather vest was a blackened patch with a couple of ragged nubs, like finger bones, poking from its midst.

"Oh, God no! No no no, Howard!"

Bone grasped the saddle horn to jump down off the horse when, with no warning, his mount convulsed as a bullet whistled and thunked, driving deep into its shoulder, two inches before Bone's right knee. The instant stink of hot blood filled his nostrils.

Then he heard the boom, just like one of the two shots he'd heard not long before, but this time, the sound was closer. It was a big-bore, large caliber, beast of a gun, likely a buffalo killer's weapon, single-shot, which might give him time to get the hell out of there. All this rattled through his mind at bullet speed.

The horse stiffened, a shudder wracking his big muscular body. He jerked his head up and down like a pump handle gone mad, then the big beast began to pitch to its left, falling like an axed tree.

Bone knew then that if he had any chance of escape, it would be on foot, because his horse was already dead, it just didn't know it yet.

In seconds, his left leg would be caught beneath that toppling horse and snapped like a matchstick, and even worse, he'd be trapped beneath the beast.

Bone freed his boot from the stirrup, a low growl the only indulgence he allowed himself. The horse had taken two shots and he knew whoever was doing the shooting wasn't about to wait around while he freed himself and jumped from the toppling mount before letting loose with a second dose of lead.

He kept his rifle gripped in his left fist and jerked himself to his right, head down, rolling and shoving away from the horse's body at the same time. He had to get away not only from the bulk of the horse but from those flailing hooves that could slash like knives.

He hit the earth on his right shoulder and felt something pop in there beneath the skin. He rolled with the maneuver and flailed to get away from the horse. He did, and also held onto his rifle. But he was still between the horse and the shooter.

The horse thudded to the earth, dust and grit clouding up about the big beast. And more followed as the horse thrashed and whinnied, flinging foamy snot and blood from his mouth as he thrashed his head.

Using his elbows, Bone jerked and crawled snakelike around the closer end—the whipping head—of the horse.

"Easy boy, easy," he said, knowing he'd have to end the beast's agony as soon as he could. If he wasn't himself drilled in the back of the head before he could make it around to the paltry safety the horse's body provided.

Bone held his breath until he'd made it safely behind the mount's still-thrashing bulk.

"Hell," he growled. "Here we go all over again." He'd been in this very pickle twice before, both times years ago, both times as a Texas Ranger. Here I am, doing the same old thing. More experienced, yet he hadn't learned a single lesson.

The horse's breathing came harder now, and his thrashing slowed. Each sawing breath sounded as if it were being dragged out, pained whinnies trembled up and out of the powerful chest. His breath rammed back in, then dragged out once more. They were great huffing, shallow breaths, a locomotive chugging up a steep grade that would never reach the summit.

"I'm so sorry, friend," said Bone, setting down his rifle and pulling out his revolver. He cocked it back all the way and, keeping low, aimed it as well as he dared without raising his arm too high above the horse's protective bulk. As soon as the deadly end of the barrel poked against the horse's skull, he seemed to know relief was at hand, for the horse's breathing quieted and leveled for a moment.

"Goodbye, Buck," whispered Bone and he closed his eyes, looked away, and pulled the trigger. The blast was loud, as he knew it would be, but it still made him wince. They would now know he hadn't been injured, or killed.

Maybe they're toying with me, he thought. Playing with me like a cat does to a mouse it has mauled not quite to death.

The horse's legs, which had been moving slowly as if it were swimming across a river, now subsided beneath Bone's hand. He stroked the beast's flopped mane as the last breaths it would ever feel slowly leaked out of its body.

But Bone's thoughts were already on what was coming next, what was about to happen. If it were him, he thought, he'd have advanced on his prey. Better yet, if there were more than one of them, which he was pretty certain there were, given the tracks he'd been following, he'd have some way of also surrounding his intended victim.

That thought caused him to look to his right, southward, then behind to the west, then once more northward.

Nobody in sight.

For long minutes, nothing moved, no mild breeze stirred the sparse, brittle grasses, no buzzards circled. He heard no sounds. The only thing that moved were beads of sweat slipping down his spine and drizzling over his face from his hair. He'd lost his hat when he dove from the horse, and the sun baked his hair-covered head without mercy.

Even the horse's hide was viciously hot. The brass and steel of his guns pained him to touch. He readjusted his grip on the revolver, swapped hands, and wiped his palms on his shirt front, then checked once again that the rifle was at the ready.

His skittering thoughts returned to young Strickland, and his heart felt small and cold. What had he done? That poor damn kid. And his fretful mother, Tina, sister of his old friend and captain, Sammy. He'd been trusted to all-but play nursemaid to the kid, keep him safe while they explored a sure-fire easy patrol.

He slowly edged to his left, tried to peer over the dead horse's neck toward where he thought the hunched form of the kid lay. He could not get enough of an angle on it, and gave it up. That kid was dead, and it was his fault.

He lay there, the unfamiliar black drip of pity and shame leaching over him. Finally, Bone groaned. He knew he had to do something, anything in this lousy situation.

He did not have the upper hand. They were waiting him out. One rash move, one raise of his head, and if someone were sighting on the horse's bulk, it wouldn't take much to part his skull with one of those booming slugs.

If he was correct and the shooter had a buffalo gun, those weapons were built for long-distance killing.

Time passed, how long he had little way of knowing. The sun was well beyond midday. Surely one of his men would have tracked him by now.

He licked his lips and scrunched his eyes, thumbed sweat from them, and wondered if he dared grope for his canteen strap. After he'd shot the horse, he'd angled himself such that his legs were bent beneath him, but his head and shoulders faced the bulk of the saddle.

He might be able to scooch lower and turn his head enough to see if the canteen strap was still there, hanging from the saddle horn, draped down the right side of the horse. He groped with the fingers of his left hand. There it still was, he felt the strap.

Bone tugged on it, but somehow it was snugged tight. Maybe pinned beneath the horse's leg? He pulled harder. Nothing. Maybe if he cut the strap he could pull it.

No, he thought. Likely it would just fall to the ground on the other side of the horse's barrel, on the side opposite him. Then where would he be? At least if he didn't touch it, the possibility of drinking bad water later outweighed his growing desperation for a drink.

His right shoulder throbbed worse than ever. If there was something wrong inside, a cracked bone or some such, he'd have to worry about it later. If there was a later.

"Don't think like that," he whispered. He didn't believe much in fanciful thinking but he wasn't taking any chances. He did not want anything, silly words or otherwise, to trigger something to happen.

The sun blazed and burned and seared everything. His forehead rested against the saddle and his eyes closed. Some time later, how much later he had no idea, he came to.

A moment later, he heard a thud, then the booming sound hot on its heels. Nearly on top of it, as a matter of fact. The horse's body rocked and the saddle seat, before Bone's face, dimpled outward, as if somebody on the other side were shoving through with a spear tip. It didn't poke through, but it came close, enough to distend the thick leather.

He heard a bray of deep, harsh laughter from somewhere ahead, to the northeast. The direction his quarry had been riding. So whoever it was hadn't moved on, hadn't decided to escape while they still could.

Who am I kidding? thought Bone. These kill-crazy rogues had committed a massacre and we gave chase. And we were ill equipped, undermanned, and ill-informed. But he should have known better.

Oh, Howard, what I wouldn't give to have you back and alive. For he knew with all certainty that the kid was dead.

Those wounds he had and the pose he'd landed in looked bad enough, but that he'd been dragged by his horse was worse. And where was that horse? The possibility of it being somewhere nearby, spooked but settled by now, was slim, but hell, it was something.

The thought of it set his teeth tight together. He had to make it through this damnable mess. He had to make it back to Margaret. Even in his fuzzy, sun-addled state, he clung to the notion that Margaret would make it right. Somehow, she would know how to make it right again.

But if something happens to me, thought Bone, Margaret will have the ranch. She'll be safe and provided for. But the truth behind that winsome thought blazed hot and bright as the cursed sun: They weren't yet married. He'd not signed anything that might make it so. Did he have something to write with? A pencil and a scrap of paper? Something that would tell whoever found him that she should have the place, all of it.

Regis. He would help her. Sure, they'd had a mighty falling out, and he'd been less-than-kind to him when he'd ridden out to try to talk to him, but they were still pards, right? All the years they knew each other had to count for something. He was a savvy businessman, he'd make certain Margaret was provided for, wouldn't he?

Hours passed, the incessant sun blazed away, up and over, then behind him. Hour on hour. With the fading light came a creeping coolness and then a dimming of the sky's brightness.

He must have dozed because when he came to once more, the night surrounded him. It was damn near black out. Far to the south he heard the yowls of desert dogs. With the coolness came a relief, a balm to his sun-fevered mind, and with the relief came a thought: The shooter hadn't yet killed him. He was low enough that he wasn't skylined against any purpling the night sky might get up to. That meant he might be able to retrieve that canteen hanging off the front of the horse.

Would the gunman be waiting him out? Wouldn't matter for the time being, unless he could see in the dark. He inched his arm up and clawed once more for the familiar strap. He found it and tugged. Same as before. He slid out his sheath knife and cut at all the straps his fingers could find, then he tugged them.

Something resisted. He tugged harder and it jerked free. He pulled it toward him, up and over the horse's shoulder. He rolled over onto his backside and leaned against the horse, risking his head sticking up a bit. He tugged the thing over onto his lap and rested a hand on it, the thought of water touching his lips and tongue and throat making him grunt.

But the canteen felt odd, not all there . . . broken. He lifted it and held it before his face, feeling it with his tired hands, feeling nothing but a cracked wooden thing, once a promising vessel but now a splintered mess.

A sigh of exhausted exasperation leaked from his split, swollen bottom lip. He worked his backside lower, leaned his head back against his saddle, and he thought: Killers be damned. I'm all done in for today.

Then Bone fell asleep.

Chapter 50

There had been a sound.

Bone forced his eyes open. Sunlight, how many hours of it, he had no idea, but it was near full light out.

He heard it again—a horse, the rubbery snort of a horse. Never had he heard a sound so welcome. Particularly because it came from back the way he'd ridden out here.

He sighed and felt for his guns, looking about for leering killers kind enough to let him sleep. None about.

So he'd slept through the night, and the fact that he could have made his escape under cover of darkness dropped on his mind like a boulder. He'd blown it, his one good chance.

Twenty years before he would have had the brain power and the muscle to have made it. Could be well on his way to safety by now, he thought. Could have made it to that camp full of railroad dead. Bound to have been water there.

He'd also been oblivious to the fact that someone hours before had tried very hard to kill him. After the second gunshot, he'd heard that big, loud laughing. The gunman's parting shot? He hoped so.

He had a dim memory of hearing night noises, snuffling, scuffling, maybe growls. He hoped the kid's body had not been savaged by critters.

Bone craned his head over his right shoulder, still keeping as low as he could, to look in the direction the kid had ended up. He still couldn't see over the horse's neck, but now that light was here once again, he didn't dare raise his head.

Once again, he heard a horse. Maybe it was the kid's mount. He squinted, held his hand above his eyes to block the light, but still saw nothing. He had heard it, hadn't be? Surely he'd not been out here long enough to loosen his brain from its tethers.

He looked westward once more and saw something, seeming to rise up out of the ground as if it was growing. But it was wavery from the rising heat and still too far away to make out. He squinted, but it did no good, even after he wiped his eyes.

Pinned down and not enough room to shift around behind the horse and face whoever or whatever was coming toward him. If it was anything at all. Well, he had guns. He'd give them what hell he could muster.

Bone shifted and managed to keep low and angled onto his left hip, while still keeping his legs bent in case they'd be seen from a distance. Any distance. He grunted as the hard earth beneath his backside pained him. Unyielding. That's what the ground was.

He dug at it again with his free hand, but as before when he'd tried, he was still hardly able to scratch away any earth, certainly not enough to make a difference. He'd thought earlier—had it been the day before?—that he might be able to dig a gully, buy himself more cover, maybe enough room to stretch before he cramped up. Hadn't happened.

This range looked to be a mix of long stretches of hardpan interspersed with troughs of looser soil, mostly sand. He looked at the canteen again. Still broken and dry as a puckered plank. Maybe one of the gunshots had gotten it.

He squinted west again and saw that the thing he'd seen had indeed become clearer, closer. The sun was behind him, to the east, but Bone still wasn't able to see anything more than a vague, black, wavery shape. Maybe a man a-horseback?

He hunkered lower, wondering if it was one of the assailants circling around to pin him down while he was descended on from the east by the shooter. How many would they send after him? Surely they knew he was one man.

Bone licked his lips again and pulled in a deep breath, though it pained him to do so. The air was already hot enough that it stung going in, like tasting stew on the boil. You can be as hungry as the devil, and know you shouldn't do it, but you give it a taste. And you get burned every time.

He glanced again toward the west, and now saw it was a horse and rider, had to be with that shape. A quarter-mile off? Less? He risked a look around the hind-end of the horse toward the east after sweeping his eyes southward. He saw no one. But he bet that the shooter was still eyeing his spot.

This sun is relentless, he thought. Even though it's morning, I have never felt such brute heat before. It is puckering my skin and frying my head like a skillet of eggs on a camp fire. Bone closed his eyes for a moment, his mind a collision of thoughts. He knew somehow that he'd become more sensitive to the sun. He had to get out of there. Somehow he had to make his play, and soon, or he'd not have enough strength to do it.

He cursed himself again for not taking his chance at night. That bitter thought collided with visions of clear, cold mountain streams, of surf rolling into shore in all its white, frothy fury, plunging into a shivery lake. It was tempting, yet dangerous, too, to allow these thoughts entry into his mind.

It also felt nice to close and soothe his eyes, the puckery, sandy feeling of them. So tired, he felt so very tired. He grunted softly at this thinnest of pleasures.

No, no, he thought. Snap to, dammit!

With what felt like an almighty effort, Bone forced his sore eyes open once more.

There before him stood a man on horseback.

"Bone?"

Bone squinted tighter. His arms shook as he raised his rifle.

"Get down!" he tried to shout, tried to make it sound as urgent as the command needed to be, but the man was already at his side.

"Bone? You hurt?"

That voice, he knew that voice. "Regis?" Bone swallowed back the gravelly, rawness of his throat and licked his chapped lips. He motioned as he spoke. "My god, man, get down!"

Regis did as Bone bade him and ducked down.

Bone grabbed him by the shoulder, bunching his plaid shirt. "Lower!"

The two men hunkered behind the dead horse. A bluebottle stirred, rose in the air, drifted down again to land on the dead beast's dun flank.

"Who's out there?" said Regis.

"Don't know. Those from before. Big gun."

Regis looked at him. "Bone, you need water."

"Shot my canteen."

"When?"

Bone thought, his eyebrows pulling together in concentration. "A long time ago, Regis. Might even have been yesterday."

"I'll get my canteen. You look rough."

Bone grabbed Regis's arm as the man began to rise once more.

Regis gently pried the Ranger's hand from his arm. "If they haven't shot me by now, I guess I'm safe. Safe as I can get, anyway. Not much else we can do except to get gone. We still have one horse."

Could it be that simple? thought Bone. Just ride on out of this nightmare. Then a thought came to him. "How'd you find me?"

Regis had returned to his ground-tied horse a few feet away and snatched his canteen from where he'd looped its strap twice around the saddle horn. He returned and, crouching low behind the dead horse, beside Bone once more, Regis felt little more than ill.

He'd seen the massacred railroad camp, now this. A dead man beyond Bone, hunched in the dirt, had to be that kid Margaret had told him about.

As if Regis's thoughts triggered something in Bone, the man looked up from nursing on the canteen. His eyes were wide, red, and wild. "Margaret!" he said, water running out his mouth and over his stubbled chin.

Regis nodded. "She told me where to find you. She's fine, Bone. Just fine. A good woman you have there."

"I do, don't I?" He almost smiled and his eyes looked to be clearing. The water seemed to do its job in reviving the sagged husk of a man.

"Yeah, I'm jealous. And happy for you, Bone. Truly. Now let's get you back to her. Come on."

"Young Howard's over there," said Regis. "We can't leave him." He nodded past his own horse. He knew Regis must have seen him, but he'd not yet mentioned him.

"I know, but he's past caring, Bone. And if we stay out here any longer jawing, we'll be the same."

"You're starting to sound like me," said Bone, cracking the barest hint of a smile as he sipped and sighed.

"We can come back for him, your things. Right now, we have to get on home. Come on." Regis helped hoist Bone to his feet. Though Bone was a big man, he felt as though he was hollow, and he swayed once he got to his feet.

"No," said Bone, bristling a little because Regis spoke sense and had somehow become the one taking charge, and Bone had become the one who required shepherding. It was not a situation he liked to be in, but there it was.

"What do you mean, 'no'?"

"The kid. We have to bring him back. I'm not kidding here, Regis. He died because of me."

"I doubt that, Bone. I'm guessing he died despite your best efforts."

Bone shook his head wearily. "No, hell no. You're kinder than I have a right to." He looked at Regis. "But I'm not leaving without him."

Regis sighed and looked east, north, then south. He bent and hefted Bone's rifle. "Cover me, then. I'll go get him."

"I'll help."

"No, dammit. Cover me. I don't want to get shot for a dead man."

With that, Regis bent low and hustled around the stiff horse and over to the fallen man. He was a bit stiff, but still limber enough that he flopped in compliance as Regis dragged him backward, all the way to his own horse.

"Oh, Lord," said Bone, watching them and not the skyline.

Regis made quick work of draping the body over his saddle. Flashes of memory of that young, impoverished farmer they'd lynched, Joss Keeler was his name, came to him. He'd tied him the same way. Would all this dying never end? All for what, Regis, he asked himself.

He finished. By then, Bone had freed up his saddlebags and slung them over his shoulder. He joined Regis beside the horse, but kept glancing back eastward, expecting a big bore bullet to core his head any moment.

"You want to ride up there with him?" Regis asked, though he knew the answer.

"Nope. I'll walk. This water's doing the trick."

Regis knew that was barely the truth, but they headed out. They made tracks southwestward, each keeping an eye to their sides and backtrail.

"I got here as quick as I could," said Regis. "It took me a long while to track you. This landscape's different than the Santa Calina."

"I'm just glad you showed up. If you had gotten here sooner, we'd likely both be trapped out there. Or worse."

Regis said nothing.

"Regis, I'm much obliged to you for sticking with me."

"Likewise, Bone. I've behaved pretty poorly toward you."

"Well, I reckon we're past all that, don't you?"

Regis nodded.

But Bone's weak smile faded as quickly. This day had brought a whole lot to chew on, not the least of it poor young Howard Strickland's death. A death Bone knew he and he alone was responsible for.

He closed his eyes a moment, getting used to a new idea that had formed in his mind. It was a dark, repugnant notion that he hated, and one he had no choice but to follow through with: There was no way he could retire from the Texas Rangers now.

Fleeting thoughts of Margaret and the ranch and the happy future they were going to have grew thinner and foggier in Bone's mind before blowing apart in a breeze. And as it powdered away, it left Bone a man alone.

Alone with his damnable badge.